Perdurare

Andria Marston

First published in 2023 by Blossom Spring Publishing
Perdurare Copyright © 2023 Andria Marston
ISBN 978-1-7393514-3-4
E: admin@blossomspringpublishing.com
W: www.blossomspringpublishing.com

For my mother, who believed I'd write a book one day.
For my husband, who believed it might be published.
For my father who believes in me.

Prologue

Semine, daughter of Kodolvan and last of the Star Maidens, was the protector of Earth. Chronos gave Semine the Key of Choices, and she became the mistress of Old Earth's past, present and future. But, Koldovan was jealous of anyone and anything that might take his daughter away from him. He took the Key far away to his palace within the Star Realm. He intended to ensure that Semine would have to return whenever she needed to use the Key. Thus, at dawn and dusk, Semine dwelt in her father's palace, but during the day, she lived with mortals. She became a friend and adviser to the warrior King Owain of Rheged. His kingdom was in the green lands of the Northern Country. Owain pledged allegiance to Semine and became her champion. In gratitude for his service, she rewarded him with long life and powers drawn from the strength of the sun. She taught him the languages of the spirit folk and revealed the secret pathways across time. At night, the lights from her rooms in the Sky Palace burned brightly as she constantly watched over him. Koldovan, perceiving Semine's increasing distraction was furious but helpless. He had only one hope: if a mortal ever harmed his daughter, he would then have an excuse to sever her connection to Earth. He watched and waited and said nothing. But, as time slowly turned and Semine became more and more devoted to Owain, his dislike of all mortals steadily increased.

*

Owain remained for many centuries in Rheged, but at last he travelled to Jorvik, and used his powers of secrecy to visit the court of Hafdan Ragnarsson, leader of the Great Heathen Army. Disguised as a Swedish merchant, he walked amongst the Viking people. His hope was that he could find the way to convince them to live in peace and so avert further bloodshed. One evening he heard a girl singing. It was Valdis, Hafdan's niece and sister to Avaldi, a warrior chieftain. Owain listened enchanted, for she had the sweetest voice he had ever heard and a matchless beauty. He decided at once to win Avaldi's friendship. Over the days that followed he did everything he could to make himself favourable in the eyes of the Viking leader. This was not difficult for Avaldi instantly took a liking to Owain, rightly respecting his knowledge of the country which, to the Viking, was still strange and new. After many happy months, Owain and Avaldi became fast friends and Hafdan gladly agreed to Owain's marriage to Valdis.

*

Owain and Valdis then returned to Rheged. Owain built a palace of marble and crystal and at its centre was an enchanted tower. It was so tall that on a clear night its turret was fully illuminated by starlight. Often Owain would go there to meditate, for he was now estranged from Avaldi and this caused him great grief. After his marriage he had cast aside his disguise and revealed his true ancestry. Hafdan had accepted him, but Avaldi was furious at the deception. He brooded upon the perceived insult, summoned the Heathen Army and a great battle ensued between Owain's knights and the Viking warriors. But the Vikings couldn't break the strength of the Knights of Rheged. After the last fierce battle, Avaldi went alone to the palace and climbed the tower where Owain had placed Valdis for safety. As he ascended he was recognised by the knights and they summoned bowmen to shoot him down. Valdis seeing Avaldi's danger reached out to help him and in doing so leaned out too far. Brother and sister both fell to the ground and were instantly killed. Owain was grief stricken. He ran to the top of the tower and called to Semine to aid him. Semine, seeing his anguish, petitioned the Moon Goddess to use her gifts of healing so that Avaldi would live again. For love of Owain, Semine passed her life force to Valdis, so she too was saved. But, by her sacrifice, Semine's spirit was forced to flee, abandoning both Old Earth and the Realm of Stars. Koldovan was furious. Taking mortal form he cursed all life on Old Earth. He took the Key of Choices and locked the great doors between past, present and future so that time became finite. Then he shattered every possible reality and scattered the shards. Finally, Koldovan taunted Owain by showing him a vision of Semine resting within a great stone chamber. "When you look to the Morning Star you may see this. It will serve as a symbol of all that you have lost," he said. Then Owain begged for mercy, for himself and for his people. The Star Gods and Goddesses hearing Owain's cries took pity on him. They reasoned with Koldovan and so at last, although with great reluctance, Koldovan agreed that the Curse might be lifted upon one condition. "There is only one chance that I will give. If you can provide my daughter's spirit with certain proof of a true and unselfish love, then I will pass. As I forfeit my place in the heavens, so Semine will return to Old Earth. Then, if she chooses, all true timelines will be restored." Owain then attempted to memorise the pathway through time which led to Semine's spirit. Seeing this, Koldovan laughed. "You think that it will be so easy to return to this place? First, you must prove yourself worthy. Trust that I will make each step a true test for you and your heirs. Your doom will be to seek, but never to find. Nor will you have the comfort of your wife to support you. She will only live until she has borne one child. When she dies you will also understand the bitterness of despair and the meaning of loss." Then

Koldovan departed Old Earth and Owain fell into a deep sleep. When he awoke he found that he had no memory of the path to the Maiden's chamber, and his palace with its tower of light was destroyed. All that remained was one great pillar. The marble, from which it was hewn, now shone blindingly white and written upon it were lines of verse.

Where no moon shines, where no sun warms
Where water moves not, where rainbows now flower
Make a sharp path
Make a master dance
Make music never played
Make a lasting power
With Knights of the Road, with a maiden's breath
With a stone of moon, with heart's loving bound
Raise the last star
Touch the golden moon
Find peace at last
A true paradise, found.

As Owain read the words they blurred, so he quickly committed them to memory. Then he looked around and saw Avaldi alive and watching him. Valdis was lying on the ground as if sleeping. Avaldi rose and Owain saw that he was changed. He had been empowered by the Moon Goddess and had no memory of the events following Owain's marriage to Valdis. Owain also knew that reality was now broken. He could no longer find and easily cross all the pathways across time. Although Valdis seemed well and happy, he perceived that the Curse was working and so eventually they would be parted. However, he concealed his grief and rejoiced in his marriage and his renewed friendship with Avaldi.

*

As spring turned to summer and the days lengthened, Owain began the Quest to find the Star Maiden. His first task was to retrieve the shattered reality splinters. He summoned his knights and sent them out in secrecy to find them. The smaller fragments he kept hidden in the vaults of his new palace, but with the larger splinters, he created special ways to use their unique qualities. Each became a device for the use of the Sun or Moon Lords, to help them guard and manage existence. Using the largest of the reality splinters, Owain crafted a protection pendant for Valdis. The pendant was set with a pearl, mounted upon silver and gold to signify the unity that existed between the Sun and the Moon Lords. Avaldi grew strong and used his Moon Powers wisely. He travelled across Old Earth and did many great and good deeds. On one journey, he found a fabulous herd of wild horses and he brought back a golden stallion, a black stallion and a silver mare. These three became the founders of a line that served the Sun and Moon Lords throughout the years to come. Then, with much joy, Valdis, at last, bore her longed-for child. But within days of her son's first birthday, she died and so this part of Koldovan's Curse was fulfilled. Owain sadly buried Valdis in Rheged and he raised above her the white marble stone upon which had appeared the verses for the Quest. Into the stone, he embedded a reality splinter, which made it possible to summon Sun and Moon Lords from across time.

*

So, the years passed and Avaldi also took a wife and bore a son. Thus, the Quest continued across the centuries, with many generations of the Sun Lords and Moon Lords, united in their efforts to save Old Earth from extinction. They became a noble force, known as the Perdurare.[1] Their great powers were hidden from mortals, although

---

[1] Latin *perdurare* to endure, from *per-* throughout + *durare* to last

they walked freely amongst them. Afraid that the secrets of the Quest might be lost, the Sun Lords forged a golden sword and into the hilt's pommel placed the protection pendant. The blade was impressed with memories regarding the history of the Sun and Moon Lords and the Curse that had fallen upon the Earth. This sword, called Sunniva, became a sacred heirloom for the leaders of the Sun Lords, known as the Paladin.[2] It was their greatest weapon and a symbol of their enduring hope.

---

[2] Trusted leader and champion of a cause

Part 1 – Paladin
Chapter One

Theora Templeton, the niece of the late Rector of Highton, watched the funeral guests leave the Rectory. The year was 1803, it was October and it had been raining heavily for many days. Day and night had merged into a misty, unrelenting gloom. The girl waited until the lights carried by the villagers had dwindled into nothingness. Then she closed the heavy front door.

Theora was just past twenty, a gentlewoman now without any living family. The Templetons, although boasting an impressive lineage that dated back to Edward Plantagenet, were short-lived. Her father, one of two boys, had inherited Temple Court at an early age, married quickly, and died soon after his daughter was born. Over the next fourteen years, his wife gradually succumbed to her weak constitution and overwhelming grief. Due to the late Lord Templeton's youthful excesses, there was no money, so the little girl had been taken in by her uncle, a clergyman with his parish in the Yorkshire Wolds. The conscientious Rector dutifully encouraged Theora to devote herself to a life of service. She had applied herself earnestly and was now as efficient in housekeeping as in French and Italian, art and music. She was attractive, intelligent, well educated, and well born, but without prospects. As her uncle had neither the funds nor the inclination to introduce his niece to society, she had never travelled further than Harrowgate and had yet to receive an offer of marriage.

The Rector's sudden death had left Theora very grieved. He had been her guide and protector and she had respected his judgement in all things. However, in accordance with his dying wish that she should not mourn excessively, she was now doing her best to look towards the future. The reading of the will had confirmed that she had the support of a modest inheritance, so she had planned to remain in Yorkshire. Then, fate had taken an unexpected turn. A week after her uncle's death, she was offered the chance of a post as a governess at Temple Court in Surrey. The fact that the Estate now belonged to a man with a somewhat curious reputation did not bother her at all. Nothing mattered except that she was, at last, going home! Thinking of this she almost sang as she ran up the stairs to change her gown, but suppressed the impulse because she knew it would have shocked the Cook, and the House Maid who were clearing away the funeral tea. Both of them had cried for days after the Rector's death as they had been genuinely devoted to him. They respected Theora, but she had never encouraged familiarity. Being naturally reserved she had made few acquaintances during her stay in Yorkshire. The exception was Mrs Colton, a widow and teacher at the local school. In Penelope Colton, Theora had found the only lady in the district equal to her in intelligence and taste and they were firm friends. Mrs Colton had willingly agreed to accompany Theora to Surrey and had helped her prepare. She had been somewhat shocked to discover that they would be travelling to Surrey on the eve of the Rector's funeral. Waiting in the parlour, she prayed that Theora would hurry. Her impatient eye connected with the portrait of the Rector. He had been a handsome man, with a single-minded duty to his vocation. As Theora entered the parlour, Mrs Colton was struck again by how very physically different she was to her uncle, who had been tall and fair. In contrast his niece was petite and dark haired. Having outgrown her childhood delicacy she had achieved a pleasing maturity. Although she frequently adopted a studied dignity, when she smiled, she was really a very lovely young woman.

She was smiling now and greeted Mrs Colton cheerfully. The House Maid who was stacking books into an old tea chest, now came forward to advise that the Miss's trunks had been taken down to the inn and ask if there was anything else that was needed, as she needed to get off (it being long past her finishing time).

"I didn't know it was that late," Theora exclaimed. "We must be going, Penny, or we will miss our escort."

She strode out into the hall, picked up a small bag and walked out into the garden. A faint moon meant that there was sufficient light for the two ladies to descend the short lane without fear of turning an ankle. Miss Templeton offered her arm to her older and stouter companion for extra support and very soon the lights of the Old Rectory were well behind them.

The inn, which was on the outskirts of Highton village, was a convenient stop for traffic going north and south. Miss Templeton quickly spotted a red-painted coach, with a distinctive crest. Nodding to Mrs Colton, she drew her quickly through the crowd where they were greeted by a tall, thin man who had been sitting up with the driver, but swiftly jumped down.

"Are you Miss Templeton?" he demanded frankly and directly to Mrs Colton. Before she could reply, Theora came forward holding out her hand.

"I am Miss Templeton. This is my travelling companion, Mrs Colton. You must be Mr Allan, I am so glad to see you, I do hope you haven't had to wait long."

The young man took her hand. "Glad to meet you both." He nodded to Mrs Colton, and stood politely to one side to allow them to enter the coach. After he had checked to ensure that they had a rug to cover them, cushions to support their backs and hot water bottles for their feet, he nodded to the driver, settled himself on the seat opposite the ladies and the coach sprang forward. For a while the sound of the wheels and the horses' hooves on the cobbled streets made all conversation impossible. Gradually, the hard roads gave way to dust tracks and words could be exchanged again. As Mrs Colton, resting comfortably, became sleepy, Miss Templeton took the opportunity to become acquainted with their new companion, Mr Allan. She already knew that he had recently been appointed the Estate Steward and had been sent by her new employer, Lord Sulien, to ensure their safe journey to Surrey. He was surprisingly young, no more than a few years older than herself. After some polite exchanges regarding the weather and the Yorkshire scene, she asked him how long he had known Lord Sulien. Mr Allan considered the question. "Depends on what you mean by knowing," he said coolly, in his soft Irish accent. He noticed that Miss Templeton was taken aback by this statement.

"Now, I'll bet you were hoping for an old family retainer who could give you a direct line into his Lordship. And here I am, a mere babe of twenty-four years, still wet behind the ears!" Miss Templeton gasped and, noting this, Mr Allan smiled broadly. "And there I was thinking I'd shocked you," he said slyly. "I see I'll have to get up a bit earlier in the morning to do that won't I, Ma'am." He glanced out of the window. "Be pitch dark soon, you should try and get some sleep too." He settled down, and firmly shut his eyes.

After Mr Allan fell asleep, the journey seemed to pass even more slowly. A thick fog had descended and it was quite dark. Although the Coachman had set up lanterns, they did not give much light and nothing could be seen from the coach windows. Theora closed her eyes but sleep did not come. Instead she reflected again on the contents of the crested, much-worn letter in her pocket. She knew almost every word by heart now.

Dear Miss Templeton,

Please accept my condolences for your recent bereavement.

I am the father of a motherless daughter. My regimental duties have meant that I have been abroad for most of her life, so she has been in the care of my step sister, Lady Meadley. Juliet is now turned seventeen and I have decided to form an establishment for her in Surrey. My intention is that she will remain there to complete her education and then be introduced to society. I have recently purchased the Temple Court Estate and I have engaged a housekeeper by the name of Mrs Chapman. I have explained that I am seeking a companion/teacher for my daughter. She suggested that this might be something that would be of interest to you. She has explained your circumstances and indicated that you would very much like to return to this district if a suitable opportunity arose. If that is truly the case, then I would be grateful if we could arrange to discuss further.

I am out of the country but returning to the district on the 28th for a few days. If you would be prepared to meet then, please send word, so that further arrangements can be made. If we are mutually suited, I would wish you to be prepared to remain indefinitely.

I am, Madam, your grateful servant
Aidan Sulien, Earl of Woodchester.

When Theora received this letter she had been considerably astonished. She knew Mrs Chapman, who had worked at Temple Court during her father's lifetime. Theora had written to thank her for the recommendation, but also (as delicately as possible) to make further inquiries. All she knew of the Sulien family was that they were wealthy and that Lord Sulien was respected in military circles. Mrs Chapman's letter had fortunately

5

come by return of post and now also reposed in Miss Templeton's pocket.

It read:

Dear Miss Templeton,

It is so good to hear from you after all these years. I am most glad that his Lordship has written to you. Please do not thank me. I am so grateful to do you such a small service, after the many kindnesses that you and your family have made to me and mine.

You wish to know more about his Lordship's situation and so I will tell you all I know. I first met his Lordship this spring. He is a most respectable man. Although he doesn't have the fine manners which marked out your dear father (God rest him).

Lord Sulien is plain speaking, but this may be due to his long military career. He is a general as well as an earl, and (if you will forgive me) it is clear from his way of speaking that he is much used to giving orders.

What else I know is only what I have been told (in confidence) by his Lordship's manservant. It seems that in his Lordship's youth he committed various offences in relation to gaming and drinking. But, since his marriage and his poor wife's death in child-bed, he has lived a very strict life and distinguished himself as a fine soldier. I have seen for myself that both Miss Juliet and Lady Meadley seem to want for nothing except, perhaps, more of his Lordship's company, as he is very often away from them.

The children are calling me so I must close now. I do hope that you have the chance to meet his Lordship in person, so that you can judge him for yourself. I have assured him that you will be the perfect person to guide Miss Juliet. It would be a real blessing if you were to return to Temple Court and I would welcome your help, as his Lordship has some grand ideas about what he

wants to do around the house. I know you will be better able than me to understand these and so make everything right and proper.
Yours respectfully,
Molly Chapman.

Theora had been very glad of this letter, but with certain passages she had struggled. Her conscience was the issue. She knew that her uncle would have been appalled at the idea of her going to live in the house of a man who (however long ago) had led an indulgent life. At last, after much consideration, she had brought Mrs Colton into her confidence. Based on her advice and encouragement, Theora had written back to Lord Sulien and shortly after had received the details on how and when she would travel to Surrey. Then it had been a flurry to get prepared whilst managing the final arrangements around her uncle's funeral. This included purchasing a few new clothes and a trunk to put them in. Despite guilt at spending the housekeeping money, for the first time since moving to Yorkshire, she had taken the carrier to Harrowgate. Here, she had tracked down the only dressmaker able to meet her modest budget. As time was short, a half-made-up gown of steel grey with a matching pelisse and new bonnet trimmed with dark red ribbons were selected. Theora had spent her last few evenings painstakingly making alterations. The result was that she was now resplendent in an outfit, which, if not London made, was at least new and fitted well. The gentle satisfaction this gave her acted as a soporific. Despite her sadness at the events of the day and the rocking of the carriage, she fell asleep. *She immediately found herself deep inside a very vivid dream. This was not unusual, for since she had been a very little girl, she had frequently had such experiences. She was in a large* room filled with bookshelves of a rich, warm wood. The ceiling was gilded and painted and sun poured through oriel windows with small, thick, round glass panes. There was a trestle table and sitting at it was a slim woman with beautiful golden hair. Her face was in shadow as she was leaning over an open book. The whole table was covered with books, each open at a page and overlapping the other. Theora could see over the woman's left shoulder. The book she was looking at was an illuminated text. In the centre of the page was a picture. It was of a young man, dressed in medieval clothes. He had brown hair and a pleasant, open countenance. Theora stared in amazement for the picture was now moving. The man had been standing by a horse, but now was walking away across a green hill. Then a tear dropped onto the page. Instantly, the movement stopped and the picture became still and lifeless. In the background a voice spoke. Theora could not hear or clearly understand the language. The woman quickly shut the book and, picking it up, thrust it into one of the bookcases. As she did so, another book pushed forward on the shelf, as if inviting itself to be picked up. The Lady took it and set it down upon the table. It was a rather shabby volume which opened to reveal the picture of a middle-aged woman dressed in 15th-Century clothes. She seemed to be praying. The golden-haired lady turned the page and the scene changed. The woman was now prostrate upon a stone-flagged floor and rocking in terror. The Lady took the corner of the page between thumb and finger. Then, to Theora's horror, she ripped it right across. At once the picture woman screamed, a sickening sound, like the sound of a trapped hare. The Lady took the page and walked to the end of the room where there was a candle stand. She spoke and the thick wax candles flamed into life. The Lady offered the page *to the flame and it burned quickly. Then she turned back to the table.*

Theora was abruptly awakened by a very sudden jolt and she came to, painfully aware that she had fallen sideways. The coach was now filled with a soft half-light and she realised it was past dawn. Mr Allan was gazing at her with some amusement and she found that her bonnet was now sitting at a somewhat rakish angle. She put up a hand, but it slipped right round, the ribbons unravelled and it fell to the floor. Mr Allan laughed outright as Theora clutched for it in vain. He quickly leaned forward, retrieved it and handed it back.

"Think you need to tie it on tighter don't you, Ma'am?"

Theora smoothed her hair. "Where are we now if you please?"

"No idea," he said briefly.

"Can't you guess?"

"No I can't," he said. Seeing that Theora's expression had become somewhat stony, he raised his eyebrows. "Look just because I rescued your bonnet, don't think I'm the fount of all knowledge now."

She tied the bonnet back. "I don't think that," she said coldly.

He ran his eye over her with smiling appraisal. "Very nice," he said approvingly.

To her surprise Theora found herself flushing. She couldn't help feeling a certain pleasure at what was the first actual compliment on her appearance that she had received since she had been in the nursery. To hide her colour she turned to the window. The view had changed considerably. The hills and moors had given way to gentle slopes and deep lines of trees turning golden lime and ruby red with the onset of autumn. The horses had slowed a little and they turned downhill and joined what seemed to be the main street of quite a large town. Early as it was there were already signs of life. Tradesmen were moving about, preparing for the day's business. The coach pulled up in front of the only inn, a long-roofed, white-painted establishment and the coachman jumped down. They were obviously changing horses and Theora wondered how long it would take. She also realised she was extremely hungry. Mr Allan jumped down and, after a few minutes of rapid inquiry, returned to say that they had an hour's grace and the coachman suggested they should breakfast. They all went into the inn and soon sat down to an excellent meal in the surprisingly clean back room. Theora, whose spirits had been revived by a large plate of ham and eggs, helped herself to a second cup of coffee from the battered silver pot and again turned her attention to their young escort. In the full light of day she perceived that he was dark haired and blue eyed. He was dressed respectably and there was nothing displeasing about his appearance or his manner. However, he seemed curiously reluctant to talk about himself. For Lord Sulien to have engaged someone so young and inexperienced for such an important post seemed very curious. She took a sip of coffee and reflected rather sadly that it was not her place to question his Lordship's servant choices, as she herself was just a servant. This was one of the things she knew she would find very difficult to adjust to. It was true that in her uncle's house she had been effectively his housekeeper, but he had never treated her as such. She had worked hard, but she had always known herself as Miss Templeton, a lady born and bred. She gave a slight sigh and Mrs Colton, who was buttering toast, stopped to ask her if she felt quite well.

"Well enough, but still very stiff," said Theora with a slight grimace. She looked at Mr Allan. "Could I prevail upon you, Sir to walk with me a little. I am not sure I can face the journey again unless I stretch my legs." He looked up in surprise, but stood up at once and offered her his arm.

"With pleasure, Ma'am, although I'm not sure there's much to see."

She smiled. "Just a short walk is all I need, Sir. A pleasant view is not a requirement."

"In which case we shall walk to the Church and back." He glanced at Mrs Colton. "Will you be all right here, Ma'am, or would you prefer me to escort you back to the coach?"Mrs Colton assured him that she was fine where she was and gladly turned her attention back to the toast.

Outside the sun was out, but a cold wind blew. The Church was just a quarter of a mile away and they made their way towards it. For a while no word was spoken, but Theora was aware that Mr Allan wanted to say something. At last, when they had reached the Church and stopped by its gate, he leaned upon it for a few moments and then turning back to face her said abruptly:

"Miss Templeton, I feel I owe you an apology. My attitude towards you and your friend. I'm so very sorry. I'm not normally like this I can assure you." Before Theora could say anything he continued hastily, "It's just that I have so much on my mind and so many things that I need to resolve. I desperately need a trustworthy friend." He took her hand as he said this in a firm grip and she was quite powerless to withdraw it.

She said firmly, "Mr Allan, please believe me when I say there is nothing to forgive. As to being your friend, of course I hope that I will be, when I know you better."

"No." He said the word so fiercely that Theora was slightly alarmed. "I need you to swear now that I can trust you."

She wondered suddenly if he was drunk, but he was leaning over her and she could smell nothing on his breath. She stood as tall as she could and looked him in the eye.

"I swear that you can trust me. Now please, release me."

His expression changed immediately and he smiled. "Thank you," he said, took her hand through his arm again and turned around. At the coach, Mrs Colton was waiting for them.

"Do you feel better, dear?" Conscious of the public place Theora managed a smile. "Quite better thank you." As the coach man was waiting for her, she asked him quickly how far they were from Temple Court.

"About a half-day's travel, Ma'am," he responded courteously. He then helped hand them up and the coach started off again.

The rest of the journey was uneventful. Mr Allan spent most of it in conversation with Mrs Colton, regaling her with stories of his early life in Ireland. He made no further attempt to speak with Theora and was so pleasant and engaging that she even found herself laughing from time to time at some of his anecdotes. Time passed and after one more change of horses they made good pace. Very soon the country became more familiar and each mile revealed remembered vistas, everyone with its own special connection to Theora's childhood. It was all so delightful that the time passed almost too quickly. It was mid-afternoon when the tired horses drew up in front of Temple Court. Here the ladies left the coach to Mr Allan who was travelling onto his lodgings. He bade them a pleasant farewell, remarking that he expected to see Miss Templeton later that week. She felt it only right to remind him that this was dependent upon his Lordship being prepared to confirm her appointment, but he only smiled and said cheerfully that he had no doubts about that. He shook her hand and as he did so she felt a scrap of paper pressed into her palm. Then with one final glance he was gone. Theora was very concerned by this, but as the manservant was waiting for them, she had no time to do more than slip the paper into her reticule and follow Mrs Colton into the house.

Chapter Two

Temple Court was a large estate. It incorporated many farms, with extensive pasture land and was bordered to the west by a small village. The house itself had started life as a priory, but had been extended twice, most notably by Theora's grandfather, who had added the much admired Palladian front. In the entrance hall, they were met by the head servant, Mr Meadows. He took them directly to the dining room where a cold luncheon was laid out. After this, Mrs Colton went to lay down upon her bed. Theora, having been advised that she was wanted in the red sitting room, took time to make herself presentable before she met her new employer. Then she knocked on the sitting room door and went in. To her surprise the room was empty except for a little, brown-haired lady who was drinking tea by the fire. She looked up as Theora entered and gave her a friendly smile, saying as she rose, "You must be Miss Templeton, welcome back to Temple Court my dear." She sat down again and waved to Theora to do the same. Looking about her, Theora saw that the room was virtually unchanged. She was pleased, for when she had previously lived here, this had been one of her favourite parts of the house. The room had an exceptional outlook with large windows which clearly revealed the distant lake glinting in the sunshine. An elegant and very large pianoforte now stood in front of them. Noting Theora's gaze, the Lady smiled.

"I would like to hear you play that later. First, let us get better acquainted, I am Lady Grace Meadley. My brother sends his apologies as he is detained on business. We expect him back any day now, but in the meantime, he has asked me to make you comfortable and introduce you to my niece."

She saw that Theora was looking a little constrained and said gently, "I do hope this change of plan doesn't cause you inconvenience." She didn't wait for Theora to reply, but rang the bell.

"Meadows, please ask Miss Juliet to join us. No, not straight away, in about ten minutes." She then poured two cups of tea and handed one to Theora.

"Now tell me all about yourself if you please and leave nothing out." She took out a small leatherbound book and silver-mounted pencil. Perceiving Theora's look of surprise she said quickly, "You won't mind if I make notes, I hope." She took a sip of tea. "Begin please."

It was not the meeting she had expected. Theora said carefully, "For the last six years I have been educated by my uncle. I speak French and Italian. I can play the pianoforte, paint in watercolours and embroider. Due to my late uncle's circumstances, I have also learned to manage a household." She waited until Lady Meadley had stopped writing. "Is there anything else I can tell you, Ma'am?"

Lady Meadley scanned over her notes. She made one or two crossings and then closed the book. "No, that's quite sufficient thank you. Would you now please play the piano for me? I think Juliet has left some music out. The naughty girl never practices as much as she should I'm afraid. Would you please choose something?"

Theora went at once to the instrument and took up the music laid out on the stand. There were several pieces which she knew, but one in particular took her eye. It had been heavily marked with amendments so the main body of the music had been subtly changed. There were written comments in a language which she realised she could not read, but recognised as Spanish. The handwriting was Lord Sulien's. She sat down and began to play. It was a technically testing piece but she had no difficulty and the changes were intriguing, they gave the music excitement and energy. Relishing the opportunity to play such a superior instrument, Theora became absorbed. Indeed she forgot where she was until she delivered the final movement. Then she was brought back to the present by vigorous applause. There were now two people in the room, the other being, unmistakeably, her potential new ward, Miss Juliet Sulien.

She came running forward saying, "Oh how clever you are. Papa brought that music back for me last year, but I have never been able to master it. Will you teach it to me, please?"

This was said with such innocent impulsiveness that Theora could not help smiling. She permitted herself to be led back to Lady Meadley who said pleasantly, "That was quite delightful, my dear. I can see that you are going to be such a help to Juliet." She looked indulgently at her niece. "Sit down would you, Kit."

Theora looked a question and Lady Meadley smiled. "Kit is short for 'Kitten'. When Juliet was a child, her father gave her that nickname. Tell Miss Templeton where you have got to with your studies, Kit. I cannot remember."

Juliet proceeded to do this, speaking quickly, but interrupting herself with frequent giggling. Theora now understood why her father sought to keep her in the schoolroom for another year. Miss Juliet was undisciplined and vain. She interspersed her list of books read and music listened to with satisfied glances at her reflection displayed in the large pier mirror. Theora took the opportunity of one such natural pause to say swiftly, "Well, you certainly do seem to have read a lot of poetry. Perhaps we could translate some into French?"

Juliet looked at her doubtfully. "I suppose we could.

Papa also likes me to ride three times a week and walk in the gardens when it is fine. Shall we go out now? I could show them to you."

Theora restrained a smile at Juliet's quick deflection. She was about to accept the offer, when Lady Meadley interrupted them.

"Not now, Kit, you have a dress fitting in an hour and I wish to talk to Miss Templeton a little longer."

She gently pushed her niece out of the room and turned back to Theora. "My dear, please come and sit next to me." She patted the sofa invitingly and, drawing Theora to her, covered her hands with her own plump ones. "Now you know the task ahead, do you think you might be happy here?"

Theora was genuinely surprised and touched by the sincerity of the question. She looked down before saying in a low voice, "I am sure I will be, Ma'am, and can only thank you and his Lordship for your kindness in considering me."

Lady Meadley leaned forward. "You are a sweet child," she said. "Quite attractive too. What do you think of my niece's looks?"

"I think her very pretty indeed," said Theora sincerely.

Lady Meadley sighed. "Yes, she is. She will also be very rich. It is common knowledge that my brother's wealth is considerable. Juliet will be prey to every fortune hunter when she is introduced to society. It is for that reason that both Aidan and I are keen that she has the companionship and tutelage of a woman of good breeding and common sense. I did not expect you to be quite so young! However, I am confident that you have just the temperament to guide my niece. My only concern is that you will not find your duties too confining. Juliet is no scholar, which is a disappointment to her father. My brother, Miss Templeton, is a man of superior intelligence and extensive knowledge of the world. He gives Juliet every consideration, but he can also be extremely particular. If he decides to engage you, it will be because he believes you will be able to satisfactorily complete her education."

Theora sat very still. "Then I am not yet engaged, Ma'am?"

Lady Meadley shook her head. "No, I'm afraid that will be for Aidan to decide, but I can promise that I will be recommending that you should be engaged. It will be important for you to make the right first impression though. Aidan is very quick to draw his own conclusions." She paused. "I hope I am not alarming you? I am conscious that you know very little about us, so I wish you to be properly prepared." She took up some needlework and began to sew, picking her words and her stitches with equal care.

"Aidan met Juliet's mother at a time when we all thought he was a committed bachelor. The marriage was a love match, although it was short-lived as Juliet's mother died at her birth. Since then Aidan has never shown the slightest interest in any other woman." She looked at Theora keenly. "He is a rich prize on the matrimonial market and he has been pursued relentlessly since poor Elizabeth died. Little wonder then, that he is so cynical about his daughter's prospects."

"You care for him very much don't you, Ma'am?" said Theora shrewdly.

"I am devoted to him," said Lady Meadley. "Although I am only his adopted sister, we have always been extremely close. However, I have never been blind to his faults and it is important that you are aware of them. Otherwise you may judge him too harshly or be frightened off."

Theora smiled at that. "I can promise you, Ma'am, that

I do not frighten easily."

Lady Meadley smiled too. "That is very good to know. Shall we take some more tea?" Realising this was a signal for the conversation to turn to more impersonal topics, Theora enjoyed the opportunity to relax and (whilst making occasional polite responses) to make a study of her hostess. Lady Meadley was dressed in a gown of ash blue silk, which in its cut and style reflected simple good taste. As Juliet too had been equally well dressed, Theora assumed her Ladyship's refined influence. After about an hour or so, Lady Meadley rose, saying that it was time for her to see to her correspondence before supper. She suggested Theora should rest and, after thanking her again, left her alone. For a little while Theora sat in thought, reflecting upon the events of the day, but eventually she rejoined Mrs Colton upstairs. She was reading, but she dropped her book at once and, drawing Theora in and closing the door behind her, was determined to know what had happened.

"Did it go well, my dear?"

"Yes, I think so," said Theora. She sank down into one of the chairs and looked up into the anxious face of her friend. "Nothing is settled yet though, I will need to see Lord Sulien for a final decision."

"You would think that his sister would have the authority to engage you," said Mrs Colton.

"It is just as I suspected: his Lordship rules," said Theora. "I must be patient. Are you all right, Penny?"

"I am as fit as a fiddle," said Mrs Colton briskly, "but you haven't properly rested since the Rector died."

"Then I will sit here for a while and take advantage of this lovely fire," said Theora, yawning.

"I'm sure you won't have trouble sleeping," said Mrs Colton. "I shall call for you later so that I can help you dress and then we can go to supper together."

Theora's bedroom was one of the rooms which faced onto the park. Although now rather dark, generally, it was pleasantly sunny in the morning and cool in the afternoon. A large fire had been lit in the basket-shaped grate and the warm flames were reflected in the gilt mirror that hung on the opposite wall. The lighting of fires in all the rooms was one of the few differences that Theora had so far detected. In most other respects, the house and its management were much the same as when her father had been alive. She lay down on the day bed, but she had only shut her eyes for a moment when she suddenly started up and ran to pick up her reticule which was on the chair. Having retrieved the slip of paper she lit a candle and read the scrawled and brief message.

Miss Templeton. I beg that you will meet me in the old summer house by the lake on Saturday forenoon.

I am your servant

Mr Ciaran Allan.

Theora looked at the paper, read it twice more and then dropped it into the fire. She sat down on the bed and looked out at the unceasing rain. She was not prone to low spirits, but the tensions of the last few weeks, the unexpected delay in meeting her new employer and now this strange note frayed her already strained nerves and she found herself disintegrating into tears. As she could not remember ever giving way in this manner, she was dismayed by her weakness and wanted to stop, but the tears flowed relentlessly. At last she was so tired that she had to lay down. Then the softness of the bed, the warmth and quiet comfort overtook her, and quite unexpectedly, she was asleep. It was indeed some hours later when the repeated sound of tapping awoke her. Now the room was dark and the fire burned down. Theora opened the door to find Mrs Colton beaming at her.

"You did sleep well then. How do you feel now?"

"I feel wonderful," said Theora, and she meant it. She could not remember a time, even when she had been a child, ever having slept so dreamlessly and awakened so refreshed. "But, it's late," she said in alarm, glancing at the clock. "We should have been down ages ago."

"Not a bit of it," said Mrs Colton. She took Theora's hair down, brushed it out, dressed it with a pale blue ribbon and helped tie up her sash. "There now, all done and no bit of fuss about it. Let us go down."

She took Theora's arm and together the two ladies descended the staircase and entered the dining room. Here Lady Meadley greeted them graciously and they all sat down to an excellent supper. After this, Juliet played the piano and Theora joined her for a duet. They finished with a long and pleasant conversation, before it was regretfully time for bed.

*

The next day there was no sign of his Lordship and Theora remained uncomfortably aware that she was still on trial. In the morning she joined Juliet and Lady Meadley for the promised tour of the gardens. Theora was quickly distracted by the distant prospect of the river, which wound down to the lake. She hoped they would go down to see it for it held many happy memories of feeding the swans and ducks. But, as neither Juliet nor Lady Meadley suggested it, she contented herself with following them down the rambling path to the orchard. This consisted of long lines of pears, plums, cherries and apples. Many of the trees were still laden with ripe apples, for, as yet, no arrangements had been made to pick and dispose of them. Juliet was keen to try one for herself, but the trees were tall for lack of pruning and none of the ladies had the necessary stature to reach the best fruit. It was therefore with relief that Juliet spied a distant man walking towards them across the fields. This quickly revealed itself to be none other than Mr Allan, approaching from the direction of the woods.

He was obviously on very good terms with Lady Meadley who greeted him warmly. After some pleasant exchanges he then turned his attention to Juliet and listened patiently as she explained that she wanted him to pick her an apple and not just any apple, the largest he could find! This request was made with all Juliet's childish impulsiveness, but, looking at Mr Allan, Theora anxiously noted his quickly altered expression. She glanced at Lady Meadley, but she showed no sign that she saw anything amiss. She looked a little questioningly at Mr Allan who returned her glance frankly. The sadness in his eyes was a contrast to his attractive smile and, although he quickly veiled it, she knew instinctively that she was seeing a man suffering from the depths of a deep, unrequited love. This then was the answer to his impassioned request for her help. Afraid that he might betray himself further, she decided to keep the couple in view. To do so, she suggested to Lady Meadley that they might walk to the end of the Park. However, her Ladyship replied that her shoes were not stout enough and she felt that she had done enough walking for the day.

"For although Dr Scott has advised me to get lots of fresh air, he is not an advocate of over-exertion. So, I will stay here and enjoy the sunshine whilst you all take a turn."

So directed, Theora followed the young couple, but kept a careful distance and a watchful eye, as Mr Allan picked a selection of fruit for Juliet's appraisal. But, Theora quickly saw that her fears were needless. Juliet was far more interested in comparing the apples than getting up a flirtation. Equally, Mr Allan gave no indication that he had any other purpose in mind than to quickly fill up the flower basket.

Seeing they were quite innocently absorbed, Theora found herself wandering along one of the paths that crossed the ride. She ascended a slight slope on the south side of the garden, between orchard and house. Knowing that this would give her a better view of the lake she struck further up the hill. At the top she found herself facing a set of finely wrought, open gates. These were new and expensive and she could see no point to them. The house and park being set upon hills, they were naturally bordered by the river on one side and heathland on the other. Her curiosity roused, she walked through. Instead of the stretch of unbroken heather and bracken that she had expected to see, directly in front of her although perhaps half a mile away was a tall white stone pillar, glittering in the autumn sunlight. She quickly walked to it and examined it carefully. It was a cylindrical spiral, the core of the stone hollowed out with shelf-like steps. These led up to a final platform, upon which it would be possible to stand. The top had been carved with yet another shelf above, but this sloped up, as if it were a church lectern with two slots on either side. With difficulty, Theora managed to climb up to the top. She stepped forward and found herself neatly wedged into the stone aperture in front of the lectern. It almost felt as if the stone was wrapped around her, protecting but not touching. She realised that if someone taller than she had been standing there, that person would have been easily able to see out for some considerable distance. Being short, she could see nothing except the smooth marbled slab. She craned her neck and stood on tiptoe but it was useless. She had given up and was about to step down when she was suddenly aware that she was not alone. There was someone immediately behind her. Theora tried to turn round, but her long skirt made swift movement impossible. Then a pair of very strong arms lifted her bodily off the platform and, with a swift and dextrous movement, turned her about so that she found herself helplessly looking up into the face of a man. As his arms remained tight about her, Theora could not pull away and she was breast to breast with the stranger. Forcing herself to meet his gaze, she looked into a pair of the most penetrating eyes she had ever seen. They regarded her with clinical directness, yet without any expression of surprise. The face to which they belonged was neither handsome nor plain, but something in between. It was not a young man's face, yet there was no real touch of age upon it.The stranger studied her briefly and then, without hesitation, carried her back down the steps and set her down again upon the heath. By his clothes and his bearing he was obviously a gentleman and his voice when he spoke was mellow, cultured, but extremely clipped.

"You are Miss Templeton." He delivered this as a statement. As she stepped back a pace, he extended his hand. "I am Lord Sulien."

Unable to continue to meet that penetrating gaze, Theora ignored the hand and sank into a deep curtsy.

"Forgive me for not being at the house when you arrived, Sir," she said.

"Do not trouble yourself, Miss Templeton. I am the one who should apologise for my delayed arrival."

He dropped his hand abruptly and stepped back. "Please also forgive me for my action just now." He glanced at the stone and rested his hand upon it lightly. It was a curious gesture of both familiarity and possession. "These steps are not safe. Others have climbed as you have just done, fallen and sustained severe injury."

"Your Lordship is too good, but I do not believe that I

was in any danger."

"Leave me to be the judge of that." His voice was suddenly harsh but his expression had not changed.

"May I escort you back to the house? My sister and daughter will have already returned."

It was undoubtedly a command and Theora had no choice but to obey it. She walked with him to the gate but could not help remarking as they passed through:

"The steps and the gates, Sir, are new?"

"Yes."

He paused and seemed to be considering something. When he spoke she sensed that he was restraining himself from saying what he had initially intended.

"It would be best, Miss Templeton, if you did not mention that you had been here or seek to do so again. I am sure you have realised that this is a very special place. I do not wish it to be disturbed in any way."

The cold finality of his tone made it hard for Theora to respond.

"I am very sorry, Sir, for intruding," she managed.

He gave the faintest of shrugs.

"There's no need for apology. The gates should not have been left open. I will ensure it doesn't happen again."

They had reached the house by this time. He walked into the sitting room. At the doorway he paused.

"When you are changed and rested, I would be grateful if you would join me. I'll expect you in an hour." Then he shut the door.

Theora made her way back to her bedroom. She tried to settle her thoughts, but they crowded upon her, demanding attention like greedy children, giving no peace. She changed her walking shoes, and hastily brushed some grass stains from the hem of her skirt. Her hair was starting to uncurl. It was not until she was once again impeccably neat from head to toe, her hair rigidly pinned and her complexion restored to its usual pallor that she felt sufficiently composed. Then she went downstairs. As she descended, she became aware that the piano was being played. As she entered the sitting room she saw that his Lordship was seated on the sofa, a glass of wine in his hand listening to the music. He looked up briefly as she entered and she was again conscious of that swift and complete appraisal, but apart from a gesture to indicate that she should sit, he showed no more interest in her. Theora, taking up a position at the back of the room, was unable to see who was playing, but she both respected and envied the skill demonstrated. She didn't resent Lord Sulien's absolute absorption in the performance, especially as it allowed her an opportunity to examine him in detail. She noted that even when relaxing he had the straight-backed posture of a military man. Like his daughter he had thick fair hair, but there was no other resemblance. Whereas Juliet reminded Theora of a wildflower, soft and fragile, her father was as unyielding and unwelcoming as a thorny tree. But Theora thought she understood his reserved manner. Having schooled herself over many years to hide strong emotions, she recognised in the Earl an equal discipline, developed to protect and hide those deeper feelings which could so easily surface and cause embarrassment and confusion. As the final notes of music died away he suddenly seemed to remember Theora's presence.

"Do you know this music?" he asked abruptly.

Not waiting for her to answer he stood up and walked over to take a seat in one of the salon chairs opposite her.

"I would like you to teach it to Juliet, do you think you could do that?"

Theora nodded. "I can certainly try, Sir, although I strongly doubt whether she will ever be able to play that piece so skilfully."

He frowned. "I appreciate your candour, Miss Templeton, are there any other areas where you feel my daughter may be deficient?"

Theora flushed. "I am sorry, Sir. I only meant to say that Miss Juliet will always lack the natural talent that has just been so ably demonstrated."

"Praise indeed from someone my sister tells me is a most superior performer."

He looked across the room. "Let me introduce you to our resident expert. Argus, come here and meet Miss Templeton."

The gentleman stood up from the piano and came forward.

"This is my friend and neighbour, Lord Thorne," said the Earl.

Lord Thorne bowed. "I am very pleased to make your acquaintance, Miss Templeton," he said.

They shook hands and, as with the Earl, Theora felt she was being carefully assessed. However, there was more open, curiosity in Lord Thorne's gaze. It was as if he was wanting something from her, yet what that might be, she could not fathom. He suddenly became conscious that she was aware of his scrutiny and, as if he was seeking something to say, spoke hurriedly, "Aidan has been showing me your paintings and I am very impressed." He broke off as Lord Sulien turned away and walked to the table where Theora had left her portfolio of pictures the day before.

"I can see you paint well and understand that you also speak several languages," said the Earl. He looked out of the window. "Indeed you seem to have all the accomplishments that I require. But, how are you with horses?"

"Horses, Sir?"

"Yes." He saw she was looking confused and his straight, thick brows drew together.

"Don't tell me you can't ride?"

"Oh yes, Sir, but I must confess it has been many years since I have done so."

Anticipating further questions she said swiftly, "My uncle's circumstances meant that I did not have the leisure or the opportunity. I am, however, very fond of horses and did often ride at home, I mean, here, at Temple Court."

She blushed for her mistake, but if he had noticed her bêtise he made no mention of it. He continued looking at her, only averting his gaze when Juliet came running into the room followed more sedately by Lady Meadley.

"I am sure you'll be happy for Miss Templeton to accompany you and Snowdrop, won't you, Kit?"

Juliet, who had reached up to kiss him on either cheek, sank back to her heels.

"Oh, it is all agreed! Darling Papa, I am so glad. I knew you would like her."

She turned back to Theora and clasped her hands. "Papa wants me to be a scholar before I am a lady, but I know you can teach me how to be both at the same time."

Her cheerful certainty was so engaging that Theora couldn't help laughing.

Juliet then drew her father away to the window and pelted him with a series of questions, not waiting for answers, but merging her inquiries into a careless monologue, to which he listened patiently. Under cover of this conversation, Miss Templeton attempted to thank Lady Meadley for the confirmation of her appointment. This was quickly dismissed.

"My dear, it is you who are doing us a great favour. Now, perhaps you should speak with Lord Thorne and agree how you are going to manage Juliet's lessons together." Theora's face showed her surprise.

"Lord Thorne has some part in Juliet's education, Ma'am?"

"Oh yes, I should have explained before. Lord Thorne is godfather to Juliet. Argus come here, will you and tell Theora about yourself please. I am sure I can't do you sufficient justice." She moved away leaving them together.

Lord Thorne came over to sit upon the long chaise. He leaned back and crossed his legs, regarding her through heavy lidded eyes.

"How are you enjoying being back in Surrey?"

"Very much, Sir."

"And you are keen to start teaching Juliet?"

"I am indeed."

"And don't mind that you will need to consult with me about it occasionally?"

"Not a bit."

"Then a potentially awkward situation has been averted," he said easily. He smiled and she thought how well it became him. "That now all being settled, shall we go for a walk?"

The abrupt request made her blink. "Of course, if you wish it, but, Lord Sulien, and her Ladyship, will they not wish us to stay?"

"Both very busy with other things at the moment. I can assure you we won't be missed, not for a short time. Please trust me."

Happily quitting the overly hot sitting room for the freshness of the park Theora found that she was enjoying Lord Thorne's company. He had struck her first as a quiet man, but he was actually quite loquacious. He was easily as educated as her uncle but far better informed. He was also relaxed and pleasant, with a friendly and respectful manner. Theora quickly found herself speaking with him far more openly than was usually natural to her. After they had strolled for a while, Lord Thorne suggested that she should lead the way out to the lake.

"For I am sure you have a far better knowledge than I of the best walks and viewpoints," he said.

Theora thanked him and, determined not to disappoint in her role as guide, led him away from the main path and out onto a pretty, but seldom-used, ride that wound up the hill. To begin with it was a little over grown, but it soon opened up and once they had passed the hill's brow, they emerged into a large grove of fine tall beeches which crowned the very peak. The trees still held their bright golden leaves and their smooth green trunks and silvery branches were stately and beautiful in the autumn sunshine. Green grass, cropped to a silken smoothness by rabbits, carpeted the whole. Far below, a ribbon of water wound directly through the valley, descended over a rocky cascade and made its stop at the rippling splendour of the lake.

"The river is called the Silverway," said Theora, forgetting that Lord Thorne might already know this, "but the locals just call it 'the Way'."

Lord Thorne duly looked and admired. "Has the lake always been there?" he inquired.

Theora shook her head. "No. The park was partly laid out by my great-grandfather and my grandfather completed it and added the lake."

"That is quite a piece of work," said Lord Thorne thoughtfully. "It must have taken many years."

"Many years, yes and a great deal of expense. But the family was much pleased with the result. My father was apparently very proud of it."

"Did he not speak of it to you?" asked Lord Thorne.

Theora, who had bent to dislodge a bramble clinging to her skirt, averted her face slightly. "Not really. He died when I was quite young you see." She released her skirt and turned away.

"I'm sorry, I didn't know," said Lord Thorne, noting that her voice was unsteady.

"Of course not," said Theora, her voice deliberately more cheerful. "Now, please tell me of your own estate. I am sure it has much to rival this." She turned and walked down the hill.

Lord Thorne followed her. Although tall, he was sparer in frame than the Earl. Yet there was about him a similar sense of authority and command.

"My home is in Gloucestershire," he said.

"I have never been there," said Theora eagerly. "What is the county like?"

"Less wooded than Surrey, more grazing land," said Lord Thorne.

"How large is your estate?" asked Theora.

Lord Thorne hesitated. "Some 150000 acres," he said.

Theora gasped. "It must be an immense work for you. You must find it very hard to leave it so often?"

Lord Thorne looked over her head and out into the distance.

"I do indeed find it very hard to leave. Especially in the spring. Then the cherries fringe the castle walls and golden daffodils clothe the river banks."

Theora looked up at him curiously, for his thin face was lit with happy thoughts and he suddenly looked much younger and less careworn. She knew suddenly that he felt about his castle exactly as she did about Temple Court. For him, there was no better place on Old Earth. She empathised with his passion and his honesty.

"It sounds quite lovely," she said gently.

They had stopped at the foot of the hill and were about to turn onto the main path back to the house. Lord Thorne sighed and his expression changed back to its normal quiet composure. "So it is, like that view you just showed me. Thank you for that, Miss Templeton. Now, I suppose we had better go back, before we are too sorely missed."

He walked away briskly, as if keen to avoid further conversation. Theora hurried to keep up with him and they reached the entrance just before the rain started to fall.

Chapter Three

Once inside the hall, Lord Thorne explained that it was his habit to visit Temple Court every three weeks to give Juliet a music lesson, or ride with her in the park. However, now that Theora was engaged, he suggested that she should consider how this schedule fitted with her own plans for Juliet's education and revise accordingly. Theora protested, concerned that she did not usurp his authority or overturn the Earl's wishes, but Lord Thorne had dismissed her fears.

"I can assure you that both Aidan and I will be glad to trust your judgement. As you know, we are both often out of the country. It is a relief to have someone here who can supervise Juliet properly whilst we are away."

Theora thanked him. "Do you expect to be away again soon?"

Lord Thorne hesitated. "Yes, I'm afraid so. Aidan also has estates in France, and we go there to attend to his business interests. One particular enterprise is likely to take a lot of our time through the next few months."

"I see," said Theora. She felt strangely disturbed by the news. Although she had not expected the Earl to always be at Temple Court, the knowledge that he was now hardly likely to ever be home at all, was disappointing. Used to her uncle's and Mrs Colton's regular companionship, she enjoyed the company of strong, able men and sensible intelligent women. It now seemed that, in future, this was likely to be a rare commodity.

As Theora and Lord Thorne returned to the saloon, they were met by Juliet, who excitedly asked if they had enjoyed the walk. She hurried on, words tripping over each other.

"We usually go for a ride every Thursday, except

when the pack's meeting of course. By the way, there's a hunt here on Saturday. Aunt Grace can't ride, but now you're here, everything's perfect. You will come, won't you? Uncle Argus, please tell her that she must!"

Theora looked helplessly at Lord Thorne who smiled understandingly and turning to Juliet said, "You forget that what Miss Templeton can or cannot do is not my responsibility. In any case, I would not presume to dictate to her." He bowed to Theora, then bent and placed a light kiss on Juliet's cheek.

"Take care, Kit. Be a good girl and try not to tease your new teacher. Now I must go and say goodbye to your father."

He headed off in the direction of the study. Theora went on to the morning room, where she found Lady Meadley engaged with Mrs Colton. They had passed a very pleasant half hour, for the two ladies were of similar age and found themselves in agreement on a great many subjects. Lady Meadley had suggested that Mrs Colton should extend her visit, but Mrs Colton whilst gratified by the offer had firmly declined it.

"For I would like to get back before the weather turns, as it looks likely to do very soon."

Lady Meadley was disappointed but agreed that it was probably for the best. "Especially as the days are starting to draw in now and it would not be wise for you to travel at night in this country."

Seeing that Mrs Colton was now looking startled she said quickly, "Forgive me, I am afraid I have alarmed you. It's just that there had been a little trouble recently, but that has quite stopped since my brother and Lord Thorne returned."

She looked up as Theora came in. "Ah, welcome, my dear. I have been so much enjoying myself that I forgot the time. I need to go and see my dresser. She has been working with me to sort out the clothes that I will take back with me to Cornwall."

Mrs Colton looked at Theora questioningly. She sidestepped the glance and took a seat by the fire. Outside, the rain had started to fall heavily and the day which had started so brightly became suddenly dark and dull. Lady Meadley stood up.

"Will you excuse me now for a while? Just ring the bell if you need anything." She gave them her sweet smile and then quitted the room.

Mrs Colton held up her hands. "So she is going away! Well I do think it exceedingly poor that this was not mentioned before. A fine state of affairs, I must say, leaving you all alone with that young girl to manage and the house all at sixes and sevens."

Theora laughed. "Do you not think that is perhaps why she is leaving?"

"I don't doubt it," said Mrs Colton tartly. "Then she'll come back again in the spring, expecting everything to be well organised. What a burden for you. It is just too bad." She looked at Theora sharply. "You really don't seem too bothered at all."

"I suppose I don't see it as a burden," said Theora. "Especially where Juliet is concerned. You forget that Lord Thorne is also responsible for her education. I am sure I can rely on him to support me."

"Well that may be all well and good," said Mrs Colton dubiously, but you've just brought up another reason why I don't like this."

She saw Theora was eyeing her with some amusement and said in tones of doom, "You, a young lady, living here unchaperoned. It's not at all right."

Theora laughed.

"I've never heard anything so ridiculous," she said when she had regained her breath. "They are both far older than my uncle!"

"They are hardly in their dotage," said Mrs Colton soberly. "The fact is they are both rich and handsome. My wonder is that they've avoided matrimony for so long."

She saw Theora was looking self-conscious and said frankly, "Do you not think them good looking?"

Theora considered. "I suppose that Lord Sulien is not so badly favoured," she conceded. "And Lord Thorne has a pleasant, gentlemanly face, but I think it stretches the point to call them handsome."

Mrs Colton leaned across to tap her hand. "I will give you a word of advice, Theora," she said kindly. "For all your book learning and common sense, you still know very little about the ways of the world. They are both handsome men in the prime of life. Let me tell you, the lady that receives an offer from either of those two should think herself lucky indeed."

"I find you very contradictory," said Theora despairingly. "One minute you're telling me about the dangers of living unchaperoned in Lord Sulien's house and now you say that I should bless my good fortune and embrace the opportunity!"

"You know that it is just an improper approach I fear," said Mrs Colton baldly. "If you were to tell me that either of those two had come to you with an honest proposal, I'd be more than happy."

Theora picked up her sewing. "So, if you were given the choice, which of the two would you prefer?" she said idly.

Mrs Colton's expression became reflective. "Now there is a question. I am sure I would find it difficult to choose between them. In truth, Lord Thorne has the more engaging manners. He is a very pleasant man indeed and so very gentlemanly. But Lord Sulien, although he is a little reserved, and perhaps less well favoured, has very fine eyes. The colour is most striking. In some lights dark green and in others green blue. Very unusual, don't you think?"

Theora thought for a moment of when she had been close enough to see into Lord Sulien's eyes and the memory made her catch her breath, but she made her answer lightly. "Yes very unusual," She got up and walked to the window. "This room really is only fit to sit in before eleven," she said. "I wonder if we shouldn't go to my bedroom instead and make the most of the better light."

Mrs Colton stood up. "Of course if you wish it." She smiled. "I take it that this is an indication that you would like me to mind my own business?"

Theora's eyes sparkled. "Only a little hint, Penny. Are you offended?"

"Not at all!" said Mrs Colton. As they ascended the stairs she said briefly, "You will remember what I say though won't you?"

"Of course I will," said Theora.

The rest of the morning was spent uneventfully. The two ladies sewed for an hour and then Mrs Colton went away to her own room and Theora applied herself to developing a schedule of work for Juliet. She was halfway through this task when she received a message that Lady Meadley was asking for her.

Lady Meadley's room was on the west side of the Court. The west wing had the advantage of possessing the largest and most modern of the turret rooms. In her father's lifetime, Theora remembered it being largely shut up and used only for the most important guests. She found Lady Meadley in the dressing room. Her Ladyship stopped in her hurried instructions to her maid and greeted Theora.

"I wanted to talk to you about the next few days. There will be some friends of mine staying and on Saturday there will be this hunt affair. As I do not ride, I need someone to escort Kit. Would you be able to do that for me please?"

"Alas, Ma'am, I am afraid I cannot help you. It is many years since I rode. So, I am very out of practice and have nothing suitable to wear."

"Heavens if that is all, I can provide anything that you might need. I used to ride at Trennance, our Cornish Estate you know, but, I was never very good and could never keep pace with Aidan. He found it quite irritating waiting for me all the time." She studied Theora closely and said, "Indeed now I look at you I see we are much of a height. We will be able to sort this matter very quickly I think." She beckoned to her maid. "Nicols, please find me the brown habit with the gold braiding."

When the maid came back, Lady Meadley clapped her hands.

"Yes I think that will suit you very well. Would you let us see how it fits?"

Theora stared at her. "Do you not think that Lord Sulien would prefer me to spend my time preparing for Juliet's lessons?" she managed at last.

"Oh there will be plenty of time for that," said Lady Meadley easily. She saw that Theora was uncomfortable and said quickly, "Don't worry about my brother. He will be well pleased, for unless you ride on Saturday, Juliet cannot. Now, let us try the habit."

Seeing that she was determined, Theora went with the dresser. Lady Meadley was well satisfied at the result.

"Well that is excellent," she said. "I am currently sorting through all my clothes and have found so many that I will no longer need. What to do with those I decide to leave is the problem. Some may be refashioned for

Juliet in due course, but others are quite unsuitable. However, I have hit upon the solution: You shall have them."

"Oh, Ma'am, I could not!" said Theora in horrified surprise.

She saw that Lady Meadley was looking constrained and said hastily, "Indeed I thank you for your generosity, but to wear your clothes would be completely inappropriate for a governess. I am sure his Lordship would be very displeased at the idea."

"Nonsense," said Lady Meadley briskly. "I have already suggested to Aidan that as well as teaching Juliet, you should also act as a Dame de Compagnie to me. Perhaps in time, after I leave Temple Court, you may also be needed to act as hostess. You know this house and all the people here about so well. You are perfectly placed to help us. It was your breeding and connections, not just your book learning, which made us invite you here, child. Did that not occur to you?"

Theora shook her head. "No, Ma'am, it did not."

"Are you displeased by the idea?"

"No, of course not. But, I do feel that I am taking advantage of you. I came here to work, you see."

"And work you shall," said Lady Meadley. "What I am asking will not be an easy task. There is much to do and my brother's standards are exceedingly high. I have no doubt that in a few months you will be wishing yourself back at the Rectory."

"Never, never," said Theora passionately. She seized Lady Meadley's hand. "Thank you so very much for all your kindness," she said chokingly.

Lady Meadley patted her hand. "There now, don't cry. We are both helping each other, remember. Now, help Nicols tidy up. Then we can start organising my trunks and deciding which of these dresses will suit you best and which I should keep for Juliet."

*

When Saturday dawned, Theora found herself waiting for the hunt to start. She was in low spirits. Mrs Colton's departure had left her feeling lonely and she was also afraid that she might disgrace herself in front of most of the county. The day had begun with the assembling of the pack. Then a farmer had set off across the fields carrying the scent, much to Miss Templeton's surprise. Although she had only been out a few times in her youth, she had been used to a traditional hunt. She had queried this with Juliet who had explained that Papa had banned fox-hunting, shooting or trapping on his estates. She had gone on to say that, although Papa was a famous soldier, he had a great love for animals. He was also a very good judge of a horse, as Theora had discovered when she was taken to the stables earlier in the week. An elegant chestnut mare had been led out and for the next few hours Theora had a delightful time, riding in the park and becoming accustomed to her new mount.

As the stable clock struck, Juliet came out from the house on her father's arm. With them was Lord Thorne and two other gentlemen, whom Theora decided must be army acquaintances. His Lordship stopped to greet his guests and Juliet went off to find her own horse which, with his Lordship's chestnut stallion, and Theora's mare, was being led up by a couple of grooms. The Earl bade Theora a good morning. Her horse whinnied and turned her head and he ran a hand down her neck.

"How do you like Solitaire, Miss Templeton?"

"Very much, Sir, who could not?" said Theora.

His tense features relaxed slightly.

"I am glad. I advise you to take care today. Black tells me that you are a good rider, but our hounds are fast. I suspect it is many years since you have followed a hunt?"

"Many years, yes, Sir," said Theora stiffly.

A groom then helped Theora to mount and the Hunt moved off. The pack of hounds quickly picked up the scent and everyone followed at a gentle canter. For a few miles the going was easy, but soon the trail turned across open country and hedges, gates and dykes tested the riders. Theora, being so well mounted, had no trouble keeping up with the pace set by most of the field, but she was soon outdistanced by the Earl and Lord Thorne. Then the field split, with his Lordship forming one group to the left with the Master. A significant number of hounds grouped along a long green hedge to the right and were scouting beside it. Suddenly they dashed underneath it and streaked away into the woods, giving tongue excitedly. Theora held back her mare as she decided what to do. It was not part of her function as a governess to lead the Hunt. Common sense told her that to do so would be foolhardy. However, something in his Lordship's face as he had told her to take care, had piqued her. As a girl she had known herself to be an excellent rider. It annoyed her to think that this strange, proud man, who hardly knew her, had made assumptions regarding her skill. She let go of the mare's head and galloped in pursuit of the 'scent'. He had vaulted over a five-bar gate and was making towards the edge of the woods. Theora heard a sound behind her and she saw a chestnut stallion bearing down upon them. Within a few strides he would be level and she would need to let him pass, as they could not both jump the gate together. She spoke softly to the mare and urged her forward. Standing off her hocks her horse cleared the gate, clipping heels as she did so. The 'scent' was standing grinning amongst the baying hounds as Theora drew rein beside him. A few seconds later, the stallion also effortlessly made the jump and was quickly pulled up. The Earl dismounted and walked over, reins looped over his arm. He addressed himself first to the 'scent'.

"Good running, Fletcher, I didn't expect you to take that route." He bent and ruffled the ears of one of the hounds. "Bella was first as usual I see." He looked up at Theora and she could not read his expression.

"That was quite a surprise, Miss Templeton. I wonder, do you have any other talents I don't know about?"

His voice was polite but something in its tone suggested to Theora he was not quite pleased. She wondered if he simply disliked being beaten.

"It's not your victory that bothers me," he said as if she had spoken out loud. "But, next time, you'll take more care when you're riding my horse. You could have broken your neck and her knees."

She was about to hotly reply, but they were interrupted by a shout from Lord Thorne, who had come galloping down the valley accompanied by Juliet.

"Very well done," said Lord Thorne. He rode up to Theora and swept off his hat. He glanced at the Earl. "Really, Aidan, I do hope you haven't been scolding her. I for one must compliment Miss Templeton on her excellent seat."

He broke off abruptly and Theora saw him glance sharply to his left. She followed his gaze. In the distance there stood a tall, black horse ridden by a gentleman with vivid red hair. Theora saw Lord Thorne stiffen. He and the Earl exchanged glances. Then the Earl looked away and the curious moment passed.

"Yes, well done, Miss Templeton," said Juliet. "How lucky that you were riding Solitaire. You must let me take her out next time, Papa. Will you?"

"I will not," said his Lordship remounting. "I think Miss Templeton has earned the right to keep the ride." He looked down at Theora. "I am sorry for my hasty words just now, Miss Templeton. When you come to know me better, you will realise that there is nothing I admire more than courage. Now, Juliet, please ride back with me. I see your own pack of admirers are forming. I suggest we make a hasty retreat so that we can all enjoy the splendid hunt breakfast your aunt has ready for us."

As they reached the house, Theora was surprised to see Mr Allan amongst the waiting crowd. He came forward at once and whilst helping her dismount said in a low voice, "Did you read my note?"

"Indeed I did, Sir. I just haven't had the opportunity to reply."

He nodded and watched as Solitaire was led away. "Now seems as good a time as any, don't you think?"

Theora looked around. The drive was crowded with guests and the Earl and Juliet were surrounded. Realising that this might be her only chance to get away, she said quickly, "Very well, I will meet you by the garden steps, the ones that lead to the summer house."

Not waiting for his reply, she slipped into the house and asked the footman to advise Lady Meadley that she had a headache and was going to lie down for a little while. Then she came back down by way of the kitchens and let herself out into the gardens. Running down the stone stairs she found Mr Allan sitting at their bottom and nearly tripped over him. He stood up, and as it was now starting to rain again, walked with her swiftly until they reached the shelter of the summer house. Theora sat down at once but he continued to stand, regarding her with a strange mixture of hope and anxiety.

After a moment he ruffled a hand through his damp black, curly hair and said helplessly, "Miss Templeton, I wish I knew where to start. I am sure whatever I say to you is going to sound quite peculiar. I have thought and thought about what I should do and can find no solution."

His voice was so contrite and he appeared suddenly so very young and vulnerable, Theora's heart was touched. She said gently, "Mr Allan, please do not be distressed. I believe I have guessed your secret."

"You know how I feel about Juliet?"

"Yes. You love her."

He sat down beside her and struggled to regain his composure. Together they gazed at the rain and listened to it tapping impatiently on the thatched roof.

At last he said, "Do you think everyone knows?"

Theora shook her head. "No, I believe I am the only one to suspect."

"But you think it hopeless," he said desperately.

Theora hesitated. Truthfully she didn't know what to say. She had no experience of such a situation. Whilst her sympathetic nature made her regard him with kindness, her duty was to protect Juliet. She therefore spoke more harshly than she wished. "You have not been presented to me as Juliet's suitor, Sir," she said bluntly. "I must therefore conclude that neither Lord Sulien nor his sister regard you in that light."

He blushed slightly. "You consider me quite unsuitable then?"

Theora sighed. "I only know you as Lord Sulien's steward. As to your prospects and connections, I cannot comment."

He eyed her face thoughtfully. "Would it surprise you to know I am both rich and well connected?"

"It would surprise me," said Theora frankly.

"Let me explain that although I am Lord Sulien's steward, I am also Lord Thorne's ward and heir."

Theora was astonished. "Do Lady Meadley and Juliet know this?"

"No. As I only became aware of the situation myself some two months ago and had made a pledge to Lord

Thorne to keep it private, I could not confide in anyone. I only tell you now because I have your promise to help me."

Theora looked out over the garden. It looked tired and overgrown and the grass, so carefully scythed in her father's time, was now tangled with weeds. It was disappointingly neglected. She turned her attention back to the young man beside her who was watching her closely. "I think that if you want my help, you had better tell me everything," she said.

Mr Allan stood up and faced her. "It is not a long tale to tell. My father was an English officer in Lord Sulien's regiment. He fell in love with an Irish lady. They married and my father continued to serve whilst my mother returned to live with her family. They were very happy for a while, but then my father was killed, just before his twenty-fifth birthday. Shortly afterwards, my mother was found dead at her father's house. I was two years old. From that point, Lord Thorne became my protector and took care of me. I completed my early schooling in Ireland and then I was brought to England and privately educated. During holidays I occasionally visited Lord Thorne's castle in Gloucestershire and that was when I first met Juliet. After I finished at college, I joined the army and served two years in the Earl's regiment. Then his Lordship offered me the post as steward here. I wanted to stay in the army, but then Lord Thorne told me that he had adopted me officially and that I was his heir. He urged me to take the role of steward. As I knew that Juliet would be here, I am afraid I didn't need much persuading. We agreed not to reveal my adoption to avoid gossip. I little thought how difficult it would be to keep my feelings secret as well."

"Do you think the Earl or Lord Thorne have any knowledge of your intentions?" asked Theora.

"Sometimes I have thought that perhaps they did, but I am not sure. Do you think I should confess? I have been afraid to do so, in case it is perceived as an abuse of trust."

Theora admired his delicacy. Turning the problem over in her mind she said abruptly, "As you have not yet spoken to his Lordship, that also means you have not yet declared yourself to Juliet?"

"No, never by any actual words." He paused and said with difficulty, "Do you think Juliet may not return my regard?"

Theora hesitated. "I am sure that she likes you very well, but it would be difficult to say whether she loves you. Juliet is still very much a child."

"She will be eighteen in three months," said Mr Allan eagerly. "Then I may ask for the Earl's permission to speak to her."

Theora stood up and shook out her damp skirt. "As you have asked for my advice, Mr Allan, I will tell you this: I do not believe that the Earl will object to you being Juliet's suitor. He obviously thinks highly of you and so has not discouraged your friendship. However, as you have pointed out, his daughter is not yet of age. I urge you to wait, not just because it would be improper to speak to her now, but because your own good sense must tell you that she needs more time to mature. In the meantime, I am certain that you will continue to treat her with respect."

He bowed. "Of course, I understand. You have my promise, Ma'am."

"Thank you," said Theora. She started to walk back and Mr Allan followed her. At the top of the stone steps she paused. "I cannot support improper behaviour of course, but Juliet rides in the park every Tuesday accompanied by a groom. If you wish to join them, I would see nothing exceptional in that. Then you could return here for tea afterwards."

He pressed her hand. "How very kind you are."

They walked together towards the house. At the stable gates he bowed, thanked her again and left her.

Theora went to her room. She was confused by what she had heard. She could not understand why the Earl and his friend had not disclosed their sponsorship of Mr Allan. There seemed no sensible reason for this obvious secrecy. She wondered if she had done right to encourage Mr Allan and allow him access to Juliet, however innocent the opportunity. She decided that all she could do was let events unfold and await more information. She tied up her hair with a grey ribbon which matched her simple gown. Lady Meadley had been firm about the need for her to join the party, but she saw no need to make herself conspicuous. Then she went down to the hall. She made her way to one of the alcoves. Half hidden in the shadows, she was able to avoid scrutiny yet also had an excellent view of the Earl. Just as Juliet was a magnet to the young men, so Lord Sulien appeared to be irresistible to the women of the County Set. Looking at him now Theora was hardly surprised. The Earl had changed into a dark green coat which admirably set off his tall figure. With his thick fair hair combed and lace in his cravat, he looked very dashing. It had been so long since she had been in Surrey that Theora could not immediately put names to faces, but she was conscious that the middle-aged blonde woman talking to the Earl was familiar to her. It was very warm in the hall, as a huge fire had been built. The woman's cheeks were burning red which did not compliment her light pink gown at all.

"Baroness Holdsworth," said a voice in her ear. Theora turned quickly to find Lord Thorne had appeared silently at her shoulder. "Ghastly isn't she!"

Theora choked back a laugh. "I think she knew my mother."

"I am not surprised," said Lord Thorne calmly. "She probably knew your mother's mother. She is nearly as old as these hills."

Theora took a breath. "I am not sure you should speak to me so, Lord Thorne," she said as severely as she could.

He looked surprised. "You dislike my honesty? I thought I judged you better than that," he said. "Still, you will not have to put up with my bad manners for long, Lady Meadley has asked me to fetch you."

"I think I should stay here," said Theora quickly. "Lady Meadley has lots of friends to greet, I would only be in the way I am sure."

Lord Thorne grinned. "I thought you would say that and so did Lady Meadley. Come now, Miss Templeton, you cannot hide forever. How can you properly look after Juliet if you are always hanging around in the shadows?"

Theora sighed. "What do you want me to do?"

"Just meet a few old acquaintances and give Aidan the proper excuse to get away, from the Baroness. Besides, you will be able to see him much better when you are standing next to him than right over here."

Theora blushed, but decided to let the last remark pass. "Very well. Please take me over."

Slowly they made their way across the room. At last they reached the Earl, who now had his back to the wall with the Baroness in front of him, alongside a youth with a purple waistcoat. Lord Thorne bowed.

"Good evening, Baroness. I don't think you have had the chance to meet Miss Templeton?"

The Baroness gave a yellow-toothed smile. "Good afternoon, Miss Templeton. Heavens, my dear, I am astonished at how much you have grown up. You were such a child when last I saw you. Do let me present my son who is visiting me from London."

The Honourable Timothy Holdsworth bowed low over Theora's hand.

"Delighted to meet you, Miss Templeton. I hear you have come to stay with Lady Meadley." He spoke loudly and his voice, like his waistcoat, grated upon Theora's delicate sense of good taste.

"Well I am very glad to have brought you all back together again," said Lord Thorne politely. "But, now, I must take Aidan away from you for a while. A business matter you see."

He nodded to the Earl who, with a look of barely concealed relief, slipped away. Theora was then left alone with the Baroness and her son. The Baroness then also abruptly left, leaving Theora alone with the Honourable Timothy. She deliberately kept her eyes lowered. When the silence became prolonged she was forced to look up and was disgusted to see that his pale eyes were assessing her from top to toe. Theora took an instinctive step back.

She said quickly, "Do you make a long stay in Surrey, Mr Holdsworth?"

The direct question seemed to make him recollect himself.

He said hurriedly, "A month or two. I am here for the shooting, although I was pleased to have the opportunity to join the Hunt. How fortunate to have such a fine morning."

"Yes indeed," said Theora. She looked around desperately, but the hall was starting to clear as the remaining guests were leaving.

You are an admirable horsewoman, Miss Templeton," said Mr Holdsworth. "I have my own carriage in London. In fact, I am considered quite a fine whip."

He smiled and she saw with distaste that his teeth were

as stained as his mother's. "Please permit me the opportunity of taking you for a drive when we are both in Town. I am sure you would enjoy it."

"Thank you," said Theora colourlessly.

"In the meantime, I would be delighted if you would accompany me out riding someday. Would you permit me to call upon you next week perhaps?"

"I have a lot of duties to attend to, Sir," said Theora firmly.

She nodded towards where Juliet was standing with Mr Allan. He saw Theora's wave and, bending, whispered something in Juliet's ear. She smiled and they both turned and crossed the room.

"Here is Miss Sulien now," said Theora watching the couple making their way towards her. "I am afraid I must leave you and attend to her."

"A pleasure I'm sure," said Mr Holdsworth. His lascivious smile broadened.

She walked off, deliberately turning her back, but she felt his gaze burning into her. Juliet came up.

"Did you want me, Theora?" she said innocently. "Mr Allan suggested you might not wish to speak further with Mr Holdsworth."

"He was right," said Theora emphatically. "Please, if you ever see me within a hundred yards of that gentleman, do not hesitate to interrupt in the future!"

"You don't like him," said Juliet with mild surprise.

"I thought him quite odious," said Theora with spirit.

Juliet dimpled mischievously. "He is a trifle dull, I know, but he did seem sincere in his admiration of you."

"That is not a compliment," said Theora.

Mr Allan looked at her with concern. "I am afraid he has really disturbed you, Miss Templeton. I am sorry for that."

Theora pulled herself together. "Nothing for you to be

sorry about. It is Lord Thorne who deserves my censure, for leaving me with the pair of them."

Juliet giggled. "Yes, he was rescuing Papa. Papa loathes the Baroness. Anyway, you won't need to talk to any more unpleasant people today. The party is over now. Mr Allan was just about to leave too. Shall we walk with him to the stables? There are some swans on the lake and I have saved some bread for them. We could feed them on the way back. Would you like that?"

"Yes I would," said Theora. "Very much."

Chapter Four

The weather after the Hunt continued wet. A strong wind battered the trees in the park and Theora awoke to the sound of it. She dressed and went down to the servant's hall, where she was greeted warmly by Mrs Chapman. They were interrupted by Meadows who came to say that his Lordship would appreciate Miss Templeton's presence in his study as soon as possible. Mrs Chapman sighed. She patted Theora's hand consolingly.

"Sure we'll have a chance for more catching up very soon, Miss Templeton."

Theora smiled. "I wish you would remember that I am in service here. Please call me Theora and not Miss Templeton."

Mrs Chapman looked doubtful. "Well if you're sure, but it really doesn't seem right to me. I don't think your father – God rest his sweet soul – would have liked that at all."

"I'm quite sure he wouldn't," said Theora, smiling, "but times have changed and we must change with them."

The study was reached through the library. Theora knocked upon the heavy door and as there was no immediate answer went directly in. The shutters were back and many branches of candles burned brightly on the window sill. In the past, this room had been crowded with cupboards, desks and great leather chairs. Now there was one desk: French with ormolu mounts, an upright chair on casters which now stood carelessly by the window as if hastily moved and a padded velvet armchair which was deliberately positioned next to the fireplace inviting repose. Over the fireplace was a gilt mirror, surmounted by a wreath of oak leaves which framed a plaque. On this was written a verse in French, which said:

For Sun I am
My light will be
Beside the Moon
Beyond the sea.

The window alcove held a large and very fine celestial globe. She went to examine it, but turned away when a firm voice hailed her.

"Good morning, Miss Templeton."

"Good morning, Sir."

Lord Sulien stepped past her, but instead of sitting down at the desk as she expected, he stood by the window looking out for some moments. When he looked back at her, his face was as expressionless as at their first meeting.

"Are you warm enough?" he said unexpectedly. "I gave orders for this fire to be built up, but it seems not to have been well tended."

"Thank you, Sir, I am quite warm."

He looked her over. "You don't look it," he said. "Come here."

With a slight hesitation she walked to him and he briefly touched her hand.

"Cold as ice, as I thought. We'd better have these shutters closed. Can you manage the smaller one if I do this?" He indicated the side window and Theora, although very much surprised, went to do his bidding. When she turned back she found that the fire was blazing. The Earl sat down in one of the chairs, gesturing to Theora to take the other. She sank down gratefully and waited for him to speak.

"You are pleased to be back in this house."

Again it was a statement not a question so Theora nodded.

"Very pleased, thank you, Sir."

"Good." He drew out a snuff box and took a pinch.

"Juliet has always lacked the right sort of female companionship," he said. "She imposes too much upon my step sister. This must now stop. Her Ladyship will be returning to Cornwall soon anyway."

He paused turning over the snuff box in his hands. "Grace is not entirely to blame. I have indulged Juliet. I am conscious that she is now quite spoiled. Is there anything to be done do you think?"

This was said so seriously yet seemed so absurd that Theora had to swallow hard before she replied.

"I am sure there is, Sir, but I will have to give the situation some thought before I can give you suitable advice," she said slightly unsteadily.

He looked up quickly, "You find the situation amusing?" he said sharply.

"Perhaps a little."

"Why so?" His voice was as cold and hard as frost on nails.

"Only that when you talk about the harmless caprices of a child of seventeen as if she had committed some terrible crime, I must find you ridiculous, Sir," she said boldly.

He stood up, put the snuff box back in his pocket and loomed over her, his tall figure casting a formidable shadow.

"That is your summation then. That I am too severe and Juliet beyond reproach?"

"I think," said Theora, carefully, "that your concerns are natural, but unjustified. Even in so short an acquaintance, I can see no major flaws. Her character is, as yet, unformed and so she is a little thoughtless. But, this can be easily excused by her youth and inexperience. I am sure that if she makes the right match, to a man of sense, she will become, as a wife and mother, a charming woman."

His Lordship turned and rested his hands on the mantelpiece. He looked down into the flames. "Your recommendation is that I marry her off quickly?"

Theora smiled. "Hardly, Sir, otherwise I would soon be out of employment," she said. "If you will permit me, I would suggest that whilst further education would be beneficial, its purpose should be improving general understanding. Juliet now needs an opportunity to meet new people and get a perception of the responsibilities she will, in time, need to assume."

She stopped wondering if she had gone too far. "I would not embark on such a course of training without your explicit approval of course," she said hastily.

He went to the window and threw open one of the shutters. Light streamed in and fell upon his face.

"I thank you for being so frank, Miss Templeton. I am content for you to take forward Juliet's training as you propose. Perhaps you will discuss with Mr Allan how and when to involve Juliet in his visits to the Estate Tenants."

He turned to the desk. "I would also be grateful for your help with another matter. Would you help me with some of the household improvements I have planned please? I trust Mr Allan in most things, but I think he will need a lady's advice when it comes to choosing new furnishings." He stopped and looked at Theora who was staring at him as if dumbstruck. "Will this be a problem?"

"No, no, not at all," said Theora hastily. "Then you wish me to stay? I am engaged?"

"Of course," he said matter-of-factly. He opened a drawer and drew from it a slim paper. "This is a formal contract of employment that I had drawn up. I advise you to read it through. You will see that I have confirmed a salary with an additional allowance for clothes."

Theora took the paper from him. "You are too generous, Sir," she said after a moment. "As to the clothes, I am quite sure I would not need half as much."

"I will be the judge of that," Lord Sulien said brusquely. He ran his eyes over her. "You will take up a position in this house as governess to my daughter, but as 'Dame de Compagnie' to my sister you will need to dress appropriately. I know Grace has started to help you with this. I will ask her to progress the provision of your wardrobe as a matter of urgency."

Theora stiffened. "I am sorry that my appearance is so unsatisfactory," she said politely.

He abruptly shut the desk drawer. After a moment he glanced at her sideways and she thought for a moment she saw the flicker of a smile. It was swiftly banished.

"I meant nothing personal, Miss Templeton."

"I appreciate that, Sir."

The Earl dropped his gaze again to his desk and, picking up a quill, wrote slowly and deliberately into the ledger that lay open upon it. Then he shut the book and pushed back his chair. "Now," he said with a return to his customary brusque tone, "tomorrow I return to France to conclude some business there. So, I will leave Juliet in your care. Please proceed as we have discussed."

He opened the study door. "You should go now and talk further with my sister. She is waiting for you."

Theora rose. "Thank you again, Sir, for your generosity and your kindness."

His expression did not change. "There is no need to thank me. My sister will have told you that I will expect much of you."

He bowed and Theora curtsied in return. At the door she paused. "When do you mean to return, Sir?"

He looked past her. "In a few months, I hope, but that will depend on how my business succeeds. Good morning, Miss Templeton."

*

During the next few weeks, Theora settled herself, although not without some difficulty, into her new role. The issue was not the task itself, for her years helping at the school in Highton had provided ample experience of teaching. But, she had not anticipated the range of distractions which would prevent her from spending sufficient time with her pupil. Temple Court was no longer the quiet, ordered, (seldom-visited) refuge, that she remembered from her own youth. From dawn to dusk it hummed with activity, from the stream of Lady Meadley's county visitors, to a vast range of workman, tradesmen and suppliers who had arrived to carry out Lord Sulien's instructions. As his Lordship was not there to consult and Lady Meadley showed absolutely no interest in the renovations, Mrs Chapman and the rest of the servants automatically turned to Theora for guidance. She found herself the appointed contact for all the major questions regarding the restoration and reorganisation of the house. Long days and short nights followed. After several weeks, where she was only able to spend an hour in Juliet's company every day, she was very conscious that she was a long way from meeting Lord Sulien's expectations in relation to his daughter. She felt extremely guilty about this and expressed her concerns to Lady Meadley but they were very casually dismissed. Theora was learning that, in some ways, Lady Meadley was as careless and unconcerned about the practicalities of life as her charming niece. Now that the responsibility of training Juliet had passed from her hands, her Ladyship happily resumed her former life of cheerful indolence, which consisted mostly of long lunches, games of Piquet and carriage rides. Every afternoon she rested in her room and in between times she made slow preparations for her return to Cornwall. There was absolutely no indication as to when Lord Sulien would return from France and his letters, addressed to Lady Meadley and passed on, remained completely uninformed on that point. They were, however, packed with questions, about the house improvements. He showed interest in everything and volunteered questions on every aspect of the plans. Sometimes Theora felt quite exhausted through keeping up with the flow of query and instruction. To be constantly challenged this way was exhilarating. She longed for the post and even felt a little dejected when no letter arrived addressed in his Lordship's unmistakeably bold hand. She also could not deny that she was finding her new responsibilities delightful. Never had she imagined that she would have a free hand to make these improvements to her beloved family home. To see it gradually emerge from faded neglect to stately elegance was the greatest pleasure she had known for many years. It was wonderful too to find that her suggestions seemed to fit so well with the new owner's wishes. He never argued with her choices, which she took care to ensure followed his own detailed directions as much as possible. It was all very satisfying and although Theora did sometimes flinch at the thought of all the money being spent, her employer's evident satisfaction and Lady Meadley's gratitude for her efforts, were reassuring. She was getting on excellently with her Ladyship and they enjoyed each other's company. The one thing that had been a slight struggle had been the provision of Theora's new wardrobe. Theora had a strong sense of propriety and she felt that acting as hostess to the Earl could easily be misinterpreted by people in the district. She feared for her reputation and felt decidedly uneasy. She raised this as delicately as she could. But Lady Meadley had laughed away her fears, assuring her that as she intended to stay until the spring, she would make it her business to ensure that everyone knew

Theora's situation before she departed. Altogether, it was a most enjoyable time for Theora. She met regularly with Mr Allan to consult with him regarding some of the Estate improvements and she found herself becoming more and more pleased with him. He was a sensible and highly sensitive young man, thoughtful, yet practical. Theora was not surprised that Lord Thorne had adopted him as his heir. He was not at all the sort of man that she was personally drawn to, but she thought that in a few years, with his handsome face and fine prospects, he would have his pick of any pretty young lady in the district. She had no such regard for Mr Timothy Holdsworth. Since the Sulien Hunt he had been a repeat visitor to Temple Court. Usually on some flimsy pretext, to request that Theora drive, walk or ride with him. Since riding seemed the least unpleasant prospect, Theora had reluctantly agreed to do so in the Temple Court Park. However, the event had been an unqualified disaster. Mr Holdsworth proved to be a poor rider. His horse was a bad-tempered grey gelding, a badly paced animal who Solitaire took an instant dislike to. When they walked she refused to come up sides and when they broke out of a walk, the mare joyfully galloped away, leaving the grey struggling in her wake. After this and several weeks of attempting to find excuses, Theora finally was forced to visit the Holdsworths at their house in Gyldeford. This was far worse than the ride. The Baroness took frequent opportunities to leave the young couple together and, during these times, Timothy boldly pressed his suit. Theora was horrified at his behaviour (as well as disgusted by his appearance and manners). She attempted to politely rebuff him, but it was hopeless. Timothy was a man blessed with little imagination and a great sense of self-worth. It was inconceivable to him that any lady should not be attracted to him. Bolstered by his mother's ambition, he ignored Theora's protests and by the end of their last meeting had secured an invitation to luncheon at Temple Court.

Theora was reflecting on this, the next time she met Mr Allan. He had come up to the house to show her the plans for the repair of the conservatory. He laid out his papers and spoke for some time, but soon realised that Theora was not attending to him. He therefore stopped and asked her if she felt quite well. She apologised for her lack of attention but assured him that she was indeed well, just a little distracted. He smiled. "I can well believe it. Tell me now, what can I help you with please? Or I can come back later when you're less busy if you wish. What would you prefer?"

Theora was grateful for his directness. "Thank you, but I would really value your advice if you can spare the time."

His face lit up. "I'd be glad to assist you. What's the problem?"

Theora hesitated. "Tell me frankly please, do you think that since I came here, that in any way, I have behaved improperly or appeared immodest?"

Mr Allan looked first astonished and then unusually grim. "Who on Old Earth has put such ideas into your head? One of the old cats round here I suppose."

"No," said Theora uncertainly, "just that I cannot help but feel that, somehow, I am no longer behaving as my uncle would have wished. I must be changed, otherwise I wouldn't have provoked such ungentlemanly attentions." She looked at him sadly. "I am so ashamed, Mr Allan."

She began to cry. Mr Allan sat down beside her on the couch and offered his handkerchief. "Will you not tell me what has happened?" he said gently.

Theora dabbed her eyes. "Mr Holdsworth has proposed to me," she said bleakly.

Mr Allan stared. "Well I cannot see why that is such a worry. I assume you refused him?"

"Yes, of course, but he is quite convinced that I am not in earnest. I have tried and tried to tell him, but he will not listen and keeps pressing me for the answer he wishes to hear. I promise you that I have not encouraged him."

Mr Allan waited for her to stop crying. When she had done so he said firmly, "Now listen to me, Miss Templeton. There is nothing wrong with your behaviour and I don't want you to worry any more. I will attend to Mr Timothy Holdsworth!"

Theora thanked him profusely, but after a moment broke off. "You promise you won't do anything rash will you? I would be most upset if you were hurt in any way."

Mr Allan laughed. "No, I will try to keep my hands off him, although if he ever troubles you again..." He stopped on the words as if they choked him, his lips tightening. "For now, please forget the whole thing. Lord Thorne is coming over later, so let's leave the work for another time. Go and put on your best dress and enjoy the rest of the day."

*

Some hours later, having taken Mr Allan's advice, Theora sat in the garden looking idly over the still water of the lake with its delicate reflections of white swans threaded between the waterlily leaves. She had put on a sage green dress and around her neck was clasped the double-sided gold locket which contained a picture of her uncle and a lock of his hair. It was nearly the most precious thing she owned, only eclipsed by the fine hair jewel which had belonged to her mother. This piece had come to her upon her uncle's death. It was made of silver on gold and contained, in its centre, a tracery of small, rose cut diamonds and some particularly fine sapphires.

Theora had brought it with her from the North and kept it carefully wrapped in three handkerchiefs in a leather purse. By day, this was hidden beneath a floorboard in her room, but at night, she slept with it under her pillow.

After the rather cold and wet October, it had been an unusually mild November. When Theora followed the path through the rose garden, she found that there were still some flowers blooming, so she picked a red rose to smell as she walked. At the back of the garden there was a small gate with a path that led around the lake. After about a quarter of a mile, the sight of a rotund, stone building made her pause. She had forgotten her grandfather's folly. It looked exactly as she remembered it and she set off to explore. The path was slippery, so she made her way carefully, aware that if she fell over here, nobody would be likely to quickly come to her aid. After several minutes of careful progress she triumphantly stepped over the threshold, only to find that she was not alone. Sitting on a bench, an easel in front of him and paints by his side was a gentleman. He got up when she entered, but she was immediately conscious that even though she had come upon him with no warning, he seemed quite unsurprised by her arrival. He had a vivid, high cheek-boned face with blue eyes and dark auburn, curly hair. He was dressed very elegantly and his smile, which he turned full upon her, was brimming with confident charm.

"Good morning, Miss Templeton, how delightful to see you."

His voice was very deep and as pleasing to the ear as the sound of a bass viol.

To give herself time, Theora drew off her gloves. "Do I know you, Sir?"

His smile became broader. "Not exactly. We have not been formally introduced, of course, but I know all about you. The daughter of the late Lord Templeton, who disappeared to the North to teach farmers' brats some manners and now is back to do the same job for Lord Sulien's daughter."

"You have the advantage of me, Sir," said Theora coldly. "I cannot place you at all."

The blue eyes flashed as he said, "My apologies. My name is De Lisle, Lord De Lisle, your employer's closest neighbour." He looked her over. "Please will you sit down and keep me company."

Theora hesitated. She now remembered that this man was the one she had seen on the black horse on the day of the hunt. The man who had made the Earl and his friends react so strangely. "I really should be getting back to the house," she said swiftly.

"Oh I don't think there's any hurry," he said easily. "I'm sure your pupil can spare you for a little longer, besides, I think it's going to rain."

She smiled at that, despite herself. "I see no sign of rain, Sir, but I suppose I could sit for 'a moment', if you wish it."

"Excellent," he said, moving the easel as he did so. He cleared a space on the bench. "I'm afraid I have nothing that I can offer you as refreshment."

"I am sure you haven't," said Theora, sitting down. "Especially as you are trespassing," she said glancing at him quickly.

He nodded. "Alas, you are quite right of course. Even though your employer and I are so very well acquainted, I suppose he would not be pleased if he found me here would he?"

"I should imagine he would be very annoyed indeed," said Theora. "What are you doing here?"

His eyebrows rose. "Why sketching of course."

"Are there no pleasing vistas on your own land which

you could capture?"

"Sadly, nothing to equal this. I do believe this is quite the most beautiful valley I have ever seen, especially now, with you to grace it." He swept her a deep bow.

Although his manners were outrageous, he was so handsome and disarming, Theora found it difficult not to warm to him. Concealing an answering smile she said quietly, "It is a lovely place and I have always thought so. However, to say that it is the most beautiful valley you have ever seen is rather an extravagant claim."

He shook his head. "I see that you doubt me, but when you know me better you will understand that whatever my faults and whatever others say of me, I never exaggerate. So, if I say this valley is the most beautiful that I have ever seen, that is the absolute truth. Or, if I say it is coming on to rain…"

He stopped and pointed with one long finger. Theora looked out and to her amazement she saw that, whereas before the skies had been completely clear, rain was now falling heavily, blanketing the hillside and drenching the treetops. He looked at her and it was as if the blue eyes were looking into her and past her at the same time. Something about their glittering depths, with the glance so deliberate and penetrating, suddenly reminded her of Lord Sulien. To hide her face, she leaned over to look at the painting. Despite herself she let out an exclamation of pleasure. The whole valley had been captured in a few deft lines and, more than that, the picture was alive with a unique brilliance of shade and colour. It was simple, but perfectly executed.

"This is remarkable," she said sincerely.

He smiled and seemed genuinely pleased. "I am glad you think so. When it is finished I would be happy to give it to you as a gift."

Theora sat back down. "You said you are Lord

Sulien's neighbour. That means you either live at Talbot Place or Glebe House."

"I do indeed live at the Glebe. You know it?"

"A little, I visited it a few times as a child."

His smile became a little twisted. "Of course and now you are back here again, as a governess. A wonderful coincidence."

"A wonderful opportunity," she countered swiftly.

He looked at her curiously. "Strange that you should see it as such. If I were in your position I would hardly be pleased to come back to my family home, just to tend to the daughter of an innkeeper."

Theora stood up quickly. "I'm afraid I find that last remark very offensive."

"I can't see why? You must know that Juliet is peasant born. I am just expressing my sympathy for your situation."

"Miss Sulien," said Theora firmly, "is the daughter of an Earl. As I am a servant in her father's house, I do not require your sympathy." She picked up her gloves. "I wish you good afternoon, Sir."

She moved towards the entrance, but he quickly barred her way.

"Please don't go. I really didn't mean to offend you. In fact I was giving you a compliment! Besides, if you leave now you will become soaked and liable to get an inflammation of the lung. Then I will be overcome with guilt and may well go into a decline. Please stay."

Theora appraised him. He was tall, undoubtedly strong and might be prepared to use force to keep her there. So, she sat down again, as there seemed no other course of action that would not be dangerous or make her look ridiculous.

"I cannot understand your extreme dislike of a sweet, innocent, lovely girl, who has never harmed anyone," she said finally.

"I do agree she is very lovely," he said coolly. "Look here." He picked up a canvas folder and turning through the pages lifted out a crayon drawing which Theora saw instantly was an extremely good likeness of Juliet. He watched Theora's face as she looked it over. "As you can see, the artist in me can well appreciate her pretty face, but you, who are her teacher, must be aware that underneath it all, she is very foolish. Whereas you, Miss, are a very different matter."

He leaned forward and before Theora could draw away, caught her chin in his hand and turned her head to the side so that he could see her profile. "Yes, you really are beautiful. I would like to paint you some time. However, let us leave that interesting subject for now. We can come back to it when you are in a better humour."

He released her and picked up a small book. "Try reading this to pass the time," he said briefly. "I'd be interested in your opinion of it, whilst I finish the valley sketch."

He turned back to the canvas and became apparently quite absorbed. Theora, although she was burning with embarrassment, opened the book he had given her. It was a small volume which contained various tales written in French, Latin and Old English. It seemed very old and the cover was well worn. On the fly leaf was an inscription in French which read: '*To all brothers and partners in chivalry. May the Knights be always true to each other. Let us honour and protect all living things, under sun and moon, now and forever*'. Theora continued to read on, keeping an eye on the encroaching rain, which showed no immediate sign of moderating.

Lord De Lisle showed no further interest in her. Some little while later, he set down his brush, wiped his hands and addressed her again.

"Well do you like it?"

Theora closed the book. "It is very well written."

"You don't like it?"

"No, I don't. I do not enjoy descriptions of conquest, as, however heroically they are portrayed, they cannot disguise the fact that all glories in war are the result of extensive bloodshed and unforgivable loss."

He started to wash out his brushes. "You are right of course. However, I am at least pleased to hear you think it well written. Now, having so summarily dismissed literature and art, what shall we talk about instead?"

He sat down and looked her up and down. "I must confess that I am wondering what to call you," he said after a long pause. "My name is Bricin. It means: 'Red King'. What do you think of that?"

"I think, Sir, that I should be going," said Theora firmly. "The household will be wondering what has become of me."

He sighed again. "I suppose you are right. I will therefore let you go, but first, please do tell me your first name?"

Theora drew on her gloves. "I should imagine that a little investigation on your part would enable you to find it out quite easily."

"But that would involve having to speak to some very boring people. I am sure you would wish to spare me the inconvenience."

Theora looked at him. She could think of no reason to conceal her name, yet she felt uncomfortable about sharing it with this strange, yet oddly compelling man.

"My given name is Jane," she said after a moment."

"Jane," he said musingly. "It doesn't suit you. I don't think I want to call you that. Can you offer nothing better?"

"My uncle always used my second name," said Theora reluctantly, "Theora."

"Much better! I do hope that I can rely on you to keep me company again in the future, Miss Theora Templeton."

Theora forced a smile. "Of course, if you invite Lady Meadley to your house, I would be glad to accompany her."

"You must know I won't do that," he said.

"Yes, but I would very much like to know the real reason why," said Theora frankly.

He laughed and she was conscious of the extreme changeability of his nature. It was as if his moods were precariously balanced. On the one side was the superiority of the cold intellectual: proud, very conscious of his own worth and outwardly despising those perceived less able. On the other was a rich montage of charm, creativity and apparent sensitivity to beauty in all its forms. He was an intriguing and (she had to admit) extremely attractive mystery. He looked at her directly and it was as if he knew exactly what she was thinking.

"Prove yourself a worthy companion and who knows what secrets I may reveal," he said teasingly.

Theora shook her head. "Not nearly good enough I'm afraid."

"Very well then." He paused. "Let me just say that my dislike of Lord Sulien and his reciprocal distaste for me are long standing and deep rooted."

"You seem to know a lot about the Sulien family," said Theora.

His gaze again seemed to look through and past her. "That would be a long study. Better to say that I have known of one of them, the current Lord Sulien, all my life."

"You were at school with him perhaps?"

He smiled. "Something like that. In fact Lord Sulien and I were close working partners for a while. Then, when he chose to marry an inferior and start a different life altogether, we went our separate ways."

"Yet you are now neighbours and Juliet's mother dead, so there is no longer any reason for enmity. The cause for your disagreement is in the past."

"In the past, yes, but sometimes the past cannot be ignored." There was sadness for a moment in the keen blue eyes, but then he smiled again. "Now, cannot I tempt you back for a further visit? I reassure you that I am seeking nothing else but some intelligent conversation."

This request was made with such sincerity that Theora could not help smiling in return. "Very well, Sir."

He looked delighted. Outside, the rain, which had been falling steadily, suddenly stopped.

"Then I expect to see you here in a week's time. Bring with you any books that you think may prove interesting." He bowed to her courteously and would have stood to one side to enable her to pass by him, but Theora paused. "Would you answer me one question before I go, Sir?" she said.

He looked at her with consideration. "Perhaps."

Theora picked up the book again. "Can you explain the meaning of this verse please?"

She turned to the very back where written in a beautiful flowing script were the words:

For moon I am
And light will be
Beside the sun
Beyond the sea.

He took the book from her and closed it. "It means nothing, just some very old poetry. Why do you ask?"

"Idle curiosity only. I wondered how it came to be there."

"It was written by a previous owner," said Lord De Lisle with finality. "You should go now, before it rains again. I feel that it may do so shortly."

Theora gave a half smile. "You are very certain, my Lord, do you, perhaps, also have an interest in meteorology?"

The blue eyes that had narrowed slightly widened again and the dark voice became mellow once more. "As you come to understand me, Miss Templeton, you will realise that I have many interests and talents."

"And the study of meteorology is one of them?"

He bowed. "Precisely. How well you understand me already. Now, regretfully, we must part."

He took her hand and pressed it lightly.

"Goodbye, Miss Templeton."

"Goodbye, my Lord."

Theora then set off again towards the house, but she had not gone more than a dozen paces before he called to her.

"Wait please, you have forgotten something."

She turned back and he strode out, carrying the red rose she had plucked earlier. "I am sure you would like to take this back wouldn't you?" He held it out and to her astonishment it was as if the bloom were lit from within. A faint glow seemed to be coming from the top of his fingers, illuminating the petals so that each was fringed with silver. Then the moment passed and she wondered if she had imagined it.

"Take it now please," he said and this time the words were an order.

She took it from him, because it seemed foolish not to and walked on. At the top of the hill she couldn't resist the temptation to look back to see if he was watching her, but there was no sign of him.

Chapter Five

After her return to the house, Theora went to the kitchen and sought out Mrs Chapman. She looked up when Theora came in.

"Well, my dear, did you enjoy your walk?"

"Yes very much," said Theora. She removed her hat and cloak. "Mary, do you know anything about the new occupant of Glebe House?"

Mrs Chapman looked surprised. "What makes you ask that?"

"Just that I heard it was occupied again and I thought I might know the new owner."

Mrs Chapman shook her head decidedly. "Most unlikely. It is a single gentleman that's taken it and he's from a long way away."

Mrs Chapman's lips folded in an expression that Theora knew well. It was a sign that she had more to say, but needed encouragement.

"Is that all you know about him?"

Mrs Chapman's gaze went to the door and she nodded slightly. Theora went and closed it.

"Well?"

Mrs Chapman smoothed her apron. "Well it's all rumour, just what I have heard in the village. The gentleman moved here from London. He was a doctor, but doesn't practise anymore and nobody knows why. We saw him first at Church, just after his Lordship went off to France. He's already turned a few heads with our young ladies hereabout, but keeps himself to himself. There's been a score of invitations for him to call, but he's turned them all down. That's not made him very popular I can tell you."

"No, I imagine not," said Theora.

She was troubled by what Mrs Chapman had said.

Also, despite awareness of the enmity between Lord De Lisle and her employer, she felt irresistibly drawn in. De Lisle's casual statement about a thirst for intelligent conversation had resonated strongly. She found herself thinking about her uncle and Mrs Colton. Of cosy nights spent in their familiar company, where, as an equal, she had been free to raise and discuss any topic that she wished. Lord De Lisle's comment about Juliet being foolish repeated in her mind. She saw sadly that, fond though she was of her pupil, her bold statement to Lord Sulien about how given time and circumstance Juliet would change into a woman of sense was proving too great an ambition. Juliet's sweetness of temper could not conceal the basic simplicity and essential frivolity of her nature. She suddenly decided that she wanted to know more about Lord De Lisle. Apart from her interest in him personally, she also had a particular ambition to fulfil. She was determined to get to the bottom of the mystery regarding the verse she had seen in his book. A verse which was the same as the one written above the mirror in the Earl's study. She was sure that it had special significance. Perhaps it had something to do with the estrangement between the two lords, for she knew, for a fact, that Lord De Lisle had lied to her when he had said it had been written in the book by the previous owner. When she had looked at his picture of the valley, she had seen his signature written at the bottom of the canvas, written in the same flowing script that had penned the simple verse in the book. So Lord De Lisle was undoubtedly very charming, handsome and fascinating, but he was also a deceiver. Either he didn't care that she had known his answer to be a lie, or the deception had been a deliberate attempt to capture her attention. Ruefully, Theora acknowledged that if the latter, it had completely succeeded. She wondered who else might be able to provide more information about both Lord De Lisle and the book.

As if reading her mind, Mrs Chapman said, "Of course, probably the very best person to ask about Lord De Lisle would be Beverley, Lord Heyworth's old manservant."

"He is acquainted with Lord De Lisle?" said Theora eagerly.

"Oh yes. His brother was Lord De Lisle's valet, you see. Mr Meadows mentioned it when I said that Lord De Lisle had moved into Glebe House."

"Where would Beverley be now?" said Theora rising.

"Still upstairs," said Mrs Chapman glancing at the clock. "Every day, after breakfast, he goes up and checks on his Lordship's clothes and makes sure everything's spick and span, in case he gets word he's coming home. His Lordship always takes Mr Samuel with him when he's soldiering, you see, on account of him being younger and better able to stand the long journeys. So, he keeps Beverley here."

Theora went upstairs, but she didn't go straight to the east wing. She went to her own room and placed in a vase the rose that she had picked from the garden. She had expected it to wilt, but once in the water, the flower instantly refreshed and filled the air with a rich, heady fragrance. Theora raised it to her nose to smell and the petals brushed her cheek. The silky touch was as soft and lightly sensuous as a fingertip and Theora instantly recalled Lord De Lisle's smooth white hand holding her chin. Hastily, she set down the vase and went off to Lord Sulien's apartments.

The Earl's suite, as Theora had expected, covered the same arrangements as in her father's lifetime. The large bed-sitting room faced off to the smaller room, where Theora had been born. She quickly walked past its closed door and all its many memories. She found Beverley hanging clothes in the closet. He greeted Theora politely, but with obvious surprise.

"I am sorry to disturb you," said Theora courteously. "I won't keep you for long. I just wanted to ask you a few questions about someone I met today."

Beverley looked doubtful. "I'm afraid I don't know many ladies hereabouts, Miss Templeton. You'd be better speaking with Mrs Chapman, or even her Ladyship."

"I have spoken with Miss Chapman," said Theora. "She suggested I spoke to you. The person I wanted information about is not a lady, but a gentleman."

Beverley looked at her and his expression changed. Beckoning Theora to follow him, he led her through the closet and dressing room and into Lord Sulien's bedroom. Placing a finger over his lips to ensure she remained silent, he shut the door. Whilst surprised at his sudden secrecy, Theora would have been a little amused by it, had she not been conscious that she was now in the Earl's bedroom. She felt quite constrained by the indelicacy of the situation, but Beverley seemed unaware of this. He simply regarded her intently.

After a moment, he said, "Forgive me, Miss, but I assume that by a gentleman you meant Lord De Lisle?"

Theora nodded. Beverley looked at her unhappily. "And you met him recently?"

"Yes, today."

Beverley sighed. "I noticed it was raining," he said. He paused. "What do you already know?" he asked.

Theora found herself flushing. "Just that he has recently moved here. And that he is not a friend to Lord Sulien."

"Did he tell you that?"

"Yes."

Beverley looked around the room. "I think you know

all that you need to, Miss Templeton." He walked to the bed. "Miss Chapman tells me that you are quite an accomplished needlewoman, I'd be very grateful for your advice regarding these curtains. I'd like to have fresh made up, but his Lordship seems to think they could be repaired."

Although choking with questions, Theora followed his gaze. The hangings were of a rich golden silk, heavily embroidered. A recurring theme were symbols of the sun, the moon, and, most dominant of all, stars.

Beverley watched her expression. "Can they be mended?" he said seriously.

Theora ran her hand over the silk. "Yes, but it would be a difficult and time-consuming task. It would take much work and might never be quite as it was."

Beverley gently touched the worn threads with a rough finger. "Yes, it will never be quite as it was," he said sadly. "So it can be with great friendships. Over many years, much of what started bright and beautiful becomes faint and faded and then it is too much effort to repair."

"Are you talking of the friendship between Lord Sulien and Lord De Lisle?" asked Theora eagerly.

"Perhaps," said Beverley. He went and sat down on the sofa. After a moment, Theora joined him.

"Lord De Lisle said that they fell out over the Earl's marriage," she said.

"That is true," said Beverley.

"Did they both love the same lady?" asked Theora.

Beverley stared at her incredulously and then burst out laughing. Indeed, he laughed so long that he broke into a hacking cough. When the paroxysm had subsided, he said hoarsely, "I'm sorry, Miss, but all I can say is that if Lord De Lisle has sought you out and spoken to you, then you should continue to associate with him, even if you might displease my master."

"You think that offending Lord De Lisle presents the greater risk?" asked Theora startled.

"I have known the Earl and Lord De Lisle for many years," said Beverley gravely. "What is certain is that although Lord De Lisle may seem to have all the answers, it's the Earl who always asks the right questions. By that I mean that if Lord De Lisle has found you, it may well be that it is because the Earl wished this and fully expected him to do so."

"You really do speak in riddles," said Theora despairingly. She stood up. The clock in the corner of the room was starting to strike. "I thank you for your help and appreciate your warning. I will think on what you have said. Now, Miss Juliet will be waiting for me. Will you excuse me please?"

She gathered her skirts and walked out. Without caring if she was seen she ran down the front stairs and didn't stop running until she had returned to the main house. Once in her bedroom she went breathlessly to the window and looked out, resting her hands on the sill to steady herself. The pleasant vista of the park was no comfort. Autumn had ended, winter had started and the cold rain showed no sign of abating.

*

Over the next few days, Theora deliberately refused to dwell on the strange events that she had experienced. She applied herself to the completion of only the essential house works and resolutely pursued her plan for Juliet's education. This consisted of an hour in the schoolroom during the morning and another in the afternoon. French, music and art were attempted with occasional embroidery and breaks for what Theora described as social studies. This created opportunities for discussion regarding world events, local news and either a walk (weather permitting) or a trip around the Estate with Mr Allan. As the weeks passed, Theora did not see a noticeable diversion of Juliet's attention from her principle interests of clothes and horses. But she was encouraged that at least she did seem to be learning restraint and some modicum of tact. This was demonstrated in her developing relationships with the tenants where her kindness and generosity were much appreciated. Theora was not surprised at Mr Allan's obvious admiration. Nor did she wonder that his affection for Juliet was increasing daily. She watched closely to see if this was reciprocated, but found this difficult to assess.

During this time, Theora was often afraid that she would meet Lord De Lisle in public and be forced to acknowledge their acquaintance. However, he seemed to have an aversion to socialising in any form, so he was rarely seen by the locals. The exception to this was his punctual attendance at Rodsall Church every Sunday. Sitting in the Sulien pew, Theora was uncomfortably aware that his Lordship was always four rows back and directly behind her. At times, she could almost feel his brilliant, blue stare burning into the back of her head. But, as he was always the first to leave the Church, she was thankfully spared the necessity of pretending that she hardly knew him. In actual fact their acquaintance had matured into something approaching a friendship, due to Theora's weekly visits to the Folly. Here, art, poetry and music had all been extensively discussed. At no point had Lord De Lisle expanded on his past history in relation to Lord Sulien and Theora, although consumed with curiosity, had been afraid to inquire. At times she felt very guilty about these secret visits, but she consoled herself with the fact that there was no question of impropriety in Lord De Lisle's behaviour towards her. He clearly saw her as an intellectual equal, but that was the extent of his interest. He never mentioned his own business nor asked her about Lady Meadley or Juliet. He was often sarcastic, making her laugh out loud at his biting humour, but there was no personal warmth in his approach towards her, and indeed at times he was quite rude. Despite this he was always exciting and stimulating company. She looked forward to seeing him, despite dreading that they would one day be discovered and she might be forced to explain herself to Lady Meadley, or worse, the Earl.

One frosty morning, Lady Meadley summoned Theora to her in the drawing room.

"I wanted to tell you, my dear, that there is a party being held by Mr and Mrs Westlake in a fortnight. It will be quite a large affair and so the ideal opportunity to introduce you and start to bring Juliet into society. After that, we will need to prepare for Juliet's 18th-birthday ball. Then, my brother will be back and so we will be able to make more definite plans for the future."

"You have had word from Lord Sulien then, Ma'am," said Theora trying not to sound too interested.

"Not specifically," said Lady Meadley. "Although I have had word from Lord Thorne, to say that Aidan has asked him to come and stay with us. So I do expect to hear something from my brother soon. Now I must go and write my letters, I leave you to tell Juliet the news."

Naturally, Juliet was very excited and for several days after telling her about the Westlake party, Theora struggled to get her to do anything but discuss it. After having failed at a third attempt to engage her attention during a music lesson, she gave up and agreed to release her from lessons temporarily, provided that after the ball, she made up for time lost.

"I am afraid your papa will be very disappointed in you when he returns," she said as severely as she could, as Juliet kissed and thanked her.

Juliet smiled, showing her dimples. "Papa is never cross with me for long," she said confidently. "Dear Miss Templeton, you are so good to me. Now do you think I should wear the pink or the blue?"

"You know I am no expert in such matters," said Theora, "but I am sure Lady Meadley will help you."

"She will help us both," said Juliet. "As this is a special occasion, do you think Papa will let me wear the Sulien pearls? That would be so perfect."

Theora had taken down her sewing and was setting stitches but she looked up at that.

"What are the Sulien pearls, may I ask?"

"Oh, a family heirloom. There is a brooch, a single string and a two rope necklace. They date from the reign of Elizabeth I and are quite priceless. "Not that I would wear all of them for this party, of course."

"Of course," said Theora smiling. "The single string of pearls sounds more appropriate."

"That's what I thought," said Juliet complacently. "I shall have to remind Papa. Except..." she broke off and her expression suddenly changed.

"What is wrong, you hardly think your papa is going to refuse?"

"No..." said Juliet uncertainly. "It's just that I forgot that the jewels are in London, so we would have to send for them and that would be dangerous."

Theora put her sewing down and looked at Juliet in surprise and concern. Her companion's pretty face was so serious that she hardly recognised her.

"Why dangerous?"

Juliet hesitated. "Well it's winter now and the roads are so bad and just recently there are an awful lot of... Knights of the Road." Her voice dropped to a whisper. "You know, highwaymen."

Theora was astonished. "Highwaymen? What on Earth

makes you think so? I have heard no such reports. I think you are letting your imagination run away with you."

"I wish I was," said Juliet sadly, "but, ever since Papa went away the first time, more and more of them have appeared and if anything happened to the Sulien jewels…" Her voice trailed off.

"I see," said Theora thoughtfully.

When Juliet finally left her, she sat for some time, looking out of the window. She was concerned by what she had been told, but her interest was caught by the term Juliet used: "Knights of the Road". This was the third occasion the phrase had come to her attention: firstly in the book Lord De Lisle had shared with her on their first meeting, but she had also noticed it more recently as an inscription on a tomb in the Rodsall Church. She was now even more determined to unravel the mystery of the link between the two families. Her impulse was to ask Lord De Lisle directly, but knowing him as she did, she was aware that if the humour took him, he might tell her some bogus tale, just to indulge his own sense of mischief. She decided that a more trustworthy source was the local rector. As she knew Mrs Chapman was bound for the village that afternoon, she begged a place in the carrier's cart on the pretext of dropping into the Church to leave the altar cloth that she had finished embroidering. Having asked to be picked up at three, she made her way up the flagged path that was still rimed with frost and through the churchyard to the north door. Even on a bitterly cold day, it was pleasing to the eye, well tended with neatly clipped holly trees. The gravestones were swagged with ivy whose leaves shone like burnished silver in the faltering sunshine. The Church itself was not as large as the one where the late Reverend Templeton had presided, but it was considerably older. It stood solidly on firm feet of golden sandstone, with a comfortable, well-rounded body of mixed stone and brick. Within the roof space there were fine beams of arching oak, blackened by age and fire. The single aisle led to the altar, beside which was a chapel in which were a few good memorials and one large tomb. On its side was a clear inscription in Latin which said:

Here is laid a true Knight of the Road
Of the Earth I now am
And here I remain
'Til sun, moon and starlight
Shine together again

Theora wrote the text down and then carefully examined the tomb. It was solid stone with a fine carving of a man on top in chain mail. The figure was in traditional pose, clasping a sword between fisted hands. The head was laying on a pillow which Theora now saw was engraved with small full suns. A sound behind her of the door opening made Theora break off her examination and turn quickly. She was aware that the Rector had entered the Church.

"Good afternoon, Miss Templeton. How good to see you. I didn't know you were coming in today."

"Good afternoon, Rector. I'm sorry I didn't let you know, I just came to leave the cloth, as you see."

The Rector beamed at her. "How can we thank you? This is quite delightful."

"I am so glad you think so," said Theora. She picked up her basket. "Now I must be going."

"You will not stay for tea?"

"No, I thank you. The cart will be here soon."

"Well you must wait here until it does. It's starting to snow and if you stand outside you'll soon be wet through." He regarded her curiously. "I see you have been looking at the Knight's Tomb, are you interested in antiquities?"

Theora swallowed. "Yes and no. I must admit I have a special interest in the inscription. I must be frank with you, Sir, I came here today to see it again and speak with you about it."

She looked directly at the Rector, who was now watching her. "I have seen the words before, you see. I was wondering if you knew what they meant?"

The Rector did not answer straight away. He looked past her and towards the doors as if to check again that they were alone. Then he beckoned and Theora followed him to the vestry. After lighting some candles he sat down and waved Theora to the only other chair.

"Before I answer you, Miss Templeton, I must ask you where you have previously seen or heard the words on the tomb."

"Is it important?"

"Important and possibly dangerous."

Theora looked down at the stone floor. "Juliet mentioned them once in relation to highwaymen and I also saw them in a book," she said at last.

A candle spluttered and the Rector stood up and attended to it. After a moment he turned back and said, "Did this book belong to Lord De Lisle by any chance?"

Theora looked embarrassed but met his gaze. "Yes it did." She saw the Rector's mouth tighten and said quickly, "Is that the danger you spoke of?"

"Perhaps."

He saw that Theora was now looking thoroughly alarmed. "I am sorry, my child, but now I must ask you to be completely frank with me. How long have you known Lord De Lisle?"

"About a month now," said Theora stiffly. "I met him in the park shortly after I came back. I have seen him several times since. Now will you tell me about the inscription please?"

She steeled herself for a lecture on her impropriety, but it did not come. Indeed, the Rector seemed to visibly relax.

"A month and always within the Sulien Estate?"

"Yes," said Theora impatiently. She stood up. "I do not wish to speak further about Lord De Lisle. If you are not prepared to tell me anything about the inscription, I should take my leave. The carrier cart will be here for me very soon."

The Rector smiled faintly. "I am quite happy to tell you anything you wish to know. It is important that you do understand the inscription, especially if you continue to see Lord De Lisle. The phrase 'Knights of the Road' was first used to describe fighting men who came from France with William the Conqueror. These men were recruited by barons to protect their lands. As the years passed there was a dispute between some of the barons in the North and those in the South. Knightly chivalry descended into the more sinister practices of highwaymen. This is what we have now, alas: pockets of bandits who prey upon the innocent." The Rector shook his head sadly. "It is a great pity indeed."

"I see," said Theora. She considered for a moment. "Is Lord De Lisle connected with these knights?"

"I could not say," said the Rector.

"But it is what you believe," said Theora eagerly.

The Rector looked at her. "Let us just say that I caution you regarding your dealings with him."

He stood up and extended his hand to Theora. "You should be getting back now. Wait for me a moment and I will take you out."

There was finality in his voice and Theora had no choice but to leave the vestry and wait for him by the church door. Outside the wind was blowing fiercely. As the Rector handed her into the waiting cart, she could barely hear his voice, but she was conscious that he was pressing into her hand a small package.

"For you, keep it safe," were the few words she caught. Then the cart rolled forward and they were heading away and towards the whitening hills.

By the time they had reached Temple Court, Theora was wet through and immediately went to her room to change, glad of the excuse to have some privacy. In front of the fire she unwrapped the parcel that the Rector had given her. It contained a small, plain wooden box, on the front of which was engraved a rather crude symbol of a star. Inside, wrapped in tissue paper, was a pendant on a golden chain. It was formed of a large natural pearl suspended within a perfect circle. The left side of the circle was made of silver and the right side gold.

There was also a note which had been quickly scrawled so that the ink was smudged.

Dear Miss Templeton.

This jewel is a Church heirloom and was left with me by the last rector. Legend suggests an association with the Knight's Tomb. Our conversation reminded me of the risks of keeping something so valuable in so vulnerable a place. Please would you take it into your keeping and ensure its secrecy and safety? Whilst you are under Lord Sulien's protection, it can come to no harm.

I am, Madam, your obedient servant, James Crawford, Rector.

Theora took out the pendant, put the chain over her head and went to the mirror. Against her plain blue gown, the jewel glowed back at her. It was exquisite. A knock at the door made her hastily push the necklace inside her dress so that it was hidden from view, but it was only Meadows to tell her that Mr Allan had arrived to ride with Juliet in the park. Theora thanked him and a few minutes later, she went downstairs and made her way to the stables. The sun now shone and the light dusting of snow was already melting. There was no sign of Juliet and Mr Allan was engaged in conversation with the Earl's Head Groom. Both men bowed as Theora came up. Mr Allan's bay cob let out a low whicker of welcome and snatched at the Groom's reins straining towards her. Solitaire also neighed a greeting and several of the other horses joined in. Mr Allan smiled.

"All the beasts have taken to you, Miss Templeton. If you ever decide to stop being a governess, you should set up as a horse dealer. You'd make a mint of money."

Theora laughed. "It's kind of you to say so." She fed sugar to the eager horse and dusted down her hands. "I see you are waiting for Juliet, I am sorry, have you sent a message to the house?"

"I was just about to do so, Miss," said the Groom. He continued to say that he had taken the precaution of having Juliet's mare walked up and down. Then he touched his hat, wished them a good morning and went back into the tack room.

Mr Allan took back his horse and loosened the girths. He turned back to say briefly, "I am very glad to have a chance to speak privately to you, Miss Templeton. I wanted to reassure you that the business we discussed at our last meeting has been resolved." He saw Theora was looking self-conscious and dropping his voice said softly, "There is no need to be concerned. I can assure you that Mr Holdsworth will not trouble you further. I am hopeful that you may never see him again."

Theora was immeasurably relieved but she regarded him doubtfully. "I do hope that this has not caused you inconvenience, Mr Allan."

The young man grinned broadly. "None that you should ever worry about. Oh look, here's Juliet at last." He turned and looked back up the carriageway. That's a sight that's worth the wait," he said reverently. "If I were to find out that tomorrow would be my last day on Old Earth, I'd still be happy, knowing that I'd had a recent glimpse of that lovely face."

Theora, watching Juliet's slow progress as she stopped to greet the gaping stable boys, could only admire his patience. Being less tolerant she raised her voice and called. Juliet, thus hailed, increased her speed by a fraction. Perceiving that Theora was looking stern, Juliet inquired with confusion if there was anything wrong.

"You are supposed to ride at three and it is quite half past," said Theora reprovingly. "Did you not think of that?"

Juliet's lip trembled. "Oh, I am sorry," she said contritely. "Aunt Grace called me to help her and then we were talking and I forgot that I had given my boots to be cleaned so they were nowhere to be found when I went to put them on. Dear Miss Templeton, please don't scold me!"

"It is not me that requires your apology," said Theora, "but Mr Allan and your poor horse, both of whom are quite bored with waiting."

Juliet looked sorrowful, but Mr Allan spoiled the force of this reproof by adding quickly, "Well I can't speak for your pony, Miss Juliet, but please do not think I am bored at all. I was quite content I assure you."

"There!" said Juliet triumphantly. "I knew it wasn't so bad. As for Snowdrop, I will make it up to her by giving her a good gallop when we have got up onto the heath. "Will you bring her out please, Thomas?"

The Groom smilingly brought forward the little grey mare and Juliet mounted nimbly.

"I will see you later, Miss Templeton," she said cheerfully."

Theora patted the mare's neck. "Be careful won't

you."

Mr Allan touched his hat and the two of them rode away.

Like her father, Juliet was a good rider and, true to her promise, she persuaded Mr Allan to come with her to the heath, where they did gallop for a while. But Snowdrop was too fat and unfit to keep up best pace for long and they soon relapsed into a walk and turned to make their way slowly back through the silver birch wood which fringed the southern edge of the Earl's Estate. The ground being sandy, it was rarely waterlogged even after so much rain. The path was wide enough for the cob and the mare to walk together as they had done many times before.

As always, Juliet monopolised the conversation and Mr Allan was seldom required to do much more than smile and nod. This was fortunate because for once his mind was not focused upon Juliet. He was thinking back to the week before when he had made the trip into Gyldeford and taken lunch at the Angel Inn...

Chapter Six

The Angel was a coaching inn much frequented by travellers and regular visitors to the town. Since taking up his position as steward at Temple Court, one of Mr Allan's more agreeable duties was to visit Gyldeford to consult the firm of agents who managed the Earl's business interests. Although a small town, with only a few shops, Mr Allan had still been able to fulfil certain commissions for Mrs Chapman. Although most of the meat, cheese and green crops were produced upon the Temple Court Estate, Mrs Chapman had found that Reeds, the butcher's in the High Street, had a way of curing ham which was highly superior. At Reed's, Mr Allan had listened with interest to the exciting news, that a corn exchange where grain could be bought and sold was being planned for the town. Taking his leave, he spied the figure of Mr Holdsworth making his way down the hill with the Baroness. Mr Allan quickly ran after them. Mr Holdsworth regarded him with disdain, but his mother, remembering that Mr Allan had the favour of the Earl, was more welcoming. Mr Allan had suggested that they should all go for luncheon together and offered to act as host. The Baroness though pleased at the suggestion declined, as she already had another engagement. But, as she hastened to impress upon Mr Allan, this should not stop him having the pleasure of dear Timothy's company. That being agreed, the two young men had made their way to the inn together. Mr Allan was a regular and popular guest at the Angel, not just because he was the steward of the Earl of Woodchester, but also because he was both friendly and generous. Very soon Mr Holdsworth found himself sitting down to an excellent meal and some of the finest wine that he had ever tasted. Time passed and, as the bottle went round for the third time, Mr Holdsworth relaxed. Once the plates had been cleared he was quite off his guard. This was exactly what Mr Allan had been hoping for.

As they sat enjoying the warmth of the fire and sipping their drinks, he said casually, "Well, I have to say I have very much enjoyed our time together. Are you likely to be in Gyldeford again next week? Perhaps we can meet again?"

"I would be glad to, Sir," said Mr Holdsworth graciously, "but I rarely come here. I have to say I do not generally admire Gyldeford. It is not a place that attracts attention from anyone of real consequence. I prefer the London scene immeasurably. Indeed I would be there now, except for the fact that I have some private business to attend to."

Mr Allan poured them both another drink. "Business in relation to your house at the Sands?"

"Hardly, my mother has that all well in hand, as you would expect. No, this, my dear Sir, is a more personal matter. Although, I must admit, it is taking longer than I expected."

"An affair of the heart perhaps?" suggested Mr Allan smilingly.

Mr Holdsworth smirked. "Perhaps." He glanced at Mr Allan to gauge his reaction but the other man's face held nothing but an expression of polite interest.

"Surely, you cannot be having difficulties in that respect?" said Mr Allan encouragingly.

Mr Holdsworth set down his glass. "You would be surprised," he said darkly. "She really is the most frustrating creature. I am all for ladies being modest and retiring; that is to be expected. But, this one is also learned in the extreme. I barely get the chance to speak without her telling me about some devilish new book that she is studying."

"How frustrating," said Mr Allan sympathetically.

"Yes isn't it?" agreed Mr Holdsworth.

"But, she's rich I assume?"

"No, not a penny to her name! But, she comes of a noble family."

"Well that helps of course," said Mr Allan. "Is she a beauty?"

Mr Holdsworth considered. "I suppose she is," he conceded, "although not really my type. Too thin and pale." He nudged Mr Allan in conspiratorial way. "If I was going to choose for myself and had my pick, then I'd go for your employer's daughter. Now there is a delicious little thing! Pretty, no brains to speak of and the heiress to a fortune. What more could you wish for?"

Mr Allan ground his teeth. "What more indeed?" he said with deceptive sweetness. "Still, where lies your difficulty with Miss Templeton?"

Mr Holdsworth sighed. "You have guessed that I referred to Miss Templeton. I cannot see why she is taking so long to make up her mind. She is clear that I am interested, she is also aware of my prospects. She has no fortune, although she is of gentle birth. You would think that she would be delighted that I was paying her any attention."

"Yes, I see your point," said Mr Allan. He looked reflectively at the fire. "If you will permit me, I have thought of another reason why Miss Templeton may be averse to your advances. Do you want me to tell you? I do, after all, have some small acquaintance with her and so have been able to get a reasonable understanding of her likes and dislikes."

"I would be most grateful for any advice you can give," said Mr Holdsworth eagerly.

"Well," said Mr Allan thoughtfully. "I understand

that the reason she would never consider marriage with you is because you are wholly disgusting and detestable. In fact, the sight of you makes her sick from head to toe!"

There was a silence. Mr Holdsworth gasped. "How dare you!"

"And furthermore," said Mr Allan calmly. "I share that view. In fact, having now spent a couple of hours in close proximity with you, I am not surprised that Miss Templeton finds you so loathsome. My surprise is simply that any lady or gentleman could bear to come within twenty feet of you!"

Mr Holdsworth got to his feet. "You will meet me for that insult, Sir," he said furiously.

Mr Allan got up, walked to the door, locked it and deliberately threw the key into the fire. "Certainly, how about now?" He went to the window and shut the curtains. "I am afraid that I am not carrying pistols, nor do I have a sword to hand, but I am sure you will forgive me that. We wouldn't wish to create a public scene. Even in so dull a place as Gyldeford." He took off his coat and rolled up his sleeves. "I propose we settle this simply, the old-fashioned way."

Mr Holdsworth looked at the locked door with dismay. "Are you suggesting fisticuffs?"

"Why do you think I brought you here?" said Mr Allan crossly. "The Landlord is waiting for my signal. When I give it, he will release us both. Then you are free to go, although of course that must be upon agreement that you never make any attempt to approach Miss Templeton again." He started to advance upon Mr Allan, his fists raised.

"What if I don't agree?" said Mr Holdsworth gaspingly as he backed away.

"Oh I don't see the likelihood of that," said Mr Allan, striking as he spoke.

*

Snowy weather persisted prior to the Westlake ball, which gave Theora the excuse she needed not to see Lord De Lisle. Although she missed his company, it was a relief not to subject herself to his scrutiny. She was certain that he would perceive her unease and question her accordingly. She was not convinced that Lord De Lisle was secretly a highwayman. Even if he was, she could not see him being a threat to her. However, exactly what he was, and what he might be hiding, was a question which she was afraid to ask. She needed more information and the only really reliable source was still away in France. Her spirits lifted when she thought of Lord Sulien. The news that Lord Thorne was attending the ball this evening had given her hope that his Lordship might soon return to England.

The Westlake's Manor was a few miles from Temple Court, so Lady Meadley, Theora, Juliet and Mr Allan, as their escort, arrived at the party in good time. Juliet was quickly surrounded by a crowd of gentleman admirers who swiftly bore her away. Mr Allan, accepting the situation with good grace, accompanied Lady Meadley and Theora in to dinner and then retired to his own seat. In an attempt to keep watch on Juliet, Theora found herself neglecting her food, a fact that was noted by the gentleman sitting next to her, who asked her politely if she was feeling unwell.

"Oh no, thank you," she said quickly.

"Then is there anything else I can get you? This is a ball as well as a dinner party and dancing when hungry is a really awful thing to do!"

Theora glanced up. He was a man in his early thirties, elegantly dressed but rather plain faced.

"I wouldn't want to put you to the trouble, Sir; I am just not very hungry."

"Too much else on your mind?" he said sympathetically, following her gaze. "Well I know that feeling."

He had a soft voice, with just the faintest accent. "Don't worry. Pretty girls can't help but charm, like flowers make nectar. She'll come to no harm from a few prospecting bees."

"I take it you speak entirely from the bee's perspective, Sir?" said Theora.

"Sure," he said, smiling, "I've done some honey hunting in my time, but then I found a perfect bloom."

He inclined his head and Theora saw he had picked out a slim blonde girl sitting opposite. She looked up for a moment and Theora saw a warm glance pass between them.

"Your wife?"

"That's correct. We got married yesterday."

Theora looked quite astonished and he smiled understandingly.

"We haven't been properly introduced. My name is Irving and that lady with the beautiful blue eyes is Mrs Gala Irving."

"How do you do?" said Theora. "I am Miss Templeton."

"Miss Juliet Sulien's governess," said Mr Irving, as he tasted the sole and white sauce with grapes placed before him.

"You know me," sighed Theora, "I am afraid I cannot place you at all."

"That's not surprising, I am not sure I can place myself. I am one of Lord De Lisle's party."

Theora choked on her wine. "Lord De Lisle is here." She glanced anxiously down the table. "I don't see him."

"No, he is coming later." Mr Irving looked at her thoughtfully. "That troubles you?"

"Yes, no, not exactly," lied Theora.

Irving waited a moment before saying, "You are acquainted with his Lordship, Miss Templeton?"

"Yes, Sir, but I have not disclosed this to anyone. I met Lord De Lisle by accident, not being aware of the difficult relationship between him and my employer."

Mr Irving nodded. "You are afraid De Lisle might embarrass you? Never fear, your secret's safe with me. Provided you promise me the favour of a dance later."

Theora smiled. "Gladly, Sir, but I am afraid you will be disappointed. I only recently started to learn the latest steps."

Mr Irving picked up his glass and drained it. "Don't worry, Miss Templeton, I've done a bit of dancing in my time, so, I expect we'll muddle through somehow."

*

Westlake Manor had the advantage of several fine rooms, one of which was specifically kept for dancing. Two of the large doors that backed onto the garden were ajar, so that there was access to the terrace where fairy lights now sparkled. The orchestra were already playing and Juliet's hand was immediately solicited. Several gentlemen then approached Theora, much to her surprise. She was carefully marking her card when she saw Mr Irving approaching.

He bowed and offered his hand. "Our dance I believe."

Without waiting for her to respond, he led her to the floor. Many eyes followed them and Theora felt most self-conscious as they took their place. She looked at Irving and saw he was smiling. There was such sympathy and understanding in the glance he gave her, that she was immediately reassured and not at all nervous. As the music started, all she was aware of was that her partner was easily guiding her steps. He danced with such assurance that there was no possibility of mistake or awkwardness. To Theora it felt like floating on the melody itself and when the last notes were played, instead of stepping off the floor, she found herself staring at her partner, with open admiration. Irving, though, was looking over her head. He was scanning for Mrs Irving who was making her way towards them. She smiled at Irving and it was as if an extra chandelier had been lit.

"Well, Guy, did you enjoy your dance?"

"Very much so. Did you enjoy yours?"

"It made a change," she said and although she spoke gravely, her warm blue eyes were dancing. Then she turned to Theora. "How do you do, Miss Templeton? I hope you don't mind me taking Guy away. I did promise Lord De Lisle that we would dance at least one dance together. He also asked me to say that he would love to partner you, so if you have a moment…" She gestured and Theora saw that Lord De Lisle was standing watching them by the windows. Avoidance now being impossible, Theora resigned herself to the inevitable. She extended her hand to Mr Irving and curtsied. "Thank you for the dance, Sir. It was wonderful."

"My pleasure, Miss Templeton. You know, with a little more practice you really would make a first-rate little dancer. Really you would."

"You are too kind, Sir," said Theora. "But there is no need to flatter me. If I came across as anything better than flat footed, that is only due to your matchless skill."

Irving actually looked slightly embarrassed at this tribute, but Mrs Irving laughed. "Well said, Miss Templeton. However, Guy never lies and if he thinks you would make a good dancer, you should believe him." She slipped her arm through Irving's. "Shall we show everyone what a little practice can do, my dear?"

She drew him away and Theora was uncomfortably conscious of Lord De Lisle coming towards her. Despite the fact that everyone else was talking loudly or dancing, he seemed to have surrounded himself with a strangely impenetrable barrier, which apparently no social convention could cross. Anyone that approached him, turned away at the last moment.

"Good evening, Miss Templeton."

"Good evening, my Lord."

"You are surprised to see me here I think."

"I am indeed," said Theora. "I thought that you made a habit of avoiding these sort of functions?"

"Usually, but knowing that you were going to be here…" He let the sentence hang, as he scanned her face. "Are you not flattered?"

"Exceedingly," said Theora. She unfurled her fan and began to ply it, more to give her something to do with her hands, than because she was overly warm. She reflected that, strangely, whenever she was with Lord De Lisle she always felt cold.

His eyes continued to sweep over her. "Would you like a drink?"

"No thank you, my Lord."

Abruptly he sat down beside her and she had to steel herself not to draw back as he leaned forward to whisper in her ear.

"You are looking very beautiful tonight, you know."

Theora looked down at her fan to hide her confusion. "Are you attempting to flirt with me, my Lord?" she said with an effort.

The blue eyes narrowed.

"Does that upset you?"

"Not in the least," she lied. "I just wondered why, after so many weeks alone in my company, you have chosen a public place to pay me compliments."

He grinned. "I suppose it must seem a little strange. But it is such a pleasant evening and you look so very charming that I'm afraid I couldn't resist. Especially as Mr Irving had warmed things up for me."

Theora took a deep breath to stifle her automatic response. "You really go too far, Sir," she said at last.

"Oh I don't think I go far enough where you're concerned," he said mockingly. "However, as you are obviously just not in the mood, I promise not to upset you any further tonight. Did Mrs Irving extend my invitation to dance?"

"Yes, but I am afraid I must decline."

His eyebrows rose. "Nonsense."

His confidence was infuriating. Looking around to ensure they were not overheard Theora said firmly, "I am in earnest, Sir, and must ask you to refrain from speaking to me in this fashion. It will not do."

She rose, dropped him a light curtsy and was turning to go when his hand caught her wrist. He pulled her back, forcing her to sit down again beside him. She made to wrench away but his fingers closed tightly.

"No, you can't go. I require your company a little longer."

She was now quite helpless. He held her hand down by his side, hiding it amongst the folds of her dress, so it was impossible for anyone to see that she was restrained in any way. He continued to look about the room and his face betrayed nothing.

"Look," he said after a moment. "Mr and Mrs Irving are going to dance for us, isn't that grand?"

He waved over to them and Theora saw that the ballroom had cleared and everyone was watching expectantly. The orchestra struck up, Mr Irving bowed to his partner and then they began to sway together with seamless grace, so perfectly in time, it was as if they too were joined at the wrist. It was an exquisite picture, but, throughout the spectacular ebb and flow, Theora was horribly conscious of the icy hand on hers. There seemed absolutely no escape and she was, for the very first time in her life, utterly afraid. Then she saw a tall figure approaching and with supreme relief she realised it was Lord Thorne. He was smiling and yet there was a certain tension about him that made her hope that perhaps he had recognised the mute appeal in her eyes.

Lord Thorne bowed.

"Good evening, Miss Templeton. You are enjoying the dancing?"

"Very much so, they make a delightful couple and so very accomplished," said Theora with an effort.

Mrs Westlake, who had just been passing, paused and bestowed a beaming smile on Lord De Lisle.

"Absolutely delightful is exactly right, Miss Templeton. I have never seen anything so charming. It was so kind of you to bring them, Lord De Lisle."

De Lisle, whose gaze had remained fixed on Mrs Irving's golden head throughout this exchange, flickered briefly. "Not at all, it was my pleasure."

Mrs Westlake bustled away and there was a slight pause before Lord Thorne said thoughtfully, "Yes, one thing we can always be certain of is that De Lisle will always please himself."

The hand on Theora's wrist tightened again, making her wince.

"What is that you want here?" said his Lordship coldly.

Lord Thorne's gentle expression didn't change.

"Firstly, I was wondering if Miss Templeton would like to dance with me."

"She is engaged to me for the next. What else?"

"I have a message from the Earl of Woodchester. He is arriving soon and would like to see you in the library as soon as convenient."

Theora swallowed a gasp of surprise. Her pulse jumped and she was aware that De Lisle felt it. He looked down at her and then back at Lord Thorne. When he spoke his voice was fiercely cold.

"So Aidan is back," he said. "How opportune of him to pick this night to return. What if I say that I am currently otherwise occupied?"

Lord Thorne smiled. "Then I am asked to ensure your presence."

De Lisle released Theora's hand and stood up. "You know, Schoolmaster, I really could become, how shall I put this, quite annoyed, if you, or Aidan, continue to force my hand in this way. And whilst, where he is concerned, I am constrained, that is not at all the case with you. I advise you to be very careful."

He raised his hand and again Theora thought she saw a very faint light glow from the tips of his fingers, but, before he could do anything else, Lord Thorne reached forward and with one swift movement pulled Theora away.

She found herself walking across the ballroom leaning upon Lord Thorne's arm. In a moment they were on the terrace and, despite the sudden cold, she was thankfully gulping the sweet fresh air.

She gripped Lord Thorne's arm tightly and managed to stand upright.

"Thank you, Sir, for rescuing me," she said at last, when she had regained her breath.

He regarded her. "No need for thanks, Miss Templeton, I am always at your service." He looked around. "I suggest we do not stay out here long. Apart from the fact that you will soon take cold, I would not wish to draw any further attention. Let us just wait here for a moment and then I will take you to somewhere safe until we can bring you home."

Theora examined her wrist. The red marks from Lord De Lisle's nails were sharply defined. Lord Thorne looked down and Theora heard him quickly draw breath.

"I am afraid I have been extremely foolish." She swallowed hard. "I allowed myself to become friendly with Lord De Lisle, even though I knew it was not a proper thing to do. I never realised until now that he could be so unfeeling. I have truly learned my lesson tonight. He is a dangerous man."

Lord Thorne said nothing. He reached into his jacket and removed a handkerchief.

"Give me your wrist," he said. Then with extreme gentleness he held the cloth against it, clasping her small hand between his palms to hold it in place. It was strangely restful and warming, as if he were applying a poultice.

"Is that better?" he said after a moment.

She nodded. "Very much so. Thank you for your kindness, Sir."

His head was bowed. He looked down at her hands for a moment.

"It is my honour to be of help to you, Miss Templeton." He hesitated. "You are right to have assessed Lord De Lisle as dangerous. I cannot tell you more at this time, but I do caution you to be very careful in his company."

"I understand," said Theora. She took a deep breath and with an effort, stood up. "Will you tell me more when the time is right?"

"I promise it."

His gentle, measured voice was reassuring. Theora forced herself to smile.

"Now, you wished to dance with me, Sir?"

He looked at her with surprise. "Yes, but only if you feel well enough of course. Are you sure you do not wish to rest, instead?"

"I think I would feel safest in your arms," said Theora frankly and then realising the impropriety of what she had said blushed furiously. "I am sorry, I only meant…" She trailed off in confusion. "What a fool I must seem to you, Sir."

He said nothing for a moment, but then he looked up at her and she was astonished by the change in his face. It was illuminated with a sudden fierce joy that made him appear all at once considerably younger. Then he seemed to remember himself and bowed low.

"I can assure you, Ma'am, that to me you appear in no way foolish."

He took her arm and she was surprised to feel that he was trembling slightly, but he led her to the floor where the sets of dancers were forming. Fortunately it was a simple country dance for which Theora was grateful. Although she felt physically recovered, her spirits were shaken. She found herself pondering the behaviour of the two men and wondering about their previous connection. Clearly they knew each other well, but how and for how long? Also, she wondered exactly how Lord De Lisle knew Mr Irving and his wife. There were just too many confusing threads to the secrecy web that surrounded her employer and his family.

*

When the dance had finished, Lord Thorne took Theora back to Lady Meadley and then excused himself politely. He went off to speak with Mr Irving and then quit the room completely. Theora sat for a while, glad of the opportunity to collect her thoughts. However, when Lady Meadley became engaged in conversation, she slipped away. She did not know the house, but having inquired of a servant she headed down towards the hall to find the library. She had thought the hall to be empty for it was late and all the expected guests had arrived, but her heart turned over as she saw Lord Sulien standing in the doorway removing his cloak. Snowflakes sparkled like jewels on his hair, but he was otherwise immaculate. As if drawn to do so he looked up and she saw his eyes flash as he recognised her. Without haste he handed his cloak to the footman. Theora stood there, her heart beating wildly as she waited for him. He looked down at her and as always she was conscious of his height and presence.

"Good evening, my Lord," she said.

He bowed. "Good evening, Miss Templeton. You were not expecting me?" he said matter-of-factly. "I see it is rather a shock. Shall I leave? I don't want to be the proverbial spectre at the feast."

Theora swallowed and said in as normal voice as possible. "Please don't do that, my Lord. It is true you were not expected, but Juliet will be so pleased to see you."

His Lordship glanced back into the ballroom where Juliet was still surrounded. "She looks very well occupied to me." He frowned as his eyes scanned the room. "Why are you not dancing?" he said abruptly.

Fortunately, Theora was spared an answer by the appearance of Lord Thorne, Mr Allan, Mr Crossley and their host, Mr Westlake. He greeted Lord Sulien with a hearty handshake, but exclaimed over his lateness.

"We thought nobody else would risk making the journey! Was the road very bad now it is snowing again?"

"It could have been worse," said Lord Sulien. "I suspect that if we have much more snow, it will be difficult for your guests who live across the valley. Still, I remain hopeful that the weather will improve. I did glimpse the moon behind the clouds as I drove in, so I expect it will be full out soon."

His eyes flickered and Theora, watching him closely, thought she saw the faintest glance pass between him and Lord Thorne. Then he addressed Mr Allan.

"Good evening, Ciaran. I hope you are well? I look forward to speaking with you later, but, in the meantime, please would you escort Miss Templeton back to my sister and tell her that I will join her a little later." Theora opened her mouth to protest, but Lord Sulien ignored her. "I would be grateful for some of your time, Crossley, and a word with you too, Argus." He bowed to Mr Westlake. "Would it be possible to use your library? There are some urgent business matters that I need to discuss with these gentlemen."

Mr Westlake assured him that he was very welcome and offered to show him the way. The older men then walked off, leaving Theora with Mr Allan. Her immediate impulse was to follow them, but Mr Allan immediately offered her his arm and his voice was firm.

"Please come with me, Miss Templeton."

Reluctantly, Theora took the proffered arm and they made their way back to the ballroom. She was hugely relieved to see that there was no sign of Lord De Lisle's distinctive auburn head amongst the other dancers, so she relaxed a little. She looked up and met Mr Allan's sympathetic gaze.

"You don't need to worry, Ma'am," he said and his Irish brogue was a little more pronounced than usual. "Now Lord Sulien and Lord Thorne are both here, there will be no more disturbances."

He had brought her to Lady Meadley at this point, so Theora was unable to follow up this interesting remark. He bowed politely and she watched his slim figure cross the room to where Juliet was sitting, for once, unattended. Lady Meadley looked at Theora with concern.

"Are you all right, my dear?" When Theora reassured

her, she said brightly, "Well, I am glad you are back for I was worried when I saw you go outside with Argus. I have been keeping watch over Juliet, but now she is with Mr Allan, she will certainly come to no harm."

Theora said quickly, "You would encourage their company, Ma'am?"

"Yes, of course," said Lady Meadley. "Aidan explained that he wanted Ciaran to watch over Juliet when both he and Lord Thorne were away. He is a fine young man."

Theora smilingly assented, but she was confused. It was clear that Lady Meadley had no suspicion that Mr Allan was in love with her niece and, even more strangely, had never considered it a possibility. She obviously did not see Mr Allan as a suitor, simply a companion and protector. As Lady Meadley was now engaged in conversation with a neighbour, Theora was able to let her thoughts turn back to Lord Sulien's unexpected and welcome arrival. The sight of him had acted as a tonic and she no longer dwelt dismally upon Lord De Lisle's brutish behaviour and Lord Thorne's rescue. Instead she remembered the Earl's green eyes glowing upon her when they had met in the hall. She even allowed herself a fleeting moment to consider whether, when they next met, he might actually kiss her hand in greeting. The possibility that one day she would permit him even further intimacy was something that she had often tried not to think about, but continually intruded. Theora knew that she should banish such thoughts immediately, but somehow, this evening, she simply could not. The girl that entered the Westlake ballroom earlier had been transformed. Mr Irving's admiration, Lord De Lisle's insidious flattery and Lord Thorne's gentle chivalry had all combined to change her forever. For the first time in her life she realised that men found her desirable in many different ways. She felt strangely empowered and she desperately wanted to learn how to use that power to her advantage.

Chapter Seven

The Earl of Woodchester, having concluded his business, continued to make himself comfortable in the Westlakes' library. It was actually a small saloon and only the two recessed alcoves lined by books suggested any literary association. There was a large mirror on the wall above the fireplace and, from time to time, Lord Sulien glanced at it to observe the time reflected from the French clock on the wall opposite. At precisely 9.30 the door opened and Lord De Lisle walked in. Lord Sulien took a small sip of brandy and put down the glass.

"Good evening, Bricin."

He waved him to a seat and the two men faced each other. There was a long silence which eventually Lord De Lisle broke.

"Well, Aidan, it seems quite an age since we last met. How well you look."

The Earl leaned forward and picked up his drink again. He looked down into the brown depths and tilted the glass exposing the dregs. Then he stood up and threw them into the fire. The flames blazed with brief intensity.

De Lisle smiled slightly. "Since you ask, I do not want a drink thank you." Lord Sulien turned round and there was no reciprocal laughter in his eyes. "I have not summoned you here for that reason."

Lord De Lisle sighed. He crossed his legs and leaned back, settling himself. "How typical," he said with studied lightness. "Yet, after all these years, I did think we might have at least one meeting where we avoided a confrontation."

"If you truly wish to avoid it, you should adhere to the rules. Whilst I have no issue with you travelling between domains, you must not endanger all our realities. You cannot keep transporting mortals randomly, without using the right pathways, or providing sufficient space."

"Those are rules which you set and which were hardly designed with my best interests in mind," said Lord De Lisle swiftly. "It is very convenient for you that the great globes reside in your domains and not mine."

The Earl's brow darkened. "Can you never think of anyone but yourself?"

Lord De Lisle stood up and it was as if a cold shadow had fallen. He glanced at the fire and it immediately shrank to nothingness and only grey ash remained. He went to the window and looked out into the darkness. "Is it so wrong that that I sometimes seek diversion from this never-ending tedium?"

Sulien regarded him. "You know that I have always let you go your own road. What you do in your domain is your business, but, by bringing this particular couple here tonight, you have gone too far."

Lord De Lisle looked back over his shoulder and smiled mockingly. "You don't like their dancing, Aidan? Such a pity. I assure you that their unique skills have been most appreciated."

"It is not their dancing that concerns me, but what they do when they stop," said the Earl dryly.

De Lisle laughed. "How extremely unromantic of you. They are newlyweds after all."

"And you should know better than to think I would let you threaten this reality by allowing you to damage its already fragile future," said the Earl. "Now, if you will permit me, it is a little cold." He raised his hand and the fire sprang back to life.

Lord De Lisle ran a hand through his red hair. "You know I can't just send them back," he said coldly.

"Of course not."

"You will give me time to prepare them and rewrite their books?"

"Naturally."

De Lisle relaxed. "Then I think we do have time for a drink don't we?"

The Earl poured another glass of brandy. De Lisle took it from him and drank it down. "Very nice," he said approvingly. He looked Lord Sulien up and down. "You are looking a little thinner since the last time I saw you, Aidan. They have kept you busy abroad?"

"You could say that," said Lord Sulien.

"But you are back for good now?"

"Actually, I am back for the good and the bad," said Lord Sulien and at last he smiled. "Especially for the bad."

Lord De Lisle laughed. "You are so suspicious aren't you? Can you not believe that I have at last mended my wicked ways?"

"I am sure you often think of doing so," Sulien conceded.

De Lisle laughed again and held out his glass. "May I have another, at the right temperature, if you please?"

"In exchange, will you tell me what you have been up to in 1803?"

De Lisle set the glass down. "Perhaps."

Sulien poured the drink. He cupped it between his two palms and then handed it over. "Good enough?"

"Perfect," said Lord De Lisle. He drank deeply. "So, I have been making some new acquaintances in the district."

"Yes, I have been informed," said Lord Sulien coolly. "What I cannot understand is why the sudden interest in the mortals in my domain?"

De Lisle's lips curled slightly.

"How can you ask such a question, when you have taken pains to provide such a delightful companion?"

"She was not brought to my house to entertain you,"

said Lord Sulien flatly. He put down his own glass, took out a cigarillo and lit it with a match from the fire.

"Of course not, but she is most entertaining," said De Lisle. He looked quizzically at Lord Sulien.

"You don't find her so?"

Sulien drew on his cigarillo. "As you are aware, I have been in France these last months, so I hardly know her."

"I, however, know her quite well. Beautiful, clever and very charming. Have you not seen her dance tonight? She is quite the belle."

"I take your word for that, I have only just arrived."

"I am so very honoured that you sought me out first then," said Lord De Lisle sarcastically.

He stood up and looked down at the Earl. "Alas, now I suppose I must go, so that I can relocate my pretty dancers. Rather disappointing. I think they really brighten things up around here."

He turned to go, but Lord Sulien put out a restraining hand. "This is serious, Bricin. You know I cannot allow you to keep returning here, unless I can be sure that there aren't going to be any more incidents."

Lord De Lisle looked down at the hand upon his chest and reached down and grasped it firmly. "You have my promise, but, in return, I must ask you to not interfere in my business. If you don't… well. Let's just say, I may forget the bargain that we struck and seek to bend the rules a little." He released the Earl's hand and went to the door, "I would also appreciate it if you asked the Schoolmaster to keep his long nose out of my business. Will you do that please?"

Lord Sulien looked surprised. "You should know that Argus is his own man and nothing I say will influence that. However, I will do my best. In return I ask one other favour."

"What is that?"

"I was hoping for a good journey back to Temple Court and we could do with a full moon to light the way please."

"If that is all," said Lord De Lisle. He waved his hand. "I believe it has stopped snowing." He nodded to the window and outside the moon now shone, lighting the snowclad hedge rows.

Lord Sulien inclined his head. "Thank you for that. Now, I wish you goodnight, Bricin. Until our next meeting."

The heavy door swung open.

"Shut the door as you leave please."

Lord De Lisle bowed. "A pleasure!" He paused and looked back at the Earl.

"I should never have brought you those cigarillos. You know they could well be the death of you!"

He walked out and as he did so, he threw a mischievous glance backwards. As the door shut behind him, a sharp gust of wind blew out the fire and all the candles.

The Earl looked at the fire and it sprang into life again. He gazed deeply into the flames. As he did so, 19th-Century Surrey disappeared and he now saw instead three young men walking down a street with linked arms. They were dressed in evening clothes. Behind them were the lamplit streets of London. It was an evening in 1922 and Christmas time. The voices rang out clearly across the crisp, cold air...

"I really don't know where we are going," said the tallest of the three. He was a spare figure, slightly gangling with brown waving hair and blue eyes. "All I know is that I wish I'd brought another jacket, it's as cold as charity out here tonight."

"Stop grumbling, Argus," said the gentleman in the middle. He was much of a height but fairer and his

distinctive green eyes were slightly crossed. "We'll be back before you know it."

"Oh he just wants a drink that's all," said the third. He seemed slightly less drunk than the others. He was also somewhat younger and more dishevelled, with his jacket unbuttoned and his tie undone. He disengaged himself and produced from his pocket a small hip flask. "Hollands," he said briefly and passed it over.

Lord Thorne took it dubiously. "If you brought that from Aidan's cellar, I'm not sure it's all right to drink it."

Lord De Lisle looked scornful. "Of course it's all right. You of all people should know that anything I have about my person at the time of transference becomes part of the final reality stream. Now take some and pass it on before we all freeze to death."

"What I was worried about was not the ethics but the taste," said Lord Thorne. He took a gulp before passing it back to Lord Sulien. "Actually it's fine. Don't drink it all, Aidan."

At this, De Lisle leaned over and took the flask from the Earl's hands. "Yes, save some for later, old man."

They linked arms again and continued somewhat unsteadily. The snow was starting to fall thickly now and they struggled to keep their footing. After a few moments the inevitable happened and all three descended into a heap on the pavement. De Lisle and Sulien roared with laughter but Thorne did not join them.

"I'm wet through," he complained. He got to his feet and extended his hands to the others. "How far is it to your house, Bri?"

"About half a mile," said De Lisle. He grinned. "We could of course get there quicker if we wanted."

The words made an impression on Lord Sulien. He shook his head.

"No," he said sharply and stood up.

De Lisle looked from one to the other, then he shrugged and the three men continued on. After a while they turned down a small street and reached a terrace fringed with tall trees. They made their way to the last house on the left. Lord De Lisle fumbled in his pocket for the key and then they went inside.

"One thing I do like about the 20th Century is electric lighting," said Lord Sulien an hour later, when they were all sitting down in the saloon. It was about two o'clock in the morning, but none of them had any thought of retiring to bed. Having finished a light supper they continued to drink, smoke and reminisce.

"Can't be the only thing surely," said Lord De Lisle lazily. He had shed his evening jacket and shoes and had propped his feet on the edge of the fender.

The Earl loosened his tie. "I can't think of much else," he said.

De Lisle looked at him in surprise. "You're not serious!"

Thorne, who had been glancing through the few books scattered on the sideboard, smiled. "You find it hard to believe that anyone should prefer Georgian England to this?"

"I do indeed," said De Lisle. "To be honest, the 1920s is about as early as I can cope with in my domain. Even so, I find it quite tiresome in a lot of respects."

"Such as?" asked Sulien.

"Oh, the smells and the dirt and the lack of social media, it can be quite boring here!"

Thorne's eyebrows rose. "Is that really what you miss, air fresheners and Tweeting?"

De Lisle inclined his head. "Of course! In 2017 I have quite a digital following you know. You should look me up sometime."

Thorne put down the book he had been holding. "I don't want to 'look you up'," he said tersely. "You know you shouldn't keep going beyond your appointed domain. It's only going to make things more difficult."

De Lisle withdrew his feet and stood up. His thin face was drawn with sudden anger. "I don't need lectures from you, Schoolmaster. Have I not done my part to support you and Aidan in your domains these many years? Who has done more, I would like to know?"

"Enough," said the Earl. His voice was soft, but it had an immediate effect. The two other men sat down. The Earl looked at the fire, and the flames leapt adding a sudden glow of warmth and light to the room. "Nobody doubts that you have done your part, Bricin, and we are all grateful for your efforts." He held up a hand as Lord Thorne was about to speak. "If you continue to be careful, as I know you will be, I see no reason why you shouldn't use your gifts as you see fit."

De Lisle relaxed slightly. "Thank you, Aidan, I appreciate that."

The Earl inclined his head. "Having said that, I don't understand why you keep coming back to 1922. What is it that draws you here?"

De Lisle smiled. "I come here purely for pleasure."

He got up, walked to the bureau and removed two brochures and some tickets. "This is why I come," he said handing the tickets to Thorne and a brochure to Sulien.

"Tickets to tomorrow's evening performance of A Good Dancing Girl," said Lord Thorne. He shook his head and looked resigned. "More showgirls," he said.

De Lisle grinned. "Not just showgirls, Schoolmaster, the showgirl, and the most beautiful you will ever see. Look." He turned to page two of the brochure. It held a picture of a young girl, slim, dark eyed, with soft curls and a mouth that melted on the edge of a provocative smile.

"Clare Page," read Lord Thorne. He scanned down the page and read aloud:

"'Miss Clare Page, the lovely English actress, singer and dancer, has returned from her fabulously successful run on Broadway to charm us all again in this lively new musical.'"

"Isn't she wonderful?" said De Lisle, enthusiastically.

Thorne and Sulien exchanged glances. "Very pretty," said Lord Sulien noncommittally. His eye ran down the page and then he looked directly at De Lisle. "What are your intentions towards her, Bri?"

De Lisle laughed. "What a delightfully old-fashioned expression! You really do need to get out of the 19th Century more often. My 'intentions', as you put it, are strictly dishonourable of course."

"I've no doubt you have amused yourself," said Lord Sulien. "I take it you have no intention of forming a long term relationship with Miss Page?"

Lord De Lisle looked scornful. "With a showgirl and a mortal? Of course not. In fact," he said airily, "I was planning to make tomorrow night our very last. However, I didn't want to spoil the show for you, by declaring myself before the performance. Might put her off."

"How considerate," said Lord Thorne drily. "I assume Miss Page's demise in your affections is because you have found some other unfortunate female to move on to."

Lord De Lisle's expression hardened. "You suppose rightly," he said sulkily. "Miss Page's understudy as it happens. Not quite as pretty, but with a much less demanding schedule."

"And also, as it says here, engaged to the show's Producer," said Lord Thorne sharply.

De Lisle sighed. *"A bit inconvenient I must admit. Still he's a big name on Broadway, I'm sure he'll get over it. Now, if you'll excuse me, I think I will go to bed. I do need to keep up my energy levels!"*

He winked broadly at Lord Thorne and quitted the room. The two older men heard him whistling as he went up the stairs, occasionally slipping on a step. Then there was the bang of a distant door and finally silence.

Lord Thorne threw himself down upon the sofa beside the Earl. *"His behaviour is outrageous. I cannot understand it, he cares for nothing and nobody."*

The Earl smiled slightly. *"He simply delights in shocking us, that's all."*

"You mean me."

"Yes, you. He knows you have certain scruples and he likes to amuse himself by teasing you."

"It doesn't bother you, this unprincipled behaviour?"

"I do not condone it," said Lord Sulien, *"nor would I wish to emulate it. However, he can do no real harm."*

"You could stop him, Aidan, if you wanted."

"Yes, I could," said the Earl. *"But Bricin's roving eye is proving surprisingly useful."*

Lord Thorne looked at him curiously. *"How so?"*

"He doesn't know it but, somehow, he is drawn to mortals who are also linked to the Quest." He extended the brochure to Lord Thorne. *"Take a look at page three."*

Lord Thorne scanned the page briefly. *"I don't understand."*

"Read it aloud," said the Earl.

"'Guy Irving is the lucky man partnering the lovely Miss Page. Guy is a young American actor, singer and dancer, who has made quite a name for himself in Europe as well as across the Atlantic. He is renowned for his incredible performances, often to music he has composed himself which has never been heard before. He is an excellent piano player, a true master of the 'sharps and flats' as well as the dance.'"

"Well?" said Lord Sulien.

Lord Thorne's face changed. "You mean there is a link to the verses?"

"Exactly." The Earl quoted:

" 'Make a sharp path
Make a master dance
Make music never played'. "

"So?"

"So, it now becomes imperative that we find a way to ensure Mr Irving comes to 1803 as soon as possible and we keep him there, without damaging the reality thread."

Lord Thorne looked dubious. "I am not sure such a thing is possible."

The Earl stood up and his fair face was suddenly grim. "We must make it possible. I am convinced that Guy Irving is the missing element we have been looking for. Without him, we will never find the way back to the Star Maiden."

Lord Thorne stared at him. "You are not thinking of bringing Bricin into your confidence?"

"Certainly not," said the Earl. "Bricin would need to prove himself trustworthy before I risked telling him anything about the Quest. Whilst he completes his training, it is best that he remains in ignorance. When he has learned to control his powers, Madelyn will advise us. No, this is a task for you and I to manage."

*

In 19th-Century Surrey, Lord Sulien stirred and sighed. He stood up and put more wood on the fire. Seconds later, Lord Thorne came in. The Earl looked over his shoulder.

"Well?"

"Not very, by the look of him," said Lord Thorne, with grim satisfaction. "He appeared, how would he phrase it? 'quite annoyed' when I passed him just now. I assume he has now gone off to make the arrangements?"

"Yes."

"And he suspects nothing?"

"He is currently far too intrigued with the mystery of Miss Templeton to think of anything else. It has been a highly successful evening in that respect."

A sound of voices approaching the library made Lord Thorne step inside the room shutting the door quietly behind him. He held it closed, his hand on the handle, until the footsteps passed and then turned the key in the lock.

"So, the plan proceeds," said the Earl. Are you ready to go and deal with Mr Irving?"

"Yes, but I tell you frankly, Aidan, I do not like the way you are putting Miss Templeton at risk."

"She is in no danger whilst I'm here," said the Earl.

"But you are not always here are you?" said Lord Thorne.

The Earl regarded his reflection in the fireplace mirror.

"I understand your concern, Argus, but really, you must trust me, my friend."

Lord Thorne looked at him directly. "I have always done so, but in this case you will forgive me if I take my own measures to protect Miss Templeton?"

The Earl bowed. "I would not expect you to do otherwise. You can hardly think that I wish her to come to any harm?"

Lord Thorne opened the door. "I think, he said deliberately, "that with the prize so nearly in reach, you may become a little forgetful of the minor details. I shall therefore continue to remind you of them."

He walked out. The Earl waited for a moment, then he

went back to the ballroom. Having collected his sister, daughter and her companion, he called for his coach. As they waited for it to be brought round, he drew Mr Allan to one side. "Can you spare me a moment, Ciaran? I would welcome the opportunity of a brief word."

He went with him to the carriageway as Theora, Juliet and Lady Meadley made their final farewells to the Westlakes. As they walked, the Earl spoke:

"Your letters assured me that there was no trouble in the district and that everything was proceeding according to plan. Is that not correct?"

Mr Allan stared at him. "Quite correct, my Lord."

"I see," said the Earl. He loosened one of the buttons on his waistcoat. "Will you tell me then, why you recently took it upon yourself to brawl with the son of one of my respected neighbours?"

Mr Allan's face cleared. "Oh, you mean Holdsworth?"

"Of course I mean Mr Holdsworth," said the Earl annoyed. "Unless you have taken up bare-fist fighting for recreational purposes, I know of no other person upon whom you have laid hands. What on Old Earth is the meaning of it?"

Mr Allan hesitated. "It was a private matter of honour, my Lord."

The Earl looked incredulous. "So private that half the county seems to know about it! I have had at least three gentleman of my acquaintance, remark upon it since I got back from France."

"I am sorry, my Lord. I kept the details most secret. I can only think the Landlord is less trustworthy than I thought."

The Earl looked at him coldly.

"From all reports, you took young Timothy Holdsworth to the Angel in Gyldeford and beat him bloody in one of the sitting rooms."

Mr Allan shook his head. "I hardly 'beat him bloody', Sir. I must confess I did hit him several times, however."

The Earl sighed. "Does this have anything to do with my daughter?"

"You have my word that it does not."

"I see." The Earl relaxed. "Well, the departure of Mr Holdsworth and his mother is not something I am distressed about. However, I must remind you that I employed you to be a steward and that is all. If there is any 'honourable' protection to be done, I'd be grateful if you would leave that to me in the future. Is that clearly understood?"

"Yes, my Lord," said Mr Allan stiffly. "Will that be all?"

"For now, yes."

"Don't you want to speak to me about anything else?" asked Mr Allan rather self-consciously.

The Earl's lips twitched. "I must confess that I am a little tired. Also, I don't wish to provoke you. I understand from the gossips that you now have quite a formidable right hook which you use to very good effect."

Mr Allan smiled. "You were an extremely good teacher, my Lord."

"Yes I was," agreed the Earl. "Go now and help the ladies."

*

When Lord De Lisle left the library at Westlake he did not immediately return to the ballroom but instead went to the small room beside it which had been laid out for gaming. He then spent an hour at cards. To the outward observer he gave every impression of being completely at ease. He drank moderately, played expertly and won heavily. However, despite his apparent calm, he was concealing a mounting anger and sense of frustration. He had come to the Westlakes' ball with every intention of amusing himself and making mischief. The appearance of Lord Sulien had put a stop to this and the fact that he had now also appeared at a disadvantage in front of Miss Templeton, bothered him considerably. He was still at the tables when Lord Thorne entered the room. De Lisle ignored him and carried on playing. However, Lord Thorne's presence seemed the signal for his run of luck to change. Instead of winning steadily, he now started to lose. At last he threw in his hand and made his way out to the terrace. Lord Thorne was waiting for him. The stars sparkled in a cloudless sky. The moon blazed and its brilliance made the snow glitter and lit up the figures of the two tall men as they faced each other. When De Lisle spoke, his usually smooth deep voice was terse with anger.

"There was no need for you to linger, Schoolmaster," he said bitingly. "I am sure Aidan wishes you to attend to his silly daughter doesn't he? After all, that's mostly what he keeps you hanging about for."

Lord Thorne's gaze strayed towards the ballroom. "As it happens, Juliet and Miss Templeton have already gone home under Aidan's escort. I just stayed to see that you also made it home safely."

"How kind," said De Lisle, coldly. "Although I am sure that all you wanted was to make sure Guy and Gala made it back to 20th-Century New York."

"That was the real reason," acknowledged Lord Thorne. He looked directly at De Lisle. "Knowing you as I do, I realised that you might well get distracted, so I have simply taken the trouble to relieve you of the burden of completing their journey."

De Lisle bowed. "Very considerate. All your own idea I suppose! How very kind of you. Especially since I know how you detest the process of reciting all the different cantus."

Lord Thorne sighed. "Not nearly as much as I detest you, Bricin," he said.

For a moment De Lisle looked furious but then he smiled. "Well," he said, "you and I have known each other a very long time haven't we? Whilst we all understand why Aidan hates me, I cannot for the life of me, remember why you do too."

Lord Thorne looked at him. "I didn't stay on to talk about the past."

De Lisle laughed unpleasantly. "Of course, what you're really worried about is the little governess. Who would have thought that she would have managed to attract an old sober sides like you? I never even knew you liked women, apart from Madelyn and you stopped having any interest there a very long time ago. Poor little Golden Hair."

Lord Thorne's eyes flashed. "I don't know why you still call her that. You were nothing to her, apart from an indifferent student."

Lord De Lisle sneered. "Oh yes, you do well to remind me of the distinction. Yet, I loved her more deeply than you ever could. I even wanted to give her my name. She would have accepted me too, if you hadn't kept her leashed to you like a pet dog all these years. And for what? You'd had your way with her as a young girl, but you never offered her marriage. Then, instead of giving her up to me, you forbade me her presence and so bound her to you forever. You pride yourself on your strength and honour as a Moon Lord, but you are as shallow and selfish as any mortal. Do you think that if I had been allowed a life with Madelyn, I would have ever have bothered with anyone else?"

Lord Thorne stood very still. "Yet, despite your dedication to Madelyn, you have been paying considerable attention to Miss Templeton?"

"Indeed, but I do assure you that our relationship has been most correct and very circumspect."

"When was any mortal woman just your friend?" said Lord Thorne contemptuously.

Lord De Lisle laughed. "True, but I assure you that until tonight, I had never even held her hand. Mr Holdsworth was far more familiar with her, although I understand Aidan's steward has now properly dealt with his presumption. I do admit that I would be quite content for little Miss Templeton to become my mistress for a while. I have been meeting her secretly you know. I think she likes me quite a lot. She is a little prim, but very full of life. You should have felt her pulse jumping when I held her hand earlier. Most promising."

Lord Thorne regarded him soberly. "Bricin," he said and his voice was as cold as the ice forming around them, "as you so often remind me, I was once your teacher as well as your friend, so upon this occasion, I feel compelled to dispense one more lesson."

He abruptly stepped forward and pressed his hand upon De Lisle's chest. As he did so, De Lisle appeared frozen and behind him a clear, glassy space appeared in the glittering sky. Lord Thorne gently pushed and without a sound, Lord De Lisle yielded to the pressure and fell backward into blackness.

Chapter Eight

The journey back to Temple Court was not as embarrassing and uncomfortable as Theora had envisaged. Mr Allan gave up his place to the Earl and rode with the coachman, which left Theora sitting opposite her employer. His Lordship seemed disinclined to talk and Juliet too was unusually silent, leaving Lady Meadley to muse over the evening's events. As she seemed happy to do this by chattering lightly without seeking to engage her companions, Theora was able to rest and even occasionally close her eyes. At last the coach drew up and Meadows was hurrying forward to assist them. His Lordship, having handed his sister down, went abruptly away and let Mr Allan attend to Theora and Juliet. Taking the young man's very cold hand, Theora forgot her own weariness and looked anxiously at him. He appeared unusually pale and tense and although he smiled at her briefly, it was forced, without his usual gentle charm. Then he turned to Juliet and Theora was startled to see an expression on Juliet's face that she had never seen before. The look of affection that passed between them was unmistakeable. Startled, Theora realised that at some point that evening a declaration had been made. Although delighted that there was definite confirmation that Juliet returned Mr Allan's feelings, she realised that now the situation had been forced on, there could be no further secrecy. Moments after she had entered her bedroom, there was a knock at the door and Juliet appeared. Theora barely had the chance to dismiss the curious maid, before she was overwhelmed by Juliet's torrent of excited words. These were so jumbled and breathless that she struggled to make sense of them and, rather than trying to do so, decided to make them both a hot drink. During this process Juliet gradually calmed down, so that by the time the kettle had boiled, she was finally more lucid and relatively sensible.

"Oh, Miss Templeton, I am so happy," she said at last. "Only one thing could make me more so, that is for dear Papa to give his consent."

Theora drank her tea. After a moment she said, "Do you have reason to suppose he will not?"

Juliet blushed and looked down, twisting her hands in her lap. "Only my age of course. There can be no other objection I am sure. Even so..."

She stopped and looked at Theora, hopefully.

"Even so...?"

"Well, I did wonder if perhaps you might speak first with Uncle Argus and ask him to speak to Papa on our behalf. Papa has a great respect for his opinion and I am sure could be persuaded by him."

Theora sighed. "I really do not think that I should interfere in a family matter, Juliet. I have no idea what his Lordship would consider a suitable partner. He has previously indicated to me that he expects you to have a good education and a better understanding of the world before you marry anyone."

Juliet walked to the window and stood looking out. Then she turned and came back. Although still trembling and tear stained, her voice was firm and she looked very much older suddenly.

"I am sorry that I may not fulfil Papa's expectations, but the fact remains that I love Mr Allan and if I cannot marry him, I will never marry."

Theora was impressed by this decided declaration. She went to Juliet and grasped her small hands firmly. "Of course I will help you, but it may take some time. Will you trust me to find the best way to reach a solution which doesn't cause either your father or your aunt unnecessary anxiety?"

Juliet met Theora's gaze for a moment.

"I know you will help me and I trust you completely," she said. She leaned forward, kissed Theora upon either cheek and then she left.

Theora prepared herself for sleep but it was a long time before she felt tired. She sat up in bed and watched the candle burn itself down to a stub whilst she reflected on the evening's events. She was deeply worried for Juliet, for she did not take as optimistic a view of the situation as her charge. Juliet had suggested that an approach to Lord Thorne should be made to solicit help, but Theora was more drawn to the possibility of confronting the Earl directly, which (she was certain) was what honesty and etiquette demanded.

Two weeks after the Westlake ball, Theora had still not found a suitable time to speak to the Earl. Her fears that he might disappear again to France were allayed by the fact that he showed every sign of making an extended visit. Theora had wondered if Mr Allan might use the opportunity to speak to the Earl about his wishes towards his daughter, but Juliet advised her that there was no such possibility. Mr Allan had apparently (although reluctantly) agreed not to speak until Juliet had provided him with an assurance that the time was right. She obviously remained hopeful that Theora would prepare the way and was waiting patiently for a successful outcome. She did not mention the matter to Theora again and seemed quite content to resume her place in the schoolroom. Relieved that she was behaving with such maturity, Theora decided that the best time to secure a meeting with the Earl would be on the coming Saturday.

After Juliet's morning lessons were finished, Theora walked down to the lake. The fields glimmered green beyond the water, which gently nudged the mossy banks. As she approached, there was the faintest sound of music.

Then it became distinctly louder, reaching its pitch as Lord De Lisle appeared across the sward. Then the music ceased and only the distant sound of the river that fed the lake remained. Although even that sound had changed slightly and was now a playful gurgle, as if laughing quietly at some private joke. Theora felt nervous, helpless and at a loss as to what to do. De Lisle was smiling at her.

"Good day, Miss Templeton."

Theora looked back at the river and then back at him. "You need to explain a lot of things to me," she said boldly.

"Such as?"

"Such as how you walk around this estate without anyone but me seeing you. How you can make it rain when you wish and the water make music," she said breathlessly.

"You have been observant haven't you?" he said lightly.

"I have eyes and ears," said Theora, steadily. "We have been enough in each other's company for me to have made a study of you. But, even before we met, I was aware that much has changed from when I lived here as a child."

He smiled again. "What else is different apart from my presence?"

She wanted to speak of the white stone on the heath, but Lord Thorne's caution at the ball made her pause. Turning away so that he couldn't see her face, she said, "I have really just one question: who are you?"

At her words a shadow came over them. The bright sunshine was suddenly gathered into a premature dusk. In the distance birds sang and the grass whispered in the wind but around them there was an unnatural and chilling silence. It was like the moment before a frost falls and all its cold strength is gathered in one huge breath, awaiting release. De Lisle was looking down at her. He ran a hand through his dark red curls and smiled in the knowing way that had frequently irritated her, but now was just terrifying.

"I will explain everything, if you do something for me. In the meantime, am I forgiven for frightening you?"

"You didn't frighten me," she said swiftly.

At that he laughed. "You really are a cool liar," he said admiringly. "I suppose you wouldn't consider throwing in your lot with me for good?"

Without waiting for an answer he dropped to his knees on the bank beside her. "Dear Miss Templeton," he said, placing one hand on his heart and extending the other gracefully, "please will you marry me?"

Theora was completely astonished. He looked so ridiculous kneeling upon the wet grass that, apprehensive as she was, she couldn't stop from laughing at him. "Don't be absurd, Sir. You must know that I do not care for you in that way."

She expected an outburst, but instead he simply smiled.

"Why don't you?"

The directness of the question surprised her. Aware that he was watching her intently she forced the words. "I cannot deny I have come to enjoy your company," she said with an effort, "but I assure you that I have never sought anything else. If I have given you that impression, I am very sorry."

They faced each other on the green sward. De Lisle was still smiling, but now it had an extremely unpleasant twist.

"Tell me, is my appearance not pleasing?"

Theora took a breath. "Yes."

"So you both like me and find me attractive?"

She dropped her gaze. "Yes, I suppose so."

"So, do you admit that the reason that you won't accept me, is that you have long been in love with someone else?"

She ran back up the slope, but he caught up with her easily.

At the top of the hill they stood facing each other. "You are insufferable," she said at last.

"Yet, I have made you a very respectable offer. If you think that Aidan is likely to do the same, you are sadly mistaken. He has never loved anyone in that way, not even Juliet's mother. He will never care for you."

She swallowed and began to walk away from him, her gaze averted. "I must ask you to leave me now," she said over her shoulder. She started up the gravelled path, but found her way completely blocked. Lord De Lisle now stood immediately in front of her.

"You need to listen to what I have to say. It's very important."

He sat down on a stone bench and Theora did so too, conscious that she had no other choice. There was no returning smile from him now and his eyes were dark with anger.

"I want you to understand the consequences of the choice you make now. If you agree to marry me, I cannot promise that I will make a good husband, but I could protect you from what is to come. If you stay with Aidan, I cannot. So, I ask you again, will you come with me?"

She passed her tongue across dry lips. "You know I cannot."

He drew breath and when he let it out again it was soft and sibilant as a serpent's hiss.

"Very well." He stood to one side and she got up and walked away from him.

At the end of the walk she turned and saw with relief that he had disappeared completely. As she ducked through the gap in the yew hedge, she almost collided with Mr Allan who was coming from the gardens. He was whistling but that cheerful sound died away as he saw Theora's tear-stained face.

"Good heavens, Miss Templeton, what is the matter?"

Theora clutched at his coat. She steadied herself. "Will you help me back to the house please?"

"Of course, but first do tell me what has distressed you so?"

Theora took another breath. "Lord De Lisle was with me, just now."

Mr Allan's face hardened. "No wonder you are upset."

"You don't like him?" said Theora, surprised in spite of herself.

"No I don't," said Mr Allan flatly. He offered Theora his arm. "Do you think you can walk now?"

"Yes of course." They set off, Theora leaning against Mr Allan's shoulder.

After a moment Mr Allan said in a low voice, "Did he hurt you?"

"No, no," she said quickly.

She saw Mr Allan was regarding her anxiously. As they reached the stable courtyard she found her breath coming in gasps. The ground seemed to be spinning up to meet her and she would have fallen if Mr Allan had not quickly caught her. Then everything seemed confused and the air hot about her, until she felt something cool and damp on her forehead and she could faintly hear a familiar voice.

"What happened?" said the Earl.

The question was addressed to Mr Allan, who said briefly, "De Lisle was here again."

"How is that possible?"

"I don't know, we have always taken every precaution, especially since the Westlake ball. I never expected he would actually come back onto the Estate…"

Mr Allan's voice trailed away.

"Experience has taught me that with Bricin you need to be ready for the unexpected at all times," said Lord Sulien.

"I'm sorry, I have failed you."

"Nonsense. No harm done. Miss Templeton is made of strong stuff."

Theora stirred at that and made to sit up but a firm hand held her back.

"Just stay still a moment longer please, Miss Templeton."

"Shall I make a search of the grounds?" asked Mr Allan.

"No, you would find nothing. Return to the house and ask Mrs Chapman to attend Miss Templeton. Then meet me in the study."

"All right."

Theora heard Mr Allan walk away and opened her eyes. She was laid on a bench and, from the strong smell of soap and leather, deduced that they were now inside the stable tack room. She was wrapped in a cloak and there was a wet handkerchief on her brow. She put her hand to it, but found another already there which drew away quickly at the contact. She looked up and saw Lord Sulien. He was dressed for riding.

"How are you feeling?"

Theora moved her head cautiously. "Better, I thank you, Sir."

"Good, then drink this."

He put a flask to her lips and she struggled to turn away, but he forced the liquor between her teeth and tilted her head back.

She gasped as the spirit touched her throat, but he didn't release her until she started to choke. Then he pulled her up into a sitting position, wiped her face with the handkerchief and, before she could move or further protest, swept her up into his arms. One of the grooms stared in surprise as his Lordship strode past him and hurried to open the gate that separated the yard from the park. Without acknowledgement, his Lordship walked through and headed into the rose garden, so avoiding the front of the house. He walked quickly, with a sure, steady step, and Theora felt completely secure. Never having seen him so closely before, she found herself staring at him in open curiosity. Beneath heavy brows, his dark green eyes glinted with flecks of gold. She could see the lines of intensity beneath them and the thickness of the gold eyelashes. The angle of the nose and the line of the lips, the firm jawline and assured head carriage, all were now fully revealed to her fascinated gaze. She was conscious of the strong, steady beat of his heart as she rested against him, a deeply reassuring sound, which, combined with the warmth generated by the spirit he had given her, made her relax. She felt, for the first time in her life, completely at peace. Despite the events of the afternoon, she found herself smiling for sheer pleasure at the experience of being held by him. Abruptly, he looked down at her and his expression changed and softened as if aware of both her thoughts and scrutiny. She shut her eyes quickly. He walked on, but she was aware that the arms that held her had tightened a little and his breath quickened. At the servant's entrance, Mrs Chapman met them

Theora felt her strength returning. She said quickly, "Please put me down, Sir, I can walk."

He set her down immediately and Mrs Chapman at once put a supporting arm round her shoulders.

"What on Old Earth has happened, Sir?" she said with concern.

"Nothing to worry about. Miss Templeton was walking in the garden and became faint. Fortunately, Mr Allan found her. Will you look after her please? I need to attend to some rather urgent matters." At that the Earl bowed, turned and left.

Mrs Chapman pulled the slipping cloak around Theora's drooping shoulders. "Let's get you straight to bed. You look as if you are fit to drop, poor thing." She gazed at Theora. "Oh heavens, Miss you're not crying are you?"

"No, no," said Theora hastily. She looked back through the garden at the Earl's retreating figure. The golden head was still just visible. "I didn't get a chance to thank him," she whispered.

"Don't you worry about that now," said Mrs Chapman briskly.

She hastened them both inside and, supporting Theora carefully, took her to her room. Theora was then undressed and, in a very short time afterwards, she fell into a deep, dreamless sleep, which, for once, was undisturbed by thoughts of either the Earl or Lord De Lisle.

Chapter Nine

Guy Irving, dancer, singer, actor and gentleman, awoke with a terrible headache. His skull jumped as if, inside it, a drum was syncopated with the motion of a lead-weighted pickaxe. For several minutes Guy lay with his eyes closed, sensing the throbbing rhythm and (because it had been this way ever since he had first stood upright), mentally translating it into something he could dance to. In a moment he could clearly see the steps, a turn here a tap there, a jump to the side… then he moved his head slightly, opened his eyes and it was as if he had been stabbed. The pain, coupled with the penetrating bright light from what seemed to be a million candlelit chandeliers, was excruciating. He put his hands over his face and very gingerly sat up.

"What on Old Earth has happened?" were his first thoughts. Another man, suffering in this way might have thought that he was feeling the effects of too much strong liquor, but Guy consistently practised moderation in all things. After several cautious moments he dropped his hands and carefully opened his eyes. He found that he was sitting on a simple couch, wearing evening clothes. Beside the couch was a table laid for one and covered platters were dotted about it. The room had no doors or windows. The only other thing of note was a large celestial globe which stood in one corner.

It stood upon a floor of maple tongue and groove which had been polished to a glassy finish. From experience, Irving knew at a glance that it was a sprung floor, made for dancing. He swung his legs down and cautiously walked around the whole room, touching the walls from time to time to see if he could find any concealed entrances. There were none. Eventually he returned to the table and lifted the covers one by one.

Choice plates of fish and chicken, jellies and fruits met his eyes. He put the covers back down and sat on the chair. A plume of steam that had escaped from the chicken rose lazily upwards and brushed past the candle flame which spat slightly as a small drop of wax fell to the floor. There was no other sound. Guy touched the wax with his finger. It was slightly warm. He wiped his hands on his handkerchief and poured himself a glass of water. As he swallowed, the pain in his head receded slightly.

He tried to focus his thoughts, but he found that he could remember nothing about the night before. He looked at the floor and then at his feet. Somewhat to his surprise he found he was not wearing dance shoes. This was disappointing because part of him wanted all this to translate into a dream. If he had been wearing dance shoes that would have somehow have made it more acceptable and more dreamlike. Not that he'd ever had a dream like this. As his days were always full of dancing (and dancing rooms with sprung floors) this was uncomfortably, far more like reality. In the rare times in his thirty-two years when he hadn't fallen into bed so exhausted that he had been effectively unconscious, he usually dreamed of something completely different. Thinking of this, his lips curved slightly into a smile of remembrance. He could see a blonde lady in his mind's eye. She had a perfect little figure but she was walking away from him now. His brain raced: what was her name? Guy clutched the glass in his hand and it smashed. His lips mouthed the word "Gala". He jumped up all pain forgotten and shouted it.

His voice echoed around the empty room, but as if the word alone were the catalyst, his short-term memory came flooding back. He remembered vaguely the rehearsal for their last show but then more vividly the sudden appearance of Lord De Lisle and how strangely easy it had been to be persuaded to leave that other world behind and step with Gala into this new, wonderful existence. He remembered Gala's face as they had stood hand in hand in the chapel yesterday. He looked around at the bare room and the blank white walls coupled with the sudden understanding off his loss were more frightening than anything he'd ever known. He clenched his fists and the shards of glass he still held pierced his left palm and blood dripped to the floor. It was at that moment the walls seemed to part and a figure stepped out. Guy watched in amazement, blinking hard to focus against the sparkling brilliance of the chandeliers, as the indistinct outline turned into an elegantly dressed gentleman in 19th-Century evening clothes and that gentleman into Lord Thorne. Guy immediately sprang forward, careless of the blood dripping from his fingers. "Where is she, what have you done with her?" he gasped. He would have caught Lord Thorne with his fists, but Thorne held him off with a firm clasp.

"All in good time, Mr Irving," he said, and his voice, though maddeningly normal, was firm. "First we need to do something about that hand."

Irving, stared at him incredulously. "Where's Gala?" He wrenched himself free and gazed around wildly. "Tell me or I swear to God…"

Then a voice spoke. It was in his head, but he knew immediately that Lord Thorne could also hear it. "We have no time for this. I have his story written now and so he must start work as soon as possible."

Lord Thorne's lips did not move, but Guy heard also his instant reply: "I understand."

Apparently this satisfied the invisible speaker. Lord Thorne turned back to Irving. "Now, Guy, let me bind that hand and then I promise that I will answer your questions."

Irving eyed him suspiciously, but after a moment he extended his palm and Lord Thorne bathed it with water and then tied his handkerchief around it.

"So?"

"So…"

"Where's my wife?"

Lord Thorne sat down.

"Miss James is safe. She is back in New York, in 1938, and waiting to restart your rehearsals."

Guy stared at him. "This is crazy," he said after a moment. "Gala's married to me and she belongs here, with me."

Lord Thorne shook his head gently. "I'm afraid not."

"But we got married yesterday, it was witnessed and everything," said Guy. His light hazel eyes were imploring. "It must be true, how can it not be?"

Lord Thorne looked at him and there was a deep sadness in his voice. "Yes you were married, but that should never have happened. Already there may have been consequences. However, with your help and a little good fortune, we may yet avoid disaster."

He rested a hand lightly on Irving's shoulder. "We can protect Gala, but there will be a price to pay. Are you truly willing to do anything to keep her safe?"

"You really need to ask me that?" said Irving. "Just tell me what's going on please?"

"I will but you need to help me first. What do you remember about meeting Lord De Lisle yesterday?"

Irving thought hard. "He came to my flat in New York with Gala," he said tiredly. "We were talking about the show and then he started chanting something. Next minute, we were married, then he took us back to his house. We spent the night. Today, we went for a carriage drive and then all got dressed up to come to the Westlake ball. It's strange, I knew I wasn't in the 1930s anymore but it all felt so right somehow."

"What time did he come to your flat?"

"About 10 a.m. I think."

"I see," said Lord Thorne. "We may still ensure no damage is done to your time, but you must come with me now."

He took Guy's right hand firmly in his and together they walked towards the globe. Lord Thorne extended his left hand and it glowed as if lit with flame. Then the room disappeared and Irving became aware of the sounds and smells of a summer's day in England. Birds sang, roses and honeysuckle draped the hedgerows and scented the air. In the distance a bell tolled faintly. In front of them was a bridge with a moat. Irving was still wearing the evening clothes of a 19th-Century gentleman. Lord Thorne, however, looked completely different in a dark green doublet and hose. Seeing that Irving was staring at him, he paused, reached over his shoulder and produced from a bag a dark blue cloak.

"Put this on," he said briefly.

Irving wrapped himself in the folds.

"I look ridiculous," he said gloomily.

Lord Thorne laughed. "Only concerned about your clothes! You are a very singular man."

Irving grinned uncertainly. "If you'd been in show business as long as I have, you'd know that a good appearance is vital."

He looked around him. "I am interested in other things though. For a start, how does this travel into history thing work?"

"Walk with me and I will tell you."

They set off down the lane. It was a warm day and there was little breeze.

"In your century," said Lord Thorne, "people are

already making long distance telephone calls and sending telegrams. A hundred years later, that process will become even faster and images will be shared. Three hundred years later, those possessed of the power to communicate across time as well as distance will find a way to contain that process and focus it into a globe, linked to every part of time and every place on Old Earth. As you use a telephone, so we use these objects."

"Why a globe though? Can't you just use a photograph?"

"Photographs are just snapshots of a certain point in time. They can also be imperceptibly altered. So, they are not secure. Globes painted by a master's hand are unique. The chosen artisan is given special powers to build a coded and secure pathway."

"That's incredible," said Irving. He walked on, thinking deeply. "Why do you and De Lisle use conventional transport then, horses, carriages, cars etc.?"

"There is a risk to always using altered objects to cross the centuries. It is an unnatural process. Time is fragile. If we cross too often, in the wrong way, we can cause damage."

"So what year is this and where are we?"

"This is 1522 and we are in Gloucestershire, England."

Irving stopped. "Shouldn't you be getting me back to 1930s New York, if we're going to protect Gala?"

"I can promise that the best protection, for us, is for you to come with me now," said Lord Thorne.

Irving eyed him unhappily. Something in the other man's calm composure seemed to reassure him. "All right," he said soberly. "Where are we going?"

"To my home," said Lord Thorne. He pointed and Irving saw the outline of an ancient castle, built of rose-coloured stone.

"You live there?" said Irving incredulously. "It's like something out of Robin Hood. You sure you've got the right man for the job here? I mean, I'm just a hoofer. Wouldn't you be better off with Errol Flynn?"

Lord Thorne smiled. "I can assure you that you are exactly the man we need."

They walked through the stone-arched corridors, until at last they reached a small simply furnished chamber overlooking a walled garden. Here a manservant brought them water to wash their hands and served them wine. Lord Thorne raised his glass. "Welcome to Ashleworth Castle."

Irving finished his drink. With unsteady hands he fished in his pocket, took out a cigarette and offered one to his companion. For a short time the two men smoked steadily and in silence.

Finally, Irving sat forward in the shabby leather armchair and said simply, "So, I don't belong in this world apparently…"

"No."

"I exist in this one and my own and in the 19th Century?"

"Temporarily, yes. A new timeline has been created for you here and your life events inserted as pages into your book in the 20th Century to keep them safe. The timeline in 1803 has now been shut and the new book created for you there is closed until we wish it reopened."

"I don't understand that at all," said Irving.

"All mortals have books," said Lord Thorne patiently. "They are written by the Lords of the Domains in the language of the Perdurare, setting out the principles of how each of you will live."

He saw that Irving was gazing at him blankly and he smiled understandingly.

"I know it is very difficult to accept this, but each of

you is given a written set of instructions at birth which are linked to time itself. This is your life book. It is our gift to you and your protection. Your book enables you to remain safely within the chosen domain and safely rooted within reality, even if that reality starts to fail."

Irving drew hard on his cigarette.

"And in this other time, in the 20th century, I just dance with Gala?"

"Correct. That is where you belong."

Irving linked his long-fingered hands and clenched them together.

"So, why can't I remember that? Why is it that the only person I know and remember clearly is Gala?"

"Lord De Lisle has taken steps to ensure that all your strongest emotions are focused around her memory. By doing so, he was able to bring you from the 1930s without damaging either you or your place in that time. However, he now thinks you are safely back in your own time with Miss James and we must take care that he doesn't learn the truth. Otherwise, Miss James will be in considerable danger."

Irving looked at him shrewdly. "But, haven't you dealt with Lord De Lisle already?"

Lord Thorne smiled. "Not completely."

Irving stood up and walked to the fireplace. The flames lit up his thin face as he warmed his hands at the blaze.

"I assume it's Lord Sulien who's the key to all of this. Is it from him that you get your powers?"

"Not him, no. Our gifts are inherited. I have certain powers, as you call them, and so do Lord Sulien and Lord De Lisle, but they were passed to us through our fathers' line. They were originally bestowed upon our ancestors, by the first Guardian of Old Earth."

"Who is that and where is he?" asked Irving, in

bewilderment.

"She," said Lord Thorne gently.

There was a silence which the fire filled with a hiss and a splutter as one of the logs crumbled into ashes. Thorne rose and selected a replacement from the basket. The flames sighed and settled back into a steady blaze again.

"All right," said Irving, a little reluctantly. "First of all, tell me, what's your part in all of this?"

Lord Thorne went and sat down again. "My name is Argus Thorne, but I was born Ames Fitz-Osbern, in the year 1042 in France. I am a Moon Lord and a teacher of Moon and Sun Lords."

Irving gasped. That makes you over 800 years old!"

"It does."

Irving sat, still digesting this.

"Ok, what are Sun and Moon Lords?" he asked.

"Appointed guardians of Old Earth's time. We are the Perdurare, the ones that continue, whilst mortals die. Reality is damaged, due to an ancient curse. This means that, without our intervention, past history may disappear and future history will never be created. Or it might disappear as soon as it is formed. Unless the Curse is lifted, eventually, time will run out, all existence will fade and only the last Sun and Moon Lords will remain."

"But, why doesn't anyone know about this?" stammered Irving. "Surely there are signs?"

"Steps are taken to ensure that as far as possible, mortals are protected through ignorance. But the days are getting short, which is why we are now doing everything we can to complete our Quest."

"What do you mean by: 'as far as possible, mortals are protected'?" asked Irving anxiously.

Lord Thorne didn't reply. Irving changed tack. "How did you become a Moon Lord?"

"It happened in 1066. I was a soldier at the French court. I came with my Lord William to England as one of his knights, to fight the Saxon army of Harold Godwine."

Irving stared at him open mouthed. "You were with William the Conqueror at the battle of Hastings," he stammered. "That's incredible. What was it like?"

Lord Thorne looked grim. "At the very last, I remember Lord Harold and his knights at Bellum[3] and their desperate courage. Then Harold was slain and we looked upon our fallen enemy as the remaining Saxons fled the field in confusion. I was appointed to guard the body. Finally, daylight faded and I was left alone with the corpse."

Irving winced. "How long did you stay there?"

"All that night. I could not sleep for fear that someone would try to take the body. William had given strict instructions that it was to be carried through the countryside before he made his way to London."

"That's barbaric."

Thorne looked surprised. "Not really, if you think about it. William was a master, not only of warfare but of strategy. He knew that by showing Harold's body to the people, he would eliminate any last vestiges of resistance. He had no personal animosity towards Harold; he respected him as a great warrior. As dawn came, I was just starting to doze when I became aware that someone had joined me in the shadows. There was enough light to perceive that the figure was beckoning to me. Something compelled me to follow and I walked out and crossed the dunes. At last the meadow disappeared and the green slopes were clothed with great dark yew trees. As we walked down, the trees closed behind us, but, curiously, I

---

[3] Battle

142

felt no fear. At last I found myself in what seemed to be a green valley. Before me were three chairs where two cloaked and hooded figures were seated. My guide immediately walked towards the furthest of the empty seats and sat down upon it. As if this was a signal, all my companions removed their hoods so that I could see their faces."

Lord Thorne paused and picked up the wine jug. "Do you want some more?"

Irving gave a groan. "Please don't stop now," he begged. "Who were they?"

Thorne filled his goblet and drank deeply. Then he sat down again and began twisting the empty goblet between his fingers. "There were two women and one man," he said finally.

"What did they look like?" said Irving, fascinated.

Thorne paused, considering. At last he said, "The lady was very tall. Below her cloak, she was wearing a robe of dark green, spun with silver thread. Amongst her jet black braids was a circlet, which bore in its centre the symbol of a swan upon water."

There was another silence. A breeze from the window made the shutter rattle.

"You remember her very well," said Irving.

Thorne sighed and set down his empty glass on the table. "How could I forget?" he said. "Nobody who saw that lady would ever forget her. Edith was her name, but she was not a mortal. She was one of the Naiads who served the first guardian, the Star Maiden, when the Earth was young. She chose to take human form so that she could live with the Sun and the Moon Lords. She was their guide and teacher until I reached my twenty-fifth year and was ready to take her place."

He looked up and saw that Irving was looking at him so blankly that he laughed. "I gather I am going too fast.

Let us break for a while and have something to eat."

He called for a servant to bring food. When they had eaten their fill, the shutters were closed and the fire built again. Irving took up a seat in a fine wing-backed chair. He prepared himself to listen intently, but after a few moments his head started to nod and he was fast asleep. Lord Thorne rose and placed a fur rug over the other man's knees. He sat back and watched and waited, as, outside the castle, night fell and the owls started to call to each other across the valley. In his mind he rehearsed the words to be spoken to close gateways across time. He took care not to utter them aloud, for to do so would cause grazes upon this timeline which would never be healed. It was long ago that he had learned this particular lesson. He remembered his first teacher, the Druid girl, Madelyn, wise beyond her years, patient beyond imagining. Then his memory turned to the summer of 1067. The trees were in full leaf, a gentle wind blew and the sun was building to its zenith…

The young man, resting in the bleached grass, embraced the loneliness of the hills. He looked up at the clear sky and let his thoughts wander. How long had he been here? It was hard to remember, for he was a different person to the knight who had served King William. Also, for him, time had no meaning, for within him was the power to move forward or back across centuries as quickly and easily as most men walked up a flight of stairs. He sat up suddenly, for his highly developed senses had alerted him to the fact that he was no longer alone in the meadow. He sank down again in the grass and waited. A moment later a golden-haired girl, dressed in a green robe, appeared at the edge of the sward.

She was obviously looking for him and after she had glanced backwards and forwards she said loudly, "I know you are here, my Lord."

The young man laughed and drew himself up on his knees so that his head and shoulders were now visible. "You know I never wish to hide myself away from you for very long, my fair one."

He beckoned and, as the girl walked to him, he sprang forward and caught her in his arms. Then he pulled her down beside him and kissed her. At first the girl returned his embrace, but eventually, as his passion grew, she drew back from him in stages, until at last with reluctance he took his lips from hers and stared down into her soft brown eyes.

"What is wrong?" he said at last.

The girl did not answer immediately. Instead she sat up and moved away so that she was now sitting opposite him.

"I came to tell you that tomorrow you must leave for your domain," she said.

The man's expression changed. His eyes narrowed and his smile was replaced by a hard line which changed him from attractive youth to an oddly plain maturity.

"I suppose it had to happen sometime," he said. "Thanks to your good teaching and by the grace of the Maiden, I believe that I am ready for the task."

The girl picked a flower at random and began to twist the stem between her fingers. "You are not afraid?"

"How could I be? I have been taught everything that I will need and more besides. No, my only sadness is in leaving you, my dearest teacher. Everything must end."
He looked at her and made no effort to conceal his bitterness. "Even, apparently, your love for me."

She hung her head. "You know me better than that I think."

"Do I? Why then will you not come with me?"

Without warning, she sprang up and ran away from

him. When he tried to follow, he found he could not, for she had made each of his steps heavier than the last and stopped him catching up with her. When he had finally recalled the words to break through her cantus, she was out of sight.

He went back to the Druid camp and to the house of the High Priestess. Queen Edith was there with her waiting women but seeing his tense face, she dismissed them.

"Madelyn has told you the news."

"That I must start my new life, alone."

"Not completely alone. Aidan will always be with you and, in time, others of your kindred too."

"But, not you or Madelyn?"

"Of course not. This is our time and we must remain in it. Only you and Aidan can go forward. I thought you understood and agreed to that."

"Understand yes. Agree, no. I need her, my Lady."

Queen Edith sighed. "I was afraid of this. It happens sometimes at the time of an awakening. You have mistaken the needs of the flesh for true love."

He flushed angrily. "You think that I am incapable of love?"

"No, I think that you are capable of the deepest love. In time, you will find it, but not with my servant."

"Nevertheless, I will not leave her and it is not in your power to make me do so," he said fiercely.

The Queen regarded him soberly. "You forget yourself," she said sternly. "If you resist, I can have you forcibly carried forward. You see, there is nothing more important than that you take up your rightful place as a Domain Lord and teacher."

She looked at his distraught face and her expression softened.

"I appreciate your pain. Separation from one's

146

beloved is cruel. But, in your heart, you must know that this is the right thing to do. If I allow Madelyn to accompany you forwards, her life story will be confused and entangled with many others. This may ultimately be a great danger to us all and risk the completion of the Quest."

"I don't agree," said Argus impatiently. "Everything you have taught me has shown that if we ensure that timelines are properly cleansed, then there is no real danger."

Queen Edith said nothing. She walked to the door and her page instantly appeared.

"Yes, my Lady?"

"Has Lord Aidan returned yet?"

"He has, my Lady; he is resting."

"Ask him to come to me at once."

She came back and sat down. Argus stood watching her suspiciously. "If you think Aidan can persuade me to change my mind you are wrong," he said.

The Queen ignored him. She sat down upon her dais. A few moments later, Lord Aidan came in.

He was dishevelled, his fair hair ruffled and his shirt and leggings stained with mud.

He bowed to the Queen and said, "I must apologise for making such an untidy appearance, but I was up at dawn and only came back to change horses before we set out again." He glanced at Argus.

"Why are you not making ready?"

"Lord Argus has asked that Madelyn accompanies him," said Queen Edith.

Lord Aidan looked at the Queen and then back at his friend. "No," he said.

Argus strode forward. "Not you as well," he said. "I thought you at least would support me."

"It is not a question of support," said Lord Aidan. He

rubbed a hand across his chin. "There is much you don't know," he said finally.

"Then why won't you tell me?" said Lord Argus.

He went over and clasped Aidan's shoulders, turning him gently so that they were face to face. Both were big men with the promise of more growth to come, but Aidan was the stronger and broader, whilst Argus stood a little taller.

"Am I not worthy of your trust?"

Lord Aidan remained silent, but Queen Edith spoke clearly:

"The Moon Lord has asked a fair question and I will answer fairly. Yes, Argus, you are worthy. I have asked Aidan here, to unlock the doors to the knowledge you require." She stood up and walked to the door. There she paused. "Soon, Moon Lord, you will realise why bringing Madelyn into the future is such a risk." Then she walked out of the tent, leaving Argus and Aidan alone together.

*

In his Gloucestershire castle, Lord Thorne, teacher of the Sun and Moon Lords rose. Leaving Irving sleeping he went down to the library. As he had done so many times before, he laid his hands face down upon the celestial globe that stood by his desk. It spun slowly and then gathered speed. As it did so, the 16th Century faded away and Lord Thorne was once again standing in the library at Templeton Court, where Lord Sulien was waiting for him.

Chapter Ten

After her encounter with Lord De Lisle, Theora kept to her bedroom. It was not until the late afternoon that she went downstairs again. Her intention had been to go into the restored conservatory and sit quietly for a while, but she was informed by Meadows that Lord Thorne and Lord Sulien were there already. Although she longed to speak with both of them, Theora dreaded their inevitable questions. However, she was also hugely curious as to what they might be discussing, so she made her way to the morning room which was next to the conservatory. Fortune favoured her; the door of the conservatory was ajar and the voices of the two men could be heard clearly. Theora crept as close as she dared, wrapped her shawl about her and settled herself down. Lord Sulien spoke first:

"Yes, we should be able to assemble in less than a week," said Lord Thorne.

"How is Irving?"

"As you would expect, still adjusting. I will be speaking with him again shortly."

"So, all that remains is to ensure that our dear friend doesn't get too close for comfort."

"How do you expect to manage that? Today seemed uncomfortably close to me."

"Uncomfortable!" Lord Sulien gave one of his rare laughs and Theora was startled at the harshness of his voice when he spoke again.

"Yes, I suppose it was, especially for Miss Templeton of course! An unfortunate incident I'd like to have avoided."

"You know that Bricin's seeking to provoke you," said Lord Thorne.

"Or, he might just be reacting to your recent action,"

suggested the Earl.

"I suppose it may not have helped," said Lord Thorne reluctantly. "I hoped a show of strength might settle things down for a while."

"I appreciate that you acted with the best of intentions, but you must have known that he would quickly respond. Anyway, what's done is done."

"What do you intend to do?"

"I shall stay here and support the preparations for my daughter's ball. My presence should be sufficient to keep Lord De Lisle's knights at a respectable distance. Once the ball has taken place, then subterfuge will have to be abandoned. But, by then, I expect that we will be as ready as we can be."

"Very well," said Lord Thorne. Theora heard the scrape of a chair as he stood up.

"I will return to Ashleworth then."

"Yes, do that. When the time comes, I will meet with you and Mr Irving at the appointed place."

"Do you want me to give any instruction to Ciaran?"

"No, it would be very dangerous for him. Safer for everyone if he knows as little as possible."

"I hope you are right, but, it's taking an awful risk. You will be careful won't you?"

"Always."

There was a sound of the doors opening out into the gardens and after a moment Theora was aware that the two men had gone outside.

*

In Ashleworth Castle a log slipped and spluttered into the grate. Irving sat up. Lord Thorne was smiling down at him.

"Don't tell me I drifted off to sleep in the middle of all of that?" said Irving disgustedly.

"You certainly did," said Lord Thorne smiling.

"Tell me more about the guy with Queen Edith. What did he look like?"

"I judged him about my age. From the moment I took his hand we were friends and we have continued to be, through many long years."

Irving whistled. "Lord Sulien eh?"

"Yes. Aidan Sulien, the last born Sun Lord. Master of the First Domain and leader of the Quest."

"And the other girl? Who was she?"

When Lord Thorne spoke, his voice was gentle and affectionate, but sorrowful. "Madelyn was her name. A Druid priestess and destined to become my teacher."

"How come?" said Irving eagerly.

"To understand that you need to forget everything that currently seems real to you. Do you trust me to tell you the truth, however strange it may seem at first?"

Irving laughed. "You're kidding me," he said at last. "In the last two days, I've been transported twice through time into different periods of English history, so I'm learning to suspend disbelief! Whatever you say is going to sound completely mad, but I do trust you. Who knows why? But I do."

Lord Thorne continued his history and Irving asked many questions. The two men sat up talking throughout the night. When the candles had burned down, it was nearly morning.

"So you're a descendant of Avaldi the first Moon Lord?" said Irving finally.

"Yes. For time to balance and the three unbroken domains to be protected, it is safest if they are managed by three connected guardians. These can either spring from the moon line of Avaldi or the sun line of Owain. When I was in my fifteenth year, my cousin was born. When I became a Moon Lord, I managed the Second Domain in the 19th Century and the Third Domain in the

20th Century. I also became Lord De Lisle's teacher, until his twenty-fifth birthday. Then, when he had completed his training, he became master of the Third Domain."

Irving sat up. "Gosh, I don't envy you having to look after him!"

Lord Thorne smiled wryly. "It was a challenge," he confessed. "Many times I have had cause to regret the pledges that I made all those years ago."

Irving nodded. "Tell me how it all worked out."

Sunlight was pressing against the shutters. Lord Thorne sighed. "Lord Sulien and I have always worked together to further the Quest to find the Star Maiden, but we have not revealed this to De Lisle. He is strong and brilliant, but unstable. So he has been kept in ignorance. Yet, despite the deception, we were once great friends."

Irving helped himself to more wine. "I sense you haven't yet come to the worm in Eden's apple," he said shrewdly. "What happened to change that friendship?"

"Look then," said Lord Thorne. He went to the fireplace and placed his hand over the mirror that hung above it. The silvery pane shimmered, dissolved and then reformed. Guy stared at the scene which appeared before him…

A young girl was walking down a chalk cliff path that led from the Village Inn to the cottages in the valley below. She was dressed in blue with a cape of fringed grey cotton and a scarf of faded gingham. As she ducked her head to avoid a tangle of bramble, the scarf was snatched sharply from her head and her shining head of hair was laid bare. The girl picked up the scarf. She made no attempt to put it back, but instead shook her head. Her long golden ringlets fell down her back. At the bottom of the hill she stopped at the village pump, washed her hands and used her scarf to wet her hot cheeks and throat. In the stone basin her reflection shone back at her and she gazed upon it, until a sound behind her made her turn sharply.

A young man riding a black horse was looking at her. Tall and richly dressed, he too was hatless and his hair was equally shining, dark bronze curls against a cheek as white as the chalk cliffs. At the sight of him, the girl's fresh colour rose and she dropped a curtsy. The man left his horse and walked to the pump. He cupped his hand, took a drink of water and dried his hands on a fine lace handkerchief.

"You left the inn early today, Lizzie," he said.

The girl avoided his gaze. "Yes, my Lord."

"Yet, you knew I would be there?"

"Yes, my Lord."

"So why would you do that?"

"I was needed at home, my Lord," said the girl in a small, tense voice.

The man walked up to her. "My need is the greater, I think," he said gently and made to catch her, but the girl jerked away. She ran to the edge of the fields and then turned and dropped down a gully that led into the meadows beyond.

The man followed. In a few strides he had overtaken her and blocked her path. The girl stopped. Around her the countryside was putting itself to sleep in its practical, ordered way.

The girl trembled. "Please let me go home," she said finally.

"But you haven't given me an answer yet."

"You know my answer, my Lord."

The man smiled. "Then, to be exact, you haven't given me the right answer."

He put his hand in his pocket and held it out to her. "Would this help the decision?"

He opened his palm and the girl gasped. Against his white hand shone a large gold ring set with one brilliant stone.

"This ring is an heirloom of my house, and I now offer it to you freely." He held it out. "Here, take it, let us see how it looks upon your hand."

The girl stared at him disbelieving. Then with shaking fingers she took the ring and put it on. Her fingers were plump and the man's were slim, so it fitted surprisingly well. She looked directly at the man for the first time.

"I cannot take such a valuable thing," she whispered.

The man smiled at her. "Why not?" he said. "Is this not sufficient proof of how deeply I feel for you?"

"Then we are now betrothed?" said the girl shakily, but with hope in her soft, country voice.

The man ran a hand down her cheek. The long fingers travelled down to her throat and then on to her heaving breast. The hand rested there for a moment as if in confident possession.

"We are whatever you wish," he said. "You know that I adore you."

The girl put up her hand to grasp his wrist and remove his hand. The ring she wore blazed as its stone caught and held the light of the sunset. "If you are really speaking the truth, my Lord, then yes, I will be your wife."

The man's smile became broader. He drew the girl to him and kissed her passionately. She endured it for a few moments and then struggled to get free. "Please, my Lord, enough..."

He released her reluctantly and stepped back. His eyes travelled over her body and it was clear from his expression exactly what he wanted.

"I have done you a great honour," he said at last. "Will you not now show me a little more gratitude in

return?"

The girl drew herself up and even though there was fear in her eyes, her voice was firm.

"My Lord, it is getting late. We can talk of this further tomorrow."

The man smiled. "As you will."

Then I wish you goodnight," said the girl. She set off across the fields, walking quickly. The man remounted his horse and cantered towards her. He jumped down, and said gaily, "I have had a thought. As we are now betrothed, would it not be right and proper to immediately advise your sister. I am sure she will be overjoyed."

The girl looked up at him and scanned his face as if trying to read his thoughts. She hesitated. "I suppose that would be right and proper," she said.

"Exactly. Now will you ride with me?"

"Thank you, my Lord, but I prefer to walk," said the girl.

"Then I will walk with you," said the man. "Let me show you a short-cut that I came across the last time I visited." He held out his hand and reluctantly the girl took it. Together they walked forwards, the man holding her hand tightly, as the sun set and a red-edged moon took its place.

*

Irving looked soberly at Lord Thorne's cold set face. He was horrified by what he had seen and fearful of what might come next. Irving was convinced that De Lisle meant to do the girl great harm and felt sick as to what that harm might be. He stared again at the mirror and instantly the scene plunged forward in time two weeks...

The white cottage at the bottom of the valley was a simple two-storeyed affair, with a small garden bright with flowers and vegetables. The curtains were closed as it was still early morning, with dawn only just breaking. Through the thick mist a man appeared. At the picket fence the man dismounted, tied the horse to the gate and went to the door. He removed his wide brimmed hat and Irving saw to his surprise that it was Lord Sulien. He knocked and a moment later a girl let him in.

She had light brown hair and a face which would have been flawless were it not for the dark red stain that ran from cheek to lip. Irving instantly realised that she was closely related to the golden-haired girl. She showed Lord Sulien into the front room and closed the door behind him.

Lord Sulien set down his hat. "How is she, Jenny?" he said without preamble.

Jenny sat down and faced him. "As well as can be supposed, my Lord," she said. "Physically, she is almost recovered."

"And in herself, how is she? Has she spoken of it yet?"

"No, my Lord. She has not spoken a word since that evening."

"My God." The passionate harshness of Lord Sulien's normally even voice made Irving shudder. He strode to the sofa and threw himself down upon it. "If only I had got here sooner."

Jenny raised sober eyes to his. "You can't blame yourself. You were not to know this would happen."

"Did I not?" said Lord Sulien bitterly. "It has been a disaster in waiting ever since I brought De Lisle here. I could have prevented it, instead I made the situation worse. If I had stayed away, there is every chance he would have done so too. My selfish desire to see the children of my old servant has brought you nothing but the most dreadful sorrow and shame. I wish I had never come back to An Baile Glas."

Jenny looked at him. "I am very glad that you did, Sir," she said timidly.

Her words seemed to draw the bitterness out of him and his expression softened. He took her hand in his and squeezed it gently. "I thank you for that, but what is to be done here? You cannot possibly stay now."

Her blue eyes, lighter and less perfect than her sister's, filled with tears as she looked at his strong hand covering her own. Then she drew back and stood up, smoothing down her white apron over her dress of grey cotton.

"This is our home," she said with quiet dignity. "There is nowhere else for us to go."

She turned abruptly and Lord Sulien let out an exclamation for the golden-haired girl was standing by the door. She seemed to have aged ten years. Her face was bruised and her lips were scabbing, where they'd been bitten. Jenny ran to her and put her arms around her. It was both a protective and defensive gesture but the girl gently put her away. She turned to face Lord Sulien.

"What are you doing here?" she said directly. Her once sweet voice was faint and cold.

"I came to see how you were, Lizzie," Lord Sulien said gently, "and offer what help I can to you both."

"If you take us away can you protect us?" said Lizzie directly. The words seemed to be driven from her. She twisted her small hands together and Irving could see that the fingernails were broken.

Lord Sulien looked at her. "If you come with me, I can promise that you need never fear from Lord De Lisle again."

The girl's white face relaxed visibly. "Then we will go with you," she said. She looked briefly at Jenny. "Will you help me get back to bed, sister?" she said. Jenny ran to her and supported her, but as they reached the door.

Lord Sulien's voice stopped them. He spoke strongly and clearly.

"I can only protect you properly if you consent to become my wife."

Jenny gasped and Lizzie froze where she stood, but after a moment she turned and, with great difficulty, faced the Earl. "You would do that, after, after..."

"It is past now," the Earl interrupted, "and neither of us need ever think, or speak, of it again."

He walked to her and offered his hand. "If you will let me perform this service, I will be greatly in your debt."

She took his hand wonderingly. The faintest smile touched her bruised lips creating a brief glimpse of her former beauty. "You are very kind, my Lord, to put it so."

The Earl looked down at her. "If you will marry me, Lizzie, I will do everything I can to show you the kindness that you deserve."

He released her and slipped the signet ring from his finger. Will you take this as a pledge of my sincerity and until I can find you a better?"

She took the gold band from him and held it for a moment in a shaking hand. Then at last she seemed to come to a decision. She opened her left hand and slipped it over the third finger.

"Thank you, my Lord" she said simply and she let him draw her back into the room and over to the couch where they sat down together. They were so intent upon each other neither of them noticed Jenny, who with a face turned to stone slipped out of the door, leaving them alone.

Then the mirror scene changed again...

It was night time and Jenny was standing at the mouth of the great Lough looking out over the still waters. Irving could see that she had been crying. A slight breeze ruffled the water's surface and Jenny sighed and *prepared to turn away. But, suddenly the moonlight became piercingly bright, the mist cleared and Lord De Lisle came walking across the sward.*

"Good evening, Jenny."

Jenny stared at him in shocked horror.

"What do you want?"

"To offer you my condolences of course."

The girl stared at him, the traces of tears still visible on her white face. "What do you mean?"

De Lisle smiled and Jenny shivered.

"It must be so hard for you, especially since you know he doesn't love her."

"And you do I suppose?"

"Of course not," he said coolly. "But at least I have never pretended otherwise. I wanted her, I cannot deny that and so did Aidan, although he is, sadly, enough of a hypocrite to pretend that his interest is of the purest nature."

"At least he is prepared to give her his name," said Jenny hotly.

De Lisle inclined his head. "True, I certainly would never have done that. An innkeeper's daughter could not be the mistress of my house. I know what I owe my lineage, even if Lord Sulien does not."

Jenny stared back and, even though she was trembling, there was a strength about her little figure as she confronted him.

"I do not know why you have come here to insult me, Sir, but I must ask you to leave myself and my sister alone. We quit the district in a week's time and so can be of no further interest to you."

"There is no need to be afraid, Jenny," said De Lisle. "I know you well and mean you no harm. Since you became a woman, you have dreamed of being a lady. More than that, ever since you knew of Lord Sulien's

position and prestige, you have longed to be an earl's wife. How galling it must have been to see your stupid sister become so beautiful. How often have you secretly cursed her beauty and wanted it to drown in this still water. You see, I know it all, because when you spoke to the moon and told it your troubles, you spoke directly to me, the Lord of the Moon."

The blood drained from Jenny's face. "I didn't, I couldn't..." she stammered.

"Of course, you didn't know," he said. "Aidan has taken care to only tell you part of the tale. But I can tell the whole. I can also give you all the power that you crave and the beauty you desire."

He stepped closer and tilted the girl's face so the moonlight shone directly upon it. "What do you think of that?"

Jenny clenched her hands. "You abused my sister, why would you do anything for me?" she said.

He abruptly released her. "I have a reason," he said and his voice was silken. "My dearest friend is now my eternal enemy. As I cannot watch him every day, I need another pair of eyes to do so."

"You want me to be your spy?"

He looked at the sapphire ring which had replaced the opal upon his white hand. "Precisely."

She shook her head. "But they will recognise me."

He smiled. "I promise you they will not. I will take you away to places and times where you can start your life afresh. Look, let me show you."

He waved his hand and Irving gasped because although she bore no resemblance to the scarred girl, he knew instinctively that the lady in the vision was still Jenny. But now she had a face and a figure so perfect that it was almost unnatural.

Then Lord De Lisle waved again and the vision was

gone. Jenny stared at him. Her sweet, mild expression was gone forever, banished by fierce longing.

"When do we begin?" she said.

Lord De Lisle took her hand. "We have already begun," he said. He drew her gently to the lake. In the still lapping waves, the reflected figure of Jenny shook, blurred and then disappeared forever as her new form took shape...

*

"What a monster," said Irving appalled. "How did you find out these things, can you read his mind in some way?"

"No. Although Sun and Moon Lords are connected and can exchange thoughts, we cannot automatically read each other's minds without causing pain. However, the minds of mortals who dwell within our specific domains are always open to us, although we rarely use this gift without permission. We respect your privacy and only forcibly look into your memories when danger threatens. Also, we are unable to look into the mind of a mortal who does not originally belong to our domain. For example, I cannot see your thoughts, yet, if I chose to do so, I could see those of any servant in this castle. Lord De Lisle believed that by creating a new life book for Jenny in the 20th Century her mind would be closed to us. If he had paid more attention to his studies, he would have realised that under the circumstances, this would never work."

"What 'circumstances'?"

"The power of love. Jenny still loves Lord Sulien and so her mind is forever strongly linked to his domain. So, even disguised, we can access her memories. So far, Lord De Lisle has imparted sufficient information to her for us to manage any possible risk."

The servants then served breakfast, but Irving ignored the plate set before him. Unshaven, slightly grubby, but no less stylish, he continued to ply his host with questions.

"Ok, so I see that De Lisle is a heartless philanderer, he's no real threat is he? He can't really do any harm whilst you and the Earl are around? He knows nothing about the true nature of the Quest after all."

There was a silence and Irving looked anxiously at his companion. "Or does he?"

"A few months ago," said Lord Thorne, "De Lisle was travelling abroad and in a museum he discovered an ancient relic, a sword, which had been found on the bottom of a glacier some years past. He used his powers to return in secret and he took the sword from the cabinet. As soon as he grasped it, a portion of the memories of the first Sun Lord were revealed to him. He immediately retreated to his own domain where he has hidden the sword. It is now somewhere in the 20th Century."

Irving jumped up and began to pace about, his quick feet beating an almost unconscious tattoo of rhythm on the stone floor. "Well that puts the tin hat on it."

Lord Thorne raised an eyebrow. "Why do you think that?"

"He can work out how to find the Star Maiden first."

Lord Thorne smiled a little sadly. "No, because he doesn't know exactly what he's looking for."

"But, he now knows all about the Curse and the Quest?"

"No. When the Sun Sword was handled, it released some memories but not all and the memories would be difficult to decipher as they are not in order. Only a Sun Lord is able to see the memories in their correct sequence. So De Lisle suspects much, but really knows little. The more major issue is that he is now searching for the jewel that fits into its pommel."

"What's the significance of this jewel?"

"It contains a very powerful reality splinter. When the stone is part of the sword, the sword becomes fully awake. It then becomes an extraordinarily powerful weapon. If De Lisle were to find the jewel, it would be disastrous, for he would be stronger than either Aidan or I and would most likely be able to do what he wished in any timeline. But do not fear, I will never allow that to happen."

Irving stared at him, for Thorne's pleasant gentle expression was now so very changed that for a moment he almost didn't recognise him. He looked fearfully at his companion, but then just as suddenly Thorne smiled and the sun streamed through the windows and the room was warm and pleasant again.

"How did the sword and the jewel go missing?" asked Irving.

"We do not know for certain," said Lord Thorne sadly. "The legends say that after Owain gave up his Kingship, he hid the sword in the mountains. Then Avaldi's daughter was riding her white horse in the sea one day and a great wave came and washed them away. So, the pendant was also lost. There were no witnesses to verify this, but what we do know is that, from that time, the Moon Lords bore no more daughters and the white horses who were descended from the Star Maiden's own herd were no longer to be found. Now only the red and black horses remain to serve us."

"I'm sorry," said Irving lamely. He felt embarrassed at his own inadequacy. "I still don't understand why there are only three timelines," he said at last, after a long pause.

"When reality was splintered, past, present and future became mixed together. Some of the reality splinters and their associated elements of past, present and future were larger than others and so the Sun Lords took the decision to focus effort upon preserving them. This ensured that the time they channel remained stable and eternally guarded."

Lord Thorne stood up. "Now you know our history, we must discuss your part in the Quest and explain the risks."

Irving took out a cigarette and lit a match from his shoe. His thin face was tense with the strain, but he looked resolute. "Ok let's cut to the last scene in this three act number. I guess I'm here to fill in the bit regarding the dancing?"

"You picked up the section from the verses?"

"Mmm, something about a 'master dancing'. What will I need to do?"

"Unfortunately, we don't know exactly," said Lord Thorne apologetically. "You're going to have to help us work it out."

Irving drew on his cigarette. "You mean you guys have been working on this production for centuries and you still haven't thought out a finale? I always thought the intelligence of the English aristocracy was overrated."

"It's only that bit we're not sure about," said Lord Thorne, laughing. "That's why we needed to get you here."

"You mean that us coming here wasn't just down to Lord De Lisle. That you somehow set up the whole thing to bring Gala and I to the party tonight?" said Guy incredulously. "How the hell did you manage it?"

"It took quite a lot of planning," admitted Lord Thorne.

"The cute governess, she's mixed up in it too isn't she?"

Lord Thorne stood up. "If you'll come with me now, Guy I can show you what we've found out."

Irving picked up his coat, "Ok, so you don't want to

talk about Miss Templeton eh? Thought I caught a certain look on your face in that direction."

He saw that Lord Thorne's face had become even more expressionless and whistled. "Hey ho, you have got it bad, brother."

Chapter Eleven

They walked down the stairs and into the library. Lord Thorne spun the globe and moments later the two men stood in the entrance of a vast cavern. It had a high ceiling, spiked with beautifully marked stalactites that glowed in distinct colours of cream and pink and amber. The space was lit by wall torches that burned with a clear, silvery light. In front of them was a gothic archway and the tallest door that Irving had ever seen. It towered up above him, a great shining expanse formed of two irresistibly smooth, black panels. Despite Lord Thorne's cry of warning, instantly Irving stretched out a hand and touched it, but sprang back quickly with a muffled oath. The surface was red hot.

"What on Old Earth is it made of?" he said, nursing his hand, which now bore an angry welt.

"Nothing from Old Earth. The stone is from the Star Realm. Only Perdurare can touch this entrance without pain and only at their touch will it open." He stretched out his own hand and as soon as his fingers made contact, the doors swung open with no sound and feather lightness. After Irving and Lord Thorne had passed through, they closed just as noiselessly behind them.

Irving looked at his hands. One was cut, the other burned. "That may be all well and good, but it will be a long time before I'll be able to handle my cane with comfort," he said wincing.

"I'm sorry," said Lord Thorne. "We can soon make you more comfortable if you follow me."

They were standing in a seemingly endless corridor. Along the walls were normal-sized doors. Some of these were closely padlocked and did not look as if they had been used for many years. Some, though, were fully opened or ajar.

"What is this place?" said Irving in awe.

"This is where all the reality splinters, not already in use, are held for safe-keeping. It is also where our knights train and we prepare for the completion of the Quest."

Irving looked around. "These caves must be massive!"

"They would be massive indeed if they could hold everything we require," said Lord Thorne. "As it is, this place is the hub, but not the entire wheel. The power held here makes it possible to see everything and access it from its location in the different domains."

He walked to one of the closed doors and placed his palm upon it. The door swung open and a light shone through. The two men walked forward and Irving saw that they were now in a hospital reception room. By its style and décor he knew it was from his own time. A pleasant faced young man who had been sitting at the front desk looked up and smiled.

"Good evening, my Lord."

"Good evening," said Lord Thorne. "My friend has burned his hand and the other one is cut. Would you help him please?"

The man reached out and pressed an intercom. "Dr Hunter to reception please."

After a few minutes a doctor appeared and took Irving away to be treated. Lord Thorne sat down and proceeded to light a cigarette.

The receptionist looked at him reprovingly and Lord Thorne smiled and put it out. Eventually Irving reappeared. His face was working with a range of emotions and he was obviously longing to speak. He restrained himself until they were then again in the corridor.

"That hospital was in New York and it was 1938," he said at last.

"Of course it was," said Lord Thorne. "You needed to

be treated in your own time and with medicines which were appropriate to you. Otherwise, you might have been permanently injured."

"But, how?" stammered Irving.

"If you are feeling better, we need to complete the journey," said Lord Thorne. He held out his hand. "To pass through this last doorway, you need to be connected to me. Please hold on tightly and do not let go."

He drew Irving forward and they walked through. Irving was terrified, for it was suffocating black and cold. Only the feel of the strong, hard fingers wrapped around his own kept him from screaming aloud. Then, suddenly, Lord Thorne let go and Irving was falling through the air, firstly with great speed, but then slowly and lightly, just as if he was floating. As he fell, warmth returned to his body and he felt his spirits rising. When at last he landed upon his feet he was no longer scared and in pain, but quite at peace. He looked around him with wonder. He was standing in the centre of a long room. The walls were brilliant white and yet burnished lightly with gold, so that they shimmered and were difficult to focus upon. The floor was flagged and thickly carpeted with a rich red rug, which folded itself around the feet and muffled all sound. Sunshine poured down from a series of arched windows. Every shelf and alcove was decorated with huge vases of golden roses, lilies, honeysuckle, lavender and lilac which perfumed the air. Rich hangings of red velvet and cloth of gold, hung from the walls and ceiling. They were embroidered with suns, moons and stars. At the very end of the room, dominating it by its sheer size and beauty, was an organ. Someone was playing and instinctively Irving moved towards the sound. But when he reached the steps at the organ's foot he paused and stood transfixed, for the music was now heart wrenching. Afterwards, when he tried to describe it, he found his words inadequate. All he could ever say was that it was like every single happy memory combined with every possible hopeful thought. These were woven into the musical notes, so each one heard was simple joy.

Irving made to mount the steps to congratulate the musician responsible. But before he could do so, Lord Thorne's hand closed firmly upon his shoulder.

"You cannot go up. You must wait for him to come down."

Irving tried to wrench free but the thin hand held him fixed to the spot. "I need to get up there," he said gaspingly.

"I know," said Lord Thorne and his voice was very kind. "It is hard to understand, but now is not the time. If you go up now, you can never return to 1938 and everything that you were, everything that you might yet be, will be lost."

Irving hesitated. "I won't be able to get home," he said haltingly.

"No."

As if it was the hardest thing he had ever done, Irving stepped back. He shook his head as if to clear it. After a moment he looked up and although his face was drawn with strain, he was smiling. "Then you were right to stop me."

He put his hands in his pockets, took a deep breath and straightened his shoulders. "How long will he be?"

Lord Thorne smiled. "Not very long. Let us wait."

The two men sat together, bathed in the rich sunlight. Irving gripped the seat to keep himself immobile. When at last the organ trembled to silence, they looked at each other. Irving was weeping.

"Why am I here?" he said, wiping his streaming eyes. "I assume it is not really a place for ordinary men?"

"No, but to become a knight, you need to receive the

necessary strength and knowledge to help you with your task. I have prepared you as much as possible, now a Sun Lord will take you forward."

He looked up and Irving saw Lord Sulien coming down the stairs towards them. He nodded to Lord Thorne but addressed himself directly to Irving.

"Welcome, Mr Irving. I am very glad to see you again."

He clasped Irving's hand briefly. "Lord Thorne has told you some of our history already, and when we have spoken, you will be ready for the task ahead. Whether you will complete that task and what the future will then hold for you and all existence, I cannot tell. All I can say with certainty is that your presence is vital to any chance of success. Now, please walk with me."

He beckoned to the American and they went forward into an antechamber. After such a rich, sensory deluge, the plain, simple room was strangely refreshing. Irving reflected that it was like quenching one's thirst with a glass of pure spring water, after finishing a delicious banquet.

"Would you like anything to drink, coffee or something stronger perhaps?" said Lord Sulien, as if he had read Irving's thoughts.

"I'd kill for something stronger," said Irving frankly, "but I didn't know it was ok to drink alcohol in the Lord's house."

Lord Sulien leaned back and took from an adjacent cupboard a couple of glasses. "It depends on which 'Lord' you are talking about."

Irving's expression was cynical. "I assume you are the resident 'Lord' and so, in essence, a God," he said.

There was a strange flicker in the Earl's green eyes as he met the other man's gaze. "Not exactly." He passed his hand briefly over the glasses and then handed one over. "Let us just say, I am someone whose ancestors happened to please the resident goddess."

"Yes, so I've heard," said Irving. He looked at the glass. The Scotch glowed against the sparkling crystal. "That's a neat trick," he remarked. He took a sip and then a longer pull.

"It's very good."

"Thank you. It's a Glen Garrioch, the very best Scotch from any time in my opinion, but I may be biased. I did have something to do with helping Meldrum set up his distillery in 1785."

Irving finished his drink. He took a deep breath. "I have lots of questions, but strangely, none of them are to do with the making of Scotch Whisky."

"I'm sure you do," said the Earl. "That is why I am with you now, to answer them."

Irving abruptly set down his glass. "All right then, first question. If you and Lord Thorne have all these special powers why don't you just put all these reality splinters back together?"

The Earl sighed. "You think it so simple? Imagine a giant jigsaw, with an infinite number of different places where each piece might fit and without any picture to guide the placement. No, alas, only the Star Maiden knows how past, present and future should be arranged. All we have managed is to assemble three complete, fixed timelines and keep safe the mortals who exist within them."

"But if that's the case, how come people are getting old, dying, being born, and living normal lives for Christ's sake? Isn't that time passing and the creation of a past and a future?"

A strange expression passed over the Earl's still face. It was a blend of sadness, resignation and despair.

"Time does not pass, it sits within fixed boundaries.

We can expand those boundaries, because we use our powers to take mortals out of existence from within the remaining reality fragments. Then we transfer the space that frees into the complete realities. That enables those realities to grow a little. That is all we can do, add time from a damaged reality, to ensure the safety of the only three domains which remain intact."

Irving stared at him. "You're a murderer," he said in a hushed voice. "Who the hell gives you the right to make those sort of choices?"

The Earl's mouth tightened but after a moment he said in a perfectly even voice: "You would prefer Miss James to never have existed? Because that would be the case if Lord De Lisle didn't make 'choices', as you describe it."

Irving dropped his gaze. "I'm sorry," he said at last. "I didn't know it was as bad as that."

The Earl took another drink and filled Irving's glass. "How could you know that all existence is balanced upon a knife edge? Unless we find the Star Maiden soon, eventually all of time will be consumed, all mortal memory erased from existence and then only Perdurare will remain. Doomed to live together on this empty planet, constantly reliving its last moments."

"But De Lisle doesn't know about the Curse? Remind me, what does he know exactly?"

"That he is a Domain Lord for the 20th Century and master of that time. That is what he was taught. But now he has touched Sunniva, the great sword of the Sun Lords, he knows that there is a secret which has been concealed from him."

The Earl looked sombre. "It is highly possible that he will soon find a way to the truth. He is very clever you see and very powerful. When he knows the full story, I do not know what he will do. He has never had much love for your kind, so I cannot imagine that he will welcome the supreme sacrifice."

"What sacrifice is that?" asked Irving.

"That when the Star Maiden is born again, Sun and Moon Lords will no longer have all their powers and the pathways across time will close."

"Is that definitely what will happen?" said Irving in surprise.

"In truth, we do not know. The Curse was bound to the first Sun Lord and only the Star Maiden can lift it and decide Old Earth's fate."

Irving was confused. "But she's dead. How can you possibly bring her back to life?"

"We believe that she is a dormant spirit, awaiting the chance to live again. We must find her spirit and, at exactly the right time, reunite it with her mortal form."

Irving swallowed. "You don't mean me?"

The Earl did not smile. "No, not you."

He opened a drawer and drew out a photograph. "This is the image of a painting which, in the 19th Century, belongs to my friend Princess Izabella. From the descriptions made by the first Sun Lord, we believe this to be a mortal likeness of the Star Maiden."

Irving gazed at the picture intently and then looked back at the Earl. He let out a long breath. "How did this happen? It's incredible."

The Earl reached forward and placed his hand over Irving's glass. It started to glow. As Irving looked down into the clouded liquid, there appeared before his eyes the vision of a glittering array of ladies and gentlemen in the clothes of the Renaissance…

*

It was a dance and leading the way was a dark, rather swarthy man, more richly dressed than the others. In his arms was a lady. She was dancing beautifully, but her expression was sad. Another man was standing on the edge of the dancers watching them with his arms crossed. He was very tall, strongly built and richly dressed. The plump man standing next to him pulled at his sleeve.

"Your muse looks a little downcast for one whose beauty is celebrated throughout the city."

The tall man glanced down briefly. He looked disdainful. "Of course she is downcast. Who wouldn't be, condemned listening to the Duke's witticisms? The man is a tasteless bore!"

The plump man yawned. "I don't disagree. The Duke has little to recommend him to anyone except a fat purse. I once heard him talk for an hour and he didn't, even by accident, say one interesting thing. Still, I don't suppose they do much talking. I know I wouldn't, if I had Miss Cecilia to warm my bed on these cold nights."

The tall man turned upon him with sudden fury. "What did you say? Take that back at once, or I will run you through." He drew his dagger and the blade flashed.

The plump man took a hasty step back, connecting with another courtly gentleman, who quickly moved between them. "For goodness sake, Leo, put that blade away, before you do us all some harm," he said urgently.

The man called Leo lowered the dagger. "He apologises or I cut him."

"Nonsense," said the courtier. "All the same," he said turning to the plump man. "I suggest you do apologise. What do you think the Duke of Milan is going to say if he hears you have been speaking in such a way about his current favourite?"

The plump man looked sulky. "All right, I apologise, since you make a point of it." He bowed to Leo and walked away with the courtier.

Leo beckoned to a servant. "Bring me a jug will you?" He waited until he was served and then taking jug and goblet, retired to the shadows. There he drank and

*drank until the jug was empty and the candles burned to
stubs.*

The vision faded and Irving gazed open mouthed at
the Earl. "That's Leonardo da Vinci," he said in
astonishment.

"It is," said the Earl. "Look further…" He waved his
hand over the glass again.

*

*Leonardo da Vinci rose and went out into the street.
Away from the revelry, it was a quiet still night and the
moon shone full upon the cobbles. He deliberately
avoided the light and walked purposefully for many
minutes until he had left the centre of the city and was
completely alone in a deserted side street. Then, he
stopped and pulled from underneath his shirt a ruby on a
chain. It glowed in the glimmering light, its quality and
brilliance in contrast to his work roughened hand. He
held up the ruby and spoke to it. At once a man in a night
shirt stepped out of thin air and stood before him. The
man rubbed his eyes and yawned.*

*"By the Maiden, it is you Leonardo," he said crossly.
"What do you want, don't you know it's only 4 a.m. in
London?"*

*"Yes, I know, I am sorry, Georgio," said Leonardo,
"but you must know I wouldn't have called you unless it
was important."*

*"Even so, it really is too bad of you. If anyone sees me
like this, even in this age of appalling taste in clothes, I
will never live down the shame."*

*"I'll take you back to my lodgings," said Leonardo
eagerly. "Once you have a glass of wine and got properly
dressed, you will be much more comfortable."*

*"If I have to wear your robes, I certainly won't be
'properly dressed'," said the man scathingly. "However,
let's get out of this cold air and I would welcome some of*

your wine, provided it's a tolerable vintage."

He took da Vinci's arm and they worked their way back through the quiet streets until at last they reached a shabby house on the corner of a courtyard. Once inside they ascended some very steep stairs until at last they entered a small apartment on the top floor. It was untidy, but cosy, with a balcony and a side room where there was a small narrow bed, a desk and a padded chair. The main room had a couch and a large fireplace, in which a fire burned brightly. There was a rug on the floor and, all over the room, many pictures in various stages of completion. The whole place smelled strongly and pleasantly of roses and lavender. Georgio wrapped himself in a blanket judiciously removed from the bed.

He took the glass of wine offered to him and said carefully, "Well now, what is this all about, my friend?"

Leonardo, who was standing upon the balcony and watching the streets below, looked over his shoulder. "I want you to take Cecilia to the 16th Century," he said.

Georgio stared at him. "Is she in danger?"

"Not exactly," said Leonardo.

Georgio looked a question and Leonardo answered it passionately.

"I can't stand it any longer," he burst out. "She is one of my painted Madonnas, I cannot see her corrupted by that lecher the Duke."

Georgio looked at his fingers. He noticed that he had a broken nail and gave a slight shudder. "You have been having a liaison with her for some time now, so she is already, as you would say, 'corrupted'," he reminded gently.

Leonardo nodded reluctantly. "That is the truth," he acknowledged. "And we have been blessed, for Cecilia is going to bear my child."

Georgio tut tutted. "Well, that is unfortunate. Does the

Duke know?"

"Not yet, but of course he will discover it soon if she goes away with him. Then Cecilia will be forever shamed and shunned by everyone of consequence."

"I suppose you could smuggle her out of Italy somehow," Georgio suggested.

"Nowhere that the Duke will not find her," said Leonardo sadly. "He is not the man to be so cheated without seeking revenge. Please save Cecilia. Let her take my place in time."

Georgio sat up. "So let me get this straight. You're suggesting that I petition the Perdurare, so that you and Cecilia can swap timelines?"

"Yes precisely," said Leonardo. "Let her live safely, in a stable reality. I will gladly give her my place in time. I am content here."

The drink in the glass held by Irving suddenly blazed, the image faded and the American set down the glass hurriedly. He looked up at the Earl.

"Who was the guy Georgio?"

"His name is George Brummell. He is one of my trusted knights."

"So Cecilia came back to the 16th Century?"

"Yes," said the Earl. "And she bore a child, a girl. Her descendant is the living incarnation of the Star Maiden."

"She is the image of Cecilia," said Irving, glancing again at the painting. "Although her eyes are different."

"That is how we have identified the living incarnation. The first Sun Lord always said that the Star Maiden had grey eyes. Cecilia's eyes were brown."

"Why doesn't she know who she is?"

"There are many reasons," said the Earl evenly.

"Which you're not going to tell me?"

"No."

Irving sat back. "Ok. So, how do I fit in here?"

"We want you to choreograph a unique dance for yourself and this lady. Then we want you to perform it, for a very select audience."

"What sort of dance?"

"That will be entirely your choice," said the Earl. "We naturally defer to your extraordinary expertise in such things, however, the music must include provision for a harp and a drum."

Irving relaxed. "No problem there, drums are my speciality."

"Yes, I know," said the Earl, "but these are very special instruments and you will only be able to practice with both for a very limited time."

"How limited?" said Irving, suspiciously.

"One hour," said the Earl.

Irving jumped up. "One hour, are you crazy? It can't be done!"

The Earl looked apologetic. "I am sorry. I do appreciate this is not ideal."

Irving sat down again. "Not ideal is an understatement," he said. "Well break it to me, how long do I have to prepare?"

"Well that is the good news. If you stay here I can give you at least three years. However, if you leave the cavern, it will be less than two weeks."

"And I'll be stuck here on my own?"

"Yes."

"Then I'll take the two weeks," said Irving. He set down his glass and walked to the door. "Will you take me back now?"

The Earl looked amused. "You decide extremely quickly. Are there no other questions that you want to ask before you go? I expected half a dozen at least."

"I have a job to do now" said Irving flatly. "The

sooner I get it done, the sooner I get back." He paused. "I do have one more question. Why doesn't your daughter have your powers?"

"Where mortals are involved, the gift does not always pass through the female line, only the male. My own mother was a Naiad, as was Lord Thorne's. Juliet's mother was a mortal. I am glad Juliet does not have to bear such a burden. To be a member of the Perdurare is not an easy thing."

Lord Sulien rose. "Now, if you are ready, let us go."

*

He took Irving's hand and they were instantly back in the corridor with its many doors. They were now standing by a large leather porter's chair. Sitting in it was a middle-aged man dressed in 19th-Century clothes reading a paper. He looked up when the Earl appeared, rose and bowed.

"Good evening, my Lord."

"Good evening, Samuel. All quiet I hope?"

"Oh yes, Sir, very quiet."

"Anyone interesting in the Club tonight?"

"Mr Horatio, King Harry and we expect King Louis later."

"Then it will soon become a lot more lively," said the Earl wryly. "It is perhaps a good thing I am here now."

"Yes, my Lord."

The Earl looked at Irving who was staring at him round eyed. "I just need to check on something, will you wait a moment please?"

Irving laughed shakily. "I don't think I have a choice do I?"

The Earl smiled, nodded and disappeared through the furthest door to his left.

"Would you like to sit down, Sir," said Samuel courteously. "I am sure his Lordship won't be long."

Irving smiled. "No, I'm fine, it's good to stretch my legs. You don't mind if I look around do you?"

"Of course not, Sir."

Samuel sat down again and returned to the contemplation of his paper, but Irving walked along the corridor, looking curiously at the doors. Each one was of a different style and he soon realised they reflected the time period to which they were the entrance. From ancient oak, banded with iron, through to graceful Georgian panels and onwards to the smart Art Deco lines of his own time. The other curiosity was the bell box that hung just behind Samuel on the wall. It was carefully labelled and Irving counted at least ten locations, but, even as he watched, these abruptly changed, as if they were on some sort of continuous cycle. One name jumped out and he exclaimed as 'Ashleworth Castle' appeared upon the board. Samuel looked up.

"Was there something you wanted, Sir?"

"Does that ring in the 16th Century?"

Samuel nodded. "Yes, it calls Lord Thorne's castle in Gloucester. Lovely place isn't it?" He turned as the Earl suddenly appeared back in the room. "All settled, Sir?"

"Yes, perfectly settled. I am now going to take Mr Irving into the Club, so that he can meet the others. Please see we are not disturbed and if Lord Thorne comes in, invite him to join us."

The Earl then walked to a plain dark green door with fine brass furniture. It swung open as he approached and a man with spectacles dressed in Georgian evening clothes came forward. They exchanged pleasantries and then the Earl introduced Mr Irving.

"He is to become a permanent member, under my sponsorship, can you please ensure that is noted in the book and the history updated as soon as possible."

"Of course, my Lord, although I must remind you that

he will require at least two other sponsors."

"Well Lord Thorne will be one and I'm sure I can find another before the evening is out."

"Very well, my Lord." The bespectacled gentleman bowed to Irving. "Delighted to make your acquaintance, Sir, my name is Wheaton. Will you follow me please?"

He led the two men across the hall and into a larger room where a variety of men were talking, drinking or playing cards. They all looked up when the Earl came in and a very tall man with bright red curly hair jumped up and immediately came over to greet him.

"Aidan, have you come to call us to council at last?" he said loudly.

The Earl took the large hand extended to him and shook it. "Later, Harry. First, I wish to introduce you to our very last knight."

The red-headed man called Harry looked knowing. "Ah the dancer." He turned and extended his hand to Irving. "Very pleased to meet you at last. Heard a lot about you."

Irving took the enormous hand which clasped his until he thought the bones would break.

"Thanks," he said trying not to wince. "My name's Guy, Guy Irving. Do I call you Harry?"

The red-headed man looked astonished but broke into a roar of infectious laughter. "Happy for you to call me Harry, though I can't say many people do, bar dear Aidan. I only permit the liberty, because he once broke a lance over my head."

Seeing that Irving was now looking thoroughly confused the Earl leaned forward and gently drew him away. "Another time for that story I think," he said swiftly. "Let's get you settled in."

He walked down the room beckoning Irving to follow until they reached a table within a padded alcove. This was slightly at a diagonal to the rest of the room, so it gave an excellent view of everyone, yet also afforded complete privacy. The Earl sat down and gestured for Irving to do the same. Then he signalled to the waiter.

"We would like," said the Earl, "a glass of your Dom Perignon, 1751. Make sure everyone's glasses are filled too. Then bring me the book and ask the Council Knights to come up please."

"Of course, my Lord."

The waiter slipped away and returned with an ice bucket, two champagne flutes and a large, leatherbound book. With practised ease he set down the bucket, presented the glasses and dextrously thumbed the cork from the slim bottle in the bucket. He carefully filled the two glasses and removing the book from under his arm, laid it in front of the Earl. The room quickly filled up as, two by two, fourteen men came and stood in rows facing the alcove.

The Earl raised his glass. "To our last knight. Mr Guy Irving, dancer. May he bring us good fortune."

As if it was a signal all the men stood and raised their glasses in salute. "By the grace of the Maiden, may he bring us good fortune," they said in unison. Then everyone sat down again and continued to play cards and converse as before.

Irving tasted his champagne cautiously. It was the most delicious he had ever tasted. He felt excited, yet relaxed. "This is one hell of a Club," he said enthusiastically.

The Earl didn't answer. He took out a fine, slender key. Carefully he inserted it into the book lock and the book opened smoothly in front of them. "This is the Quest Journal. You may wish to look at it before I introduce you further."

He pushed the book forward and Irving leaned

forward. In the front were a series of exquisite maps by the Venetian Antonio Zatta, and Andreas Cellarius a 16th-century cartographer. On the facing page were listed names of each knight, their role in the Quest and the date of admission into the Club. As each name was read, a scene appeared, in which each person featured.

So, as he looked at the gilded pages, Irving saw the red-haired giant he had met downstairs appear as the great King Henry VIII, jousting at Windsor. Then the scene changed and he was whisked forward in time to rough seas on the English coast. Here, he saw a galleon captained by Drake, a man with a brown beard and bright blue eyes, sailing out to join a flotilla of ships. And so it went on, until at last the histories of all of the other knights were revealed.

Irving sat back from the book open mouthed. He looked at the Earl and then at the book and he let out his breath.

"How is this possible?" he said at last. He looked down the room where Henry VIII and Louis IV were laughing together at some joke. "And why these men?" he asked. "If you can have whoever you like?"

"It is dangerous to take too many mortals away from their natural timeline, even if only occasionally," said the Earl. "We choose those who can truly help with the Quest and yet are also able to conceal their vocation from others. It takes great strength of will and purpose to be a Quest Knight."

"I see that apart from me, all these guys and gals are from before the 20th Century," said Irving. So, how do I manage to get a seat at the table?"

"It has been difficult, to get you here," acknowledged the Earl. "The 20th Century is Lord De Lisle's Domain. That is why your part in the Quest must be quickly fulfilled. You are here through a special deception. Lord

De Lisle initially brought you to the 19th Century and so we are safe to keep you here for a short time. However, if Lord De Lisle discovers the truth, that it is only an illusion of your presence that remains in 1938, then the whole Quest will be put at great risk. So, we must act now; we cannot delay."

The Earl stood up and banged his palm on the desk. There was immediately silence. "Now is the time," he said in a clear, strong voice which carried to the rafters, "for this council to assemble. Now is the time for all our strength to be gathered and for the great journey to commence. I thank you all for your efforts through the dark years, but now much more is required of you. This is our moment and we cannot fail."

He beckoned to the all the members and they came and sat down about him. Then, as the night unfolded, the final stages of the Quest to restore the Star Maiden were revealed and the details of the plans debated at length. It seemed a very long time before the Earl pronounced himself satisfied and the council was dissolved. Irving, his eyes sore from lack of sleep, was very glad to be taken to one of the Club bedrooms by Samuel.

Chapter Twelve

The next day Irving came down to breakfast expecting to find himself surrounded by the other knights. However, the Club dining room was deserted. Having been offered coffee, he helped himself to eggs and bacon from the buffet and was making a good repast when there was a discreet cough and Samuel appeared again.

"Good morning, Sir."

"Good morning," said Irving cheerfully. He looked around. "Was it something I said?"

Samuel permitted a faint smile. "Not at all, Sir. It is simply that his Lordship issued instructions that you were not to be disturbed."

"Very considerate of him," said Irving yawning. "I assume he has plans for me today?"

"Yes indeed, Sir. You are to be taken to the rehearsal rooms and I am to help you with anything you need."

"Rehearsal rooms eh." Irving cocked an eyebrow. "Well that sounds good. Will his Lordship be joining me later?"

"No, Sir. Lord Sulien has returned home."

"I see," said Irving. He wiped his mouth, folded the napkin precisely and stood up, clapping his hands briskly. "Ok, Samuel, I'm ready to get creative, but before I do, there's something I need."

Samuel produced a small note book. "Very well, Sir, I am ready."

"Good," said Irving. "To start with I am going to require two pairs of size 10N leather tap shoes. Here's the address. If you say they're for me they'll be no problem. They always keep a few in stock just in case I need them in a hurry."

Samuel wrote it down carefully. "Very well, Sir. I have that noted."

Irving looked at him quizzically. "You can get those quickly then, even if they're coming from the future?"

"Oh yes, Sir. Inanimate objects aren't a problem to bring back from any reality. I should have those for you within the hour."

Irving smiled. "Right. Let's go then."

They left the Club and Samuel took him through a plain door, painted red and unmarked in any way. It opened up into an elegantly tiled changing room, with a shower, robes on hooks and neatly stacked towels. It was in the Art Deco style with chromed mirrors and cream leather benches. At the end of the room was another door, marked 'Mr Irving's Rehearsal Room'. Samuel pointed at the bell on the wall.

"Do ring if you need anything, Sir," he said. "I will be back shortly."

Irving, having taken off his coat and hung it up carefully, opened the rehearsal room door and looked through. He wasn't surprised to find that it was where he had been met by Lord Thorne the night before. Secretly he was pleased. He vividly remembered the feel of the floor and he was itching to try it. When Samuel returned later with the shoes, he stopped in the doorway, open mouthed. The usually restrained Mr Irving was now tieless and barefooted, leaping and jumping and occasionally rolling across the shining surface, making extravagant shapes and floating effortlessly on his seemingly winged feet.

*

Sitting in his study at Templeton Court, following the great council, the Earl suddenly stopped reviewing and approving the instructions set before him by his clerk. He sent the little man away to get some refreshment and sat for some time, rubbing his quill pen between his fingers. He looked out over the park and pondered the problem of

Lord De Lisle. He thought back over the centuries and remembered a day long ago in June. There was a green valley below the walls of a castle of pink, mellow stone…

An assembly of men dressed in armour, their horses gaily caparisoned, were jousting in turn, each man waiting for his opportunity to take the field. On a dais, watching, were two men and a woman beside them. They were all richly clad, but the man in the centre outshone them all. He was speaking to the fair woman upon his left and, although he spoke English with accuracy and precision, it was with a marked French accent.

"How tedious it is that I am not permitted to ride this afternoon," he complained. "Can you do nothing to persuade our host that it should be otherwise?"

The woman smiled. "You asked me that before, Majesty, and I can only give to you the same answer. We cannot risk your royal person on a simple tournament. You know full well that you are needed for much more important things."

The King sighed. "But it is so dull, just sitting here."

"I know, but remember we are all looking forward to your fencing exhibition later. Suppose we were to be deprived of such a treat through some mischance."

The deep frown that clouded the King's brow lifted somewhat. "I suppose that is true. You do well to remind me of it, mademoiselle Madelyn." His heavy lidded eyes swept over her. "It is a pity that I cannot tempt you away from all of this. A woman of your beauty and talent deserves so much more." He unfurled his fan and raised it so that they were both partially hidden behind it. "What do you say to that?"

The Lady Madelyn rose. "Je regrette, but his Majesty must already know my answer. Now if you will excuse me." She dropped a deep curtsy and withdrew.

The thin, immaculately dressed man sitting on the King's left leaned forward.

"I hope that you are not offended, Sire?" he said in exquisite French.

The King drew out a scented handkerchief and held it to his nose.

"Offended, no, not all. But I do detest her false English morals. I know full well she used to be Lord Thorne's mistress. It is so ridiculous that she stays here to play hostess for a man who obviously no longer cares for her."

His thin companion looked out onto the distant fields.

"Love is not love, which alters when it alteration finds," he quoted.

"Or bends with the remover to remove," finished the King. "You make a fair point. Look, here comes Lord De Lisle. Let us go down."

He descended the stairs and they picked their way across the damp meadow to the practice ring. Lord De Lisle was waiting to mount up, but upon seeing the King he stopped, thrust his reins into the hand of a groom and went to greet him.

"Louis, how good it is to see you. Just the person I wanted to speak to above all others."

His blue eyes swept past the gorgeous figure of the King and alighted upon his companion. "Oh, Brummell, I didn't know you were here too."

Mr Brummell bowed. "Indeed yes, my Lord. I trust I find you well?"

"As always," said Lord De Lisle, looking him up and down. "You look well yourself, but a little heavier than when last I saw you."

Brummell raised his eyes. "Your Lordship is correct," he complained. "Alas, too many of Prinny's endless banquets and not enough riding in the park I fear."

Lord De Lisle smiled maliciously. "You are of course welcome to take part today. That may help shift a pound or two!"

"What a novel idea," said Mr Brummell, "but it would be such a shame to see my very stylish new coat poked full of holes." He gave his charming smile and bowed himself away.

Lord De Lisle watched him go and turned back to the King. "Will you walk with me, Louis? I don't need to ride for at least another twenty minutes."

"What is it that you want, Bricin?" said the King.

Lord De Lisle looked around him. "Not for discussion here," he said urgently.

The King stood his ground. "I must insist that you give me a hint, before I make any more journeys across this extremely muddy field."

"Very well then. I think I may have found a way to make fine use of those exceptional mirrors of yours at Versailles."

He saw the King's eyes narrow and nodded approval. "I see you understand me. Now you know why we must have some privacy." He took the other man's arm and led him away.

From across the showground, Lord Sulien, standing with Lord Thorne, stiffened as he watched the two brightly clad figures disappear into the shadows.

"And so it has begun. Bricin is deserting us," he said with cold certainty.

"Shall I fetch him?" asked Lord Thorne.

The Earl shook his head. "No, it would make no difference. We must let events take their course, for to tamper now may affect what transpires later. That we cannot risk."

Lord Thorne brushed a hand across his eyes. "I cannot believe that he means to cause us harm."

"He may or may not," said the Earl. "He must make his own decisions and take his own path, however dangerous that may be."

He turned and walked off across the field. Lord Thorne walked beside him, but after a moment he caught the Earl's arm.

"You must do something, Aidan. It's not just the fate of Old Earth that is at stake here, but Bricin's salvation."

The Earl would have walked on, but Lord Thorne stood in front of him.

"Answer me, Aidan."

"Very well then, since you insist. For now, all I am concerned about is ensuring that Bricin continues to be sufficiently deceived. It is vital that he continue to believe that King Louis, Beau and the others are brought here just for our entertainment. By believing this, he will never suspect that there is a higher purpose."

He looked again at Argus and his expression was quizzical. "What is that you would have me do?" he said abruptly. "I see you have some suggestion to make."

"I believe that there is still a chance that you could influence Bricin for the good if you chose to do so. Invite him again to Ireland to stay with you at An Baile Glas. He has always loved it there, ever since we first took him."

"You do not think there is a risk that if I take Bricin to Ireland, he may just simply create a new problem?"

"If that is all, then I will both vouch for him and watch over him," said Lord Thorne.

The Earl looked at him. "That is quite an assurance, Argus."

"Nevertheless, you have my pledge," said Lord Thorne. He extended his hand and the Earl grasped it. "Now what is your answer?"

The Earl shook his hand. "I trust your wisdom, my

friend, as I always have," he said. "So, I will take your ward and I swear he will never lack for my company."

Lord Thorne laughed. "Please don't overdo it, I beg you."

They walked back to the pavilion, where the Earl was quickly encircled by a group of admiring knights and squires, but eventually he managed to slip away. He went up onto the hillside, away from the showground, where some time later he was found by Madelyn Drew. Passing across the meadow, holding her skirts up to navigate the long grasses, she was so wrapped in her own thoughts that she nearly stepped upon the recumbent figure of the Earl, whose green velvet doublet had made him almost invisible. Only his gleaming head of golden hair stood out against the sward.

Madelyn gave a gasp of surprise.

"Forgive me, my Lord," she said and sank hurriedly into a curtsy.

The Earl sat up. "Good afternoon, Madelyn," he said easily. "Are you enjoying the day?"

"Yes, very much," said Madelyn with an effort.

"Then you will be sorry to leave for France?"

"France?" said Madelyn in surprise.

"Yes, did Lord Thorne not tell you? He is planning to visit Repaire Noble very soon. I assumed that he would bring you with him."

The tears started in her eyes. He felt in his pocket and produced a handkerchief. "Take this, I beg you."

She accepted it gratefully. "You must think me very foolish," she said.

The Earl regarded her sadly. "I am just sorry to see you grieve like this. Would you not consider exchanging your old love for a new one, who now needs you so desperately?"

He pointed and, far away across the showground,

Madelyn saw Lord De Lisle standing by a great stand of oak trees. He was scanning the horizon and, with a shiver, Madelyn knew that he was looking for her.

"Your master has suggested that I take Lord De Lisle with me to Ireland. Would you consider joining us there?" asked the Earl.

Madelyn stared at him. "Lord De Lisle is still just a boy."

"I know he must seem so to you, who have lived so long and are so wise. But, there is within him the ability to become the greatest of all the Perdurare. I see nothing but unhappiness for him, and us all, if you will not cleave to him."

"But I do not love him," she whispered.

He nodded. "I know. But would there not be some satisfaction in knowing that you were contributing to the achievement of the Quest, rather than risking its possible downfall?"

She looked alarmed. "You think Bricin can threaten the Quest?" she said urgently. "That is surely impossible. He still knows nothing about it?"

"He has no knowledge at this time," agreed the Earl, "but he continues to prove a random element, which even I cannot control. I believe that only your love can keep him true. Will you not try to care for him, for the sake of us all?"

"What would you have me do?" she said listlessly.

"Come to An Baile Glas. You can stay with some friends of mine. Their father owned the local inn and did me some service. Before he died, he asked me to watch over his girls, so, I visit them occasionally. Bricin has been there too and, over the years, we have all become good friends. The younger girl, Lizzie, is especially delightful."

"And the other daughter?" asked Madelyn.

The Earl's expression became hard to read. "Oh, Jenny's another matter altogether," he said. "Very intelligent. I bring her books from my library and she devours them. I also taught her chess and she is getting close to beating me."

Madelyn sighed. "I will think about what you have said. I grant that, perhaps, I have let my heart rule my head for too long. When will you leave?"

"After the prize giving. Talking of which, we should make our way back. We cannot start the presentation without our Tournament Queen to grace it."

He extended his hand and she put hers into it. They walked down the hillside laughing and talking in the familiar, easy way of very old friends. At the bottom of the hill Madelyn dropped a low curtsy.

"I will send you my answer very soon, I promise."

She rose up and watched the Earl cross the field. Then she turned and prepared to walk back, but a hand caught her arm. Turning swiftly she stifled a gasp. It was Lord De Lisle. By the expression on his face she knew he had overheard her promise to the Earl. There was a cold tension about him which, she knew from experience, meant that he was secretly furious. However, she faced him calmly.

"Good afternoon, my Lord."

"Is it?" he said bitingly. "I have not found it so. I see you have amused yourself well enough though."

"Yes I have," she agreed. She saw him struggling to restrain his anger and made haste to turn the subject.

"Have you come to escort me to the prize giving? If so, then let us hurry for I must change my gown first."

"Why?" he said sulkily. "The one you have on becomes you well enough." He stared at her with a mixture of frustration, fury and desire. She concealed a smile, knowing that he was struggling with the impulse to *kiss her or hit her, neither of which he dared.*

"What were you arranging with Aidan?" he said abruptly as they walked back together.

"He has asked me to join you both on your next visit to An Baile Glas."

Lord De Lisle drew breath. "Will you?"

"I am considering it," she said.

She saw the flash of passionate excitement light his face. The woman in her was momentarily warmed by his delight. Then she suddenly thought of Lord Thorne. In that instant her mind was made up. That night, she sat down and, using the technology that her Lord had borrowed from the future, wrote an electronic message to the Earl. It said:

My Lord,

Thank you for your invitation, which I must decline. You know my heart. It cannot change. As our friend Oscar Wilde once wrote:

One with our heart, the stealthy creeping years
Have lost their terrors now, we shall not die,
The Universe itself shall be our Immortality!

Your dear friend,

Madelyn.

*

In the 19th Century, night fell. The Earl waved and candles began to light. Then he opened a ledger that was upon his desk, dipped his quill in ink and began to write. As he did so, the candles guttered in their stands. The Earl swore under his breath and in an instant the candles flamed tall and fair again, illuminating the room with a bright and constant light.

Part 2 – As it was, where it was
Chapter Thirteen

After the Westlake ball, Lord De Lisle did return to the 20th century, but he did not stay for long in 1938. Usually, when he came home to Paris he felt immediately at ease, but this time it was different. Sitting in his apartment, eating breakfast, he felt restless and uncomfortable. When he had held the ancient Sun Blade for the first time, amongst the various jumble of memories, he had seen the original Sun Lords and had been aware that they were searching for something. The finding of the sword was a turning point in his relationship with the Earl. De Lisle detested Lord Thorne and his reasons for this were clear cut. As a young man he had always resented Lord Thorne's status. He had never understood why Lord Thorne had been appointed as his teacher and why he was forced to accept his guidance. Whilst he had initially tolerated him for the education he could provide, over the years, his dislike had turned to a bitter hatred. However, with the Earl, he had veered from deep friendship to lingering frustration, but always tinged with grudging respect. He had occasionally teased him and allowed him some freedom in return, but on only one point did they ever disagree: the Earl's treatment of mortals. Lord De Lisle had taken up his reign as a Moon Lord, totally convinced of his superiority to mankind. He saw himself as the ruler of mortals, benevolent (usually) but all powerful. When the Earl had married the daughter of an Irish innkeeper (despite the circumstances), De Lisle had been outraged. He despised the Earl utterly for this and the two had been immediately estranged. Yet, in the depths of his cold heart, he had never completely lost his affection for the Earl, who he saw as his only equal in a world of inferiors.

Then, when he had held the Sword, he suddenly became aware that over the years the Earl had been concealing vital truths. He also strongly suspected that Miss Templeton was connected to this mystery. Lord De Lisle was no believer in coincidence. When he had first met Theora he had been intrigued by the fact that Lord Sulien was apparently interested in her. He had therefore sought her out, simply in a spirit of mischief. But, when he had first flirted with her at the Westlake ball, he had done so with a curious sense of anticipation and excitement which he had not felt for many years. Her subsequent refusal to accept his marriage proposal had not affected his interest. Although her words and behaviour had confirmed that she was in love with the Earl, De Lisle's own immense self-confidence would not allow him to admit defeat. He was sure that what was now needed was a more direct approach and if that meant physically removing Theora from Temple Court, then he was willing to risk the subsequent repercussions.

He called for his valet and whilst he dressed he considered carefully what needed to be done. Eventually, he decided upon a dual plan. Firstly, he would put Theora and Juliet into danger, through a series of subtle attacks. In the meantime, he would use his own methods to find out what secrets the Earl and Lord Thorne were still keeping from him. He was once again in high spirits as he donned a suit of silvery grey finished with an ice blue silk tie which was an exact copy of the one worn by Guy Irving in his last movie. Although Guy was a mortal, De Lisle had developed almost an affection for the quiet but stylish American with his matchless dancing skills. Talent of any sort was interesting to the sensitive Moon Lord and over many centuries he had learned from many great artists. It was admittedly frustrating that he could not play the piano as well as the Earl. Worse still, that

Lord Thorne was superior to them both on virtually every instrument. He consoled himself by demonstrating extreme good taste in his dress sense. It was a balm to his self-esteem that he was known across fashionable Europe as the epitome of panache. Placing his hat at a jaunty angle and picking up his cane he headed out of the house and waited for his driver to bring round his car. This was a black SS90 Jaguar. It was customised with a glistening silver banding on the jet black exterior and midnight blue leather seats. The effect was breath taking, yet restrained and every time he took the wheel, De Lisle felt a sense of satisfaction at the picture he presented.

It was a very pleasant route to Versailles, through green fields and small villages, where the occasional peasant would stand open mouthed to marvel at the sight of the strange man who drove past so swiftly and with such apparent ease. It was still morning when his Lordship arrived at the gates of the palace. He parked the car in the side-street garage (which had been especially built for the purpose) and made his way through the park to the entrance. As always, the gates of the Museum of French History were crowded. The weary-looking manager who acted as ticket officer, upon seeing Lord De Lisle, simply waved him through. Lord De Lisle gave him the faintest of smiles, but this expanded upon sight of a short, plump fair-haired young woman who, having been peeping out in anticipation of his arrival, ran out of her office to greet him.

"Mr De Lisle, welcome back to Versailles, Sir." She spoke in French and De Lisle answered her easily.

"Good afternoon, Michelle. It is good to be back. How are you?" He allowed her to prattle, encouraging her small talk with the occasional nod and smile.

As she spoke his blue eyes looked into hers, scanning her brain and taking in and dissecting everything she had done, seen and thought since the last time he had seen her. When he had got enough information, he raised his hand to halt the flow and said sweetly, "That all sounds excellent. I would love to hear more, but alas, time and my duty does not permit. Would you mind getting me the key now please?"

"Of course, Sir, I have it here. Would you like me to accompany you to the vault today?"

"No thank you," he said smoothly. He saw the disappointment in her face and felt for a second, slightly sorry for her. To ease the pain, because he knew that she had a massive crush on him, he bowed, took her hand and gave it a squeeze. "I would kill for one of your amazing cups of coffee. If you could make me one in say, an hour, perhaps we can sit together whilst you have your break?"

Michelle looked as if she might cry. "That would be my pleasure, Sir," she managed.

"Wonderful." He gave her another dazzling smile and walked away, reflecting that, even for such a simple girl, Michelle was incredibly easy to please. He knew that she would be terribly disappointed when he didn't return and would probably spend the rest of the day alternately praying that he was safe and reapplying her make-up in case he miraculously reappeared.

As he opened the vault with the elaborate key she had given him, he quickly put her out of his mind. It was necessary to preserve a strong cover to enable him regular access. Keeping Michelle, 'interested' was just one element of this process. Inside the vault, it smelled slightly musty. De Lisle shut the door behind him. Disguised as a renowned security expert, nobody questioned his presence. However, instead of carefully examining the room and checking all its features (which was what he was supposed to be there to do), he simply placed a completed report on the small table and beside it a fountain pen. Then opening the trapdoor in the vault roof he hauled himself smartly through. He came out (as he had done dozens of times before) in a small cupboard which allowed just enough room for his tall frame and contained a mop and a bucket. He picked these up, opened the door and passed noiselessly through the various state rooms until he reached the Hall of Mirrors. As always, as soon as he saw them, De Lisle felt the same glow of sublime satisfaction that enveloped him when he drove his car. But this was coupled with another thrill, the knowledge that neither the Earl of Woodchester nor Lord Thorne had the ability to harness the power that was held within these ancient panes of glass. He stood looking at them and marvelled as before, at their beauty as well as their purpose.

By joining together small reality shards, he had magnified their strength through the reflective power of the Venetian glass. This was now impregnated with a powerful cantus. Instead of only being able to move through one reality and then having to return before he could access another, he could now travel seamlessly. He could step from 1938 into the future and then back again. More than that, he could move into a future beyond the 19th Century and the past before the 16th century. De Lisle had worked with Louis XIV to modify the mirrors in secret. The King had believed the excuse that they presented a way for the Sun and Moon Lords to travel at speed if they ever needed to do so. When the work was completed, to ensure that the Earl and Lord Thorne never knew about them, De Lisle had wiped all memory of the endeavour from King Louis' mind. Hitherto, he had only accessed the mirrors to visit the future, but now he was resolved to return to the reality from which both Lord Thorne and Lord Sulien had originally sprung and find out the truth. It was a perilous undertaking, for visiting any time outside the three domains was now against the specific decree of Lord Sulien. Although he had occasionally tempted the Earl and Lord Thorne to travel with him to the 21st century, due to fractures suddenly appearing in the other domains, the Earl had forbidden any further attempts without permission. If De Lisle was detected, he risked being banished outside time as a punishment, something which he knew, from his recent experience with Lord Thorne, was likely to leave him drained and weakened.

The Hall was full of people but De Lisle ignored them. Stepping deliberately into the middle of the room he raised his hand. At once every person in the room stopped dead as if frozen. De Lisle looked at them with ill-disguised contempt. He walked down the Hall, wending his way between the still figures. When he got to the end he looked back and said in voice of silk: "Retrahere.[4]" At once, and in perfect order, each figure began to shrink. Each one became smaller and smaller until at last there was only a point of light no smaller than a pin head on the floor where they had stood. They sparkled and glittered, reflected in the mirrors and twinkling in the cold electric light. De Lisle took out the mop and bucket. Whistling as he did so, he swept the mop across the floor, capturing each speck and dropping it into the bucket. When the floor was clear, he took the bucket, went to a window and poured the contents out onto the gravel. Here they turned into bubbles and rose up into the air, where they burst and promptly disappeared. Without another glance, De Lisle returned to the mirrors and extracted from his pocket three reality splinters. Then he took careful aim and threw them each

---

[4] Retreat

at the centre mirror. As they landed they made a coloured mark and then, as easily as a boomerang, they were safely back in De Lisle's hand. Closing his eyes, he began to chant slowly and in Latin. Then he stepped forward and, placing his hand on the mirror's frame, climbed swiftly inside.

*

Although he was supreme in his own domain, Lord De Lisle had no real mastery over other timelines and realities. When he entered the mirror he only had a vague knowledge of where he might end up. The cantus enabled the mirror to translate his wishes, and he had hoped to arrive on the edge of some reasonable habitation. Instead he found himself standing upon a hill looking at the remains of what had obviously been a hasty departure from a soldier's camp. Further up the slope, he could see smoke and the sounds of battle. Despite his great powers, he had no wish to become engaged in some unknown conflict, so he picked his way carefully up the slope, avoiding the open fields and hugging the hedgeline. Soon he reached a ridge which offered him the chance for greater concealment. He was cautiously tracking its path when a bay horse came plunging up the bank. It halted at the top, struggling in the mud, and its rider set spurs to it. The horse reared and fell back and its rider landed heavily. At once De Lisle sprang forward and put a hard hand upon the man's throat holding him immobile and looking deep into his eyes. Blood gushed from the man's mouth and his lips frothed with it. De Lisle swore long and fluently. He felt for a pulse and finding none, quickly put his hand over the man's forehead, but the man was dead, his eyes staring at up at the grey sky. After a moment, De Lisle bent and took off the man's long cloak which he wrapped around his shoulders. He removed his tie and put it carefully in his pocket, loosened his collar and then stood up, looking down disgustedly upon the corpse. A movement behind him made him turn. The horse, steaming and wet, its flanks red with blood from the spurs, shook its head and looked back at him forlornly.

Although De Lisle had little time for a humans, he had always retained a fondness for animals, so when he saw the tired and wounded horse gazing at him, his angry expression changed to one of pity. He took the reins and led it unresisting onto the field. Then he removed the saddle and passed his hands lightly over the animals back and sides. As he did so, white light shone from his fingers and the wounds healed quickly and neatly. When he had finished, the horse shook its head and whinnied as if in thanks.

"Better now I think, my friend," said De Lisle. "Now I must ask you to help me as I have helped you. Will you take me to your camp, for that is where I suspect that I will find all my answers?"

The horse tossed its head as if in acknowledgement and De Lisle vaulted lightly onto its back. "Let us go then," he said. The horse set off down the hill. At last they reached a wider plain which was dominated by a stand of great white stones, all of varying sizes. They formed the boundary to an assortment of wooden houses and tents. At once De Lisle drew up. "This is a Druid camp," he said wonderingly. "How very curious that you should bring me here." He rode forward, but he had not gone more than a few yards before a man carrying a spear appeared, shouting words in an ancient dialect.

De Lisle held up a hand. "I cannot understand you," he said. "However, I must ask you to lower that spear. I may not kill you, but I can certainly make your remaining days extremely unpleasant." The man stopped suddenly, clearly having understood. De Lisle's eyes narrowed.

"How very interesting," he said. "Will you now perhaps introduce me to whoever is in authority here?" He jumped off the horse.

The Druid looked at him. Then he beckoned and, turning, walked away down the valley. De Lisle followed walking beside the horse. Other Druids came out and stood watching as they passed by. Eventually they reached a large pavilion. De Lisle handed his horse's reins to the Druid and went inside. It was empty, except for a tall, slim woman, sitting upon a gilded throne. To her left was a large table upon which burned one tall, white candle.

"Welcome, Moon Lord," she said.

She had spoken to him in Latin and De Lisle answered her in kind.

"You know me, but alas I do not know you. Yet, you were expecting me?"

The Lady gazed at him. He knew at once that she was not a mortal, for her mind was completely closed to him.

"You are powerful," he said at last with grudging respect. "I can tell that you have a long association with Lord Aidan and Lord Argus," he said concentrating deeply, "but that is all that I can perceive clearly. What is your lineage?"

"That is not the question that requires answering," she said. "Time is short, Moon Lord, even for you and you should not waste it."

"Will you then tell me what I wish?"

She sat back in the chair. "I will, if you will make me this one promise. If you are victorious, you will restore this time according to its current history and allow me to live my life once again with my husband, Lord Harold."

He stared at her. "Is that why you have waited here so long, Milady, caught in this echo of a long dead reality: to petition me?"

She nodded.

"Yet, even though I cannot read your thoughts, I sense you are an ally of Lord Aidan, so why did you not make this request of him?" The Lady looked at him steadily.

"I have no guarantee that Lord Aidan would risk his own domain, if a choice needed to be made."

De Lisle laughed.

"Hedging your bets, eh? However, you must know that my word is perhaps not to be trusted?"

He looked at her beautiful but impassive face.

"That doesn't bother you?" She turned away from him and the artist in him admired the way the candle light illuminated her long smooth neck and graceful figure in its gown of forest green.

"Yes, of course, but, all I can do is make my request and pray that you will honour it."

De Lisle inclined his head.

"Very well, I give you my word, for what it is worth. Now for your side of the bargain. What is it that you wish to know?"

"Firstly, I want to know about the Quest."

"And secondly?"

De Lisle smiled "Everything else!"

The Lady beckoned to him and they walked to the table. She took from it a burning candle. She put one hand upon De Lisle's forehead and placed the other over the flame. The candle began to burn down rapidly and, as it did so, De Lisle understood that the lady was Queen Edith, wife of King Harold Godwinson. Their son, Aidan Sulien led the centuries-old quest to find the Star Maiden. Then he knew that if the Star Maiden was restored to mortal form her power would be infinite, but, if she willed it, his own would pass.

Queen Edith spoke a word and the candle stopped burning and its flame flickered into immobility.

"Now you will complete my knowledge," said Lord De Lisle. "Tell me about Madelyn Drew and how she came to end up in Lord Thorne's Domain."

Queen Edith hesitated. "I believe it will only cause you great pain to understand her story fully. Why do you wish to do so?"

"That is my business," said De Lisle coldly. "Complete the bargain, or I promise you, your dear husband will be forever a memory."

So Queen Edith spoke again to the candle and it burned once more and within its flame De Lisle saw...

Queen Edith sitting in the great, green pavilion on a summer's day. She was sewing, but she set aside her needle and called a servant.

"Bring the Lady Madelyn and her father to me please and see that we are not disturbed."

When the old man and his daughter had come to her she bade them sit and said at once:

"Our new Moon Lord has declared to me that he loves Madelyn and wishes her to accompany him to his new domain. I have called you both here for your council. What he wishes is forbidden, but my fear is that, should he be denied, he may abandon his destiny."

Madelyn and her father looked at each other. The old man spoke:

"My Queen, it was long foretold that this Moon Lord is key to the success of the Quest. How that will be, we do not know, but it is of the utmost importance that he takes his place beside Lord Aidan."

Queen Edith sighed. "I knew you would say that, my friend. But what then is to be done, for I have looked into his heart and it is clear that he will not change his mind?" She looked at Madelyn. "What do you think, my child?"

Madelyn rose and sank in a curtsy before the Queen.

She took her hand and kissed it. "My Lady, I am and always will be, your true servant. As your servant, I say to you that I never sought the Moon Lord's love."

Queen Edith beckoned to her to rise. "There is perhaps one way to resolve this," she said, "but I warn that it will be a long, sad journey for you, Madelyn. However, it will enable you to remain with Argus, if you are willing to do exactly as I ask."

Madelyn looked up. Her soft eyes were suddenly filled with hope. "I will do anything, my Queen."

"Then come with me."

She led the girl out through the pavilion to a small chamber. In the centre was a deep well sunk into the floor and around it stood five iron sconces. Each held a candle. Three burned brightly. One was partly burned and extinguished and one was unlit. In the deep water of the well, the candle flames were reflected like distant stars in an infinite sky. Queen Edith walked to Madelyn and stood facing her.

"You know where you are?"

"Yes, it is the place where the Earthly symbols of the Perdurare are revered by the servants of the Star Maiden."

"Yes," said Queen Edith. She pointed to a small candle with a flame which glowed richly gold. "This is the candle of Aidan, last born of the Sun Lords, which soon he will take to his domain." The candle next to it was also small and the flame had a purple edge. "This one is the candle of the Moon Lord and teacher, Argus Thorne. As you can see, these candles have many years before they will achieve their full length. For the power of our line, bonded to the forces of life itself, will always wax rather than wane, unless we choose to reverse the process."

She paused and gazed into the water for a moment. "I

show you this," she said at last, "so that you understand the limits of the gift which I can bestow upon you. We can, if you're willing, provide Argus with your continuing companionship and love. But there will be a price for you to pay. I can give you a longer life, but I cannot give you an extension of youth. My life force is bound to this domain. Tomorrow I will have to close the door between realities, so only Lords of the Sun and Moon can enter. Can you bear the consequences of leaving this time? Your fate will be very different to the life you would have had here and you will need great courage to endure the dark days to come. Do you understand?"

Madelyn knelt down on the rushes before her. "I do, my Queen."

"Then hold out your hands."

Madelyn did so and the Queen dripped onto her open palms eight drops of wax from her candle. The wax instantly cooled and disappeared without trace. But as they did so, Madelyn's hands glowed white and red and then blue, as if a rainbow had passed through them. Her slight figure shuddered from head to toe.

Then the Queen replaced the candle and faced her again.

"Those eight drops signify the 800 years which are now granted to you. Use the time well."

So Madelyn accompanied Argus to the 16th Century and then Queen Edith locked the door of that time and guarded it with cantus, then the Domain was hidden…

Lord De Lisle gasped. Furiously he pulled his hands away and as he did so the candle shattered and Queen Edith fell to the floor stone dead. Then De Lisle was flung backward out of that time. He came through the mirror and was again in 1938, spread-eagled upon the floor within the Palace of Versailles. He lay there for a moment for he was severely winded. Then he stood up, took off the blood-stained cloak and put on his tie again. He returned the mop and bucket to the broom cupboard, pushed the cloak behind them and retraced his steps back through the palace. He slipped past the front office where the ever hopeful Michelle was watching for him and returned to his car. Reaching into the glove compartment he took out a 21st-Century mobile phone and dialled a number. A woman's voice answered him.

"Good afternoon, Jenny. You are well? Of course, why would such a powerful sorceress ever be in ill health? Yes, I want to see you, on a matter of great urgency. I'll meet you in the usual place in 1938, in an hour. Goodbye."

De Lisle put the phone back and drew out a watch. It was made of gold and guilloche enamel. Inside was a crystal mirror. Craftsmen from two different domains had worked together to make it. He had been given this special gift by Lord Thorne when he came of age to allow him to move quickly to different places within his own time. Every Moon or Sun Lord owned similar devices, but De Lisle had commissioned Faberge to amend the watch mirror to include, within it, an extremely small, but powerful reality splinter. He looked into the mirror and said, "1938, the Ritz, Palm Court, table for two, afternoon tea." Seconds later he was sitting there, surrounded by the rich and sophisticated members of society London. He smiled broadly as he saw a lady in a floor-length gold and black dress, making her way toward him. The lady's name was Jennifer Layton.

Many years had passed since Lord De Lisle had changed Jenny Lawson, the scarred and embittered daughter of a poor Irish publican, to the exquisite creature that turned all heads but one as she passed through the restaurant. Jennifer Layton meant absolutely nothing to Lord De Lisle. Having changed her appearance as a means to an end, he had educated her sufficiently to enable her to enter Lord Sulien's world. This included teaching the necessary cantus to enable her to function as his spy. He had then watched her progress through the society of the 1800s with curious anticipation. He had hoped that her physical charms would tempt the Earl into committing an indiscretion. But, he now realised that the Earl had obviously had no time for any other thought than the completion of his Quest. De Lisle had then left Jenny to fend for herself, but he had underestimated her. She had used her wealth to complete her education and was now both a sophisticated woman and an accomplished sorceress. Scorned by the Earl, she now demonstrably hated him. De Lisle admired the vindictive spirit that drove her and saw her as a useful ally. So, he had taken her from the 19th Century and placed her in his own time, whilst giving her the power to travel secretly between the 19th and 20th and even the 21st centuries upon occasions. In return, she had become his eyes and ears and a most efficient support across the centuries. Occasionally, he also used her as an escort to functions where a female companion was a necessity, but that was the extent of their relationship. Neither of them felt the slightest warmth for the other, but they had developed a certain degree of trust and reliance, in the way that snakes will reluctantly share a nest to keep themselves safe from other larger predators.

Today Jenny (or Lady Jennifer as she preferred to be known) was wearing an afternoon dress of rich gold with an abstract black pattern. A neat black silk hat, trimmed discreetly with small black plumes, topped her chestnut head and her lips were painted dramatically dark red. She ignored the admiring glances of the other guests, extended her cheek for a perfunctory kiss and sat down, drawing off her long back gloves and placing them on the table.

"What would you like?" said Lord De Lisle courteously.

"Champagne," said Jenny decisively, "and my usual sandwiches please, Ashley." Also, do they have any of the special chocolate cake left?"

The head waiter bowed. "I believe so, Milady."

"Then a generous piece of that," said Jenny. She manufactured a smile and put it on. "You must try some of it, Bri, it's quite divine. I can't tell you how many slices I've had. Have you been counting, Ashley?"

"Of course not, Milady," said the waiter. He gave a discreet cough and lowered his voice. "Milady's figure has not suffered from the experience. I only wish you would pass on your secret."

Jenny's smile widened. "It's all down to magic, dear Ashley," she said brightly. "Now pop off, there's a good fellow, and find my champagne. I am really very thirsty."

The waiter disappeared and Jenny's smile switched off like a dropped electric torch.

"What do you want, my Lord?"

Lord De Lisle sighed. "Really, Jenny, for all your sophistication you still sometimes display the manners of a serving girl. Perhaps that is why you can never hold onto your lovers. Do try to be a little less common!"

He had not bothered to lower his voice and several people nearby looked shocked and hastily bent over their sandwiches to pretend they hadn't heard him.

Jenny inclined her head. "I am sorry, my Lord. What would you like to talk about?"

"Oh I don't know," said Lord De Lisle carelessly. "It just seems to be an affront to our very pleasant surroundings to simply get down to business. There is no immediate hurry is there?"

"Not if you say so," said Jenny icily. She fished

around for something to say. "Very well then, how do you like my dress?"

Lord De Lisle felt in his pocket and produced a pair of horn-rimmed spectacles. His eyesight was perfect, but he liked the fashionable effect, when combined with his cream and beige suit.

"Chanel I assume?"

"Excellent," said Jenny approvingly. She wrinkled her nose. "I suppose you know Coco? Probably in the biblical sense?"

De Lisle grinned. "We exchanged a few kisses a couple of years ago and I suggested that she wore pearls with tweed. That was the extent of our association."

He broke off as the waiter appeared. After they had been served, they ate for a while in silence.

Then De Lisle said abruptly, "I have summoned you because I now know it all. I am ready to act and I need your help."

Jenny put down her cake fork. "Will you tell me too?" she said eagerly.

"Yes, but not now, I need you to do something for me first."

"I'm listening."

"Go to the 21st and start devising the most lethal range of cantus you can think of. I need a wide range, from simple diversions to complete devastation. You will need to demonstrate them to me."

Jenny stared at him. Then she took another bite of cake and ate it with relish. "Very well," she said. "I know of some already, but I'm sure I can think up some more interesting ones if I put my mind to it. What's the deadline?"

"Three weeks. They need to be ready before February 2nd."

"Understood," said Jenny. "Thank you for tea. I will

expect you at my house in a couple of weeks for the demonstration."

"I will be in touch," said Lord De Lisle. He rose and took Jenny's hand in his. "Au revoir, my dear."

She left her hand in his and held his gaze. "What will you be doing in the meantime?"

"I, my sweet, will be assembling an army."

Her eyes widened and she let out a long breath. "So, you are declaring war on him at last?"

Lord De Lisle bowed. "I am indeed. Feels good doesn't it? War it is." He winked at her and waved for the bill.

Chapter Fourteen

At Temple Court the arrangements for Juliet Sulien's ball progressed at pace. As the only distractions for Theora Templeton were practical ones, she concentrated upon them and, by doing so, put aside her fears. It had been helpful that Lord Thorne was making an extended stay at Temple Court. His presence had a calming effect on Juliet, and he also supported Mr Allan with the management of the Estate. Soon the whole house hummed with activity and a pleasurable sense of excitement and anticipation was felt by all.

Three weeks before the first guests were due, Theora was working her way through her list of essential tasks. She had been up since dawn, for she was aware that Lady Meadley had invited the cream of London society. The intention was to introduce Theora to them at the ball, before her ladyship departed to Trennance the week after. Lord Thorne, who had decided to take a turn around the grounds before breakfast, was startled to find her fully dressed and writing notes regarding seating arrangements as she sat alone in morning room. Apart from the grooms and the kitchen maids, nobody else was stirring. As Lord Thorne came up to the house via the meadow, Theora did not see him approach. He stopped short by the gate to the kitchen garden to watch her. She was dressed in a gown of blue and cream and she had tied her hair loosely with a scarlet ribbon. It made her look less severe and very young. When he came in to join her she greeted him with pleasure, but he thought also with perhaps a touch of disappointment. He knew instinctively that she had been wishing, secretly, that he was the Earl. He immediately suggested that she accompany him for a morning ride. Theora's eyes brightened at the idea, but she shook her head reluctantly, protesting that she had too much to do.

"I fear you are going to wear yourself out if you carry on at this rate," said Lord Thorne. "Is there nobody who can assist you?"

Theora smiled wearily. "I am afraid not, but please do not worry about me. I am really quite strong. It is just a great pity that I am unable to give more support to Mrs Chapman. She is sadly run off her feet."

Lord Thorne looked thoughtful. "But if there was some other lady who could assist Mrs Chapman, that would enable you to make a little time for yourself?"

"Do you know of such a person," said Theora eagerly.

"I might," said Lord Thorne surprisingly. He bowed. "Which means that I should go now and write the necessary letters. Would you excuse me, Ma'am?"

He walked off towards the study. Theora watched him go a little wistfully. She was grateful for his solicitude, but would have been glad to have sat chatting to him a little longer. His presence was a pleasant diversion. Collecting up her notebook and pencil, she walked up the servants' staircase.

When she reached the landing, she glanced out towards the lake. To her surprise, she saw that the seat under the cedars was occupied. Juliet (who she had presumed still abed) was being embraced by Mr Allan. In fact they were kissing passionately and without any consideration for who might be watching. Theora was pardonably annoyed. Having assured Juliet that she would help her broker the secret engagement with the Earl, she had not pledged her pupil to any particular secrecy or advised her upon her future behaviour. She had assumed that Juliet's common sense and good breeding would guide her. To see her behaving so casually, in full view of the Temple Court servants, was embarrassing. She went to her bedroom, sat for a few moments and then, unable to bear it any longer, ran back down the stairs, but Mr Allan and Juliet had now vanished from view. Theora went on to the kitchen, where Mrs Chapman, taking one look at her black expression, quickly drew her into her own private parlour and asked her bluntly what was amiss.

"For knowing you as I do, Miss, it must be more than your accounts not adding up to bring down such a thunder cloud! What's the trouble? Is it Miss Juliet?"

Theora hesitated. "If I do tell you, Mary, you must keep it most secret. Will you?"

"No need to ask that," said Mrs Chapman comfortably. She got up, peeped round the door and latched it firmly. "Well, what's happened?"

"I am afraid she has entered into an engagement without her father's knowledge," said Theora.

She looked at Mrs Chapman and was astonished to see no reaction at all. "If you are expecting me to be surprised, Miss Theora, you are going to be fair and far away. Who is the gentleman, for you cannot tell me that, foolish though she is, she would engage herself to anyone but a gentleman!"

"It is a gentleman. It is Mr Allan."

"Well, thank mercy for that. As fine and sensible a young man as you could ever find, even if you searched this country from top to bottom. Surely you aren't going to tell me that you dislike the idea?"

"No of course not. Only I do feel that Juliet is too young and inexperienced to be any man's wife at this time. She really is no more than a child."

"More reason for her to quickly find a good, steady man to take care of her."

"I suppose so," said Theora. She got up and walked to the fire to warm her hands. "She has already asked me to raise the idea with his Lordship."

"Well you'd best do so, as soon you can," said Mrs

Chapman also rising. "Now I must get on. Lord knows we have enough to do, getting ready for this party, without worrying about secret engagements." She patted Theora's shoulder in a motherly way and took herself off to the pantry.

Theora then went back to her room and sat for a while considering what to do. Eventually she decided that the only course open to her was to write to the Earl and put the matter in his hands. It was no good waiting for his return, for he had gone away again on business and was not expected until the day of the party. She wrote a brief note, stating the facts and skirting over the improprieties. This she handed to Meadows to be sent by the next post. Then she returned to the important business of deciding whether Countess Lieven should really be sat opposite the Marquis de Serenare.

*

A diversion from all the domestic chaos came three days later when a carriage appeared and from it descended a lady who came to the front door and asked for Lord Thorne. Meadows quickly explained that Lord Thorne was away from the house. However, the lady, upon hearing this, asked to see Miss Templeton instead. Meadows advised her to sit and, leaving her in the hall, went to find Theora. She was in the parlour helping one of the maids unearth some china that was needed to make up a supper set. When she saw the Butler, she stopped unwrapping and looked up at him questioningly.

"There is a lady to see you, Miss," said Meadows.

Theora looked perplexed. "Who is the lady?"

"Her name is Miss Drew."

Theora wiped her hands on a cloth and pushed a cobweb away from her face. "Where is she from and what does she want?"

"As to that I couldn't say, Miss. She came in a hired

conveyance which left her and her luggage. The Lady asked for Lord Thorne on arrival. I explained Lord Thorne is out, so she then asked to see you."

"Very well, I'll see her in the drawing room, but give me a few minutes to tidy up first."

When Theora went up to the drawing room. Miss Drew immediately rose. Theora was instantly aware that she was being looked over very carefully.

"Please sit down, Miss Drew. Would you like some tea?"

"Yes thank you."

Miss Drew took the cup. She then sat looking out of the window, apparently not wishing to speak further. This forced silence enabled Theora to make her own study of this unexpected visitor.

She saw a woman of medium height. She had very fine, exceptionally luxuriant hair, which was silver grey with glints of gold. This was piled high and added to her distinguished air. It was difficult to judge her age precisely. There were deep hollows in her cheeks and stretched lines about her mouth so that her face appeared somewhat thin and severe. In contrast, the brown eyes, under the finely arching brows, were still wide, bright and expressive. She was wearing a dark grey gown which fitted her well and was decorated with a lace collar and cuffs to match. The gown was simple, but the lace, though old, was expensive. She was, without doubt, a lady of some high standing, but although she racked her brains, Theora could think of no one in the district who bore the name of Drew.

"You are wondering who I am aren't you, Miss Templeton," said the Lady abruptly.

"Yes, I am afraid I am," said Theora honestly. "I am sorry, have we met before?"

"No, Miss Templeton, we have not."

Silence fell again. Theora felt at a loss. Questions burned upon her tongue, but Miss Drew's rather foreboding manner made her unable to think of a way to frame them suitably. At last she said lamely, "You are acquainted with Lord Thorne I believe?"

"Yes."

"He is not here at the moment."

"Your servant advised me of that."

"Do you wish me to send for him?" said Theora a little desperately. "

Miss Drew nodded to the window. "There is no need. I believe he will soon be with us."

"You have already agreed to meet him here then?"

"That is correct."

There seemed nothing more to say. Theora took up a book and began to read, although her ears were on the prick for the sound of Lord Thorne's carriage. Thankfully she did not have long to wait. Some twenty minutes later, she heard the wheels of his chaise draw up on the gravel.

Excusing herself quickly, Theora went out to the hall. Ignoring Meadows' surprised glance, she quickly beckoned Lord Thorne to follow her into the saloon and, as soon as he was inside, shut the doors behind him.

"Thank goodness you have come back," she said.

He looked amused and said lightly, "I am extremely flattered that you are so glad to see me after so short an absence, Miss Templeton. I am even more delighted that you have chosen to kidnap me, although I am afraid these obvious tactics are going to cause some gossip in the servants' hall."

Theora rolled her eyes. "Please do not be ridiculous, my Lord. I have not kidnapped you; I just needed somewhere to speak to you alone."

His eyes twinkled. "Really, how very disappointing. I don't think I've ever been kidnapped you see and it would have been such a novel experience. So, if we are not here for flirtation, how can I help you?"

Theora looked at him. "You must be aware that Miss Drew is here?"

Lord Thorne looked at Theora's white face with surprise.

"There is truly nothing to be worried about," he said gently. "Miss Drew is here to help you. She is my housekeeper. It occurred to me that I could spare her for a while. So, I have asked her to come to Temple Court and to remain as long as you need her."

He paused. "I am conscious," he said, "that there are many issues and pressures that you have to face and neither Lord Sulien nor I can always be here to support you. Miss Drew can, to some degree, act in our stead. I have the utmost confidence in her."

Theora stared back at him. "Do you think I am in danger?" she asked breathlessly.

He pressed her hand reassuringly. "Not necessarily, but I think that you know from your last encounter with Lord De Lisle that he at least should be avoided. I ask you to have faith in me please. Faith that at the right time and in the right place I will tell you everything you need to know."

There was finality in his tone and Theora knew that he was bringing their conversation to a close. She was disappointed, but she resolved not to pester him, as it occurred to her that should she win Miss Drew's confidence she might have a better chance of getting the information she yearned for. When he suggested that they join Miss Drew in the drawing room, she did not resist, but followed him through.

*

Later that month, Theora made the trip into Gyldeford to collect her own and Juliet's ball gowns. Theora had been content to make the journey alone, but she felt slightly guilty about it all the same. Before setting out she had wondered whether she should invite Miss Drew to accompany her. Since her arrival at Temple Court, Miss Drew had proved herself invaluable support. She was efficient, practical, deft and very quick. Tasks which Theora had feared would take days had been reduced to hours and the house was now virtually ready, with only a few final arrangements to complete.

Having spent the rest of the day shopping, it was getting dark when the coach arrived to take her home. It was cold and a hoar frost glittered in the brightness of the full moon. As the miles passed she slept. Then, the familiar vista of the park disappeared and she was transported to a different time and place. She found herself watching a beautiful young girl on a white horse galloping across a field of corn, towards a sunlit sea. Then she awoke, her dream quickly forgotten. The sound of a gun firing made her hurriedly sit upright and shrink back against the squabs. The coach came to a sudden halt, sliding in the mud and tilting precariously. The door opened and a man in a dark coat and muffler leaned in. Two other men appeared beside him, similarly dressed and carrying pistols.

The leader caught Theora's arm, pulled her from the coach and threw her roughly onto the grass. Theora could see that the coachman had been knocked to the ground and was lying either dead or insensible. One of the highwaymen was at the horses' heads, trying to calm them. The others, ignoring Theora, began to unload the coach. In the faint moonlight, Theora groped her way to the coachman, he was too heavy for her to lift, but feeling through his coat she could sense the faintest heartbeat. There seemed to be no sign of injury, but his breathing was shallow and she was aware that out here, in the deep frost, he had a slim chance of survival. Suddenly she realised that in his hand was a gun. He had evidently been trying to find and fire it when he'd been knocked from his seat. She quickly took it from him and covered it with her cloak. By the feel she could tell it was a large gun and she had no experience of a firearm of this type. Desperation drove inspiration so she started to crawl slowly towards the man with the horses. When she thought she was in reasonable distance she raised her arm and fired. Then several things happened all at once. Firstly, the man holding the horses dropped to the ground with an oath and the horses sprang forward, jerking the coach into motion and knocking the two men at its door off their feet.

Boxes and parcels scattered and the coach, now free of the mud, jumped across the ground. The horses, aware that home was near, put their heads down and bolted. The man Theora had shot was cursing, clutching his bleeding arm. The leader of the group, running forward, caught Theora. He stared at her furiously, but then turned as there was the sound of hooves coming from behind them in the trees. A dark shape appeared and then a great chestnut horse leapt forward. It reared up and the Highwayman was knocked down. He lay cowering in the grass whilst his companion, holding Theora in front of him, jumped hastily back. She felt the gun pushing into her shoulder and tried to pull away but the man's grasp was firm.

"One move and I'll kill you." She felt his coarse breath on her cheek as he shouted out, "Hear that do you? I'm going to kill the little lady if she moves. What do you think of that, my fine gentleman?"

The words echoed around the combe but there was no reply. The man shouted again: "I'm going to kill her, you hear, I mean it. You get yourself off now."

He broke off as his companion made a hoarse choking cry. With a mixture of amazement and horror Theora saw that the stallion was now standing on top of him. There was the horrible noise of the man's skull cracking on the stones, then the horse stepped over the body.

In the darkness Theora was aware that its rider had dismounted. There was a sudden flash of light and she found herself staring at a welcome figure. The Earl regarded the Highwayman with careless contempt and said coldly:

"In answer to your question, I don't think much of your plan." He looked at the Highwayman. "Do you wish to try again?" The Highwayman gasped. Lord Sulien smiled very slightly. "Very wise. I suggest that you let this lady go at once. If you do, then I may leave you and your friend to die in the snow. That is the best option I can offer you. If you don't..." His voice trailed away. Theora could feel the Highwayman trembling and the indecision within him. The horse pawed the ground impatiently and let out a whinny. His Lordship nodded, "Quite right, Apollo, time we concluded our business."

One hand shot out and the Highwayman was jerked off his feet, he gave a grunt of surprise as his Lordship struck him across the mouth. Theora fell to the ground and saw Lord Sulien draw his sword. As the Highwayman lunged forward there was the glint of steel and then the body thudding backwards. His Lordship withdrew his blade with one swift movement and jumped down to kneel beside Theora in the mud. He put an arm round her shoulders and drew her upright.

"Are you hurt?" Her response was so low he could barely hear her, so he lifted her onto the waiting horse.

The man who Theora had shot was standing gripping his blood-soaked arm and still cursing. "You're mad you are," he shouted. "Mad and deserve to die. I'll see that happen, by the Knights of the Road, I swear it. You're going to come to a bad end, you and your doxy." He broke off as his Lordship, who had started to ride away, now pulled up. He dismounted and took the man's head in his hands. He looked deep into the rolling eyes.

"Whether a knight or not you forfeited your right to life when you came into the presence of this lady and placed her in the slightest danger. You and these others are not permitted to walk the road anymore. Do you understand?"

The man nodded and gave a gasping cry of terror. Then Theora saw that his Lordship's hands were starting to glow, the whiteness became brighter and more golden so it was as if the man's entire face was alight. The light became quite unbearable and she was forced to look away. When she glanced back, there was no sign of any light, nor any highwaymen. His Lordship remounted and they rode away down the now deserted combe. It was now burning cold and Theora could not feel her hands and feet. Only his Lordship's hand upon her shoulder stopped her from falling. She was conscious of creeping numbness and sore patches all over where the Highwayman had grabbed and thrown her. After what seemed like hours, but was perhaps no more than twenty minutes, his Lordship drew rein and Theora saw the lights of Temple Court sparkling ahead. They were reflected on the river which she perceived with a dim sense of shock was larger, more fast flowing than usual and covered the road. They rode a little further down the valley, but neither direction showed any path to Temple Court which was not underwater.

His Lordship swung round and headed up the hill. He made for a low roofed building which was nestling in the lee of the cliff side. A smattering of sheep scattered before him as he pulled up and, lifting Theora down, carried her inside. It was small, but dry and densely packed with straw. He set her down, remarking, "Shepherd's hut, lucky to have remembered this." He struck flint and lit a branch which he propped up by the door and wedged with rocks. Turning back she saw his serious face touched with eerie shadows. Aware of everything that had happened that evening, conscious that she had seen him commit murder at least twice, she wondered vaguely why she felt no fear. He took off his cloak, wrapped it about her and piled up the straw setting her down upon it.

"Does that feel better?" She tried to answer him, but her lips were too stiff to move.

He frowned at that and looked back at his horse standing patiently outside, almost hock deep in snow. The Earl knelt down. "Listen, Theora, I am going to have to leave you now and get help. The river's too high for Apollo to swim with both of us on his back and I can't leave you outside all night with all those cuts and bruises; the cold will kill you. I wish I could get you home myself, but I can't risk any more damage at this time." He looked at her closely. "Do you understand?" She nodded and he gave one of his rare smiles. "Good girl." He paused and she was aware of some inner struggle going on within him. When he spoke again his voice was very measured. "I can cross the river, but to save your life, you also have to stay awake. You won't be able to do that unless I help you. I can do that, but you have to trust me. Will you do that?"

She wanted to say that of course she did, but there were no words or thoughts or feelings inside her, everything was empty, black and cold. With a supreme effort she managed to raise her head and looked into his eyes. In the gloom they seemed to be blazing with an intensity she had never seen before. The green brightness of his gaze was almost blinding, but suddenly she was too close to see them. Then she was aware of the touch of his lips on hers and she would have struggled, but his arms were locked about her. The kiss deepened and her heart, whose beat had seemed to have all but disappeared, began to race. The cold and the pain were beaten back as new energy rushed through her. With her returning strength she clung to him. Then she found that they were no longer outside in the snow, but miraculously standing on the threshold of the Earl's bedroom at Temple Court...

Winter had gone, it was springtime and a warm sun blazed through the oriel window, turning his Lordship's golden hair to a shining crown. Theora was wearing a gown of lace and carrying a basket of roses and orange blossoms. The scent was intoxicating. Then his Lordship swept her up into his arms, sending the basket flying and carried her into the bedroom shutting the huge oak door behind them.

Sometime later, Lord Sulien took his lips from Miss Templeton's and lowered her gently back on the straw. He took one of her hands and pressed it to his cheek for a moment. It was now perfectly warm. He let it drop suddenly as if it was painful to him and covered her with his cloak. Then he stood up and went out to his horse, mounted and rode down to the river.

Chapter Fifteen

Two days after the highwaymen's attack, the Earl received Mr Allan in his study. He had kept to himself since his return to Temple Court, avoiding contact with anyone. Mr Allan, used to seeing his employer clean and well dressed, was very surprised to see him in his shirt sleeves and breeches and without cravat. A decanter was on the desk, standing one third full next to some empty, used glasses.

"Good afternoon, Aidan."

The Earl nodded but for a moment made no response. He looked the younger man over very deliberately and there was a long silence. At last he said, "You may be wondering why I have called you here, Ciaran."

"I assumed you needed a progress report?"

"Perhaps."

"How is Miss Templeton?"

The Earl's eyes flickered. "Fully recovered."

"And she remembers nothing of the incident?"

"No."

"But it was De Lisle's men. Why would he sanction such a thing? I know he doesn't like you, but this attack is beyond comprehension."

The Earl drained his glass and motioned for Mr Allan to sit. He picked up the decanter. "Do you want a drink?"

"Yes thank you."

The Earl poured him some claret and then directed his gaze out to the distant fields. In the distance a bell tolled, but otherwise, there was no sound of activity and not even a breeze was blowing outside to disturb the tranquillity of the day.

Then the Earl spoke and the still peace of the cold, pale day was instantly shattered.

"Please explain this."

He tossed across the table a crumpled letter. After one alarmed glance at the Earl, Mr Allan picked it up and scanned it hastily. He turned first red and then white.

"I don't understand?" he stammered.

"Don't you? This is the reason why I have been forced to cut short my business and return to Temple Court."

Mr Allan started to stumble a hasty response but the Earl held up his hand.

"I advise you to think before you answer me, Ciaran."

Mr Allan swallowed, "I owe you an apology. I should have spoken to you first."

"That's for damned sure," said the Earl coldly. "However, my concern is with your timing, not your behaviour towards my daughter."

He paused and, looking at Mr Allan's strained face, his expression softened.

"I am not unsympathetic to your feelings, so this I will say: if my business progresses as I wish, then you may marry Juliet."

Mr Allan thanked him profusely. When he had finished the Earl said, "But I ask you not to tell Juliet any of this. You may only advise her that I am considering your request, but have asked for more time."

Mr Allan smiled. "I suspect that she will press you for a firm date."

"I have no doubt that she will," said the Earl. "Like her father she longs for certainty in all things. Now please send Argus to me. I am going to walk in the garden."

*

As they walked down the avenue of lime trees that flanked the formal garden, Lord Thorne looked sharply at the Earl. "What is wrong, Aidan?"

"Ciaran," said the Earl quietly, "has asked for Juliet's hand."

"Oh," said Lord Thorne. "I assume you don't object?"

"Of course not, but I have asked him to wait."

Lord Thorne sighed. "You are delaying the inevitable. He is only weeks from his twenty-fifth birthday. Would it not just be easier to tell him the truth now and prepare him properly for what is to come? Unlike Bricin he is honest and true and has already proved his worth. We will need his strength before the end."

"That I know, but I still fear that we might find his allegiance tested," said Lord Sulien. "No, for the time being, Ciaran must remain in ignorance. Until he has the strength to repel a direct attack, I cannot risk either him or my daughter coming to harm."

"Very well," said Lord Thorne. He stopped and leaned on the kissing gate, looking closely at his friend. "So what else troubles you?"

The Earl rubbed his hand across his chin. He hadn't shaved that morning and a golden stubble was forming. "I am worried about Miss Templeton."

Lord Thorne looked surprised. "Why so? I saw her this morning and she looked restored to full health. I never saw her better."

The Earl gave a slightly twisted smile. "She probably will never look better, Argus. That's the trouble."

Lord Thorne stared at him and his face changed. His hands gripped the gate and tensed. After a moment he said very evenly. "How could you do that?"

The Earl's expression darkened. "I had to," he said. "She would have died otherwise. You know how it is. De Lisle used a cantus so powerful that I couldn't transport her to safety. Believe me, I would never have wished such a thing to happen."

"You know there may well be repercussions," said Lord Thorne angrily. "Are you prepared to deal with them?"

"Of course, if I have to, but I can't worry about that

now, obviously."

Lord Thorne gave a harsh laugh. "'Obviously'. How can you be so bloody objective, Aidan? That girl will never be the same. Even though you have wiped her mind the memory will haunt her and there may be worse to come."

"She is one girl. My responsibility is to the many."

"Yes, you've learned that lesson very well. Please do tell me more! It would not surprise me at all to learn that you took no joy from the actual act of saving Miss Templeton."

He broke off as the Earl suddenly turned and struck him with his open palm. Lord Thorne stepped back, his cheek bone reddened.

The Earl said in a voice that shook slightly, "Forgive me?"

"Forgive you? I am glad that the ice has at least shown a hint of thaw! The last time I saw any such emotion from you was the day of poor Lizzie's death. As to Miss Templeton, I will not let you just ignore the situation. It must be managed, even if you find the process to do so distasteful."

The Earl looked at him. "What do you wish?"

"That if she shows any reaction, we act at once, whether that affects the Quest or not. I ask for your promise, Aidan?"

The Earl nodded. "I promise. Now let us go in."

They walked back to the house. The Earl glanced at Lord Thorne's face. "You will need to bathe that bruise. I hope your face does not swell up for the party."

"So do I," said his friend with feeling.

"Now, we must make haste," said the Earl. "With the Drum on its way we have much to do."

They went to the study and using the globe returned to the cavern of the Perdurare. In the Club, the Knights were assembled and waiting. The Earl took his place at the top table.

"I have asked Mr Brummell to provide an update."

"I have good news," said Mr Brummell. "The Drum is on its way and I have also identified the cantus to release the Harp of Suantri. This enables the completion of the music for the dance."

There was a hum of appreciation from around the table. Guy Irving leaned forward. "That is good news indeed. I have gone as far as I can with choreography."

The Earl turned to Lord Thorne, "What do you have to report, Argus?"

Lord Thorne stood up. "Since the attack on Miss Templeton, I have increased the network around Lord De Lisle, but he seems to have deliberately distanced himself from our usual informers. There is only one now that I trust and it is proving extremely difficult to get to this person without Lord De Lisle detecting my presence. However, what I do know is that Lord De Lisle is summoning an army even as we speak. I am sure that he means to strike very soon."

"Then we cannot delay" said the Earl. "We must gather our forces, make our way to Venice and face him there. Are the Hind and Victory made ready?"

Drake and Nelson looked at each other. "Victory is ready," said Nelson, "but the Hind is still at dry dock in Plymouth awaiting repairs."

"Very well," said the Earl. "Then it must be Victory who brings our precious cargo."

He turned to King Louis. "Are the Knights of the Sword ready, my friend?"

King Louis bowed. "They are, my Lord Earl."

"Then have them ready to meet on St Mark's Square at the appointed hour."

He rose and looked round at the council. "We will

have one last meeting, but, in the meantime, go now and make ready. Do nothing to draw attention. It is vital that we preserve every semblance of normality until the last possible moment, so that Lord De Lisle remains in as much ignorance of our intentions as possible. We do not yet know what knowledge he possesses, but, he is quite capable of making highly informed guesses. We must not give him any opportunity to affirm his assumptions. I bless you all and wish you success."

*

The Earl and Lord Thorne then returned to the study at Temple Court. There they reviewed the arrangements to bring the Drum from Devon and discussed the cantus required to play the Harp. Only when he was satisfied with every detail did the Earl relax.

"Well," he said, "it seems as if we are finally ready. There are still many risks ahead, yet I do at last feel a little hope."

"As do I," said Lord Thorne. "Of course, we do still have one major obstacle ahead…"

The Earl glanced at him sharply. "Which is?"

Lord Thorne raised his eyebrows. "Ensuring that we pick the right waistcoat for Juliet's ball of course," he said with a faint smile.

*

The day of Juliet's ball dawned clear and bright. There was great excitement as the preparations drew to a close and the house was at last ready to receive the expected guests. Theora had been delighted by Lady Meadley's suggestion that Mrs Colton joined them from Yorkshire. She had arrived the day before and had exclaimed both at the refreshed elegance of the house and Theora's appearance.

"I have seldom seen you in such good looks, my dear," she had said as soon as the two of them were alone. "Being back in Surrey obviously agrees with you!"

Theora had thanked her, but quickly turned the conversation. She did not wish her friend to know that she had started to hear strange voices. She could not clearly make out the words spoken, but she was becoming terrified, for the frequency of the voices was increasing and made it hard to concentrate. She longed to confide in someone, but had no idea who to turn to. Her only relief came from wearing the pendant given to her by the Rector of Rodsall. She had decided that after the party, she would try and arrange a meeting with the Rector, who seemed, to her, the only person she could trust to help her, without involving the Earl in some way.

From dawn, the house was thronged with servants and tradesmen. Miss Drew continued to support, dealing with every crisis and through her cool efficiency restraining the mounting excitement within the household staff. She finally advised Theora that everything was ready and suggested that the ladies retired to dress. Theora duly went to Lady Meadley's dressing room where the maids were attending to her pupil. At last Juliet stood ready in a gown of shell pink, her golden curls stranded with ribbons and rosebuds. Leaving Juliet to the raptures of the maids and Lady Meadley's fond compliments, Theora slipped away to her own room where Mrs Colton, tastefully arrayed in green silk, was ready to help her friend prepare for the evening ahead. Theora's dress was midnight blue, with a silvery underskirt. The neckline was beaded with matching crystals and it was of a severe cut that perfectly set off her slim figure. Mrs Colton brushed the dark curls and piled them high, setting in their glossy midst the Templeton crescent with its fine Ceylon sapphires. When she had finished, she stepped back, staring at her friend with pride. She reflected that, although this was to be Juliet's night, Theora might well eclipse her, for never had she looked more beautiful. There seemed to be flowing from within her a particularly vital brilliance. This magnified her already striking good looks and made her absolutely radiant.

It had already been agreed that the Earl, Lady Meadley and Juliet would greet the principal guests in the hall, so Theora and Mrs Colton went unescorted to the ball room. Here, Lord Thorne, Mr Crossley and a sprinkling of the County Set were already assembled. As they entered, Theora looked around with great satisfaction, for although she had watched the room being prepared, she had not yet seen it with all chandeliers lit. Now the banks of white flowers were fully illuminated and the marble pillars and restored golden plasterwork dazzled the eye. As she glanced around she saw that Lord Thorne was there and was looking directly at her. She was surprised to see an expression on his face that she could not read. She saw that Mr Crossley too was looking at her in apparent amazement.

She was confused and whispered hurriedly to Mrs Colton, "Penny, what is wrong? Is there anything amiss?"

Mrs Colton patted her hand reassuringly. "Absolutely nothing, except you are turning everyone's heads by looking so lovely, my dear."

Theora hung her head. "I didn't want to draw attention to myself, I thought this dress was so suitable."

"And so it is, quite perfect. Now don't think any more about it. Look, here comes Juliet."

She nodded towards the door where the Earl, his sister and his daughter were entering with a crowd of visitors. Theora had very little acquaintance with most of the guests outside the county and so was able to stand unremarked, watching Lady Meadley making introductions. The Earl quickly became surrounded and so disappeared from view.

Mrs Colton opened her fan. "I declare it really is warm in here already," she said. "Shall we go in to supper?"

"Yes, let us go in," said Theora with an effort.

They went through to the dining room and took their places. It was an excellent meal and at any other time Theora would have been delighted, for the room looked exquisite, the service was flawless and each course a triumph. But the food all tasted like ashes to her, for the noises in her head were growing. It was all she could do to pick up a fork. Fortunately, Mrs Colton quickly became engaged elsewhere. As Theora was seated by a politician who barely raised his eyes from his plate, conversation was limited. Eventually, everyone rose to go back into the ballroom. Immediately couples started forming and Juliet was quickly claimed by Lord Brough. Theora turned quickly as she felt a gentle tap on her shoulder. With relief she saw it was Mr Allan. He was smiling at her.

"Good evening, Miss Templeton, Mrs Colton, how good to see you again." He shook hands cordially with Mrs Colton. Then he turned back to Theora. "The house is looking wonderful, Miss Templeton, I congratulate you."

Theora smiled. "We should congratulate each other, Sir. I could not have got the house into any order without your support."

She waited until Mrs Colton was distracted and said in a low voice, "I am sorry, I have had no opportunity to speak to the Earl directly about your situation. Although I did write, so that he was appraised of all the facts."

He withdrew his gaze from Juliet's golden head, which could just be glimpsed as she danced by.

"As to that, it happens that the Earl has already spoken to me. He has given us his blessing, upon condition we delay the marriage for a while. On this basis, we shall not of course, be making any announcement tonight."

Theora looked relieved. "I truly congratulate you, Sir. Juliet is a very lucky girl."

"Thank you." He bowed. "Would you perhaps honour me with a dance to celebrate, Ma'am?" He looked around and lowered his voice. "Then we can perhaps speak more freely?"

Theora's heart sank. She had no particular desire to dance so early in the evening. However, she had a real fondness for Mr Allan and was curious to know what exactly the Earl had said. She managed a smile. "I should be glad to, Sir."

He led her to the floor where a Quadrille had just completed. The orchestra struck up again and Theora was startled to hear that they were playing a waltz. Dancing on one's own, in a private parlour, was completely different to standing up in a public room. She consoled herself with the thought that at least, in Mr Allan's case, there could be absolutely no question of any amorous intent. So, when he took her in his arm, she was able to step up to him without embarrassment. She found she was enjoying herself, as they circled lightly around the floor.

"So, I am permitted to tell Juliet that I have her father's consent but that we must wait," said Mr Allan.

"That is good news indeed," said Theora.

They made their way down the room and passed a small group including Lord Thorne that were standing near the entrance. There was an excited murmur as they went by and Theora saw again the curious expressions upon the faces of some of the men. Glancing up at the face of her partner, she saw that he too was gazing intently at her. She dropped her eyes quickly. "Please don't stare at me like that," she said hurriedly.

He smiled slightly. "I am sorry. Of course, you know

that, to me, nobody could be lovelier than Juliet. I am afraid that I have a secret strategy which I must now confess to you. I am hoping that by dancing with you and making all the other men envious, this will persuade the Earl to permit me at least one dance with his daughter."

Theora smiled. "I admire your guile, Sir. Let us hope your effort is not in vain!"

They came to halt as the violins brought the dance to a close. Mr Allan bowed low. "Thank you, Ma'am."

He took her hand and started to lead her back to Mrs Colton, but a tall figure barred his way.

"Oh good evening, my Lord." Mr Allan stopped quickly and Theora found herself face to face with Lord Thorne.

Lord Thorne bowed. "Good evening, Miss Templeton. Ciaran, if you wish to solicit Juliet's hand for a dance I suggest you do so quickly. Her card is nearly full."

It was clearly a dismissal. Mr Allan bowed himself away and Lord Thorne then took Theora's hand and led her quietly but firmly from the floor. Theora found herself leaning on his arm with relief for the room suddenly felt very hot. He brought her to one of the seated alcoves, left her briefly and returned with a cooling drink of lemonade which Theora took gratefully. After a little while, once it was clear that they would not be disturbed, he asked her directly if she was feeling quite well.

Theora hesitated. "I am afraid not, my Lord. But, I beg you not to concern yourself. This is Juliet's night and I would not for the world do anything to interfere with that. If you wouldn't mind just leaving me alone for a while, I am sure I will be able to return to the ballroom soon. I just need a few moments."

"I doubt that," said Lord Thorne. "I will leave you, but only to find some assistance. Wait here."

He spoke with authority but Theora, who had started to feel not just hot, but very sick, had no choice but to obey him. She sat with her eyes closed and, after what seemed to be hours but could only have been a few minutes, he returned, accompanied by Miss Drew.

"Madelyn will take you to your room, Miss Templeton." Seeing that she was about to protest, he raised his hand to stop her.

"Please don't worry, my dear, all will be well here I promise you." He gave her an encouraging smile and watched as, supported by Miss Drew, she left the room.

There were murmurs of surprise from some of the guests, but, fortunately, they were diverted by the announcement that there was to be a firework display on the terrace. As the room cleared, Lord Thorne made his way out to the garden. Under cover of the distracting spectacle, he managed to lead the Earl away from the crowd and they met Miss Drew in the summerhouse.

"Well," said the Earl, tersely.

"She is very sick indeed," said Miss Drew.

The two gentlemen looked at her. "Can you do nothing, Madelyn?" asked Lord Thorne urgently.

"No, she is beyond my skill, beyond the skill of any mortal physician."

"How can this be?" said the Earl. "This reaction is completely unprecedented."

"But, not unique," said Lord Thorne heavily. "In any case, our duty now is clear, we must ensure that Miss Templeton is freed from these demons as soon as possible."

The Earl looked thunderstruck. "Are you suggesting I should try and repeat the process? That is the only way I can think of which might aid her now?"

Lord Thorne looked at him coldly. "I think that would be unwise, as would be the use of any healing cantus. The only sure way to enable Miss Templeton's full recovery is to ask Bricin for his assistance."

The Earl's face hardened. "You are not serious?"

"It is the only definite way to cure her," said Lord Thorne. "Bricin's gifts in healing are beyond question. If he chooses to help her, she will certainly live."

"Then she is dead already," said the Earl. "For I know he will choose not to help her, to spite me."

"I am not so sure," said Miss Drew thoughtfully. "Bricin hates you, but we know he has admiration for Miss Templeton. I do not think he will let her die so easily. Also, we do not know whether he is aware that she has a connection to the Quest. If he does, then he will certainly seek to keep her safe."

"There is another aspect to this which is worth considering," said Lord Thorne. "Should you ask him for help, Aidan, I have no doubt Bricin would see that as a psychological victory and it would afford him great personal satisfaction."

The Earl let out a brief laugh. "I am sure it would. Well, I suppose I have no choice." He looked back at the ballroom. "For now I must stay here as host. It would arouse suspicion amongst Lord De Lisle's spies if you are also absent, Argus, so Madelyn, would you please request Lord De Lisle's presence at the appointed place?"

Miss Drew inclined her head. "Of course, my Lord."

"Thank you." The Earl turned to go but paused. "Is someone with Miss Templeton that can be trusted?"

"I have given her a sleeping draught and Mrs Colton is with her."

"Good. Argus, will you please see Mrs Colton and my sister later and deal with any questions they may have?"

"By deal with, I assume you wish me to wipe their minds?"

"Yes. You know I do not like to tamper with the

minds of mortals, but in this case we have no choice. Now come with me, we are keeping the guests waiting."

The two men went off towards the dining room, but Miss Drew went back to her room, donned stout shoes and a hooded cloak and slipped out into the garden. Once clear of the house, she raised her hand and muttered some words. Instantly, the grass in front of her feet began to glow. With every step she took the path before her became more obvious and she half walked, half ran until she reached the orchard and the gates which led onto the heath. She put both hands upon them and they swung open and the great white summoning stone loomed up before her.

It took her a few moments to climb up onto the pedestal and then she stood, regaining her breath and making sure her hands were in the right position before she recited the cantus. For she knew that the stones would only do her bidding if she did everything exactly right. As she spoke, the night seemed to become even darker, but a circle of light formed with the pedestal stone at its centre. Then within the circle a fire sprang up. It burned fiercely and made a pillar that revolved slowly and out stepped Lord De Lisle. Miss Drew let out a sigh of relief.

"Welcome, my Lord." Lord De Lisle looked up at her. He gave a slight, somewhat ironic bow.

"Good evening, Madam. To what do I owe this unexpected and unusual pleasure?"

Miss Drew stepped down from the pedestal and walked towards him. "It is good to see you again, Bricin. It has been many years now."

"Indeed," said Lord De Lisle. "Many years since you cast me out and pledged allegiance to those mortal-loving fools."

Miss Drew looked at him sadly. "You were never cast out, Bricin. It was your choice to leave us and make your own way."

"Perhaps, but not once, in all these years, have you sought me out, or attempted to contact me. It has been lonely." He reached out and, as if compelled to do so, took her hand. "I have missed you."

She let him hold her and looked up into his tense, white face, her still beautiful brown eyes searching his. "And I you," she said honestly.

"Yet still you tarry here, masquerading as a servant and letting the burden of the years fall upon you. Why must you?"

"You now know the reason well enough."

"It's ridiculous. You know he doesn't love you. He just uses you."

Madelyn hung her head. "No he doesn't love me anymore. That feeling died long ago, but he still cares for me and I have his companionship. That is what sustains me. Whilst I can give him true service, I will always do so and never count the cost."

"I could have given you so much more. It is still within my power to do so. Look."

De Lisle waved his hand and against the shining surface of the pedestal stone a vision appeared. It was of Miss Drew but she was again young. Her golden hair shone and her brown eyes were filled with life and longing. The fair image shook its head and laughed.

"You see," said De Lisle passionately. "You see what I can give you, my first and only love."

Miss Drew raised her hand and the vision dissolved, leaving nothing but the black night. "You and I both know that if I took such a gift from you, it would still be nothing but an illusion, for I cannot and never will love you. I am sorry."

Lord De Lisle laughed harshly. "Then you will become old and withered and finally you will die, my

Druidess, as the mortals do. Even though you were once accounted the wisest of your kind, yet I still denounce you as a fool, my Lady."

She smiled sadly. "Love makes fools of all of us, my Lord."

De Lisle took a long breath. "Then let us speak of other matters. Why have you summoned me tonight?"

"Lord Sulien bade me make the summons and I speak upon his behalf. He needs your help."

De Lisle looked at her incredulously "You are joking of course."

Her brown eyes held his light blue ones. "No, my Lord. It is for the sake of Miss Templeton we make this request. She is extremely ill and only you can save her."

"Show me," he said curtly.

She let him take her head in his hands and after a moment he released her, twisted the black opal ring on his finger and stared for a moment into its glowing fire.

"And why should I intervene to save one more mortal that Aidan and Argus have made into a servant and taken a fancy to?"

"Perhaps because you have taken a fancy to her too?"

He eyed her thoughtfully. "You still have your gift of perception, Madelyn. Very well, I will help, but it will be for a price. Tell Lord Sulien I will meet him and Miss Templeton at Aquae Flammarium tomorrow night, but he must come alone."

She dropped a deep curtsy. "Thank you, my Lord."

"Wait, you have not yet heard the price."

She rose up. "What is it?"

"That you leave Lord Thorne forever."

She stared at him incredulously. "Don't be ridiculous. I won't do it. I can't do it."

"Will you not? Then alas, everything you and those other fools have worked for will be lost. Can you really risk that, Madelyn?"

She stepped back and rested her hand upon the white stone as if for protection.

"No," she whispered at last.

Lord De Lisle eyed her with satisfaction.

"Good. This is what you will do. Tonight you will leave Lord Thorne's house and never return to it. You must also conceal our bargain from Argus and Aidan. Do I make myself clear?"

"Yes."

"Yes, of course. You were always so very quick witted. I am very glad to see that age has not yet dulled that fine mind."

He swept her an extravagant bow.

"Stella benedictionum[5], until our next meeting."

The moon burst from behind the clouds and shone full upon his face making it alive with light. He turned to go, but she raised her hand.

"Wait."

He stopped and looked back at her. "What now?"

"I will come to you, but you must give me time to prepare. I require a year in this time. Will you grant me that?"

His eyes flashed with amusement. "You know, I can make one year last one minute if I wish, so, yes, I will give you that 'minute'. I think I know what you propose to do and I will not stop you aiding Miss Templeton. But, remember, when the minute ends, you will leave forever and never return to the 16th or 19th Centuries."

Miss Drew nodded. As she did so, the moon had disappeared and so had Lord De Lisle. She went back to the house and directly to Miss Templeton's room. Mrs

---

[5]A star of blessings

Colton was there, tending the fire, but she looked relieved when she saw who it was.

"I am glad you are back, Miss, for I must confess this sickness of Theora's has me baffled. I have known her come through quite a few illnesses when she was younger, yet never have I seen her wander in her wits in this horrible way."

Miss Drew crossed to the bed. "She is sleeping still?"

"Yes, but she cries and moans and seems in the grip of some awful fear which is far worse than any normal nightmare. Do you not think we should be seeking some additional help? We can't be keeping her drugged like this forever."

She looked up at Miss Drew anxiously and was struck at how pale and ill the other woman looked.

"Are you sure you are well, Miss Drew?"

Miss Drew straightened her shoulders. "Quite well thank you," she said. She bent and adjusted the pillows under Theora's head. "Additional help, as you call it, has already been requested," she said.

Mrs Colton looked at her sharply. "Someone you know and trust."

"Indeed," said Miss Drew and if her voice sounded brusque, Mrs Colton was too thankful to notice.

"Well that is good news," she said. She looked uncertainly at Miss Drew. "Are you planning to stay?"

Miss Drew, who had been wringing out a soft cloth in cold water to apply to Miss Templeton's forehead, nodded briefly. "There is no need to worry. I will stay for as long as she is sick. Please do return to the ball. I am sure that is what Miss Templeton would wish. I promise I will let you know if there is any change."

She waited until Mrs Colton had left the room and then laid the cloth over Theora's forehead. Having pulled up the blankets, she sat down on a chair next to the bed.

Her eyes closed, but she was not asleep. She was thinking about the events of the evening and, as she did so, her memory returned again to 1540 and the great hall of Ashleworth Castle...

Chapter Sixteen

The sound of the hounds baying in the courtyard and the scurrying of the chamber servants told the young housekeeper that Lord Thorne and his new pupil had at last returned to the castle. Madelyn Drew stood at the head of a long line of servants, her hands loosely clasped before her, head bowed. Outwardly she appeared calm and composed, but inwardly her heart was pounding and she was filled with excitement. For it had been over a year since Lord Thorne had gone away. During that time he had also become the guardian and teacher of the last born Moon Lord and so he had not returned to Ashleworth even for a short visit. There was some satisfaction in the fact that, although five years had passed since she had come forward into the future, she remained beautiful. Knowing this she had chosen to wear a gown of blueish grey, woven with fine thread and had unbound her hair under its silken veil.

The door of the hall swung open and Lord Thorne came into the hall. His blue eyes were bright and cheerful in his lean, sun-browned face.

"It is good to be home," he said heartily. His gaze fell upon Miss Drew and he smiled. "And even better to see you, my Lady," he said. He walked to her and bowed. "I do not need to ask if you are well, for I see it clearly." He turned quickly away, looking around the hall and failed to see the disappointment flash in Miss Drew's eyes. "Ah, it is good to see nothing has really changed." He threw his hat down on the sideboard and bent to remove his spurs. "It is always so peaceful here," he said with satisfaction. "It is truly a haven. Do you not agree, Bricin?"

The tall red-haired young man, who had been standing behind him with his eyes fixed in wonder upon

Miss Drew, nodded slowly. "A haven indeed."

Lord Thorne, noting the direction of his gaze, smiled. "Miss Madelyn Drew, meet Lord De Lisle. Bricin, whilst I am away, I entrust Madelyn with your teaching. I can give you no better guide to our ways." He drew De Lisle forward. "Come now, shake her hand. This is an introduction that I have long planned for."

Madelyn extended her hand and De Lisle took it eagerly. "I bid you welcome, my Lady," he said and then switched to Latin and stammered, "Beatus foltchain."[6]

Lord Thorne laughed. "I wonder where you picked that up from. It has been many years since anyone called Milady 'Foltchain'. Although, of course, her hair is very beautiful." Madelyn looked up at him with an unmistakeable expression of longing but he deliberately avoided her gaze. "Now introductions are over, let us go in to supper shall we? I am famished. I assume everything is prepared."

Madelyn bowed her head. "It is, my Lord."

"Good, it will be a pleasure to sit down to some simpler fare. I have spent too many nights being force fed at banquets and soirees." He threw an arm around De Lisle's shoulders. "Let's eat now and then tomorrow, I'll take you for a ride round the Estate. There is so much I want to show you." They walked away, but even whilst De Lisle appeared to give his full attention to the man at his side, Madelyn was conscious of the voice in her head, speaking to her directly. "I look forward to our next meeting, Flidais Bandrui."[7]

That evening, she had waited for Lord Thorne to call

---

[6] Blessed creature, beautiful hair

[7] My sweet teacher

for her. At last, in her desperate need to see him alone, she sought him out. As she had guessed, she found him unpacking his books. It was against the house rules for anyone to disturb him when he was in the library, so when Madelyn entered, his Lordship turned quickly with an expression of annoyance. Seeing who it was, he relaxed and greeted her with a slightly forced smile.

"You wanted to speak to me, my Lady?"

His deliberately casual tone, so unlike the intense and passionate way he had used to address her, caused fresh pain. "I wanted to ask you about Lord De Lisle," she said directly.

He had been looking at her with ill-concealed constraint, but at this his face cleared. "You wish to discuss his future training?"

"Not his future training," said Madelyn. She looked at Lord Thorne. "I wanted to know where he learned to speak into the minds of mortals."

Lord Thorne put down the book he'd been holding. "It is not something I have taught him. As you know, it is not our custom to communicate that way, except with other Moon or Sun Lords. He spoke directly to you?"

"He did."

"Did you answer him?"

"I did not. I did not wish him to know that I had heard him and could respond in kind, but I believe he knows that I received his message."

"I see," said Lord Thorne thoughtfully. "Well you did right to tell me. If he attempts such a thing again, feign ignorance. I don't want to punish him at this stage of his development. If he restricts himself to just speaking to you, well, there will be no harm done."

"Very well, my Lord," said Madelyn. She hesitated. "There is just one thing. From the nature of what Lord De Lisle says, I believe that he may..." She swallowed. "I *believe that he may already be forming an attachment to me."*

Lord Thorne rolled his eyes. "I am sorry, Madelyn, it is unfortunate, but you are far too sensible to have your head turned by anything he might say. Now I advise you to go to bed now and think no more about it."

He deliberately looked down at his crate of books. "Sleep well."

*

In 1803 Miss Templeton stirred and sighed. Miss Drew sponged her face again. She pulled the curtains closer, obscuring the moonlight, and Miss Templeton settled again. Miss Drew sat down again by the fire and placed another log upon it. The flames glowed red and within them a scene was forming and was reflected back in Miss Drew's dark eyes...

In the forest glade, the sleigh, drawn by dapple grey ponies, was deserted, for its occupants were some distance away. Lord De Lisle was now a little older than when he had first come to Ashleworth Castle. He stood straight and tall in his hose and doublet, covered with a cloak lined with fur. His eyes were closed.

"Veni ad me,"[8] he said loudly.

Nothing happened. Miss Drew, sitting on a cloak-draped tree trunk, raised her eyebrows slightly.

"Try again," she said encouragingly. Lord De Lisle opened his eyes. He was clearly very angry. "I have tried and tried and tried. How long are we going to have to stand out here in the snow?"

"Until you get it right."

"My feet are freezing," said Lord De Lisle, sulkily.

Miss Drew tucked her hands in her muff. "I am cold

---

[8] Come to me

248

too," she reminded him gently.

De Lisle looked at her, with tired resignation. For a moment it seemed as if he was going to walk off. Then he shut his eyes and took a deep breath. "Veni ad me."

There was a cracking sound and one of the great oak trees bent its snow-topped crown as if in salute. As De Lisle stepped forward and placed his hand upon the trunk, it started to shine, a current of energy running from root to tip, until the whole tree blazed. When De Lisle removed his hands, they too glowed, translucent and gleaming. De Lisle looked at them with wonder. He looked at Madelyn and spoke confidently.

"Calefacies ea,"[9] he said.

Madelyn stood up, clapping her now warm hands. "Well done, my Lord. Your power is now linked to this planet's inner spirit and whatever reality you pass into, you will always be protected by it."

Lord De Lisle looked at his shining hands. "I could already command the weather and the water, but this is something completely different." He stared at Madelyn and his blue eyes were blazing. "This is incredible!"

Madelyn began to walk back to the sleigh. "Now you must learn to measure and regulate your strength. Then it will be maximised and exercised only when you most need it."

He ran after, slipping a little in the snow. "You will teach me this, of course," he said.

She shook her head. "No, my Lord. You have passed beyond my skill. Now is the time for you to return to the Domain of the Lord of the Sun. He will continue your lessons."

De Lisle kicked at the snow. His vivid, mobile face,

---

[9] *Warm her*

that so closely mirrored his thoughts and moods, was furious. "I don't want him, I want you," he burst out.

Madelyn ignored him. Having reached the sleigh, she waited, whilst behind her, Lord De Lisle let out a string of oaths and expletives. Used to his temper, she knew that the best way not to encourage him, was to assume unconcern. Eventually he subsided and entered the sleigh to sit beside her. The ponies then set off at a steady pace back down the hill and the bells upon the sleigh rang out and broke the uncomfortable silence.

"I am sorry."

"Of course you are," said Madelyn calmly. "You always are when you lose your temper in my presence."

Her soft voice was matter of fact. Lord De Lisle, peeping at her, had the grace to look a little shamefaced.

"When must I leave?"

"In five days. I will send word to my Lord when we have returned."

They turned out of the wood and the road to Ashleworth stretched out across the fields. The setting sun flashed and flickered. Lord De Lisle raised his hand and shaded his eyes.

"If I could but know what the future will hold." His voice was deliberately casual. "You could tell me something of that couldn't you, my Foltchain."

"I asked you not to call me that," said Madelyn. "But, in answer to your question: using the gift of foresight outside your own time is forbidden."

Lord De Lisle groaned. "Yes, another of the silly rules, which we have to apply. Like not bringing mortals back from the future. But who knows if that actually does any harm? Is it proven, or just a whim of the Sun Lords?"

"I do not know what else to say to you," said Madelyn. "I have attempted to make you understand the *great responsibility that you bear. I have taught you the ways of your kind. However, it is not for me to judge or prevent any action that you now take. Only this will I say: be very careful, for all power, however great, has its limits and what was once given can also be taken away."*

Eventually they reached the keep gates. When they entered the courtyard, De Lisle jumped out to hand Madelyn down. Holding her hand tightly he said fiercely. "You must know that I would give it all up, for you to look at me, just once, as you do him." Then he released her, turned and ran into the castle, leaving Madelyn staring after him in astonishment and fear.

On the bed Miss Templeton moaned and stirred. This time, though, Miss Drew ignored her. She rose and left the room. Stopping only to ask a servant to take her place, she went down downstairs. Slipping unnoticed into the Earl's study, she left a small envelope addressed to Lord Thorne on the desk and then went out into the dark, still night.

*

"It is time to wake up, Miss Templeton."

The words, spoken quietly but firmly, had an instant effect. Theora stirred, opened her eyes and sat up. The last thing she remembered was leaving the room on the night of Juliet's party. Now she was on the top of a high hill in the centre of a green moor, with the Earl sitting opposite her. Instinctively she raised her hands to her ears but dropped them again as she realised that the whispering voices were now much fainter. The hill was crowned by a series of stones which ran in concentric circles, the smallest on the outside with six large ones creating an inner core. There was nothing else save a large pit in which burned a curious fire. The flames were very pale and even. They did not flicker but blazed with constant force and uniform heat.

"What is this place?" said Theora and was pleased to find that at least she had command of her voice.

The Earl did not say anything for a moment but looked thoughtfully at her. Then he got up and walked to the fire. He spoke a word and the flames on one side instantly extinguished.

"This is the oldest of our sacred places." He beckoned to her. "Come and look."

Theora stood up and walked to the pit. On one edge only coals remained. As she looked down, she saw that the pit was in fact a deep well and within, perhaps five feet below, there was a perpetual waterfall springing all around the edge and dropping away to an unimaginable depth. Far below, where the cascade disappeared into the darkness, she saw small but distinct lights. As she gazed, the lights moved together and to her amazement formed a perfect arc upon the water.

"They look like stars," she said and then felt immediately foolish.

His Lordship smiled slightly. "Indeed they are very much like stars, each being different and unchangeable. But, unlike stars that you see above, they once took human shape. Now, alas, these images are all that remain."

Theora stepped back from the pit and sat down again on one of the stones. "You are suggesting then that these were some sort of God-like creatures?"

The Earl looked down at her. At last he said, "Yes, God-like in that they once walked upon this Earth and gave us strength."

"Us?"

Lord Thorne, Lord De Lisle and I. We are the last of an ancient line of Sun and Moon Lords."

Theora stared at him in bewilderment. "But you and Lord De Lisle are enemies?"

"To a degree. But our personal feelings are not the issue. Our goals are very different. That is why we distrust each other."

"What is your goal?" said Theora breathlessly.

"To save mortals from certain oblivion," said the Earl.

"And Lord De Lisle's?"

"To save himself."

"I still do not understand," said Theora. "What do I have to do with any of this?"

"You, Miss Templeton, are the weapon which Lord De Lisle wishes to use against me. He is seeking ways to hurt me and distract me from my purpose. It was for this reason that he had you attacked."

"But, these voices I am hearing…" Theora broke off and pressed her hand to her head. "Is this something Lord De Lisle has caused to happen?"

The Earl hesitated. "It is not easy to explain, but I promise you, Lord De Lisle is not responsible. I am afraid that I am to blame."

Theora stared at him. "But I understood that it was you that saved me from the highwaymen. It was you who brought me back to Temple Court. That was what I was told."

"That is the truth. But there is more. Lord De Lisle caused the river to be raised. I was unable to bring you back immediately, so I used another way to protect you." He paused and looked at Theora directly. "I am sorry, but that is why you are now so distressed."

"I don't understand," said Theora. "Are you saying that you have passed on some sort of sickness?"

"Not a sickness," he said quickly, and for the first time in their acquaintance, he dropped his eyes. "It is an after effect that sometimes happens to mortal women that we choose." He stood up and turned away. "Forgive me."

Theora's mind was in confusion. "Forgive you for

what? I don't understand. You saved my life. What then do you have to reproach yourself for?"

A burst of laughter behind her made them both quickly turn. Lord De Lisle was suddenly standing before them. His expression was an unpleasant mixture of mirth and disgust.

"How touchingly naive you are, my dear," he said. He looked at Lord Sulien and made an elaborate bow. "And what an excellent storyteller you are, my dear Aidan. I really must compliment you. So direct and yet so heartfelt, I was really very impressed. You must forgive me for the interruption, but I'm afraid I couldn't wait for the denouement."

He strolled over to Miss Templeton and took her hand to kiss it. "How charming you are looking, my dear, quite blooming in fact. Can it be you are expecting a happy event?" He laughed again and the sound made Theora shiver. "Come now don't be shy, surely you must have guessed by now."

Lord Sulien stepped forward. "Take your hands off her, Bricin, or I will be forced to make you," he said.

Lord De Lisle looked him up and down, the smile still lingering.

"Oh, Aidan, you mistake me. I don't wish to brawl, simply to make sure that you do tell the whole story. After all she has a right doesn't she?"

Theora stood up between them. "I would be grateful if both of you stopped talking in riddles and gave me plain answers," she said a little breathlessly. "You first." She turned to Lord De Lisle. "Why are you here?"

Lord De Lisle looked amazed. "Why, I am here to help you, at Aidan's request too. I must congratulate you! It appears that you may not just bear a child, but possibly one that could inherit our power. You should also be grateful that you have the distinction of being the only woman to whom Aidan has, how can I put this this delicately? Shown any special favour, for at least eighteen years by my reckoning. He really must care about you to break his own special rules of restraint. He did save your life. Even if you are now losing your mind because of it."

There was a silence. Theora looked at Lord Sulien. He met her glance squarely and suddenly all her memories became straight and clear once more. Her heart began to pound and she blushed until she was red to the roots of her hair.

"I am going to have a baby and I am going mad," said Theora stunned. "Wouldn't it have been better to just let me die, than live and have to bear this disgrace?"

She held them both with her eyes and then said bitingly, "I suppose that wouldn't have been so safe. If I had died that would have raised all sorts of questions. You would then have to break off your own private war."

Lord De Lisle rocked with laughter.

"Oh excellent stuff, you really are rather a treasure aren't you. But, don't be afraid, Aidan will soon lose interest in you. As you can see, he is far happier playing with his knights and, of course, his fires."

Lord Sulien stepped forward into the light and, as he did so, a sheet of flame spread in front of him and stopped just short of De Lisle's feet. "On that subject, I am sure I don't need to remind you of the way back down, Bricin."

Lord De Lisle stepped back a pace but now he was no longer smiling. "I take the point, but in return I would remind you that, according to our ancient laws, using our gifts, except to heal, is not permitted in this place."

The flames extinguished as quickly as they had appeared and there was another flash as Lord Sulien drew his sword. "I am happy to resolve this any way you choose."

Lord De Lisle raised his hand, but Theora stepped quickly between them.

"If you want to kill yourselves I'd be grateful if you did it after you get rid of these voices in my head. What do I have to do?"

"Nothing at all," said Lord De Lisle and he now sounded bored. "I just need to touch your forehead for a moment." He drew off his gloves. "Forgive my cold hands but it has been a long journey." Reaching forward he extended his fingers and placed the tips on Theora's brow. She saw the faintest glow as he took his hand away, saying brightly, "All done." He looked at Lord Sulien. "I suppose my presence here is now no longer required and you want me to take myself off, Aidan?" He sighed. "Such a pity, I really would like to hear what this lady now has to say to you."

"I am sure you do," said Lord Sulien. "But, I am sure that you also recognise that to stay any longer would be extremely unwise."

De Lisle cast him a look of hatred. Deliberately turning his back, he bowed to Theora. "I am sure we will be meeting again, so no goodbyes for the present."

He then walked away down the hill and, although Theora strained her eyes, she couldn't tell when he had disappeared. For a moment, she heard the sound of very faint music and Lord De Lisle's voice spoke mockingly in her head:

"Until our next meeting." Then the music ceased and there was just the sound of the wind buffeting the hills.

Theora found that her legs suddenly felt very weak and she sat down. She looked at Lord Sulien directly. "Would you please tell me what you are planning to do with me now?"

She saw that he seemed confused and unusually

uncertain.

"Do with you? Why, take you back to Temple Court of course."

"And have you found a new governess for Juliet?"

He looked astonished. "Of course not, why would I?"

She looked resolutely ahead. "If you would be so good to pay my outstanding wages, I can make arrangements to leave by the end of the week, Sir."

"Now that's enough." He grasped her shoulders. "You need to understand, you can't leave."

She shook her head. "You will have to lock me up then."

He swore under his breath. "I have no intention of keeping you prisoner." His eyes searched her pale face. "Look at me, you little idiot."

She met his gaze reluctantly and saw that his eyes were blazing. She took a breath. "Well what do you intend, Sir?"

To her surprise he released her abruptly, walked to the edge of the ring and looked down. Then he came back again and took her hands in his. She noticed how scarred they were and wondered, vaguely, why, if he was some sort of God, he looked so battered and knocked about. She sought to draw her hands away but he held them firmly. His voice was very low almost a hoarse whisper.

"Will you do me the very great honour to become my wife?"

"No, no," said Theora, chokingly. She wrenched away, ran to the edge of the circle and looked down. There was no visible sign of any path. She gave a moan.

"Please let me go, I beg of you."

He was as pale as she. "You have to understand, you are in danger and will remain so until…"

"Until I have your child. I know that's all you care about."

The words were out before she could stop them. He hesitated and then said clearly, "I suppose you wouldn't believe me if I said that my feelings for you are sincere."

"No," said Theora, simply. "I wouldn't. I can believe that you feel this situation touches your honour and so sincerely want to make things right. However, I am still a free woman." She looked keenly at him. "Is that not so? Am I not free to make my own choices?"

"What do you wish?"

"Before I answer, you must swear that you will help me."

"I will, provided you swear that you have no intention of harming yourself in any way."

"Very well, I pledge it. Now, hear my request."

"I am listening."

"I never, ever, want to see you again."

His face, shorn now of expression, was strangely bleak and grey. "You have my promise. When you leave this hill, I promise you will never see me again." He whistled and Apollo came trotting up the hill. His Lordship mounted and without a backward glance rode away into the valley.

*

Then the world spun away and Theora found herself once more in her bedroom at Temple Court. She had no way of assessing how much time had elapsed. The light was cold and grey and for the first time since she had returned to Surrey, there was no welcoming fire in the grate. She did not stop to look around but instantly went to the wardrobe, took out her trunk and began to pack. She had not been more than a few minutes when there was a soft knock at the door. Her heart stopped at the thought that it might be the Earl and she hastily pushed the trunk beneath the bed. She opened the door carefully and was relieved to find that it was Miss Drew carrying a tray.

"I have brought you a hot drink," she said. Looking past her into the room, her eyebrows rose at the sight of the dresses strewn about the bed. "Let me help you get this tidied up."

Without waiting for Theora to respond, she came past her into the room, set the tray down and said. "Before we get started, shall we have a cup of tea?"

"It is really very kind of you, but I can manage on my own," said Theora stiffly.

Miss Drew said nothing. She poured two cups and added lemon to hers and cream to Theora's.

"You cannot manage on your own, Miss Templeton, and that is why I am here. Now drink your tea."

Theora found herself obeying despite her confusion. The warmth of the liquid and the quiet calm of her companion began to make her relax.

Miss Drew set down her cup. "Now then, let us talk."

She held up her hand as Theora prepared to speak. "There is no need to attempt to construct some sort of fabricated tale, Miss Templeton. I know what has happened. You see, I have been in Lord Thorne's service for a very long time."

"You know about Lord Sulien and Lord De Lisle," breathed Theora. "Will you tell me what you know?"

"I will tell you what I can," said Miss Drew steadily, "but it is now more important that we get you quickly to a place of safety where you can have your child."

She saw Theora was blushing and said with concern, "Please don't be embarrassed." She poured herself another cup of tea. "It takes us in different ways you see," she said reflectively. "Sometimes, as in the case of Juliet's mother, nothing happens except a normal child is conceived. Occasionally, the mothers are temporarily gifted with the power of a Sun or Moon Lord, which is why you heard the thoughts of other mortals. In very rare circumstances, the mother's gift is prolonged and this can be dangerous. That is why we needed aid from Lord De Lisle. He has the gift of healing mortals which unfortunately my master and Lord Aidan do not."

"I suppose I should be grateful," said Theora, her voice shaking.

Miss Drew looked at her. "You should. I, for one, envy you exceedingly. I would have given up every year of my extended life, just to have borne a child for my master. Alas, it was that gift that prevented me from conceiving a child."

Theora picked up one of the dresses and began to fold it. "You were Lord Thorne's mistress," she said after a moment.

"I was," said Miss Drew, "but that was a very, very long time ago. Now I am nothing to him. I am just another servant in the great Quest. You, Miss Templeton, also have a part to play and it may be that your child does too. I know you have turned your back on Lord Aidan and I understand your reasons, but you cannot go forward alone. I am here to assist you."

Theora continued to pack. "Does Lord Thorne know that you have offered me help?"

"Yes," said Miss Drew. "He respects your desire to distance yourself from Lord Aidan at this time. That is why he has not come himself."

Theora turned. "I do not think I have any choice but to trust you," she said. "I would be glad of your help, Miss Drew. I must confess that now I have quit Lord Sulien's service I have absolutely no idea what to do. Do you have a plan? I think I need to get right away from England."

Miss Drew came to her and the two women sat down side by side upon the bed. "I agree that you should leave England as soon as possible," said Miss Drew. "I thought that you might go to France, but that would be too easy for Lord De Lisle to attack you. My suggestion is Venice."

Theora looked her surprise. "Why so far away?"

"In a previous century, Lord De Lisle made an enemy of the reigning Doge. This Doge made an alliance with the Sun Lords. If you go there, the Venetians will give you protection. Also, my master has asked one of his new knights to join you. I believe you know him? Mr Irving, from America."

"I do indeed," said Theora. "Yet, to get to Venice will take a very long time and would be quite a complicated journey. I am not sure if my health" – she choked slightly on the word – "will be up to such a sustained voyage by sea and land."

"Of course not," said Miss Drew. "That is why we will need to go via another, faster way. Let us finish the packing and I will show it to you." She smiled reassuringly. "Please don't worry, Miss Templeton, I promise you, all will be well."

Theora smiled uncertainly. "Then, as we are to be travelling companions, will you please call me Theora from now on?"

"Gladly, and I am Madelyn. Now, let us get you ready."

They bent to their task. Theora watched her new friend with a mixture of curiosity and awe. She fought down her desire to ask questions and happily allowed herself to be directed. As Madelyn was preparing to close the trunk, she stopped her. "You have something else to add?" asked Madelyn.

"Yes," said Theora. She reached within the collar of her dress and pulled out the pendant. "I was wondering if this should go with the luggage or remain with me," she said a little shyly.

Madelyn looked at the jewel on Theora's palm.

"Where did you get that?" she said hoarsely.

"The Rector of Rodsall gave it to me for safe-keeping," said Theora.

"I see," said Madelyn. She let out a deep sigh. "You have been wearing it?"

"Yes, on and off. Is that a problem?"

Madelyn looked at her intently. "I presume it has aided your strength these last weeks?"

"Yes, although not since…" Theora broke off.

Madelyn nodded. "No, that is not why it was created," she said. She turned and closed and locked the trunk. Taking the key she slipped it into her pocket. "I think that, for now, you should keep the stone with you, but tell nobody else about it. I don't know how the Rector came by this relic, but he obviously wanted it kept secret. Now, let us go."

They made their way down the stairs and towards the Earl's study. At the door they were met by Meadows. He nodded to Theora understandingly and bowed to Madelyn. Theora hesitated, but Meadows pushed the door open and ushered them in.

"Please do not be concerned, Miss Templeton," he said. "Lord Aidan has advised that he will now be away from the house for some time. Good luck with your journey." He shut the door behind them.

Madelyn walked towards the great globe. "Come here and hold my hand," she commanded. Theora did so and as she stood looking at the globe it started to spin and upon its brown surface a scene appeared of shining coloured buildings with strange, tall chimneys and unusually shaped windows suspended upon a glimmering web of water. Then the cold winter chill was replaced by a warm summer breeze and the ceaseless sound of swifts and swallows filled the air.

Chapter Seventeen

Lord De Lisle, Moon Lord and millionaire, drove through the hills of Nouvelle Aquitaine on a scorching hot afternoon in June. For once, he was not pushing the Jaguar to its limits, but proceeding at a reasonable pace. He reflected that, although he seldom travelled outside the 20th century, when he came to the 21st (dangerous though it was) he always enjoyed the trips immensely. He was feeling extremely satisfied. Although he had been surprised at the way the events were proceeding in 1803, it amused him to think that he had been asked by his enemy to assist Miss Templeton. He knew that the Earl must have been desperate to make such a request and it could only have been prompted by the deepest anxiety. Irrespective of whether she bore the Earl's child, he was now more than ever resolved to win Miss Templeton's affection and so humiliate the Sun Lord.

He turned the car into a valley spangled with olive trees that led to the cliff top. Set a little way back from the crest was a fine Chateau, its towers outlined against the very blue sky. There was a long drive which finally gave way to a courtyard with a fountain. De Lisle pulled the car up in the shade and stepped out onto the gravel. He was wearing the casual, but expensive, clothes of the period, jeans, a silk T-shirt, deck shoes and vintage Ray-Ban sunglasses, which he swept off his face and pushed into his hair. He walked to the door and rang the bell, glancing with amusement at the sign on the wall that read: 'Val sans Retour'. [10] He was let in by a pencil-slim

---

[10] In Arthurian legend, the Val sans retour (Vale of No Return or Valley Without Return), also known as the Val des faux amants (Vale of False Lovers) or the Val périlleux (Perilous Vale), is an enchanted land in which the sorceress Morgan le Fay imprisons her knightly lovers until the spell is eventually broken by Lancelot.

man who greeted him courteously and informed him that Madame was waiting for him by the pool. Refusing the offer of escort, De Lisle made his own way round the house to the marble pool lavishly and tastelessly flanked with statues of Roman and Greek Gods and Goddesses. On the left was an iron pergola, dripping with highly scented, blowsy pink roses. Under the pergola were a number of sun loungers and reclining upon one of these, face down, was the film star.

She turned her head slightly. "Good afternoon, my Lord."

"Good afternoon, yourself," said Lord De Lisle carelessly. He sat down. "How are you, Jenny?"

"Well enough," she said shortly. She sat up. "Good journey?"

"Very," said his Lordship. He ran his eyes over her. "Yes you look very well," he said. "It is most satisfying to see. I doubt if there is another mortal woman in any reality to touch you."

"Naturally," said Jennifer. She stood up stretching languorously.

"I'm thirsty, do you want a drink?"

He smiled. "Naturally."

"Try this." She extended her hand and in it was a small bottle. He opened it and sniffed.

"I was expecting a cocktail."

"You can have one in a minute," she said impatiently. "Just take a sip."

De Lisle put the bottle to his lips and drank. The next minute he sat down hurriedly.

"What on Old Earth is it?"

She smiled. "Think of an animal, any animal."

"Ok, I'm thinking of a leopard," said De Lisle. "What happens next?"

"That's up to you. But I'd suggest you try jumping the

pool."

De Lisle laughed. "I wasn't planning on swimming with my clothes on!"

Jennifer took the bottle from his hand. "Just try it. I promise that you'll be pleased."

De Lisle grinned. "Fine, here goes." He ran at the pool and jumped. As he did so, he let out a shout of surprise and exhilaration, for instead of landing in the middle as he had expected, he found himself easily on the other side, coming down lightly crouched upon the balls of his feet on the smooth marble slabs.

Jennifer clapped. "Very good, well done," she said in a bored, flat voice.

De Lisle looked down at the water. The reflection that gazed back at him was of a sleek, shining, spotted cat with his own sparkling blue eyes. Jennifer walked up and handed him a glass. "You can have that cocktail now. How about a strawberry Daiquiri?"

De Lisle took the glass and drank it down. "I should be the one applauding."

Jennifer lowered her long eyelashes. "I take it you're pleased?"

"Extremely. I knew you would be an able student but I never dreamed that you would take your skills this far."

"I thought we could dispense it amongst our knights," said Jennifer seriously. "If you still want to go ahead?"

"More than ever. Now I know all the details of this pathetic quest, it is vital that we mount an attack as soon as possible. That will create a suitable diversion."

"A diversion for what?"

De Lisle smiled. "All in good time. What else have you got to show me?"

"Well I've been working on my counter cantus, as you advised, and I've got a really good one, but I don't know how we could apply it."

"Show me."

"Very well." Jenny leaned over and picked up a small silver-mounted bell which she rang briefly. Seconds later the manservant appeared.

"Paul, would you bring me the green box from my inner wardrobe please?"

The man withdrew and returned with the box which he put on the table.

"Will there be anything else?"

"No thank you. Lord De Lisle and I will be out in the garden for the rest of the afternoon, so please make sure we aren't disturbed."

"Certainly," said Paul. He hesitated. "Mr Gardiner has been ringing on the hour, every hour, since this morning. Shall I continue to ignore him?"

Jennifer inclined her head. "Yes, by all means ignore the phone."

She watched Paul's departing back. "Jealous men are such a bore."

De Lisle finished his cocktail. "I can't keep track of all your admirers. Who's this one?"

"He's the director of my current film and very talented, so I can't just turn him into a toad or something."

De Lisle laughed.

"Been doing a lot of that?"

"No, I don't like wasting the gift that way. Talking of which…" Jennifer opened the box. "What do you think?" she said lifting out a black satin cape.

"Bit old fashioned for the 21st century isn't it? Are you planning to use it in a film?"

"I was actually planning to make a present of it, to someone in the 19th Century."

De Lisle looked intent. "Why?"

"Watch." Jennifer draped the cloak gracefully around

a bust of Apollo. Instantly the stone statue turned to solid glass and shattered.

Jennifer looked at De Lisle proudly. "Good isn't it?"

"Wonderful. We will definitely need to find a use for it."

"But that's the problem," said Jenny crossly. "I can't quite think how."

"Never mind and please don't be cross, I prefer your delightful smile." De Lisle patted the seat beside him. "Come and sit down. You have been working hard."

"Thank you. I do deserve a bit of a holiday. Will you be able to stay a while? I really do want to get the cantus multiplied and you do that stuff so well."

Lisle curiously studied the exquisite but intense face, with its glowing amber eyes. "Are you still so hungry for revenge?"

The golden eyes shadowed. "Always."

"I almost feel sorry for Aidan," said Lord De Lisle. "Nothing like the wrath of a woman scorned."

He ran a finger down her silken arm from shoulder to wrist.

"Strange how he was immune to all this perfection. It was such a pity that our close contact spy plan didn't work, but he was never remotely interested was he? I believe he paid more attention when you were poor little Jenny the innkeeper's daughter with the red face."

Jennifer's face hardened. "Don't," she said tersely.

De Lisle lifted her hand, it sparkled with jewels. "It doesn't matter," he said. He pressed the hand to his lips. "Remind me to bring you some more opals for being such a clever girl. And yes, I will stay for a while, my pretty Jenny. You deserve it. And now, for the rest of your reward." He put her hand down and leaned forward to kiss her.

*

267

Many hours later, the sun went down and a cool, delicious night replaced the shimmering heat. Lord De Lisle, leaving Jenny sleeping in her white satin bed, went down to the beach to look at the sea. He threw himself down on the sand and stared up at the full moon. Then he concentrated and sent his thought across time and space to the 19th Century. Lord Sulien, who was sitting in the Knight's Club, stiffened. Lord De Lisle spoke clearly into his mind.

"Good evening, Aidan."

Lord Sulien relaxed. The momentary shock of the sudden contact had passed. "What do you want, Bricin?"

"I have a proposition for you," said Lord De Lisle. "One which will avoid much bloodshed, if you are willing to accept it."

"I am listening."

"Very well, it is simply this. Allow me to bring Miss Templeton to dwell in my domain and I will never again raise a hand against you, or your knights."

Lord Sulien's lips tightened. "You know I won't agree to that."

"Why not? I now know that you only brought her to Temple Court to distract me from your precious quest. So, I thank you for that and gratefully accept the gift. She is a charming creature."

"She is also under my protection."

"Oh, don't be ridiculous! What is the life of one mortal in comparison with the fate of Old Earth? Will you risk everything for a woman who means nothing to you?"

Lord Sulien's hands clenched on the velvet arm rests, but after a moment they relaxed and he said in a voice from which all emotion was banished, "I have watched you use and abuse a number of innocent women. Miss Templeton is a lady for whom I only have the greatest respect. My answer is, again, no."

"You remain, as always, a self-indulgent fool," said Lord De Lisle coldly. "You may not admit it, but you are attracted to her and her obvious affection for you has touched your vanity. It is history repeating itself all over again. Except, this time, at least the woman is a cut above the silly little miss you wedded and bedded, after I'd had her first."

Lord Sulien stood up. As he did so, there was a sudden sound like cracking and within the Club, the walls and floors shook. In the 21st century, Lord De Lisle was flung across the sand as if he had been picked up by a giant hand. He fell back down holding his head. The mental blow Lord Sulien had dealt him would have killed him, had he been in the same reality. As it was he was left faint and drained. He struggled for breath.

"So," he said at last, his voice choked with pain, "you wish to keep up the charade. Well I warn you that I will not take this refusal lightly."

Lord Sulien sat down again. He waved away his knights who had clustered around him in confusion and concern.

"And I warn you that if you ever threaten me again, I will not be so merciful. Now leave me and never again contact me this way." With that the Earl abruptly severed the connection.

For a long time afterwards Lord De Lisle lay upon the wet sand. When at last he managed to sit up he was bathed in sweat.

He went down to the sea's edge and vomited into the tide which was edging its way up the beach. Then he walked back to the mansion. Jenny was still sleeping, but he passed by her room and slipped into the shower. Fifteen minutes later Jenny found him there, naked under the streams of water, leaning against the black and silver tiles. She stared at him in astonishment. "Are you all right?"

"Get out," he said.

She looked at his white set face. She hesitated for a moment and then left him.

*

In the Club, Lord Sulien had gone to a private room and been joined by Lord Thorne. "I heard what happened," he said. "Does he know the truth about Miss Templeton?"

"No," said Lord Sulien. "He knows a great deal, but not that."

"What were you able to find out?"

"Not much, we were not connected very long. He has become very strong and much of his mind was closed. However, I do know that he travelled backwards and somehow he has had contact with Queen Edith."

Lord Thorne let out one long breath. "How has he managed it? That door was closed long ago?"

The Earl nodded. "So we thought, but somehow there was an opportunity to open it and Bricin has used it to his advantage. We must just be grateful that he went that way for his information and did not try another. On that subject, please find Brummell and bring him to me."

Moments later George Brummell came in.

"George, I need you to disappear," said the Earl without preamble.

"My Lord I am all ready to go to Cornwall with Lord Nelson, the plan was…"

"I know the plan," interrupted the Earl, "but it must now change. You need to go back with Lord Thorne to his domain and stay there to guard Leonardo. It is imperative that he is kept safe and out of Lord De Lisle's reach."

Brummell gave a slightly twisted smile. "You want me out of reach too, don't you, Aidan. Why, may I ask?"

"I am afraid that Lord De Lisle has learned about the Quest. Our only piece of fortune is that he has no knowledge regarding Miss Templeton's true identity. I have managed to deceive him. He believes that she is important to me, but nothing else. I have hope that he will now leave her alone. However, it is vital that the secret is kept until the very last moment. I have no concerns regarding Lord Thorne's ability to conceal the truth, but you are the only other who knows the full tale."

"And I am a mortal," said Mr Brummell. "Yes, I see. Well, much as I wished to help with the battle, I equally have no desire to be tortured by Lord De Lisle."

"Very wise," said Lord Thorne approvingly. "You are of course welcome to stay with Leonardo at Ashleworth for however long you wish."

"No thank you," said Mr Brummell. "We will go to Rome."

"I am not sure that is wise," said Lord Thorne. "Ashleworth is the safest place."

"I am sure it is," said Mr Brummell, "but it will also be incredibly dull. You know I loathe the country! Rome is the only place for both safety and sociability. I have friends there, we will be well looked after."

"Very well," said the Earl. "Come with me and I will make the necessary arrangements."

He led Mr Brummell back to the cavern. Samuel instantly rose from his desk.

"Yes, my Lord, you require a key?"

"I do. The Vatican Palace, guard's entrance."

Samuel bowed. He opened a drawer and drew from it a thin gold chain with a delicate key of cut steel attached. The Earl took it and nodding to Brummell they walked to a small door that was hidden away in the shadows. It was padlocked and the Earl inserted the key in the lock. The padlock fell away and the door swung open. Through the entrance was a courtyard. The two men walked through. As they did so, the door made to swing shut, but the Earl blocked it with his foot and held it open.

Brummell looked round.

"This is within the Vatican precincts then?"

"Yes. Very soon you will be joined by one of the guards. He will ensure you have safe escort wherever you need to go. I will ask Argus to send Leonardo to you."

"Thank you," said Brummell. He looked steadily at the Earl. "Is this goodbye then, Aidan?"

"I hope not," said the Earl. "I would indeed be sorry not to see you again, my friend. But, alas, when this door closes, there will be no chance for you to return this way. If we should meet again, it will only be by the grace of the Maiden."

"I see," said Brummell. "In which case I thank you again for all your many kindnesses and giving me the honour to serve you, my Lord."

The Earl opened the door behind him and turned to go. "Farewell, George. I cannot foretell what the future may hold, but my heart tells me that we will meet again. Until that time comes, take care of yourself please."

*

Back at the Club, Lord Thorne was waiting for him. "You're not still in pain?"

"I am not," said the Earl. "However, I am very, very angry."

He walked over to one of the card tables and began absently turning over some of the discarded cards. As he did so, a few turned red and started to flame at the edges.

Lord Thorne leaned over and hastily patted them out. "Don't burn us down will you?" he said cheerfully.

The Earl looked down at the blackened cards. "I'm sorry," he said bleakly.

Lord Thorne rested his hand upon his shoulder. "There

is no need to apologise, we have plenty more cards to play with."

"I didn't mean that," said the Earl. "I was referring to Miss Templeton. I wish I knew what I could do to make amends."

"There is nothing," said Lord Thorne. "Put it from your mind. The girl is as safe as we can make her, which is all that could be done."

"I'm not so sure. I offered her marriage and she refused me. As my wife I could have given her both my name and my protection. Without both, she remains vulnerable. I do not understand why she would refuse me."

Lord Thorne went to the window and looked out. In the distance was the sea and the sun was sinking slowly upon it. When he spoke his voice was hard and he did not turn around.

"In all our many years together, I have always thought you as unlike Bricin as was possible. Yet now I hear you speak with similar conceit! I am not at all surprised that Theora refused you. What amazes me is that you expected any other response. You really don't know her at all."

The Earl looked at him strangely. "And you do?"

"Perhaps."

"Then it is a pity you weren't there to rescue her when she needed assistance," said the Earl coldly.

"Indeed it was. You should have waited for me to join you and then we could have effected a suitable response without all these repercussions. It was unlike you to have acted impulsively. I can only think of one reason."

"Which is?"

"That you are truly in love with the girl."

"That's ridiculous."

"Is it? She is very patently in love with you, a fact that

I am sure you are well aware of."

The Earl was about to speak, but he broke off as a waiter appeared at his elbow.

"Dinner is about to be served, my Lord."

The Club dining room was already full when the Earl and Lord Thorne entered. For a while no further conversation was possible. But eventually, after the steady consumption of duck and peas and half a bottle of claret, the Earl spoke again.

"So, you believe I took advantage of the situation and abused Miss Templeton's trust?"

Lord Thorne wiped his mouth with a napkin.

"Hardly," he said. "I have no doubt that whilst you now regret the incident, given the same situation, you would not have acted any differently. My concern now is that having taken these steps, you have set us upon a course where there will be consequences. However, my advice is to concentrate upon the work in hand. Irving will look after her."

"Very well," said the Earl. "But, will you keep her under your protection please?"

"I will," said Lord Thorne. "I will do whatever I can."

"Thank you," said the Earl. He looked tired but his face seemed suddenly relieved of care. "Let us now return to Temple Court, so you may see my new racing curricle. It arrived from London yesterday."

"Excellent," said Lord Thorne laughing. He looked slyly at the Earl. "I assume that you will be pleased to let me drive it?"

"Sadly, no. You are the best of friends, but when it comes to carriage driving, you have never had my confidence."

They returned through time to Temple Court, 1803. In the stable yard the new carriage was being duly admired by the grooms and stable boys. A pair of grey horses were being coupled to it. The Earl eyed them with approval.

"They are looking well." Then as an aside to Lord Thorne he whispered, "I am glad I was able to take them out of time, until we needed them."

He mounted the carriage. "Shall we take a turn round the park?"

Lord Thorne shook his head. "I think I will leave you to fully test it. I will meet you later, back at the Club."

He watched the carriage disappear, remembering, as he did so, the first time he had seen the Earl drive this particular pair, nearly twenty-six years ago…

"What do you think of them, Argus?"

"Very fine," said Lord Thorne. "This is the new team from Scotland then?"

"Yes, I bought them off old Charlie McCall," said the Earl. "They are the fastest horses in the country."

"They look a couple of devils," said Lord Thorne with feeling.

The Earl ignored him. He watched a groom jump away from a viciously aimed kick and moved between him and the nearest horse.

"Socraich sìos mo charaid,"[11] he said clearly.

At once the horse dropped its head and stood as still as stone.

The Earl looked back at Lord Thorne and winked. Despite himself Lord Thorne grinned.

"Even so, I am not sure I fancy getting up behind them."

"Nonsense," said the Earl. He beckoned to one of the grooms. "Hurry up, man, there's no need to fear, they won't touch you now."

---

[11] Settle down my friend.

He waited until the horses were put to and both men climbed up.

"Ready, Argus?"

"I suppose so." Lord Thorne sat back, holding on tightly, and at a word from the Earl, the horses sprang forward. When they reached the edge of the grounds they turned onto a sandy road.

"So, let's now see how they perform at best pace," said the Earl.

Lord Thorne sat up. "Be careful, Aidan," he said nervously.

"Are you afraid?" asked the Earl. "If not, I dare you to come and sit beside me." He pulled the team to a halt. "Hurry now, I can't hold them for long."

He waited until Lord Thorne had climbed up and then let go of the horses' heads. They ate up the track. The Earl sat behind them, perfectly poised in complete balance, but Lord Thorne held onto the seat and looked down. When at last the Earl pulled up, he looked distinctly green.

"Han eil e gu math dona,"[12] said the Earl.

He glanced at Lord Thorne.

"How are you feeling?"

"As I always do after one of your drives," said Lord Thorne. "Sick."

"It will pass," said the Earl. "The important thing is that this rig is ready to help us with the Quest."

"I'll be interested to know how," said Lord Thorne. He was about to speak again, when, suddenly, he whipped round. "Declare yourself," he said clearly.

The Earl followed his gaze to the side of the road. He leaned back into the curricle and drew out his whip, but

---

[12] Not at all bad

lowered it when the figure emerged from the trees. It was a woman, with auburn hair and large amber eyes. She was wearing a green riding habit and leading a bay mare.

Lord Thorne stared incredulously. "Jennifer Layton," he said after a moment. "What on Old Earth are you doing here?"

There was a silence. The woman turned her gaze onto the Earl, but he was looking past her.

"Have you nothing to say to me, my Lord?" she said at last, but her voice was low and trembling, as if the words had been forced out of her.

The Earl ignored her. "It is time we went back, Argus," he said.

Lord Thorne immediately descended from the curricle.

"I'd like Jennifer to tell us why she is here first," he said.

The Earl gathered up his reins. "As you wish. I will see you back at the house."

At that Jennifer ran to the curricle. "Do you still hate me so much?" she said in a low voice, her eyes searching his face. "Is there no forgiveness in your heart, even for the sake of my sister whom we both loved?"

The Earl looked down at her. "You dare to speak of her, after what you have done?" he said. "You do not change. You are as selfish as ever."

At that he made a sign and the horses turned, so quickly that if Lord Thorne had not reached forward and pulled her back, Jennifer would have been thrown to the ground as they passed. As it was she was only saved by his protective arm which held her tightly until the carriage had drawn away. Jennifer watched it hungrily until it had passed completely out of sight. Then she disengaged herself from Lord Thorne's hold and sat down upon the verge.

"Thank you," she said tonelessly.

He stared at her in concern. "What are you doing here?" he said. "You have taken a great risk. If Aidan had chosen to, he could have killed you just then and I would have had no way of saving you."

She ran a shaking hand through her hair.

"Yes, I know."

"So, why put yourself in such danger?"

She licked her lips. "I suppose you haven't got a drink anywhere around have you?"

He hesitated and reached into his pocket, withdrawing a flask which he passed to her.

She slowly sipped the brandy.

"I am surprised that you didn't just cantus yourself one of those," he said after a moment.

"You know that if I used sorcery here Aidan would punish me. I wouldn't want to take the risk just for a drink."

"No I suppose not," said Lord Thorne. He looked her over. "Why are you here?" he said after a moment.

"I need your help."

Lord Thorne hesitated. "For myself I would always wish to help you, Jenny. But you have seen how it is with Aidan. He cannot forget that it was through your alliance with Bricin that Lizzie came to die before her time."

"But Lizzie's death was not my fault," said Jennifer angrily. "You know that!"

"I did not say it was, but she was still lost," said Lord Thorne sadly.

"I see," said Jennifer. "Well then I must 'put all my eggs in one basket', as we used to say. You have received my letter?"

"I do not recollect... stay, I think the post came this morning but we have been away, so I have not yet seen it."

"Then I ask you to return as soon as possible to Temple Court," said Jennifer. She walked back to her horse, felt the girths and mounted. "I will await your response in the village. I have taken rooms at the Good Intent so you can send a message there. If I don't hear from you within the day, I will leave and never trouble you again."

"You cannot just tell me what is wrong?" said Lord Thorne gently.

"I do not have the heart to, not now," she said simply. "I had hoped..." She broke off. "Anyway, it doesn't matter anymore, but I don't want to stay any longer than I have to in this domain. I can feel Aidan's hatred all around me now." She pressed a hand to her throat. "It's suffocating me."

"I understand," said Lord Thorne. He reached up and pressed her hand. "I promise you an answer within the day."

"You have been so kind," she said gratefully. "I am sorry if this causes you problems with Aidan. I would never wish to be the cause of any dispute between you."

Lord Thorne smiled. "I can handle Aidan."

"Yes of course." She touched the horse with her heel and cantered away.

Lord Thorne watched her go. He walked out to the edge of the park and whistled three times. A few minutes later a black stallion came galloping out of the trees. Lord Thorne swung onto its back and they rode back to Temple Court.

He found the Earl in the conservatory. His eyes were shut and he looked as if he had been asleep, but as Lord Thorne came in he opened them quickly.

"You are angry with me?"

Lord Thorne sat down.

"Not angry exactly. Just concerned. Has it occurred to

you that she may actually be of use now?"

"I don't trust her"

"That is quite obvious. However, I do. I think she has come to us for help and if we assist her now, that could be for everyone's mutual gain."

The Earl sighed and rubbed his eyes. "You may be right," he said heavily. "If I promise to not interfere with whatever plan you make between you, will that suffice?"

"It is a beginning," said Lord Thorne. "I have arranged to meet with her and when I do I will advise you of what is agreed, but that will be the extent of your involvement."

"Here is the letter she sent," said the Earl. He handed it to Lord Thorne. "Take it and go."

"Very well," said Lord Thorne. He went to the door. "I will message you later."

"Yes, do that," said the Earl.

Chapter Eighteen

The late afternoon sun burnished the brilliant façade of the Doge's Palace. High upon the skyline above St Mark's Square, four ancient, bronze horses gazed down impassively at the Café Florian far below. Here, groups of Venetians, mingled with foreign visitors, clustered around the precious pools of shade. Throughout the afternoon there had been a long, languid lingering over cups of chilled coffee, the ceaseless consumption of cake and a stream of sophisticated conversation. Now the elegant ladies and gentlemen were leaving for their palaces. They peeled away from the Café in their fine, bright silks, like petals falling from the heart of some exotic flower. At last there was only one couple left: a slim, dark-haired young woman accompanied by an older man. These two sat quietly together, so close that, to an outward observer, it would have been easy to have taken them for lovers. The man held his companion's small, white hand loosely in his beneath the table, but it was not an amorous clasp. Indeed the waiter, who removed their spent coffee cups, thought that it seemed more of a protective gesture than anything else. The man's glance when it strayed to the young lady's face held no hint of anything but gentle concern. She continued to look away from him as she had all afternoon, and her face was expressionless. At last she sighed and stirred and shivered. The man immediately reached for her wrap but the woman shook her head.

"I'm not cold, thank you, Guy."

Guy Irving put the wrap down again. "Do you want to go home?"

Theora Templeton looked up. "I suppose we must," she said with reluctance. "I do hate this time of day."

He looked down at the ground and brushed it lightly

with his right foot. It was an instinctive movement and toe to heel made a tap. Somehow the sound was strangely derisory. "Let's get off the street shall we? Before everyone starts staring."

He offered his arm and they walked to a gondola stop. Soon they had set off across the lagoon. Lamps were starting to be lit and were reflected back across the water. In the dark interior of the boat, Theora leaned back against the silk cushions and Irving took off his hat. It was strange, thought Theora watching him, that even with his hair ruffled and his tie loose, he still was the most elegant and sophisticated man she had ever seen. As they sat together in companionable silence, Theora remembered that day when she had descended from the hill after her meeting with the Earl. Having travelled with Madelyn to Venice they had stayed together in a palace owned by one of Lord Thorne's friends and guarded by the Venetian Knights. They spent the time helping Theora understand the nature of the Quest and answering her questions regarding the history of the Perdurare. Then, after they had been there for a few weeks, Mr Irving had joined them. Theora had found that Madelyn was serious by nature, so she was grateful for Mr Irving's engaging presence and help as a guide to the city. But this pleasant interlude lasted only for a few weeks. Whilst they were studying Titian's Assumption at the Frari, Theora had suddenly felt faint. During the confused jumble of days that had followed, she drifted in and out of high fever, into reality and back again. When she was eventually conscious and the pain had passed, she was told by the Doctor that not only had she lost her unborn child, but her chances of ever bearing another were now virtually nonexistent. Afterwards, she had been listless for a few days, yet she physically recovered quickly and when Irving was at last allowed to visit her, despite having lost a little weight, he thought she was as lovely as she had ever been. But her bitterness of spirit remained. All she could think about was the fact that she had lost her baby. Even the fact that Madelyn had left them unexpectedly did not distract her. Irving had continued to act as her escort, but, although he concealed his fears, he was very concerned. His instructions from Lord Thorne were clear: he was not to pressure Theora in any way. Yet he knew that time was running out for her to make a decision as to whether she would aid the Quest, or abandon it.

They both started, as the boatman suddenly leaned into the cabin and said that they were about to reach the palace. Inside the windows were open to welcome the breeze and supper was laid. Theora removed her hat and watched as Guy helped himself to wine from the decanter. This was a routine they had adopted over the last few weeks. A shared supper and then Irving made the short walk to his own apartment. Tonight, though, it was different and they both knew it. Theora made up her mind. "May I have some wine please?" she said decidedly. Irving looked surprised but silently poured a small glass and handed it to her. Theora drank slowly, wrinkling her nose slightly until the warmth of the liquor flooded through her and she had passed noticing the taste. She drained the last drop and then clasped her hands firmly in her lap. This was a childish gesture she had never lost.

"So what do I need to do to help?" she asked.

Irving looked her over soberly, taking in the tension that held the little figure so tightly still, knowing the effort it had cost her to say the words and the courage behind it. His admiration for her soared. And she was so beautiful. The wine had brought colour to her normally pale face and the dark eyes which had recently been so shaded, now glowed. He realised with a sudden pang of guilt that he had an overwhelming urge to make love to her. He fought it, knowing that it was simply a reaction to his desperate relief. To hide his expression he walked out to the balcony and looked out. The sun was setting now and a misty gauze lightly caped the Grand Canal. When he looked back he saw that she was closely watching him. He took a deep breath and walked over and sat down beside her.

"You don't have to do anything," he said. "You can just go back to England if you want."

"But I don't," she said. "I really want to help. I want to get you back to your time, so you can live a full life and have a family if that's what you want." She tripped slightly on the words and swallowed. "And, most of all, I want to heal this world and give it a future, instead of this void we're all locked into, with no beginning and no end."

"In that case, I think we need to send an email," said Irving and, although his voice was grave, she saw that his eyes were dancing.

"What's an email?" asked Theora.

"It's a way of communicating across long distances. It means we can get some good advice quickly," said Irving.

He produced a leather case with a metal folder within it. This he opened it and he proceeded to tap upon it. Then he handed it to her.

"Look at this."

Theora saw a list of addresses all written by different people. Halfway down was a name in a hand she instantly recognised. She looked up to find that Irving had drawn from his pocket a small silver-handled knife. To Theora's surprise and concern he drew it quickly across a forefinger and a bead of blood appeared. He allowed one drop to fall onto the folder. He then tapped it again for a few seconds and closed the top, so it was held firmly closed.

"And now we wait for an answer." He put the folder down on the sofa between them.

Theora stared at him. "Don't you think you should bind your hand?" she said finally. Irving smiled. He turned over his palm and to Theora's astonishment she saw no sign of any wound. She sighed. "More sorcery I suppose."

"Not exactly." He looked a little uncomfortable. "Look at the leather binding, how does it seem to you?"

Theora glanced down. The small folder was heavily embossed with suns and moons on a soft tan leather. "What should I be looking for?"

Irving hesitated. "It's made of the skin of one of the Moon Lords. Even when killed they have the energy to heal." His voice trailed off.

Theora wrinkled her nose and drew back.

"I thought they were immortal."

"No. Whilst time exists, they are linked to it. So they live on and age very little. However, although mortals cannot harm them, they can harm each other."

He broke off as the folder that lay between them started to throb and there was the sound of faint music. It then fell open. Irving read quickly and then handed it to Theora.

"The Doge's chamber at moonrise," she said. "Well that's clear enough, although I cannot think how they suppose we are going to get in at this late hour."

Irving smiled. "I'm expecting that we'll find some doors unlocked," he said. He stood up. "We'd better go. Do you feel up to this?"

He was looking at her searchingly and Theora met his glance. "If you mean am I comfortable about meeting

Lord Sulien..." She paused and forced a smile. "There are so many more important things to worry about now than my wounded pride!"

"Good girl," said Irving approvingly. He ran his eyes over her. "You might want to change your dress before we go."

Theora laughed. It was so typical of him. "Of course, if you will wait for me."

She went to the bedroom calling for the maid as she did so and shortly re-emerged, having changed her afternoon gown for a dark green walking dress and matching velvet cloak trimmed with gold twill.

"Is this suitable?" she said, knowing that his taste was always excellent.

"Perfect," he said. He took her hand firmly. "Let's go."

*

It seemed odd to return to St Mark's at such a late hour. As they alighted from the gondola and walked through the now quiet streets, the beauty of the city was distracting, but very soon they had reached the palace gates. As Irving had predicted, they were open and nobody seemed surprised by the fact that two strangers were entering into the unlit apartments. It was getting dark and Theora was glad of Irving's confidence. Without hesitation he took them to the ancient council chamber. Theora, who had been steeling herself in preparation for the sight of Lord Sulien, was deflated to find the room was quite empty. Irving guided her to one of the carved stalls and they sat down.

"What do we do now?" Theora whispered.

Irving felt in his jacket. "I suppose we wait." He took out his silver cigarette case and lit one. The match flame illuminated Theora's pale face. He saw her expression was strained. "Don't worry," he said and she was moved again by the kindness in his voice.

"I'm not worried," she said stoutly. She looked around the room. "I suppose it's not yet moonrise. When do you think that is?"

"Perhaps twenty minutes," said Irving. He followed her glance. "This sure is a big, empty room." He jumped up, extinguishing his cigarette between thumb and finger. "We might as well use it."

Theora stared at him. "What do you mean?"

"I mean that by dancing attendance on you for all this time, I haven't actually done any real dancing, so I need to get back into practice." He walked into the middle of the room and started limbering up, shaking his hands and legs gently. "Sing something for me."

Theora laughed. "Don't be ridiculous, Guy."

Irving swung round and danced a few experimental steps towards her. "I'm quite serious," he said "Anything you like."

"You know I don't know any songs from your time," said Theora despairingly.

Irving sighed. "I suppose I'll have to teach you one."

"Can you sing?" asked Theora dubiously as he swayed away from her.

He was about to reply when suddenly a noise behind them made them both turn. They were no longer alone. Lord Sulien and Lord Thorne had entered the chamber. As they came closer, the Earl waved his hand and around the rooms each of the lamps sprang into life so that the whole room shone with a soft but clear light. "Good evening, Miss Templeton," he said. He nodded briefly in Irving's direction. "Mr Irving."

Lord Thorne, who had been watching this exchange, glanced quickly at Theora and then indicated to Irving that they should withdraw. The two men walked away leaving Theora and the Earl alone together. She kept her eyes lowered although she knew that his had never left her face. After a moment he spoke very carefully:

"I can imagine, Miss Templeton, how disagreeable this meeting must be for you. There is nothing which can make amends for what has happened. All I can say is how truly sorry I am for the pain that you have experienced and how grateful I am that you have agreed to see me again. I can only assume that you have decided to put the past behind you? If that is the case, you have my word that I will do the same."

His voice, so halting and so unlike his usual calm certainty, made her look up.

"Do not distress yourself, Sir. I blame myself."

He looked astonished. "How can that be?"

Theora looked down at her hands and then up again, facing the truth which she had only ever half acknowledged. "You have always treated me with courtesy and respect, but I pretended to myself it was something far more. When you saved my life…" She hesitated on the words "…you risked everything to keep me safe despite putting the whole Quest in danger. That part, I will never forget. What I want now though, is to not just 'put the past behind me' but to thank you sincerely."

She sank down before him in a low curtsy.

"Will you accept my thanks, Sir?"

The Earl stepped forward quickly. "Of course I do." He hesitated and then held out his hand. "I would hope that perhaps we might even become friends one day. What do you say?"

Theora found herself smiling. "That would be very welcome, Sir," she said. They shook hands briefly just as Lord Thorne and Mr Irving re-entered the room. Theora looked about her. "So what happens now?" she asked.

The Earl didn't answer, but walked away to the far

end of the chamber. As he passed through, the wooden seats around the room became occupied with many different people. Their origins Theora could not imagine, but many of them (from their bearing and dress) were obviously not from the 19th Century.

Finally, when the room was full, the Earl spoke, "My friends, in two days the last stage of the Quest will begin." At this there was a murmur of excitement, but the Earl held up his hand for silence. "I am sure you have many questions and they will be answered. Who will go first?" His eyes scanned the crowd and fell upon a thin, slight man in the first row. "Lord Horatio, do you wish to begin?"

The man he had addressed stood up, but, as he did so, Lord Thorne also rose and beckoned to Theora and Irving to follow him. They left the hall and entered an anteroom.

"This meeting will go on for some time," said Lord Thorne. "Do you want to rest here for a while?"

"I thank you, Sir, but I would like to stay and listen," said Theora. "Besides, I have not yet heard how I can help."

Lord Thorne smiled. "Very well, but you will be able to see and hear everything from the gallery and I think it will be a lot more comfortable. Come with me."

He led them out and through a small door which led to a small, curved stairway. At the top there was a recessed balcony with a padded couch. Theora saw that the gallery looked out over the chamber. Lord Thorne then returned to the assembled council. Theora settled herself down comfortably and prepared to listen.

A lively debate had broken out between a tall man exquisitely dressed in 19th-Century evening clothes and the one Lord Sulien had addressed as Horatio. The tall man was speaking. He had a strong, precise voice which carried clearly.

"I tell you, gentlemen, that I am by no means convinced that bringing the Drum by sea is the safest course of action. I would strongly recommend a different approach."

Various voices shouted back in response but Lord Sulien raised a hand for silence.

"It was agreed that, if we are to avoid interception by Lord De Lisle's spies, we would need to forgo use of the globes. As making the entire journey by land would take too long, sea is the least risky option."

The tall man shook his dark head decisively. "I cannot believe that. We do after all have the fastest team of horses that ever existed right here. Now is surely the time to use this to our advantage."

There was a murmur of reluctant assent across the room. Lord Sulien looked at Lord Thorne. "What do you say to that, Argus?" he said.

"I understand everyone's concerns," said Lord Thorne, "but now is not the time. The horses of Helios will only have the strength for one race and we must use them when the danger will be the greatest. Anything else would be a waste. Besides" – he turned to the slight man beside him – "we have Horatio's assurance that he can bring the Drum to us safely. Is that not right, Horatio?"

The slight man inclined his head. He spoke lightly, but the gentle, clipped voice compelled attention.

"Once the Drum is on board Victory, I pledge to you that neither mortal, nor Perdurare, powers will be able to touch it. I guarantee that we will bring it to shore by sunset on Alban Eilir."[13]

His taller companion bowed. "I don't think anyone doubts the power of Victory, Horatio, but I am concerned

---

[13] Druid beginning of spring

with the margins of time. Irving has barely hours to rehearse the sequence with the Drum and the Harp."

Guy Irving stood up. "If that's the problem here, I can set your minds at rest. There will be no rehearsal."

Everyone in the chamber turned and stared up at the American. An excited babble of questions broke out but Irving waved them to silence.

"I know that it's a huge risk and believe me I've had some sleepless nights worrying about it. But, it's the only way. I'll teach Miss Templeton the steps and we'll practice together without accompaniment. That's all we can do. Besides, I've always been a good improviser if the big occasion calls for it and this is definitely a big occasion." Laughter broke out and faint applause.

Lord Sulien inclined his head respectfully before saying, "Well, there we have it. The Drum will be returned by Nelson. I will bring Irving to the Kieve and then we will take our chance. We know that Lord De Lisle has returned to this time, that he knows at least part of the purpose of the Quest and that he is assembling his great army. We can expect that he will try to stop us reaching the Kieve. Even I do not know what we will have to face. The gravest risk is to the unprotected mortals in my domain. Lord De Lisle will not scruple to massacre them if it suits his purpose. We must protect them and I will be briefing the captains later to ensure this is a priority." He turned and ran his eye over the assembly. "Is there anything that anyone wishes to add before we depart?"

Nelson stood up. He cleared his throat.

"Just this. On behalf of us all, I want to thank you and Lord Thorne for your selfless protection. We, your knights, share every hope that you have for success. Now is the time for each of us to stand steadfastly together and do our duty." He paused and smiled. "England confides it."

There was huge applause. Theora looked at Irving. Together they descended from the gallery and went back out to the square. Outside it was dark and lanterns sparkled across the lagoon.

"What next?" said Theora.

Irving smiled briefly. "We go home and you learn the dance."

*

After the council, the Earl and Lord Thorne returned to the Club. They spent the rest of the next day briefing the captains and waiting and watching as the key knights assembled. During this time Lord Thorne was unusually quiet and seemed distracted. When they were alone again the Earl tackled him directly. "You have said farewell to Madelyn?"

"Yes. She has gone now, I hope, to a place of safety." Lord Thorne sighed. "Why is it," he said sadly, "that those that most deserve love, are so frequently denied it?"

"It is not your fault that you could not love her as she loves you," said Lord Sulien.

"No, but I was too selfish. I should have released her from my service years ago."

"I do not think that she would have gone," said Lord Sulien. "Do not grieve for Madelyn. Very soon we will repay all the many sacrifices that have been made on our behalf."

The two men sat silently for a while. Both were reflecting upon what had happened and what was still to come. At last Lord Sulien stood up. Despite his relaxed attitude, Lord Thorne sensed an underlying tension.

"You are still troubled about something, Aidan?"

"A little. There is something, something not quite right, in my own domain. Let us go to the library and see what we can find out."

He led the way through the caves and they stepped through to the chamber beyond. When they had passed through the great door they entered a large room, panelled in oak and filled with books. Lord Sulien walked at once to a large table in an alcove. Here there were three candles. His own and Lord Thorne's burned bright and tall as usual, but beside them, smaller, whiter and shining with a flame of faint silvery whiteness, stood another.

"This is the difference that I felt," he said. "It seems that Ciaran is becoming aware of his true self."

Lord Thorne looked sombre. "These candles are only lit when the life force starts to ignite within the body of its celestial host. Ciaran is not yet twenty-five. Something must have happened to trigger the process. There is only one thing I can think of that would do that. I'm sorry Aidan but it must be Juliet."

The Earl turned on heel and walked to a globe that stood by the window. He spun it and Meadows' face appeared.

"Would you tell me where my daughter is please?"

Meadows looked surprised. "Miss Juliet? I thought she was with Lord Thorne. She left a message earlier to say that she was travelling to Gyldeford with Mr Allan to meet him as arranged."

"I see. Thank you, Meadows."

The Earl shut his eyes and then opened them again.

"You are right. An elopement has taken place."

Lord Thorne looked grim. "I thought that he had given you a promise. This is not the behaviour of a gentleman!"

The Earl gave a wry smile. "We must put aside 19th-Century morals for the moment. The point is that, although he doesn't know it, Ciaran is now in grave danger. There is therefore no time to lose. We must start our journey as soon as possible, to save him and all the domains."

Lord Thorne passed a hand across his eyes. "If De Lisle finds out the truth about Ciaran, he may kill him before he comes to full strength," he said.

"I think it could now quite easily be the reverse, which is what concerns me," said Lord Sulien.

"I could stand a future without Bricin's presence," said Lord Thorne with feeling.

"But could any future stand without him?" asked Lord Sulien. "Which is why, despite many interesting opportunities to do so, I have never put him to the sword. No, De Lisle's story is not yet over. Only the Star Maiden herself can now decide his fate."

He went to the shelf and picked out a large book with a blue cover. "Go now and join Horatio. I suggest that you also ensure Miss Templeton's presence on board. I think it will be the best way to get both of our most precious items to safety as soon as possible. I will stay here and get ready." He handed the book to Lord Thorne who took it from him. He turned to go but at the doorway he stopped. "Be very careful please, Aidan."

Lord Sulien smiled. "I will indeed be very careful. Have courage, I have never lost a carriage race and this one will be the most exciting yet!"

Without further words he stepped forward and passed his hand briefly over his own candle flame. Then he was gone from that time.

Lord Thorne opened the book in his hand and spun the globe. At once the surface became misted and from the depths of that mist the vision of Victory, Nelson's great flagship, appeared. Lord Thorne spoke within his mind.

"Horatio?"

"Yes, my Lord?"

"Please prepare your ship. I am going to bring Miss Templeton on board." He spun the globe again and entered the palace.

"Are you ready?" he said briefly.

Irving nodded. "Of course. Theora knows the steps now and we will continue to practice, but I am still unclear what will happen?"

"I am afraid we are unable to predict anything," said Lord Thorne. "All we know is that you need a female partner to accompany you in the dance. The legends have shown that this is key to awaking the spirt of the Star Maiden, so that she can make her judgement."

"And her spirit will need to be joined with her reincarnated body," said Theora unexpectedly.

Lord Thorne looked wary. "Why do you say that?"

Theora reached inside the collar of her gown and drew out the pendant. "This showed me," she said. "I thought it was a dream, but, after my confinement, I remembered what I had seen and knew that it was true."

Lord Thorne stared at the glowing jewel.

"Yes, I see that," he said. He sat down beside her. "Listen to me, Miss Templeton. I don't know how this jewel came to you, but the fact that it has revealed so many things is not simple chance. Yes, you are the living image of our goddess, the Star Maiden for whom we have sought for so long. We kept that fact from you, not because we wished to conceal the truth, but because, until now, we had no definite proof that this was anything but coincidence. Aidan brought you to Temple Court because he has always believed that there was a possible link. I was not so sure. Now that the Moonstone has spoken to you, we have proof that your presence is vital to our success."

Theora fingered the pendant in her lap. "If Lord Sulien thought I had a link to the Quest, why did he allow me to continue to meet with Lord De Lisle? He must have known that I was doing so."

"Yes he did. But when you first came to Temple Court, Lord De Lisle knew nothing about the Quest. Rather than interfere and arouse his suspicion, Aidan decided it was safest to let your liaison continue. We were pleased that, with the arrangements for the Quest reaching their conclusion, De Lisle was so easily distracted."

Theora pondered this. "Why did he attack my coach then?"

"Unfortunately, Lord De Lisle has discovered some of the secrets of the Quest. Although he does not know your true connection to it, he suspects a link. He attacked your coach to show defiance. Nothing is more important to Lord De Lisle than proving his superiority and causing irritation to the Earl."

"But you can protect her," said Irving sharply.

"As much as we can. But Lord De Lisle has a knowledge of the future realities which Lord Sulien and I do not share. All we can be certain of is that he is now raising an army. That is why we must reach the Maiden's resting place before the end of Alban Eilir. So, we must make haste. We have a ship that is waiting now to carry you and other precious cargo to the appointed place. This ship has great power and the finest master that has ever sailed. You have my promise that you will be quite safe."

He extended his hand. "Come with me now and I will see you safely bestowed upon HMS Victory where Lord Nelson will join you."

"Where will you be?" asked Theora rising.

"I have to prepare for the battle," said Lord Thorne.

Theora hesitated, she still held the pendant in her hand. "Then I would like you to take this," she said firmly.

He stared at her. "I cannot do that," he said at last. "The Moonstone has come to you. It is meant for you."

Theora smiled. "Then let us say that I am now lending it to you." She pressed it into his hand. "I would like it to give strength to the wisest and bravest of all the Perdurare."

Lord Thorne took the pendant and wrapped the chain round his neck. As he did so it glowed and then burned with a fierce light, illuminating his face.

"It does that sometimes," said Theora with a nod. "I suggest you wear it inside your shirt for concealment."

Lord Thorne laughed a little tremulously. He thrust the jewel away.

"Thank you," he said, "but this is really just a loan. I will return this to you, I swear."

"I know you will," said Theora. "In fact you must promise that you will do so, in person, as soon as the battle is over."

He bowed. "I promise." He looked deeply into her eyes for a moment then turned to Irving. "Guy, you must go first to the cavern and get ready with the other knights."

He took Irving's hand and spoke softly and Irving disappeared. Then he looked at Theora. Moments later, the palace in Venice faded away and she found herself standing upon the wooden deck of a great ship. The sails were furled for it was in harbour on a warm sunny afternoon. Theora tasted the salt upon her lips as above her seagulls wheeled in the sky. Then Lord Thorne led her to the Captain's cabin. It was empty, for the ship was deserted.

"Where are the crew?" she asked as she removed her bonnet.

"Getting ready to join the ship," said Lord Thorne. "They are not needed yet." He looked around the cabin. "I am going to need to leave you here alone for a while, but I promise it will only be for a short time. Outside the cavern, this is the safest place for you now. This ship contains one of the strongest reality splinters and is secured with many deceiving cantus. Lord De Lisle cannot possibly find you."

"That is a relief at least," said Theora with feeling. She saw he was hesitating and took a deep breath.

"Please go now. I know you have lots to attend to."

He still lingered. "I could stay a little longer."

"No please don't," she said. "There is really no need."

"Then this is goodbye," he said and she was surprised, for his voice was strangely broken and harsh.

"Yes I suppose it is," she said, "although of course, if your plans do work, then I assume we will be meeting again very soon, in one form or another."

He regarded her intently. "You are very brave, Miss Templeton," he said.

"I am afraid I am not," she said with a trembling smile. "I am truly terrified."

"I understand," he said. He touched his breast briefly. "I thank you again for this gift."

He went to the door but she ran after him.

"Please take the greatest care, my Lord, until our next meeting."

She reached up and kissed his cheek.

He looked down upon her. "Farewell," he said. Then he turned and walked up the stairs. She heard the sound of his feet crossing the decking and then he was gone from both the ship and that time.

Chapter Nineteen

Ciaran Allan drew himself up on his elbow and looked down at the exquisite figure of his young wife. Juliet was still completely asleep, a soft smile curving her perfect mouth, her golden curls shining amongst the silks and laces on the pillow. Ciaran longed to kiss her, but contented himself with smoothing back one wayward strand of hair that was touching her nose and causing it to wrinkle. Then, moving quietly so that he didn't disturb her, he went downstairs. Outside, the air was filled with the sound of birdsong. The young man sat down upon a tree stump to listen to them. He felt, for the first time in his life, completely at peace, but also filled with a strength and energy he had never before experienced which was growing with every second. His senses were alive and alert to every sound and movement. A red squirrel darted across the lawn in front of him and he gazed upon it with wonder and delight. It stopped and stared at him and then ran smartly up a tree. Ciaran ran to the tree and looked up. But, as he placed his hands upon the trunk, he drew back in alarm and rubbed them quickly upon the grass in an attempt to remove the strange tingling energy that had flowed from the bark to his fingertips.

He turned to find Juliet watching him. He went to her at once. "I didn't mean to wake you," he said contritely.

She smiled. "I am glad to be so woken, although, had I known my husband planned an early morning walk, I would have put on stouter shoes."

She gestured and Ciaran saw that her feet were wet with dew. He laughed, bent and picked her up, sweeping her into his arms. "Does this help?"

"Somewhat. Now if you will just come back upstairs everything will be perfect."

He looked down into her soft blue eyes, read the unspoken message and kissed her deeply. Then he carried her back to the lodge and set her down in the doorway. "I promise I won't be long."

She grasped his hand. "What is wrong please?"

He looked at her, the smile still lingering upon his lips. "Why should anything be wrong?"

She looked anxiously up at him. "There is something troubling you."

He laughed and cupped her face in his hands. "You know me too well already, little wife. Do not worry, I will be with you soon." He kissed her on the tip of her nose and walked back into the garden.

Once again he walked to the tree and placed his fingers on the trunk. Again there was a burst of exhilarating energy. He forced himself to remain still and let it wash through him. Then he found that he was no longer experiencing the sights and sounds of the English countryside. He was now in the centre of a city, standing by a park bench looking at a woman...

She was beautiful, elegant and dressed in 18th-Century clothes. She faced him and her voice shook with anger and frustration.

"I suppose I should be grateful that you came at all."

Ciaran's lips moved in response but the voice that passed through his lips was not his own and the familiar sound filled him with loathing.

"You know that I always like to show good manners," said Lord De Lisle.

"Having received your urgent invitation, I came at once. Now, what is so important?"

"You dare to ask that, after, after...." She broke off and turned away in confusion.

Through his undesired link, Ciaran felt the other man's quiver of amusement, but the deep voice was deliberately indifferent.

"After what?" He looked past the woman's fury and sat casually down upon the bench, crossing his legs and placing his ebony cane with its silver sickle-moon handle carefully down beside him. "Really, Jennifer, I do find these histrionics rather boring! We spent a pleasant few days together that is all. I enjoyed it and so, I believe, did you."

The woman's face burned with fury. She was very striking with auburn hair and exceptionally fine eyes.

"I cannot believe that you are treating me so shabbily," she whispered and the angry words seemed strangely out of keeping with her outward air of sophistication.

Lord De Lisle had been lazily surveying the bandstand, where a number of ladies and gentleman had started to assemble. He looked back at Jennifer coldly. "I would remind you to remember who you are talking to," he said, "and what you owe me. Under the circumstances, I find it quite absurd that you would dare to suggest that I should treat you in any other way! You are my servant, nothing more, nothing less. If I wanted to visit you every day and every night until the end of eternity, you would have no right to refuse me."

Jennifer clenched her fists. Her cheeks were flaming. "I agreed to help your plan, not become your resident whore," she flung at him. "Forcing yourself upon me was never part of the bargain."

"Forcing – good God how hilarious you are today," he exclaimed and his harsh laugher disturbed a few fat pigeons who were nosing around the bench. They flapped untidily away.

"As I remember, no force was necessary."

Her hand shot out and caught his white cheek. He rubbed the faint mark that was left, slightly ruefully, the remains of his good humour still evident despite the blow. He stood up and extended his arm to her.

"Enough of this. Come now, let us walk a while shall we? It is too cold a day to stand about and perhaps you will be able to restrain the need to abuse me so."

Reluctantly she rose, took his arm and they walked on towards the lake. After a few moments, he said slowly, "Explain to me what it is that has annoyed you so, my dear? We have always been honest regarding our ambitions, so tell me, what else do you want?"

They stopped at the bridge and stood for a moment watching swans and cygnets that were passing underneath. Jennifer leaned upon the smooth stone. When the swans had vanished she looked up. "I want a husband," she said at last.

The amusement vanished from Lord De Lisle's eyes completely.

"You are not suggesting that I am your choice? That's ridiculous."

"Why is it?" said Jennifer desperately.

He stared at her incredulously.

"Well, even if I loved you, you must know that I would never consider you as a possible wife. I am a Moon Lord and I know what I owe my name. I have only ever thought one mortal woman worthy of me and she has refused my offer of marriage. I am certainly not minded to try again with a peasant like you!"

She shook her head. "You are terribly cruel."

He laughed at that. "Has it taken you this long to find that out? I always thought you were so perceptive! Come now, there are hundreds of mortal men who would gladly take their place at your side. I advise you to choose again and more wisely."

She watched his face. "Is that your final word?"

"Indeed it is." He bent and lightly kissed her pallid

cheek. "Now I suggest you get yourself home. It looks to me very much like rain and it would be a shame to spoil that lovely hat." He bowed extravagantly. "I wish you a good morning, Madam. Shall I call on you in the Dordogne again next week? After all, even if we are not to be lovers, we still have a lot of work to do."

She pulled herself upright. "No, I am afraid I will be staying here on an extended trip."

"Staying with anyone I know?"

"Yes, Lady Meadley has asked me to join her at Temple Court."

"Excellent. How very extraordinary that she should do so. You will have a ringside seat for the coming events."

"I am glad that you are pleased," she said.

He drew from his pocket a pair of lambskin gloves which he drew on, working his fingers into the soft leather with deliberation. "Another word of advice, my dear Jenny. As you know, I have always looked to the future, not the past, in all my dealings. I have learned that that it is always best to be grateful for what you have. Now, enjoy your time in the country and I expect to see you again very soon."

He nodded to her and walked away.

Jenny watched his progress down the street for a moment and then turned and walked back to a large house set back from the road and shaded by horse chestnut trees. She sat for a while in her bedroom with a pen in her fingers and a ream of paper unfolded upon the desk. Then she set down the quill and drew from the drawer a well-thumbed letter. She opened it and read:

My dear Lady Layton. I am writing to confirm the results of your examination. I am pleased to inform you that you are indeed with child and that all indications are that you and the baby are in perfect health. There is therefore no reason why you should not be safely delivered in August. I understand that you intend to make an extended trip to Surrey. I support withdrawal to the country rather than staying in town during the hot weather. When you return to London, I should of course be glad to attend you. If there is any other way I can assist you, please do not hesitate to contact me.

Yours sincerely, Edward Myers, Senior Physician.

Jenny carefully folded the letter and then she took up the quill and started to write.

Lord Thorne, Ashleworth Castle, Gloucestershire
Dear Sir,

I am appealing to you for help and offering my assistance. I will be visiting Lady Meadley in two weeks' time, please contact me at Temple Court. Please note that the matter that I wish to discuss is very secret business. It would only concern a true knight who is committed to the Quest. I know that Lord Sulien may not believe this, but I give you my word that Lord De Lisle knows nothing of this.

Lady Layton.

*

Ciaran stepped back from the tree. He looked up at the green branches moving gently in the breeze. To his amazement he saw that each of the great beeches was reaching out, one to the other as if linking their presence within the grove. He saw that the next tree in line was shining faintly and he quickly went to it and placed his hands again upon the smooth trunk. He now saw a different scene. It was the 18th Century and he was viewing the solar room at Ashleworth Castle. Jennifer Layton was there with Lord Thorne who was sitting opposite her...

"So, your proposition is that if I will look after your child and keep his identity secret, you will support us by providing information regarding Lord De Lisle's plans?"

Jenny looked at him briefly. "Yes."

"You are certain that there will be a child?"

"Absolutely certain."

"Forgive me, you are also certain that Lord De Lisle is the father?"

Jenny nodded. "I suppose I cannot be surprised that you would mistrust me, but yes, there is no doubt that Lord De Lisle is the father." She carried on, her voice breaking, "I do not know exactly why I let him seduce me. I suppose I was still jealous of my sister and this seemed the only way to become her equal."

"Jealous? How could you still be jealous when your poor sister has long since passed away?"

The expression on Jenny's face changed suddenly, shame and sadness hardened into anger and frustration. "I know it is wrong but I cannot help it. She had everything, everything I should have had. It wasn't fair that Aidan married her. He never loved her, he never even talked to her until after that night. He used to come to see Mother before she died, but he stayed to talk to me. I know that he could have loved me, he just didn't have enough time to find it out." She broke off, her beautiful face livid and twitching with anger.

Lord Thorne regarded her soberly. "Are you saying that you still love Lord Sulien?"

Jenny nodded. The amber eyes lost their fire and became soft again. "No one else is important or ever could be," she said helplessly.

There was a pause. Lord Thorne seemed to come to a decision. "I will help you," he said finally. "But, it must be our secret and you must pledge to keep it, whatever the cost. We will need to discuss how you will help me, but, before we tackle the particulars, I suggest that we have lunch." He rang the bell and a servant appeared. "Please take Lady Layton to the dining room and I will join her there shortly." The servant withdrew and Jenny followed.

Lord Thorne turned as a door opened in the wall panelling and a young woman stepped out. Ciaran recognised her as Miss Drew. "What has happened?" she said.

"I need your help once more," said Lord Thorne. "I am going to find a place within this timeline to raise a child and I want you to superintend his education. This will be a real test of your skills. Are you ready for it?"

The woman dropped a deep curtsy. "My Lord knows that I am always at his command."

"Yes," said Lord Thorne. He sounded weary. "Do you never desire that it was not so?"

"To wish that would be to wish that we had never met," she said.

Lord Thorne looked at her steadily. "I am sorry, Madelyn," he said at last.

She rose from her curtsy. "There is nothing for you to be sorry about," she said. "Now tell me what you need me to do."

After Miss Drew had left, Lord Thorne went to the window and stood looking out at the slanting rain. Then, the door that led into the solar from Lord Thorne's study opened and Lord Sulien came in.

"I am not at all convinced that you have made the right decision, Argus," he said. "This woman is undoubtedly responsible for the deaths of many of our knights and has lied repeatedly. How can we now be confident that she will not simply turn again and run back to De Lisle?"

"We cannot be confident," said Lord Thorne.

"However, as the teacher of the Sun and Moon Lords, I would not be doing my duty to our line if I abandoned De Lisle's heir and left him to an uncertain future in a mortal world."

"You believe it will be a boy then?" said Lord Sulien.

"My senses tell me so. I believe too that this boy will have a major part to play in the years ahead. So, as I did with his father, I will take him and protect him until the time comes for him to understand his birthright and stand with us."

Lord Sulien relaxed slightly. "Very well. It is agreed then. We will protect the boy. But this I do insist upon: that woman is never to know him or be allowed to be near him. She gives him up to us and that is an end of the matter. Any other help she can give will need to be carefully planned and considered."

Lord Thorne looked at him. "This is not like you, Aidan," he said. "Why must you be so unforgiving? Jenny doesn't intend any harm to her child and, as you have just heard, she is capable of great love."

"Great love," said Lord Sulien contemptuously. "She is a traitor."

"She cared greatly for you," said Lord Thorne gravely. "Whilst we must condemn her actions, we may at least understand and, to some degree, forgive her motivation."

"Are you suggesting that I am in some way responsible for her falling in love with me?"

"Well aren't you? Surely, by visiting her family so often and singling her out, you gave her cause to consider that you held her in some esteem."

Lord Sulien considered. "I suppose she might have received that impression," he said reluctantly. "She was always so very glad to see me, that I should have seen the possibility. I just thought that because..." He broke off.

"Because of her disfigurement she was incapable of great feeling?" said Lord Thorne coldly. "How shameful. I fear you must take a large portion of blame for what she has become. Had you not paid her such attention, she would not have fed upon false hope. As it is, a sweet, innocent girl has become a complex and highly unbalanced woman. We can only be thankful that we have this chance to make some reparation."

*

Ciaran stepped back from the tree. He sat down upon the grass and looked at his hands. They were still faintly glowing. With a detached certainty, he knew now that he was a Moon Lord, capable of giving and taking life if he so wished. The thought made him drag his mind back to more practical matters. His initial desire was to go and find Lord De Lisle and kill him, but he had a responsibility towards Juliet. He went back into the lodge and up the stairs. Juliet was waiting for him. She had brushed her hair and donned a silk wrapper sprigged with rosebuds. The sight of her warmed his heavy heart. She ran to him with shining eyes and slipped her arms about his neck.

"What a long time you have been," she said and kissed him.

He returned her embrace, losing himself in her soft sweetness and then stood back from her. I am afraid, my darling, that I have had some bad news," he said with an effort. "I must leave at once and join your father in France. You need to return to Temple Court as soon as possible."

Juliet's face fell. "Today, but how can that be? Oh you must be joking?"

"I am afraid I am not," said Ciaran. "I have had an urgent message you see." He took her arms from his neck. "Now I must dress and so should you. Please would you call for my valet and your maid?"

Juliet sat down upon the bed. "You are keeping something from me?"

He touched her cheek. "I promise you I am not. It is simply that I cannot deny your father this assistance when he has made such a specific request. Also, bearing in mind that we have ignored his wishes and got married without his blessing, I think it is important that I do see him as soon as possible."

Yes I suppose you are right," said Juliet reluctantly. She sighed and then summoned up a smile. "Can we at least have breakfast together?"

"Yes, of course," said Ciaran and then he left her to dress. He went to the sitting room and wrote two notes. One was to Lord Sulien, where he advised of Juliet's impending return. He made no reference to the elopement, but stressed that he intended to wait upon the Earl as a matter of urgency and requested an audience. The longer message was to Lord De Lisle. In this he stated that Lord Sulien had agreed to give up Miss Templeton in exchange for a declaration of peace and that he had instructed Ciaran to make the arrangements. He asked for a meeting that evening. As he wrote, he wondered if Lord De Lisle would accept the bait. He thought it unlikely that he would believe that Lord Sulien would give up Miss Templeton. However, he was counting upon De Lisle's curiosity being sufficient to divert him from his current plans. After breakfast he had the carriage brought round. It was just before midday when the horses drew up at the turnpike. Mr Allan then descended and, having promised a tearful Juliet that he would send word as soon as he reached Calais, mounted his own horse and rode swiftly to the next town. Here he sought a suitable messenger to deliver his notes. Then, he remounted and took a short-cut across the country towards Temple Court. When he arrived, he entered the house without incident. He had already been aware that Lord Sulien and Lord Thorne were not in residence, as Lord Thorne had advised him that they would be away for some weeks. He went to the study and having made a scan of the books there, selected a few and read them carefully. With his heightened senses, he was quickly able to find what he needed. He made notes and, by the time night had fallen, he felt sufficiently prepared to deal with Lord De Lisle.

*

Lord De Lisle reached the village of Elsted in the late afternoon. He had driven alone, dispensing with his groom. Having briefly issued instructions for the disposal of his team, De Lisle accompanied the Innkeeper through the small smoky corridor and into the private parlour at the back of the house. His Lordship stopped short at the sight of Mr Allan sitting in the shadows. He stood for a moment, weighing up the situation, and then went forward extending his hand.

"Good afternoon, Mr Allan, what an absolute pleasure."

Mr Allan looked at him and after a brief moment shook the hand offered. "Good afternoon, my Lord. I can imagine you are surprised to see me here?"

De Lisle smiled. "Not entirely. Whilst I would have expected another emissary for this particular transaction, I know that Aidan has always kept you close. Especially where Miss Templeton is concerned."

He drew off his driving gloves and looked around. "I assume she is here somewhere? When will we be expecting her to join us?"

Mr Allan sat down. "She will be with us for supper. Does that satisfy you?"

"That depends." De Lisle helped himself to the jug of

wine on the table and drank. His eyebrows rose. "This wine is quite good." He looked over his shoulder at the hovering Landlord. "Go now and leave us undisturbed."

When the door was finally shut he stood in front of the dusty mirror making small adjustments to his cravat. He saw the younger man watching him with undisguised contempt and his expression hardened. "You must know that I would prefer you to leave as soon as possible. Now that Miss Templeton is to be released to me. I have much to discuss with her. Matters which do not require an audience."

"I would presume not," said Mr Allan. "Nevertheless, I will stay until Miss Templeton comes down. In the meantime, I would ask that you spare me a little of your time." He stood up and drew his sword. "In fact I insist you do so." The cold anger in his voice made it shake.

De Lisle laughed.

"I advise you to be very careful, boy, you are in too deep here. If you continue to interfere in my affairs I will have to take you right out of the game forever. I advise you to go home, find yourself a wife and stay well away from matters that do not concern you."

The two men faced each other. They were exactly the same height. "I have already followed some of your advice," said Mr Allan. "I was married yesterday."

"I congratulate you," said De Lisle. "Now, if you would be good enough to ring for Miss Templeton, perhaps I may be equally as fortunate."

He went to the door, but Mr Allan sprang forward and barred his way. "You are not interested in learning more about my wife?"

De Lisle rolled his eyes. "Be assured that I have no interest in your alliance with Lord Sulien's peasant brat. Now get out of my way."

Mr Allan shook his head. "It was not Lord Sulien's

daughter that I married, Sir. My wife is the lady that you knew as Miss Theora Templeton."

De Lisle stared at him, but after a moment he laughed again. "Don't be absurd, Theora would never consent to marry you."

"Nevertheless, she has done so," said Mr Allan, steadily. "Let me prove it to you."

He gestured for Lord De Lisle to follow him. The bedrooms were at the back of the inn. Outside the room Mr Allan put a finger to his lips. "I would ask you to be very quiet, my wife is asleep."

Gently he eased open the door and Lord De Lisle saw the large half tester bed upon which Theora lay. As they looked in, she stirred, murmured Mr Allan's name and turned over.

Mr Allan shut the door. "Satisfied?"

He gasped as Lord De Lisle's hand shot out and grasped him by the throat. "You wanted my attention, now you will have it."

He looked deep into Ciaran's eyes, raised his hand, twisted the ring upon it and, as he did so, time moved onto another future. Seconds later, Mr Allan found himself a prisoner. Across the room Lord De Lisle was standing with something pressed to his ear and apparently talking to nobody. His altered appearance made it quite clear that they were no longer in the 19th Century. Mr Allan rubbed his throat, which was sore, but he was filled with triumph. He had done what he had planned, which was to distract De Lisle and, by doing so, protect Juliet and his friends. He did not know whether he had the power to destroy Lord De Lisle, but he had done his best to help Lord Sulien and Lord Thorne.

Chapter Twenty

Time passed very slowly for Theora, alone on HMS Victory. Wrapped within the confines of a dense sea fog, the view from the Admiral's window was shrouded and the galley room was chill. For a while she attempted to pass the time reading, but since the book selection consisted of little but naval strategies and records of great battles at sea (mostly led by Lord Nelson himself), she found it difficult to apply herself. At last she laid down on the narrow bunk and the gentle rocking of the boat, and her own nervous exhaustion, eventually made her drowsy. When she did finally awake, the metallic striking of the Admiral's clock told her it was nearly midnight. She sat up quickly, every nerve strained to hear the slightest sound. Even without the Moonstone to amplify her senses she was conscious that she was not alone. Someone else was on board the ship. Instinctively she reached out a hand to touch the cabin wall. What had Lord Thorne said? "You cannot be harmed whilst you are in England and England's heart is in this ship."

The remembrance of the words brought her courage. She got up from the bunk, and sat down in the Captain's chair to wait for the inevitable and unwanted visitor. It was thus, straight backed, pale and resolute, that she was found by Lord De Lisle.

He came in without haste, bending slightly to miss the crossbeams, his dark red hair damp from the mist.

"So, Miss Templeton, I find you all alone. How very fortunate. I had expected to find at least the Lord Admiral on board his flagship. How careless of him to abandon it so precipitately."

Theora passed her tongue round her dry mouth. "You should leave as soon as you can," she said. "You must know that not only Lord Nelson, but Lord Sulien and

Lord Thorne will very soon be here."

Lord De Lisle smiled unpleasantly. "I admire your confidence, Miss Templeton, but I'm afraid that you underestimate their power and my initiative. You see, I know that they will not return unless Victory warns them that you may be in danger and, even with the power that is woven into this ship, it will struggle to send that message now. Thanks to the knowledge supplied by Mr Allan's link to Lord Thorne, not only have I managed to break their cantus and so find you, I have also been able to manufacture some of my own. Look, I beg you."

Reluctantly, Theora followed his gaze and to her amazement she saw that although she knew it to be just past midnight, outside the sun was shining on a beautiful clear morning. There was no mist and it was obviously well past daybreak.

"You have moved the ship in time," she said in a whisper.

He inclined his head. "Just so. We are resting in a place which, by lunchtime, will no longer be a safe haven for Nelson's precious ship. In fact, things will become very unpleasant all round, unless you give me what I want."

Theora stared at him in horror. "You are doing this just to get revenge on Lord Sulien," she said.

His laughter rang out.

"Is that what you truly think I'm interested in? Good God I rated your intelligence higher than that."

His gaze raked the room, I suppose there's nothing decent to drink is there?" He looked contemptuously at the ship's decanter and the few glasses that were stacked neatly on the sideboard. "Obviously not. However, needs must..."

He strode forward, helped himself to a large glass of rum and drank it down. He shuddered. "Gut rot they call it on board these ships, you know, and I can see why. Thankfully the future has so much more to offer." He fingered the glass for a moment, looking at the dregs in the bottom. Then he met Theora's gaze squarely. "You could have had all that you know, if you had consented to become my wife. As it is…" He broke off and set the glass on the table. "Time to conclude our business, I think, but the question is where? I suppose this rather purgatory looking couch is the best we can do. Oh well."

With deliberation he removed his coat and set it down. Then he turned back to her and looked her over from top to toe. "How very satisfying it is to have one's plan come to a successful conclusion."

Theora found that she was shaking. "What plan?"

He smiled unpleasantly. "I want a child of course, sired by me, mothered by you. You are, after all, the living image of the Star Maiden. A child of your blood is the only way to ensure my survival."

Theora stood up. She knew now that she was completely in his power and her only hope was that she could goad him to some act of aggression which would perhaps trigger the ship's defences.

"You must know that this is a hopeless plan," she said as calmly as she could. "I have recently been told that I can never have children."

He walked to her and she was surprised to see that he was smiling. He took her cold hands in his and, although she longed to pull away, she held steady in his grasp.

"The Earl," he said, his voice dropped and chilled, "is as much your enemy as mine. He has cast me as a villain, but I wonder how much truth he actually revealed to you of our long history. Did he tell you that his wife actually desired me more than him? Did he also tell you that if you travelled with me to the future, you could bear a child without any danger? No, I'm sure that these important details were conveniently kept from you. He has deceived you as he has done so many others. That is his way, as it has always been."

Theora looked up incredulously. "That is ridiculous. How is it possible that I could bear a living child, when I was so injured before?"

"Because here, with me now, in my domain, there is no history, just as in the past there is no future. That is one of our most powerful gifts. At the command of Sun or Moon Lord, the living page of any mortal may be refreshed and all wounds can be healed."

Theora closed her eyes. She knew that she was entirely helpless. With an immense effort she moved to pull away from him, but instead found herself leaning forward until her head was upon his shoulder. It was as if he was a magnet and she was irresistibly drawn. Any resistance now not only seemed ridiculous, but almost painful. As if this was a signal he bent and lifted her off her feet and carried her to the couch where he laid her down. Unhurriedly, he removed her clothes, then his own and turned back to her again. The sun poured in through the windows and shone brilliantly upon the two pale figures. It rose into the glittering blue sky and became full. Behind the sun, hot heavy clouds built, massing together to cast a vast pall. Then at last, when the day had reached its zenith and the heat could no longer be borne, forked lightning pierced the clouds and struck the great ship, rending the mainsail from top to bottom.

The timbers groaned with the strain. The sea writhed as the waves were lashed by the rising wind. Victory rocked in its moorings, tensed and then relaxed, settling again as the wind subsided. Gradually the sky cleared, the sun came out again and apart from the scorch marks on the deck, there was no visible sign that a great storm had passed by. Lord De Lisle stood up. He dressed and walked up onto the deck, taking deep breaths of the fresh, clean air. He was smiling, but after a moment his face cleared and became expressionless. He spoke one word loudly and precisely:

"Exordio."[14]

And the great ship on which he stood rose up into the air and leapt forward as if sailing into nothingness and reality itself leapt with it and the sun rose and set once, then twice, and then many more times and Lord De Lisle stood unmoving and watched its passage, until finally he lowered his arms, looked at his watch and said, "Terminus."[15]

Victory settled down again in the harbour and the sea gently lapped her prow. Lord De Lisle then hurried down to Nelson's cabin. Theora was dressed and lying peacefully as if asleep, and upon her breast, was a tiny baby. Very gently, De Lisle lifted it up. He covered it with his cloak and without looking further, at either the child or Theora, he took out his watch, opened the mirror compartment and disappeared into time.

*

Lord Nelson, writing meticulous notes in preparation for the journey ahead, suddenly stopped and put his pen down. Drake, who was sitting beside him in the Club lounge, eyed him with concern. "Something's wrong?" he said in his gruff West Country voice.

Nelson nodded. "Yes. It was as if my ship cried out to me and then her voice was somehow instantly silenced, so no message could be given. That has never happened before. I must go and fetch the Earl."

---

[14] Begin

[15] Finish

Drake rose and picked up his log book. "Do you need me too?"

Nelson clapped his shoulder. "No, we need you quickly at the head of the Venetian fleet as we arranged. God speed to you and a fair wind."

He went swiftly out, dispatching a servant to call for the Earl. Lord Thorne and Lord Sulien both met him in the cavern entrance.

"We must go to the ship," said Nelson.

"Is Miss Templeton in danger?" said Lord Thorne sharply.

"I believe so," said Nelson. "Victory too."

Lord Sulien closed his eyes and opened them. "The guarding cantus have been destroyed," he said after a moment. "We must go now." They went to the library and moments later they all stepped through time and onto Victory's deserted deck.

"De Lisle's not here," said Lord Thorne instantly. He ran down to Nelson's quarters calling Theora's name. The Admiral looked at the Earl. "What will you do," he said, "if she has been hurt?"

The Earl's hand went to his sword. "There will be a reckoning," he said, patting the hilt, "but not yet."

The Admiral nodded. "Good judgement. I often think you should have become a sailor instead of a soldier."

The Earl raised his eyebrows. "I think we are all best placed where we are. I could never match your seamanship and you are an extremely poor horseman!"

"I am indeed," said Nelson with feeling. "Go now and see to Miss Templeton. I will wait for the Drum and meet the fleet at Plymouth."

"Thank you," said the Earl. He went below deck to the flagship cabin and found Lord Thorne beside Theora who was unconscious. "How is she?" he said sharply.

"Seems to be fine," said Lord Thorne brusquely. "Just

drugged." He showed the Earl an empty glass. "I can't make out what has happened here?"

The Earl looked around and his brow darkened. Lord Thorne glanced up quickly. "You sense something, Aidan?"

The Earl hesitated. "Yes, something, a trace, nothing more. There has been an event involving Miss Templeton, but not in this time, in the future. Whatever has happened there is hidden from me and there are no backward ripples in this time. Yet, I can feel that there will be consequences in all the realities. What these will be I do not know. Our only course now is to take Miss Templeton to safety and continue with the Quest. Then, we must deal with whatever unfolds."

He bent and picked Theora up and strode with her up on deck. The crew were starting to board now and the sails were unfurling. Drake appeared suddenly carrying a large covered box. He nodded briefly to Lord Sulien and Lord Thorne but turned immediately to Nelson.

"Do you want this in your cabin, Admiral?"

Nelson smiled. "Yes, thank you, Captain. I expect you will be sorry to relinquish it, but I swear I will guard it with my life."

Drake grinned. "You'd better, or it will be the last time that I'll make sail with you. Good luck to you, Sirs." He smiled briefly at them all and then disappeared below deck leaving Lord Sulien to take himself, Lord Thorne and Theora back to the cavern.

*

When Theora finally awoke she found Guy Irving regarding her anxiously. When she sat up he smiled with relief.

"How are you feeling?"

"Well enough," said Theora truthfully. "Where are we?"

"In the stronghold of the Sun Lord and the Knights of the Quest." Irving looked at her narrowly. "Do you remember anything?"

"Only that I was on the ship and then Lord De Lisle came." She wrinkled her brow. "What he said to me and what happened. Nothing."

"Yes, Lord Thorne said that might be the case," said Irving. "They think De Lisle has cleared your mind deliberately, but nothing to be concerned about." He patted her shoulder. "Don't worry, it's all under control, I promise."

"Where are they?" asked Theora.

"Gone to battle," said Guy. As Theora sprang to her feet he stepped forward and put a restraining hand on her shoulder. "Uh, uh, I have the strictest instructions to keep you here until after it's over, so you might as well sit back and rest."

"I can't," said Theora flatly. "I have to know what's going on. Isn't there a way to do that?"

"Might be," said Guy cautiously.

Theora impatiently stamped her foot. "Well then show me!"

Guy sighed. "Couldn't we just wait for the signal?"

"What signal?"

"The one from the Earl when he gets back."

Theora jumped up. "If there's a way to see what's happening, I beg of you, show it to me!"

Guy looked unhappy, but he went to Lord Thorne's desk and opened the drawer. He drew out a blotter and a blank piece of paper. "Firstly we need a signature, let's hope this gives it to me," he muttered under his breath. He laid the paper over the blotter and, to Theora's amazement, Lord Thorne's name, written in his graceful, flowing script, appeared on the page.

"Well done, Guy" she said admiringly.

Mr Irving nodded. "Helps to keep your ears and eyes open round here," he said modestly. "Now comes the tricky bit."

He went to the great globe and carefully started it spinning. He screwed up the signature and threw it at the globe. The paper hit full square and the globe stopped dead as if seized. Then it started to come apart, just as if it was an orange with dozens of segments. Each one was either the image of a place or a person. Each place image floated upwards, neatly stacked as if it was a pack of cards, and sorted itself, until at last the one at the top was clearly St Mark's Square in Venice. Then, each of the knights' images stepped forward and entered the St Mark's image, one after another, finishing with the Earl and last of all Lord Thorne. The place image grew and solidified and shone above the globe, but what was immediately clear to Theora was that what they were now seeing was the view from Lord Thorne's eyes…

The square, usually so full of people, was deserted apart from Lord Thorne riding Utopia. The horse stood calmly and Lord Thorne held the reins loosely with one hand, but that hand was a mailed fist. Theora saw the glint of steel as the sun flared across his drawn sword which he held at Utopia's flank. There was a sudden sound of hooves slipping on cobbles and, from the entrance by the great clock, Lord De Lisle came riding in upon his black stallion, Othello. He too was clad in armour, but his head was bare, save for a crown of gold set with opals and sapphires. He rode across the square and stopped in the centre so that the two horses were directly facing each other.

"So, Schoolmaster, it is you, not Aidan, who chooses to stand against me. Yet, in this place, where our powers are as nothing, I will easily beat you in combat. Considering your long friendship, I am disgusted that

Aidan will sacrifice you, but I suppose not entirely surprised. He holds our lives cheap where his precious quest is involved. I only realised the full extent of his ambition when I spoke with your Swan Queen. Another great lady sacrificed."

De Lisle's voice was so filled with loathing that Theora shivered, but Lord Thorne appeared unmoved. "And I am disgusted that, after so many long years, you understand so little about sacrifice and duty," he said. "It is you, not Aidan who seeks to be perceived as divine. Had you not, you would never have come here today. For now you know the true nature of the Quest, you will also know that it is part of your birthright to help it succeed. You still have the opportunity to do this. Take your knights home."

De Lisle sneered. "A brave speech indeed, but still just words. All my life I have heard you prosing on about duty and honour and sacrifice. And now, you're trying to make me believe it was all part of some higher calling, when actually it's just about you and Aidan preserving your own little timelines. Well I tell you now, that I have no intention of helping your precious quest. Here is my reply. You can tell Aidan that, in return for all your years of deceit, I will destroy you and all your knights!"

"Tell him yourself," said a clear voice. Theora gasped for the voice had come from high above the square. Guy exclaimed too, for they could both see the Earl. He was standing on the roof top of the Basilica.

Lord De Lisle glanced once at Lord Thorne and then upwards. He dismounted from Othello and walked to the edge of the Square. He sheathed his sword and stood hands on hips, regarding the Earl.

"Well then, Aidan. You make an appearance at last."

"Indeed. It seems that for all your apparent perception, you have misjudged me," said the Earl.

"Then come down and let us discuss the situation," said Lord De Lisle. He tapped his sheathed sword. "Look, I can surely give you no better sign that you can trust me? Let us, for once, meet without enmity and discuss terms."

"What terms can there be, when you have made your position so clear?" asked Lord Sulien.

Lord De Lisle regarded him. "If you will give up the Quest, I promise to go away and never bother you, or the Schoolmaster, ever again. After all, Aidan, we were friends once too. You have been closer than a brother to me. Indeed, if we had not squabbled over a pretty face, I am sure we would still be much in accord. Will you not come down?"

The Earl leaned over the balustrade. Around him silken pennants waved gay defiance to the wind from the lagoon. "I will come down, but on condition that you explain what happened with Miss Templeton."

Lord De Lisle's expression did not change. He whistled and Othello trotted to him. His Lordship mounted. "Very well. Let us speak of that, but not here," he said and touching up his horse, moved under the portico.

A few moments later, the Earl appeared. He was without armour, with a flame-coloured cloak about his shoulders and long-top boots over his breeches. He walked to Lord De Lisle and waved his hand.

"So, I am here as you requested, Bricin. Will you give me what I asked for?"

"Will you give up the Quest?"

"No."

"Then there can be no bargaining," said Lord De Lisle coldly. "I do not know why you have been so foolish as to think otherwise. And now you are come down, I see no reason to let you go."

He raised his hand and, to Theora's horror, she saw hundreds of armoured men enter the square. They poured in, like a pool of ink spilling onto the silvery flags, completely covering its clean lines until all the space was filled and the Earl was surrounded. At the first movement, Lord Thorne had attempted to ride forward, but he had been stayed by the Earl, who with one swift movement had drawn his sword and put himself between them.

Lord De Lisle leaned forward. "Well then, Aidan, as you are my prisoner, I think all that remains is for me to decide upon where you should be kept. Be sure that I will do everything I can to make your days quite miserable!"

The Earl's smile was a little twisted. "And a few moments ago, you reminded me of our friendship! I find you very fickle."

"Yes, I am," agreed Lord De Lisle. "Now, how about you give up your sword, I call off my knights and then we can all leave? Unlike you, I have always found Venice a very sordid, vulgar, city. I have no desire to linger. I could never understand your fascination with the place."

"Alas, your outlook upon life has always been distorted by self-focus," said the Earl. "You never look up, or out, but always within. It is your greatest weakness and it makes you vulnerable."

Lord De Lisle laughed. "I do not feel weak or vulnerable."

"Yes, I can see that," said the Earl. "You are so able to read the signs of nature, but always unable to read the signs of the times."

He stretched out his sword hilt first, but, as Lord De Lisle went to clasp it, there was a sound of rushing air, spiralling down from high above. Mingled with it were other more complex sounds: the clanging of metal upon metal, the turning of wheels, the thunder of hooves and *the heavy breath of horses straining at their bits.*

Guy gasped and he and Theora caught at each other's hands in sheer wonderment, for what they saw seemed to defy all reason…

Falling from the sky, on a direct path from the roof of the Basilica, was a huge, golden chariot drawn by four magnificent horses. But these horses were made from what appeared to be solid bronze. The speed and power of their passage caused many of Lord De Lisle's knights to be cast up into the air and swept away through sheer force. Those that remained galloped pell mell from the square to escape the terrifying wind. At last, only the Earl, Lord De Lisle, Lord Thorne and the two black stallions remained, wrapped in a protective veil of golden light.

The Earl lowered his sword. He stepped out from under the veil, leaving the others still held within, and walked out to the chariot. The four horses, towering above him, stood immobile now. One of them pawed the ground impatiently and sparks flew from his huge metal hoof. The Earl regarded them and then bowed low.

"Thank you, my friends, for obeying my summons. After your long years of sleep, a Sun Lord again requires your services. Soon dawn will rise upon Oimelc and we must be there before it does. This journey will require all your strength and speed, for the cargo we bring will be precious and must reach its destination undamaged. I ask you now for your help with this."

He bowed again. As he rose up the four horses looked at each other and then him. Then they all lowered their heads to their forelegs as if bowing in return. The Earl gave a deep sigh. "Thank you." He mounted the chariot and gathered up the reins. "I will see you at the appointed place, Argus. I would be grateful if you would keep Bricin and his remaining friends entertained here for a little longer."

Lord Thorne nodded. *"Very well, Aidan."* He looked at Lord De Lisle who was staring at him with a face black with anger. *"I think Bricin may be feeling vulnerable now."*

"Very probably," said the Earl. He looked down at Lord De Lisle. *"Farewell, for the moment, Bricin. I have no doubt I will see you soon."*

"You can be sure of it," said Lord De Lisle venomously. *"I cannot believe that you violated our laws and used a cantus in this place,"* he said incredulously.

"I know," said the Earl. *"It appears that I too am 'fickle'. Yet, I did try to give you fair warning. I did tell you to look 'up and out'."* He smiled and as he did so, the sun rose above the Basilica and blazed across the square, sweeping into every corner so that the whole expanse was glittering and golden. Then the Earl spoke to his horses and the chariot rose into the air and in a second it had disappeared completely.

The golden veil dissolved, leaving Lord De Lisle and Lord Thorne facing each other. Lord Thorne turned his head slightly and the Sun Knights, who had been waiting by the lagoon, started to ride up to join him. In the distance a fleet of English ships were just visible. Lord De Lisle's knights were nowhere to be seen. They had fled the square and not returned.

"I would advise you to leave whilst you can," said Lord Thorne.

"You know that my power is a match for yours," said Lord De Lisle angrily. *"If Aidan has used a cantus, what makes you think I won't?"*

Lord Thorne nodded. *"I know you will, which is why, if you do so, I will turn this place inside out and trap you within it forever."*

"Which would kill you and all your knights too," said

326

Lord De Lisle swiftly.

"Yes, but many more, for whom I care deeply, would still be safe," said Lord Thorne.

"I see," said Lord De Lisle. He scanned the impassive faces of the knights. "Yes, I suppose there would be little satisfaction in it ending here." He gathered up his reins and mounted Othello. "I will leave, but be assured, we will face each other again, very soon."

As Lord De Lisle rode away, Lord Thorne spoke a word and he and the knights stepped out of Venice in 1803 and that time and place were no longer visible to Theora and Guy Irving.

Chapter Twenty-One

It had been a long day for Mr Allan, as he had been forced to spend it chained to a chair. To start with he had been drugged from a potion and when he awoke, he found himself alone in the cold, dusk-lit room with no sign of his captor. His immediate thought was to free himself, but he soon realised, somewhat ruefully, that he had no idea how to do so. The irony was that even though he was now one of the Perdurare, he was aware that this power could only be channelled through special training and study which he had yet to receive. In his angry desire to cause harm to his father, he had used a book filched from Lord Sulien's study and so managed to deliver the cantus which had created the illusion of Theora Templeton. Lord De Lisle's temper and impatience had done the rest, for he had not stopped to investigate further. Fortune had therefore favoured Mr Allan so far, but he acknowledged that his luck had probably run out. It was quite possible that Lord De Lisle would kill him very soon. He shrugged mentally at the thought. So be it. If he was to die, he resolved to do so bravely. Through one of the great windows he could see up into the dark sky where a single star now burned clear and bright. He smiled at the sight, fixed his eyes upon it and so the night passed. It was many hours later that he was awakened from an uncomfortable doze. The door behind him opened and someone came in and switched on the light. He called out, but whoever it was remained deliberately out of view and silent. The visitor went backwards and forwards out of the room for a while, apparently bringing in various items. Then the door was locked.

"Who is it, who are you?" cried Mr Allan, straining in his bonds to see behind him. There was no answer. Instead a soft hand covered his mouth and a moment later this was replaced by a silken gag which prevented all further speech. Then the stranger sat down immediately opposite Mr Allan in a large, wing-backed chair. He gasped, for it was Jennifer Layton. She was quiet, composed and incredibly beautiful. Mr Allan gazed at her with loathing. One word formed in his mind: "Traitor." She regarded him, looking him over almost hungrily. Finally she went to him and lifted his chin, studying his face. Mr Allan struggled to pull away, but she held him tightly. There was a latent strength in the slim, white fingers. Then, when she had examined every detail, she gave a sigh and reached forward and removed the gag.

Mr Allan uttered a range of expletives in his native Irish. Lady Layton's eyes danced. "How unfortunate, that is one of the few languages I have not bothered to study. How well you speak it, my son."

"Don't call me that," said Mr Allan savagely.

"Why not?" she said. "We both know that is what you are."

"What are you doing here?"

Jennifer leaned forward and picked up a pear from the table. She began to peel it with a gold-handled knife. "It may surprise you to learn that I am here with Lord Sulien's blessing," she said calmly.

"It would surprise me," said Mr Allan coldly. "I know that he took steps to prevent you ever having anything to do with me. I am deeply thankful for that."

She winced, but carried on with her task. When she had finished, she wiped her hands on a gold-edged napkin and poured some water into a glass. She held this to Mr Allan's lips. "Drink it," she said. "I am sure you are thirsty. That potion, although very effective, always leaves the victim with a very dry throat."

Mr Allan reluctantly sipped from the glass and when she offered him a slice of fruit, took that too and chewed slowly.

"Why are you doing this?" he said at last.

Her amber eyes became shadowed. "I am here to help you."

"You'll forgive me if I find that hard to believe."

"Nevertheless, it is the truth."

"Then remove these bonds."

To his surprise she did so instantly. Mr Allan rubbed his sore wrists. "Was it you who drugged me?"

"Yes, I mixed the potion. I also persuaded Lord De Lisle to leave you alive."

"Where is he now?"

"Looking through time for Miss Templeton, before he joins the battle."

Mr Allan stood up. "Then I need to get back as soon as possible. Will you help me?"

She looked rather surprised. "I am honoured that you trust me. Yes I will help you."

"It is not a question of trust, just expediency," said Mr Allan sharply.

She smiled. "Yet you acknowledge me freely as your mother and Lord De Lisle your father."

Mr Allan looked around the room for his coat and put it on. "Acknowledgement is not acceptance. I want nothing from you, but passage back to my own time."

"I suppose I deserve that, Ciaran. Yet I would ask you to believe that it is not my fault that you were born and seeing the man you have become, well, it is impossible for me to feel any regret."

"I don't care what you feel," said Mr Allan. "However, if you give me your word that you are now operating under Lord Sulien's direction, I will accept it."

"Then the word is given," said Jenny evenly. "If you will take my hand, I will bring you to Lord Sulien, who is awaiting you."

She held out her hand which he took reluctantly. She lifted up her compact mirror and spoke into it. The next moment they were standing inside a richly decorated sitting room and a grandfather clock was striking. Jenny shut the compact.

"Would you take a seat please?" she said pleasantly. "We are a little early."

She went and sat down on one of the damask sofas. Mr Allan, after a moment's hesitation, did the same, so that he was facing her. Despite himself he could not help looking around, for his eyes were drawn to the rich furnishings, pictures and incredible plasterwork. Everywhere he gazed, there was some new treasure to be seen. He was aware that Jenny was watching him. "Do you like it?" she asked.

He stared at her, conflicted with emotions and uncertain how to react. At last he said sincerely, "It is magnificent. Who lives here?"

Jenny smiled. "I do. It is my home when I am in England."

She gestured to the window. "When you were still a very small baby, we used to stand here and look out together."

Mr Allan stared. "Why do you tell me this?" he said. "I can have no memory of it."

"Of course not," she agreed. She hesitated and stood up and walked to the window. "I want you to know that it was not easy for me to give you up. Nor has it been easy to pretend my indifference to you all these years, whilst keeping Lord De Lisle's favour. He would not hesitate to blast me out of existence if he knew the truth."

"That I can well believe," said Mr Allan with feeling. He relented a little. "This house is protected?"

"Yes. It has a reality splinter linked to a cantus which conceals those who enter from Lord De Lisle's sight.

Within this house we are safe, but once we step outside we become visible to him. This is a safe place for the Knights and their servants to meet. Lord De Lisle has never suspected anything because he has never come here. He has a keen dislike of this area of the country, it being the Sun Lords' ancient stronghold. He was, however, quite happy for me to stay here, to spy on Lord Sulien as required."

Mr Allan stood up and walked to her. "I don't fully understand. You owed much to Lord De Lisle. I know you wanted to marry him. Why didn't you just tell him that you were pregnant?"

"Because he would have killed my unborn child," she said bleakly.

She saw Mr Allan was looking disbelieving and said passionately, "You cannot fathom such a thing can you? Lord De Lisle has never loved me, he sees me as quite inferior. I am a useful tool that is all. If he ever spares me a thought, it is to smile at the idea that he has made a slave out of the woman who loved his rival. So, if he knew that I had a child and that child would one day be as strong and powerful as him. Well, that would be a wound to his pride and he would seek to destroy you."

"Would you tell me what you meant when you said that it wasn't your fault I was born?" asked Mr Allan.

"Simply, that I thought it was impossible for me to conceive. I was always told that my facial disfigurement was a manifestation of my barrenness. You see, in all my many affairs with mortal men, I never became pregnant. I incorrectly assumed that I was infertile."

She looked up. "I do not ask you to forgive me. I have done many bad things. But I do want you to recognise that I have also used these last years to make some amends."

His blue eyes met hers. "I can see that," he said. "I am

sorry that you have suffered."

She smiled. "The pain I have felt is nothing in comparison to the pride I have now in my son." She glanced out over the parkland. "Soon Lord Sulien will come for you. I have only one request. When everything is over, please consider this your home. That is all I could ever wish for." Without allowing him to answer she stepped forward and flung open the window. There was a sound as of a rushing wind and an immense chariot drawn by four giant, metallic horses landed upon the carriageway. Lord Sulien stepped down. Mr Allan ran down the stairs and out to him. "Get in, I will be with you shortly," said the Earl and entered the house.

Jenny looked at him fearfully. "My Lord, you should not tarry, Lord De Lisle will surely be hot on your heels."

"I am more concerned about your situation," said Lord Sulien.

She stood up and faced him. "Please go, my Lord and, if you can, protect my son."

He looked at her with a mixture of admiration and exasperation. He thought how that standing thus, with her hands loosely clasped in front of her, she looked far more like the simple innkeeper's daughter from the cottage in Ireland. Seeing his strange expression, she smiled at him uncertainly.

"I am so sorry for all of this, Jenny," he said abruptly.

"You have nothing to reproach yourself for, Sir," she said.

"Yes I do," he said bluntly. "I married your sister because I was angry with Bricin, but also because I was angry with myself. I did want her, in much the way that Bricin did, but I wouldn't admit it. Just as I wouldn't admit that I also knew you loved me. If I had been truly honourable, I would have married you and we could both have looked after Lizzie."

"My Lord, your marriage to Lizzie gave her much happiness. You have a sweet daughter who is the living image of my sister. I have a son who has all the power that I always longed for. That they love each other means that the circle has now closed. Everything is as it should be."

Lord Sulien stepped forward. His lips brushed her hair. "Goodbye, my brave Jenny and thank you."

She leaned against his shoulder for a moment, struggling with her heart. Swiftly she flung her arms around his neck and pressed her lips to his. He let her touch him for a moment. Then he turned away and went out to the chariot. Behind him the windows slammed shut and a fierce wind rose up as the quadriga departed for the last leg of the journey. Jenny stood and watched the glittering speck until it had entirely disappeared. Then she went and sat down again on one of the damask benches. She opened a book and began to read until the light became too dim for her to see the finely printed pages.

*

High above the clouds, Theora and Irving sat together, hands clasped as they had been since they entered the chariot to which the Earl had transported them directly from the cavern. Mr Allan sat opposite, his head bowed. All of them were silent, Theora and Irving were incredulous about everything that was happening. Mr Allan because he was filled with conflicting emotions which made him unable to speak. As they were unable to assess the passage of time, it might have been minutes, hours or days, when suddenly they realised that the journey had finished and the chariot alighted on the quayside of a harbour. The bronze horses were standing, blowing hard, a strange sound like glass breaking. Mr Irving nimbly climbed out, followed by Mr Allan. They found the Earl standing at the horses' heads and looking out to sea. Beyond the headland there were many ships of various forms. Some bore flags with golden suns and they were facing off to others with black sails. Mr Allan let out an oath when he saw the latter.

"De Lisle's here already!"

The Earl nodded, he did not look concerned. "The fleet has been engaged for some time. The black sails cannot win, not with Nelson and Drake to contend with. De Lisle knows this."

"Then why does he bother?" asked Irving.

"He knows that I will not wish to see mortal blood spilt, so thinks to hold up the Quest by tempting me to join the sea battle. Every second is now precious to him, for although he knows where we are headed, the final location is still concealed. He will be now using all his powers to find out what that might be, in the hope of heading us off."

"Will you join Nelson?" said Mr Allan seriously.

"I will not," said the Earl. "Although it will mean mortal casualties, none of us can now leave the appointed path. We six are all instrumental to the completion of the Quest. It is the other knights who must now fight De Lisle's forces. We go forward on horseback, for the quadriga are spent. Their power was only for this one journey. Now they must return." He climbed back up the chariot and leaned inside. "Please would you allow me to lift you out, Miss Templeton?"

She looked up at him and stood up. "Can I not climb out, Sir?"

He smiled. "Only with extreme difficulty. It is easier this way, if you will permit me." He climbed down the ladder which extended down the inside of the chariot. "Would you please put your arms around my neck?"

After a moment's hesitation she did so. He lifted her

335

easily and moments later he set her down lightly upon the cobbles.

Leaving her with Mr Irving he turned back to the horses. They were looking at him through their burning gold eyes. "I thank you, my friends, for your efforts. Your part is done. Go back to your home and take your rest, with all my blessings."

He raised his hand and at this signal the horses leapt into the air and in that second they were gone.

Mr Allan was looking at him. "You said six of us, my Lord, yet I count only four."

"Yes, I include Lord Thorne," said the Earl. "He will join us with King Henry. They have brought the Harp and the Drum. Now, let us find our horses. Come with me, Ciaran. Mr Irving, please stay with Miss Templeton and escort her to that cottage just inside the harbour wall. They have a change of clothes for you and will give you refreshment. Ciaran and I will be back shortly."

He beckoned to Mr Allan and they walked down the harbour together. Mr Allan spoke first.

"What should I do now, my Lord?" he said hesitantly.

The Earl didn't break stride. "What do you mean?"

"You know that I am now better able to help you than I was," said Mr Allan.

"Ah, you mean that now you are fully a Moon Lord," said the Earl. "But, what sort of help did you plan to give? Already, your action has allowed Lord De Lisle to find a way to Miss Templeton. We can only hope no actual damage has been done. If you are now thinking of another attack on your father, be assured that I would never permit that."

Mr Allan stopped. "Why, wouldn't you?" he said abruptly. "He surely deserves death for everything he has done."

"'Everything he has done'," repeated the Earl. "But

what is so bad in comparison with the good? I cannot forget his years of service protecting the 20th-Century Domain."

Mr Allan's lips tightened. "What about the rape of your wife and the abuse of my mother?" he said in a whisper. "Is that not sufficient reason for him to be punished?"

The Earl turned and faced him across the path. "Listen to me, Ciaran, and then never speak of this again," he said sternly. "In the case of Juliet's mother, I was the one who put her in Lord De Lisle's path. With your mother, I could have prevented the situation occurring, but chose to do otherwise. So, if you wish to punish someone, I am your man."

They made their way to the coaching inn which stood at the end of the valley. The stables were around the back and here they found King Henry awaiting them.

"Welcome to Botreaux," he said boisterously. "Everything is ready and I have our drum and harp safe and ready. How goes the sea engagement? I can get no news here."

"It goes well," said the Earl. He saw that King Henry's face held a hungry expression and he smiled. "Still longing to be with them, Harry?"

"I am indeed," said King Henry with feeling. "Just as I'd rather be with Louis on the field of combat. Are you sure there is nobody else that can play the Harp for you, Aidan?"

"Quite sure," said the Earl firmly. It is a Welsh harp and it needs an expert Welsh hand to play it. You understand that don't you?"

"Yes I understand, but I am a warrior as well as a musician. As the battle is now engaged, I am afraid I do not feel like music at the moment," said King Henry fiercely.

The Earl laughed. "Yes I know it's very hard for you. Still, it may be that once you have played your part, you will be able to join the fighting!"

"I never thought of that," said King Henry brightening. "Let us therefore make haste." He led them to the stalls. "Here are the horses." He called to the grooms who led out Apollo and Solitaire.

King Henry vaulted onto his own horse, a blood bay. "And here is your mount, my Lord." He pointed to a black mare who was led out of the furthest stall.

Mr Allan looked questioningly at the Earl. "This is not my horse," he said positively.

"She wasn't your horse," agreed the Earl, "but she is now. She is sister to Utopia. Her name is Sable. Now let us go and collect Mr Irving and Miss Templeton."

"How far must we go?" asked Mr Allan.

"It is a short journey, but it wants but five hours 'til midnight and we do not know what Lord De Lisle will do to hinder us."

He led the way back to the fisherman's cottage where Irving and Theora were waiting. Theora had changed into a riding habit and Irving into breeches, boots, a warm jacket and a cream scarf. He looked neat and stylish as ever but somewhat anxious. The reason for this was evident as the Earl and his company were brought up to the house.

"You know I don't ride," he said baldly, "and if you want me to dance later, I can't risk breaking anything from a fall, so what's to be done?"

"Don't worry," said the Earl soothingly. "Apollo will carry us both. I can promise you that you will be as safe upon his back as in your own rocking chair."

He waited for Theora to mount and they all set off at a steady pace up the valley. Having circled around the pretty fishing village with its painted cottages and slate roofs, they headed down into a green glade. They rode single file down a steep path. This wound beside a river of such rippling loveliness in form and sound that it caused even Irving to forget his fear of falling and exclaim at its beauty. The water skipped merrily between the pebbles making a deep sweet music.

"This is Dowr an Velinji,"[16] said the Earl. "It is also known in English as the River Valency."

Apart from the sound of the horses' hooves on the soft earth and the bubbling water, there was little other noise. They had gone no more than a couple of miles when Mr Allan spoke within the Earl's head.

"You know we are being followed."

"Yes. Since we entered the wood."

"What do you want to do?"

"In half a mile the track opens out. I suggest we make a run for it."

"Can we outrun them?"

"Ordinary horses yes. If it is Lord De Lisle with Othello, I doubt it."

"Then let me stay behind and create a diversion."

The Earl hesitated. "You give me your word that you will not harm him?"

Mr Allan grinned. "Are you serious? I have only just mastered thought transference and I learned that from page twenty of a stolen book. I promise you I won't do anything desperate. I'll join you as soon as I can." At that he turned and headed back towards Botreaux.

King Henry looked questioningly at the Earl. "Something's wrong?"

"No not at all," lied the Earl, "please, let's keep up the pace."

---

[16] Cornish

He called back to Theora who had reined in Solitaire and was watching Mr Allan's departing back. "Miss Templeton, would you come up here and ride behind me."

He spoke to Apollo and the stallion broke into a canter and then into a gallop. Solitaire snatching at her bit raced to follow. They made their way through the darkening woods and across the hills until at last they reached the winding way which led to the glen. Here the Earl pulled up, for the road was petering out and twilight had fallen. There was, however, no sound of pursuit. Mr Irving breathed a sigh of relief. "Can we go more slowly now?"

"Yes, indeed," said the Earl. "We must now make the rest of the journey on foot and lead the horses." He dismounted and gave his hand to Mr Irving. "How do you feel, Guy?"

Irving winced. "I'll be much better for walking a while. I don't know how you fellows ever take to this riding lark. Plays merry hell with your dancing muscles."

King Henry, who having also dismounted was assisting Miss Templeton, laughed. "Once our Quest is completed, Sir, I will have to show you how easy it is to be both a good rider and a good dancer. I am renowned for my skills in both. Is that not true, Aidan?"

"It is," said the Earl. "I believe there is much you could teach him. But now we need to go forward. Here is our host waiting to escort us." He looked ahead and they saw two tall men coming down the path towards them. One had dark grey hair, crowned with a simple silver circlet, and was wearing green robes. The other was unmistakeably Lord Thorne.

The grey-haired man bowed. "Greetings, my Lord," he said, "and to all of you, his quest companions."

Lord Thorne looked around sharply. "Where is Ciaran?"

"Coming," said the Earl. "Greetings, Lord Nechtan.[17] It has been many years since the first Sun Lord marked this glen as the likely resting place of the Star Maiden. You have guarded it long and well. May your unceasing protection be rightly rewarded."

"Let us hope so indeed," said Lord Nechtan. "Follow me now and keep close. The spirits that guard this place will do the mortals harm unless I quickly make my mark."

He led them a little way down the path to a small well that stood by the crossroads. Reaching into its depths he pulled out a bucket of clear water and wetted his hand. Then he traced on the forehead of each of the mortals a star shape.

"There, it is done. Now the spirits will pass you by. Try not to look at them, for they can unhinge your mind, if you choose to allow them access to your thoughts."

"Ok, understood," said Irving briskly. "God damn it, if things weren't bad enough, we now have spooks to worry about," he said under his breath. "I'm glad to see you again, my friend," he said to Lord Thorne. "But you seem a bit downcast. Worried about young Mr Allan?"

"I am," said Lord Thorne. "Shouldn't I go back for him, Aidan?"

The Earl shook his head. "No, not yet. We must ride on. If he needs us, I will know."

---

[17] Nechtan is derived from Old-Irish necht "clean, pure and white". The name relates to mythological beings, who were dwelling near wells and springs. Lord Nechtan is the protector of the Kieve.

Chapter Twenty-Two

When he left the Earl, Ciaran had made his way back through the woods until he reached the meadows. There, he pulled up, tethered the mare and crept to a safe spot to wait and observe. Within minutes, Lord De Lisle came galloping up. Behind him were a troop of his black-clad knights. De Lisle looked up the trail. "They are making their way to the waterfall," he said after a moment. "We must meet them before they reach it and then hold the line." He swung Othello round, but in that instant, Mr Allan spoke into his mind:

"Sistite, Dominum Luna hoc tempore non tuo."[18]

The knights looked around in confusion as Lord De Lisle pulled Othello to a sharp halt. Holding his stamping, snorting horse, he said clearly, "Ride on as fast as you can, I will be with you in a moment." He watched as the knights disappeared and when at last the glade was empty again he said out loud, "Habes enim adhuc discere tempus captivitatis."[19] He dismounted from Othello. "Will you not come down and talk to me in person, my son?"

Mr Allan walked through the trees until the two men were facing each other. Lord De Lisle made a slight bow. "Welcome to you, Ciaran. How are you?"

Mr Allan regarded him. "I am well enough, Sir. I am also strong enough."

Othello snorted. It was a slightly ridiculous sound and brought a faint smile to Lord De Lisle's lips.

"Othello says it all. You must not make assumptions. I

---

[18] Halt, Moon Lord this is not your time.

[19] And you have yet to learn that time is for the taking.

have had years of instruction to hone my skills and many centuries to practice them. Although I do applaud the trick you played upon me with regard to Miss Templeton. It was well done indeed."

Mr Allan removed his gloves. "Thank you."

"And now you are here to kill me," said Lord De Lisle conversationally. "I am fascinated to see what arts you will employ to bring me down."

Mr Allan thrust the gloves inside his tunic and flexed his fingers. "I promised the Earl I would not kill you," he said coldly. "However, I did not promise him that I would not hurt you. Iam intelleges dolor fecisti."[20] He swung and landed a blow to Lord De Lisle's solar plexus. White light sparkled from his fingers and Lord De Lisle fell backwards onto the earth.

Mr Allan, breathing deeply, looked down upon him. De Lisle lay still, but then he rolled over and, to his horror and irritation, Mr Allan could hear that he was laughing. "Good, very good, you are an excellent fighter. I am afraid I have never really bothered with the noble art of boxing, although Aidan did try hard to get me interested. It is such an untidy sport you see, I prefer something more civilised and stylish."

He stood up and held out his hand. Within it was a silver-mounted gun. "This rather pretty but useful weapon holds bullets fashioned from time splinters. They are only the particles, but they are enhanced with lots of quite nasty and destructive cantus and a few small tweaks of my own devising. The purpose is to cause the victim long-lasting pain. It depends on how strong you are, of course. Most ordinary mortals succumb quite quickly, unless they are like dear Jenny, well versed in our ways."

---

[20] Now you will know the pain you have caused.

He saw Mr Allan's face change and his smile deepened.

"I rarely use this because, unlike you, I have been trained and I prefer to use that training whenever I can. But, in this case, time really is of the essence, so let's see how we get on. I have always wanted to see the effect upon one of my own kind, so thank you for providing me with such an ideal opportunity for a controlled test."

He raised his arm and pointed the gun deliberately at Mr Allan's chest, but, as he took careful aim, to Mr Allan's amazement he suddenly lowered it again, fixing the gun at his side. "Ah," he said and his voice was chillingly cold, "Good evening, Schoolmaster!"

As he spoke, Lord Thorne walked to Mr Allan keeping his eyes fixed upon Lord De Lisle. "We need to leave, Ciaran," he said.

Mr Allan didn't move. "I want to know what he meant about Jenny."

Lord Thorne took his arm. "No, come now and leave him."

He whistled and Sable trotted into the glade. "Mount up and we can go. I can only hold him still for a little longer."

Mr Allan shook his head. He went up to De Lisle and looked into his eyes. Lord De Lisle was quite immobile, but his expression was still one of amusement. "Tell me," said Mr Allan angrily.

Lord De Lisle closed his eyes and opened them. "I don't think so."

Furiously, Mr Allan leaned forward and jerked the gun from the other man's lifeless hand. He pointed it directly at De Lisle's chest.

"Tell me."

De Lisle looked pained. He flicked a glance at Lord Thorne. "Another lover of mortals. What is the fascination? I mean, I know he is the son of a mortal, but he is also now a fully-fledged Moon Lord. He really needs to develop some perspective."

"Shut up," said Mr Allan furiously.

Lord Thorne placed a hand on his shoulder. "You do no good here," he said. "Forget him and remember what we are here to do."

Lord De Lisle laughed harshly. "Oh, Argus, always so prudent! Duty first has always been your maxim. Yet, it wasn't always so. After all, you kept a Druid priestess as your whore for quite a few years. You weren't always so sanctimonious."

Lord Thorne said evenly, "And you should know better than to try and provoke me. It won't work."

"No, but it has wasted a little more time and in a few seconds your cantus will be broken. If you want to delay me further, you will need to think of something else."

Lord Thorne relaxed. "There is no need to delay you further, De Lisle, Aidan has reached the Kieve. Even you cannot stop the Quest now."

"Well we will see, won't we," said Lord De Lisle. He watched as Mr Allan threw the gun far away into the river and then the two men mounted up and rode away up the hill.

In a moment, Lord De Lisle shook himself as if to remove invisible bonds. He fell to his knees as the cantus left his body and shuddered as his limbs came back to life. He breathed deeply and then, summoning his strength, sent his thought in pursuit of Mr Allan.

*

Utopia and Sable made short work of the miles between Botreaux and Tredhewi. When they pulled up at the entrance to the glen it was pitch dark.

"Keep behind me," said Lord Thorne, "and keep your eyes upon the path." They dismounted and walked forward. The light that emanated from them both made

345

the walkway distinct. The night was still and initially there was no sound, but gradually as they came further into the valley, strange, sharp cries, started to emanate from deep within the trees. Sable began to sweat. Mr Allan ran a comforting hand down her neck. "What is it?" he asked.

Lord Thorne looked around anxiously. "It is the protection of the glen. Lord De Lisle's knights have not had the strength of mind to resist it. We must keep going. Keep your mind focused upon the path."

They walked on, but the cries became more piercing. They mingled with moans and sobs. Mr Allan stopped dead. "We must help them, Argus," he said hoarsely.

"We cannot," said Lord Thorne, "and it would be dangerous to do so." He turned back but suddenly swung round hastily as Mr Allan jumped off his horse. "No, you must keep to the path!"

It was too late, Mr Allan had darted into the trees. He ran clumsily, half tripping, until he reached a ditch, choked with stones and ivy. Here, one of Lord De Lisle's knights was lying, tears streaming down his face and spittle foaming from his lips. Mr Allan lifted him upright. "Don't be afraid," he said and placed a hand upon the man's brow.

The man looked up at him. "I cannot forgive myself," he said in a voice that was choked with sobs. "I didn't mean for her to die. She was so beautiful. I thought he just wanted me to drive him to the house. I didn't know what he would do."

Mr Allan looked into his eyes. "I can ease your pain if you show me. Remember what happened and I can take away the memory for you."

The man moaned and shook his head. "I don't believe you."

Mr Allan smiled. "Trust me," he said gently. "I

promise you that all will be well."

The man relaxed. He looked into Mr Allan's eyes and the Moon Lord saw…

Jennifer Layton sitting within her house, upon a gilded bench, a book in her hands. She was staring at the page, but Ciaran sensed her attention was not on the words. Then suddenly all the glass in the windows shattered and a furious wind blew into the room. It knocked over the table and porcelain was sent flying in all directions. Jennifer shrank back against the settle, but she did not attempt to move further. Then out of the centre of all the destruction a figure stepped. Lord De Lisle brushed the glass from his coat and came forward.

"Good afternoon, Jenny."

She sat immobile. Her lips moved but there was no sound.

He sighed. "You have no words for me. Well perhaps it is best if I do all the talking."

He sat down beside her. "I now know everything of course. Now that the cantus that protected this house has been lost, I understand both what has happened and what is planned. I now also see why you wanted me to marry you. Poor Jenny, did you really think I would have looked after your son after I realised the truth? Still, I suppose, after all that, he is a likely enough fellow, but a little too serious for my taste." He paused. "Still nothing to say?"

"You will not harm him?" she said as if the words were forced from her.

He flicked at his coat. A shard of glass still twinkled upon the cuff. "I have no desire to harm him," he said with cool indifference. "He cannot be blamed for his mother's mistakes. But enough of this. I have other things to do." He jerked her to her feet.

"Get up please. Now where should you stand? Ah, I think in front of the fireplace would be appropriate." He

pushed her round until she was standing on the hearth and then stepped back and faced her. "That's perfect. Stand up straight please!" He pulled out a silver-mounted gun. "Any last words?"

She regarded him through heavy eyes. "Please get it over with quickly."

He gave a chuckle. "I hoped you'd say that." He levelled the gun. "Alas, I am afraid that is a request that your treachery prevents me from granting." He pulled the trigger.

He then sat down on the bench and watched her with interest. The minutes passed and a clock struck. As the bells tolled, Jenny writhed and moaned. Blood ran from her eyes and ears streamed onto the fine carpet. She clawed at the grate and crawled painfully towards the window, her body grating upon the broken glass and her dress ripping. A tremor ran through her and her breath gurgled as she tried to speak. Then she fell still. Lord De Lisle rose. He went to the window and looked down at Jenny's mutilated body for a moment.

"Goodbye, my dear Jenny," he said. Then he stepped over her. The Knight who had accompanied him was staring at the devastation with his mouth open. Lord De Lisle ignored him. He mounted the carriage and signalled for them to depart...

*

Mr Allan withdrew his hand from the Knight's brow. He was trembling and his heart was pounding in his throat. He was filled with an anger unlike anything that he had ever felt in all his gentle life. His whole body started to pulse and the energy within him made the ground upon which he stood shake and twist. He clenched his fists and a cold white light, tinged with blue, shone about him and flamed in the air. Then he fell to the ground. He started as Lord Thorne suddenly appeared beside him. He had brought water, which he splashed upon Mr Allan's face. The sensation made Mr Allan gasp and choke.

"Perge linquere luna ut luceant in spiritu rursus stella virgo praecipio tibi,"[21] said Lord Thorne. He thrust his hand inside Mr Allan's jacket and placed it upon his heart. "Come back to me, Ciaran," he said in English. Then he waited. After a moment, Mr Allan's heartbeat slowed and the white and blue light receded. Lord Thorne relaxed.

After a moment Mr Allan stirred. He sat up, blinked his eyes to focus and looked painfully at Lord Thorne. "What happened?" he whispered.

"It was De Lisle," said Lord Thorne. "He reached deep into your mind. If I hadn't been there you would have run mad and been lost to us forever."

Mr Allan coughed. "I saw what he did to Jenny," he said hollowly.

Lord Thorne nodded. "I know."

"Was it a lie?"

"I wish I could say so," said Lord Thorne, "but, I am afraid, it was not. She is dead, but nothing will change that and to try to revenge her would be useless. Soon you will be going into a place where only the purest of heart are welcomed. If you wish to repay your mother's sacrifice, banish now from your heart the hatred which Lord De Lisle has planted there. Otherwise, you will be unable to help us. That is Lord De Lisle's intention and if you cannot do this, the Quest will be doomed and he will have already won."

Mr Allan looked at him. He shuddered and then seemed to come to a decision. "I understand and I am

---

[21] "Go spirit leave the moon to shine once more, by the Star Maiden I command thee."

ready to do whatever is needed. Let us go and end this."

Lord Thorne nodded. He smiled encouragingly and side by side, leading their black horses, the two men walked forward and soon they had passed under the shining curtain of the waterfall.

*

"Why do you think that this is the last resting place of the Star Maiden?" asked Guy Irving as they made their way through the tunnel behind the Kieve.

The Earl had insisted they kept going at a strong pace, assuring them that Lord Thorne would catch them up. They had walked further and further into the darkness and, despite the comforting light and heat from the torches that they carried, it was icy cold.

Irving's question was addressed to Lord Nechtan, who was leading. He stopped and looked back, then quoted these lines:

Where no moon shines
Where no sun warms
Where water moves not
Where rainbows now flower

Irving looked intrigued. "Ah, so it's part of the Sun Lord's verses."

Lord Nechtan nodded. "Yes, this is the one place on Old Earth where neither Sun nor Moon Lord can use their full powers."

Irving looked at the Earl. "So, you're now effectively just as mortal as we are?"

"Not exactly," said the Earl. "When the first Sun Lord discovered the secrets of this place he explored it thoroughly. What he found made him appoint a guardian to protect it, until we could create an exact plan for how we might release the Maiden from her long sleep. In this place, I can no longer easily contact my kindred or channel the energy of the Earth. If I stay here for more than a day, I will start to age more quickly. Which is why we must complete our task quickly."

"So you can't now help Lord Thorne," said Theora sharply.

"No, he has gone from my sight. We can now only have faith that he is safe. In the meantime we must keep going. Do you think you can manage this journey on foot, for now we must leave the horses and descend into the heart of this place?"

Theora nodded. "I can do whatever you require of me, Sir."

He gave his rare smile and the warmth in his green eyes suddenly reminded her of when he had kissed her in the shepherd's hut.

She glanced away to avoid his gaze and said hastily, "What will happen to the horses?"

"They will wait for us," said the Earl. He walked up to Apollo. "Farewell, my friend. Protect your sister and I hope to see you again very soon." The stallion tossed his head. He breathed gently upon the Earl's chest for a moment and then he, Solitaire and King Henry's bay gelding turned and walked back up the passage.

"Let us now go," said the Earl, "Nechtan will lead us."

They walked on, down and deep into the heart of the chasm. Although the air remained fresh, it was wet and cold and slippery. Soon the path became narrow, with a sheer cliff drop beside it of many hundreds of feet. Theora, holding Irving's hand, was glad of his natural balance to help her keep her footing. Even King Harry walked slowly, balancing panniers carefully upon his mighty shoulders.

At last they came out of the darkness into a vast, natural chamber. It was formed of intricate rock formations, some rising like stately pillars from the floor and others cascading from the ceiling. In between these were pictures, drawn simply but with great skill. They showed animals and birds and symbols of the sun and moon.

Irving gazed about him in wonder. He touched one of the pillars. "Stalactites?"

"Stalagmites," corrected the Earl. "Stalactites grow downwards."

Irving whistled. "Where water moves not!"

"Precisely. And look here."

The Earl walked to the centre of the cavern and raised his torch to the mass of stalactites that hung like a natural chandelier from the roof surface. At once the space was irradiated with brilliant colours from across the spectrum. Blue, pink, gold, red, violet, orange and aquamarine glittered and danced from floor to ceiling.

Theora clapped her hands in delight. "Where rainbows now flower."

"Yes," said the Earl. "We have already taken the 'sharp path'. Now we must 'make a master dance'. This is where we will use all our skills and the musical instruments of power, to gain an audience with the Star Maiden at last."

King Henry bent and put the panniers carefully on the ground. "I would advise that we do not yet reveal the Harp and Drum," he said. "If we are pursued and Lord De Lisle finds us, we will need to keep them protected. Besides, fine musician though I am, I cannot play both. We require Lord Thorne to be our drummer, so that Mr Irving has the correct rhythm."

Irving looked at King Henry. "You want me to dance here?" He touched the floor with one foot. "It's not going to be easy."

The Earl nodded. "I'm sorry."

Irving seemed resigned. He took off his jacket. "Ok, well we'll have to do the best we can whilst we wait for the orchestra to assemble. Aidan, Harry, I need you to get as much light for us as you can. Theora come here please."

She came at once and stood before him. "What can I do, Guy?"

"I need you to hum the song I taught you. Can you do that?"

Theora smiled at him. "I'll try."

"Good girl," said Irving. He walked to the edge of the cavern, placed his jacket on a smooth rock and then went up to the Earl and Lord Nechtan. "Now you've lit those lamps, I suggest you two go and save our drummer. Theora and I will get in some practice whilst you are away."

The Earl picked up his cloak. "Very well. I don't need to warn you about wandering off whilst we're gone!"

Irving raised his eyebrows. "I forget you've never seen me rehearsing," he said. "I tend to get pretty absorbed."

He saw the Earl's gaze rest upon Theora and he nodded understandingly. "Don't worry. I'll be keeping her close."

Thank you," said the Earl and he followed Lord Nechtan and King Henry out of the cavern. When they reached the waterfall, the three men were relieved to see Lord Thorne and Mr Allan emerge from outside. The Earl hurried to greet them.

"Thank the Maiden you are unharmed," he said swiftly.

"Yes, we're fine," said Lord Thorne, "although De Lisle is following and I sense he is calling for reinforcements. Will the protection hold, Nechtan?"

Lord Nechtan shook his head. "Alas, no. It was not designed to hold back such forces."

"Then we must summon King Louis and his knights immediately," said the Earl. "I had hoped that speed would give us the advantage of secrecy and we would not need to do this, but we have no choice. This sanctuary must be protected at all costs. Where is King Louis now?"

"Still at Versailles, engaging the Moon Knights," said Lord Thorne. "After you left Venice, De Lisle launched an attack on the mortals in my time. King Louis is defending them."

"A very clever tactical distraction by Lord De Lisle," said King Henry with grudging approval. "It has split our troops and leaves us vulnerable. It may now be impossible to get Louis' army here in time."

The Earl glanced at the curtain of water. "How long before De Lisle reaches us?" he said.

"Minutes," said Lord Thorne. "We have only one chance, to start the process early."

He glanced at the Earl. "That is our only hope."

"You are right," said the Earl. "But wait for me a moment, I beg you." And with that he stepped through the curtain once more.

"What will happen to him?" asked Mr Allan.

Lord Thorne hesitated. "If he is fortunate, he will have enough strength left to summon King Louis and get back to us. If not and De Lisle catches him unprotected…" He broke off. "All we can do is wait, as he has asked."

The black empty night surrounded the Earl as he ran away from the cavern and into the trees. He made his way through the thicket, feeling his way for he was unable to light his way and so was virtually blind. He was soon short of breath too, for his energy was only just returning. He was aware of the sound of hoofbeats and he knew that Lord De Lisle was coming up the valley and would reach him in seconds. He sank down into the undergrowth and inched his way towards the grove that he had seen as they had approached the Kieve. It was a stand of gnarled oak trees that he was seeking. They were not tall, for this close to the sea, the trees were often stunted by the wind and exposure to the salt. However, they were ancient specimens, their roots spreading deep into the Earth and blanketed with moss. He sank down at the foot of the largest and placed his head against the trunk. At first nothing happened, but then the roots of the tree rose up out of the soil and wrapped themselves around the Earl's legs. Gradually the Earl was taken down into the ground until at last he was invisible and the moss grew green over where he had been standing. Lord De Lisle galloped up the hill and jumped off Othello at the entrance to the waterfall. He looked carefully around him.

At last he walked to the curtain and standing in front of it said loudly, "I know that you and your companions are in there, Aidan. You must also know that I am not so foolish as to enter alone. My knights are on their way and there is nothing to stop them now. Very soon they will be with me and then I will come for you. I can afford to wait, but you, I fear, are running out of time to complete your precious quest."

He let go of the reins and sat down on a mossy stone. "This is a charming place," he said. "I will enjoy the wait."

Inside the tunnels King Henry was pacing angrily. "Can we do nothing to help?"

"Our silence is Aidan's defence," said Lord Thorne. "He will be growing stronger with every second that he is away from the Kieve."

"There is perhaps one other way we can help," said Lord Nechtan. "I can cause the curtain to drop with great speed once Lord Aidan is again inside. If King Louis is successfully summoned, this could balance the engagement and perhaps give our forces the advantage."

"I would like to see what's happening out there right

now," said Mr Allan. "Is that possible?"

Lord Nechtan nodded. "Of course, look here." He walked to the wall and pulled from it several stones. He drew out a silver bell and rang it once. As he did so, a small window, clear of the water droplets, appeared in the centre of the curtain.

"De Lisle cannot see in," he whispered, "but he might hear you, so I suggest that we keep as quiet as possible."

They crowded around the aperture and peered out. Lord De Lisle, lit as he was, appeared clearly, but there was no sign of the Earl. As they watched they saw Lord De Lisle stand up and walk back down the path. He stared into the distance and then turned back an expression of deep satisfaction on his thin, pale face. Minutes later, the reason for this became clear as they could all hear the sounds of the horses galloping up the valley. Lord De Lisle mounted up and rode to the edge of the curtain.

"It seems that very soon this will all be over," he said loudly. He bent over, adjusted Othello's girth and mounted. "Basically, I intend to kill you all, with the exception of Miss Templeton," he said flatly. "What happens to her, I leave to your imagination at this stage." He walked Othello forward. "I am so looking forward to this," he said with relish.

"I have no doubt of that, Bricin," said a calm voice from behind him and the Earl walked out of the woods and stood upon the pathway.

He raised a horn to his lips and blew one sharp note. The sound of oncoming hooves became deafening and Mr Allan gasped, for the knights that came through the trees were clothed in white and gold, not black as he had expected. They had overtaken the army of Moon Knights. Lord De Lisle swung Othello round. He raised his sword, but the Earl made a sweeping motion and the blade flew into the air and fell to the ground. He bent and picked it up.

"I believe this belongs to me," he said. "Thank you for returning it!"

"It makes no difference" said Lord De Lisle, coldly. "All I need to do is stop you from getting into the Kieve."

He made a sudden diving leap from the saddle and fell upon the Earl. The light of both became mingled and flashed and flamed as they struggled together. Behind them King Louis and his knights were battling the Moon Knights that were now surging up the pathway.

"They are evenly matched," said Mr Allan anxiously watching the wrestling Sun and Moon Lord.

King Henry grinned. "I think not," he said comfortably. "I'll lay you odds that the Earl throws him in the river and takes his horse!"

Lord Thorne said quickly, "More to the point, this is an opportunity to ensure that Aidan is able to get back inside the curtain. Nechtan must stay here, but we may now go out and help. Do what you can, but whatever the cost, you must get back inside once we have Aidan free."

"Marvellous," said King Henry boisterously. He drew his broadsword and immediately plunged into the fray.

"Can we stop Lord De Lisle?" asked Mr Allan.

Lord Thorne hesitated. "Perhaps, but it will be perilous. Do you trust me?"

Mr Allan nodded. "I do, my Lord, with my life."

"Good, then take my hand."

Together, hand fasted, the two men ran through the curtain. Lord Thorne dropped to his knees beside the Earl and caught at his free wrist. Lord De Lisle uttered an oath but Lord Thorne was already starting to speak. Light passed from Mr Allan and ran through Lord Thorne's body to his hand. The light surged across the Earl and created a glittering arc. De Lisle was thrown backwards and away.

The Earl struggled to his feet. "Harry," he shouted.

"One moment," shouted the King. He made two more passes with his sword and a Moon Knight fell to the ground. Then he ran up the slope and all four men jumped back into the cavern. The water behind them became a solid wall. The sound of the water and ringing silver bells became deafening and they were not followed.

Chapter Twenty-Three

The Earl and Lord Thorne landed on their feet within the cavern, but King Henry, who had caught hold of Mr Allan's coat as he jumped, brought himself and the younger man down. They fell and rolled, eventually coming to rest with Mr Allan on top of the King.

"Any damage, Harry?" said the Earl sharply.

King Henry sat up. "Fit as a flea," he said cheerfully, "although I must look a trifle less majeste than when we set out." He looked around and gave a shout of laughter. "By the Maiden, what a picture we present!" He gave Mr Allan a friendly push. "Stir yourself, lad, you are no great weight, but I am king you know and must keep some dignity!"

He laughed again and soon the others joined in. Even Lord Nechtan permitted a smile. The sound of their mirth echoed through the cavern and caused Theora to cease her song.

"They are safe," she said joyfully and turned to run back up the passageway, but Irving barred her way.

"You hang on, Miss, we need every moment to get this right. I've no doubt they'll be with us soon. Remember what I taught you. And don't be afraid to jump high. I'll catch you right enough."

Reluctantly, Theora stepped back and they performed the sequence once more. Then Irving left her and started his solo. Theora watched him, as she had done so many times before, marvelling at his balance and grace. She was so engrossed that she didn't notice the Earl, Lord Thorne, King Henry and Mr Allan quietly enter and seat themselves out of Irving's eye line. However, when he had finished, Lord Thorne applauded. At once Theora ran to him.

"Oh I am so glad you have come back," she said.

"You are not hurt?"

Lord Thorne glanced quickly at the Earl, but he was looking away. "I am quite well, Miss Templeton, as are we all."

Irving wiped his forehead on a white towel which he slipped around his shoulders. "Well, we have the dance ready and if you two can just play the music in time, we should be fine to get it all in one take."

"That's good," said the Earl, "because I'm afraid there may only be time for one attempt. Soon Lord De Lisle will break through and before he joins us, it is vital that the whole dance is completed."

"Ok," said Irving, "then we need to get moving. We need to arrange the set and Miss Templeton and I require some better clothes."

"We also need to move into the next chamber," said the Earl.

Irving smiled. "I guessed this was just the rehearsal room. How do we get to this chamber?"

"We climb," said the Earl pointing. They saw that at the corner of the cavern, there was a group of stalagmites that created a small screen. Behind them they found steps fashioned out of the side of the cliff.

King Henry examined them. "They are easy enough for us, but we need to have a care for Mistress Templeton."

"Let her go between myself and Argus," said the Earl. He led them all to the stairs and they slowly began the ascent. Eventually the stairs opened up and they reached a vast open space which was suspended by stalactites above the cavern. Above it was another aperture and, far away, they could just glimpse the night sky, now faintly lit by moonlight.

They all walked into the space and the Earl beckoned to Mr Allan and Lord Thorne. They joined hands and the light that emanated from them flooded the chamber. It started to transform immediately and Theora clapped her hands in delight for within moments the place was a ballroom, shining with millions of wax candles in glittering candelabra. She looked at herself in amazement for she was now wearing a dress of silvery gold trimmed with diamonds that sparkled and flashed, so that at every step she blazed with light. All the other men wore a knight's livery in red and gold, except for Mr Irving who was in 1930s evening clothes.

The Earl looked up at the sky. "Now is our chance," he said. "Good fortune to us all." He beckoned to Mr Allan and the two of them retreated to the edge of the stairs, their swords drawn.

Lord Thorne and King Henry sat down with their instruments. Irving looked at them. "You chaps ready?"

King Henry drew an expert finger across the harp strings and a sweet, rich note echoed around them. "Quite ready, I think. Let us begin."

As he started to play, the Earl looked back down the stairs. Mr Allan following his gaze saw that Lord De Lisle had entered the lower chamber and was starting towards them.

"We cannot engage him," said the Earl in a whisper. To do so would corrupt what we are trying to achieve."

"What can we do then?" asked Mr Allan.

"What I have attempted for these many years – appeal to his reason."

They slipped down the stairs and into the cavern. Lord De Lisle was waiting for them.

"So here we all are and you have begun at last," he said. "Yet my army will soon break through. Do not think that I will show any mercy. I will kill every single one of your knights."

To Mr Allan's amazement the Earl began to laugh. "Is

that your only purpose? Don't you want to kill me?"

Lord De Lisle looked scornful. "Killing you will not stop the Maiden being raised and might result in me being punished. I will not raise my hand against any inside this place, but I want you to know the consequences of what you are doing. If you had left well alone, many mortal lives would have been spared, remember that as you kneel before her! Now, shall we go? You have my word that I will not harm you or anyone else that is up there. Besides, I think I have as much right as any to see the Maiden."

The Earl looked at him carefully. "Very well, I will allow this. But, if you break your promise, I will not hesitate to use all the strength that is left in me, to cast you out of this time and into a place which even you would find difficult to return from."

Lord De Lisle bowed. "Understood." He watched as the Earl stood aside from the steps and started to climb. "I must say," he said over his shoulder, "that in a way I have been looking forward to this. I do so love to see Guy dance!"

They came out onto the ballroom just as Theora and Mr Irving were circling by. Theora gasped at the sight of Lord De Lisle but Irving held her gaze. He said through set lips, "Not a word, not a motion, please, that we haven't rehearsed." She blinked in acknowledgement and he smiled. "You're doing excellently well. Now don't mess up on the turn when we repeat!"

De Lisle, Mr Allan and the Earl sat down and Lord Thorne picked up Drake's Drum and took up the beat. The chamber throbbed to the sound.

"Let us hope that all our efforts do not go unnoticed," said the Earl. He looked up at the sky. "Now, all we can do is wait."

Irving and Theora continued to dance to the music of

the Harp and the Drum. The conclusion was particularly complex. It consisted of a series of leaps that they made together, followed by spins and a lift which finished with Theora being spun over Irving's shoulder and left on the ground in an elegant curtsy. The Earl was the only one, other than Irving and Theora, who knew the whole sequence. So, as they prepared to finish, the Earl made a signal to Irving. It meant that he wanted them to continue dancing and not complete. Irving nodded briefly, whispered in Theora's ear and they danced on. The minutes ticked by and the routine continued. It was technically complex and exhausting. After they had gone through twice more, the Earl wondered privately whether Theora would be able to sustain the pace. He could see the strain on her face and noted that Irving was holding her as tightly as he dared in an effort to support her. He knew that soon they would have to stop and he could see that the smile on Lord De Lisle's face was becoming broader with each passing moment. Mr Allan was equally becoming more and more furious. He sat with clenched hands as Lord De Lisle tapped his knee lightly in time to the music.

The two dancers passed through the top of the room and reluctantly, the Earl made the closedown signal. Irving nodded and he and Theora began their final leaps. Lord Thorne met the Earl's gaze and their eyes held the same message of sad resignation. Then, just as Irving made his final lift, holding Theora high above the ground, a light started to form. It shone very faintly at first and then began to pulse with a silvery brilliance. As Theora dropped into her last position, the mortals and the Perdurare found themselves immobile. In the centre of the room, one slim darting beam shone straight and clear as a spear, reaching down from the distant blackness of the sky. It was so fierce that the mortals had to avert their eyes.

The beam began to rotate, spinning slowly. It travelled across the upper chamber, moving with precision, until at last it was directly in front of Irving. It hung before him, a glimmering, rippling sheet and then suddenly enveloped him entirely. Theora gave a cry of horror.

The Earl raised his hand. "Wait, we must have faith," he said.

"What is it doing?" said Theora numbly.

Lord De Lisle cast her a look of contempt. "It is assessing," he said. "We must hope that Mr Irving is deemed worthy of preservation."

After what seemed to the watchers hours, but was only minutes, the light parted and Mr Irving stepped out. He looked a little pale, but otherwise unharmed. He ran a shaking hand across his hair. "She wants to speak to you next."

"She?" queried the Earl eagerly.

Irving smiled. "Yes, she hasn't got much of a figure, but I know a lady when I see one."

"What did she say to you?" asked Lord Thorne.

"Not much," said Irving. "But, I think it's going to be ok."

The Earl held out his hand. "Thanks to you, my friend. How can we ever repay you?"

He broke off as the beam returned and, without hesitation, the Earl stepped into the light. Again the minutes passed. Eventually, the beam parted again and the Earl re-emerged. The beam then retreated upwards and spread into a cloud which hovered far above in the night sky.

"Come," said the Earl. He led them all down to the lower chamber.

Lord Thorne looked at him in concern. "What has happened, Aidan?"

The Earl faced them. "Harry, I want you to take Mr Irving and Miss Templeton back to the curtain chamber and see them safely bestowed back to their own times. Protect them with your life." He saw that the King was about to protest and said quickly. "No, you must go. There is nothing that you can do here. My Lady wishes to speak only to the Perdurare now and so all mortals must depart."

Lord Thorne looked up at the sky. "We must make haste, I believe she is returning."

As he said this there was a sound which made them all turn, a wind was blowing from high above and it pulled at the Harp strings and rattled the Drum to make a strange, unearthly but hypnotic rhythm.

"She is waiting for us," said the Earl.

Without another look he ran back to the stairs. Mr Allan and Lord De Lisle followed, but Lord Thorne hesitated. He looked at Theora.

"Goodbye," he said. "I will look for you on the other side." He smiled at her encouragingly, turned and followed the Earl as King Henry gently shepherded Theora and Mr Irving into the dark passage beyond.

In the upper chamber, the spear of light was shining bright and clear. The Earl walked forward and knelt down before it. "Lady, we come to you in humble hope. We, your chosen children, beg that you will forgive the faults of our forebears and give us once again your divine blessing."

The music stopped abruptly and the spear began to move, backwards and forwards in clear decisive strokes across the polished dance floor. Letters began to form and, as they did so, each one rose and hung in the air above, so that the Lords could clearly see the written message.

WHERE IS THE PUREST LOVE?

The Earl looked up. "I love Old Earth and every creature is precious to me," he said clearly.

The letters formed again.

THAT IS NOT WHAT IS REQUIRED. WHERE IS THE LOVE LINKED TO A TRUE SPIRIT? THE LOVE THAT WILL WILLINGLY SACRIFICE ITSELF?

Lord Thorne passed a weary hand across his eyes. "To break the Curse requires a blood sacrifice," he whispered. "I was afraid it would come to that."

"What can we do?" asked Mr Allan.

"What we must," said the Earl. He stood up and faced the light. "You have tested my heart and know me now. Take me. I give myself to you willingly."

The beam moved across and enveloped the Earl. It blazed upon him until it was as if he was lit within. More letters formed before him.

THE LOVE WITHIN YOU IS STRONG, BUT INCOMPLETE. IT WILL NOT SUFFICE.

The light dwindled and the Earl returned to the others. "I am sorry, my friends. I do not know what else we can do. I thought that she would take me. I have failed you."

"No," said Mr Allan, "there is still hope." He pushed past the Earl and ran to the light. He fell to his knees. "My love for my wife is shared and proved. Take me, I beg you."

Lord Thorne gave a moan of despair and tried to follow him, but the Earl held him back. "We must let him try, Argus. It is his choice."

The light beam moved deliberately across Mr Allan. It touched his face and chest and lingered about him. Then it wrote:

YOUR LOVE IS TRUE AND STRONG, BUT YOU DO NOT GIVE YOURSELF TO ME WILLINGLY. YOU WISH TO REMAIN WITH YOUR MORTAL WIFE. YOU CANNOT PAY THE PRICE.

I GIVE YOU ALL ONE MORE CHANCE TO PROVIDE A PURE LOVE AND A WILLING SACRIFICE. IF YOU CANNOT, THE CURSE WILL BE UNBROKEN AND I WILL RETURN AGAIN TO MY GREAT SLEEP.

The Earl looked at Lord Thorne and he appeared suddenly very old and grey. "That is it then," he said. "There is no more to do or say. We should go now and prepare the mortals for the few years that are left to them."

There was a faint cough from behind him. Lord De Lisle who had hitherto shown no interest in the proceedings, came over. Lord Thorne eyed him coldly. "I warn you that this is no time for you to make some foolish witticism."

"I am shocked by your lack of confidence in me," said Lord De Lisle smoothly. "I am so tempted to leave you to your fate. Only my noble and selfless nature is restraining me!"

Lord Thorne clenched his fists. "I warn you, Bricin…"

"Enough," said the Earl sharply. "Let's hear him out, we have no other choice."

"A wise decision," said Lord De Lisle swiftly. "I have a way to provide the Lady with what she needs."

The other men stared at him. "You!" said Lord Thorne with steely contempt. "You've never loved anyone except yourself."

"As always, your biased view prevents you seeing the truth," said Lord De Lisle icily. "If you hated me less, you would have recognised the true love that I had for Madelyn."

"This is ridiculous and irrelevant," said Lord Thorne furiously. "Madelyn never loved you. You were obsessed with her, which is your misfortune." He drew his sword. "He is wasting time as usual. Let me dispatch him now,

Aidan, and put an end to this folly."

Lord De Lisle laughed. "I'd almost like to see you try that, Schoolmaster, but, as you say, we would just be wasting time. Permit me to finish." He raised his hand and a small bundle appeared upon the ground before them. "This is my offering," he said.

The Earl walked forward and bent down. He lifted the black cloth and revealed the form of a young boy. They all stared in astonishment, for he was the most perfect child they had ever seen. He was perhaps seven years old, slim and dark and lay as if sleeping, one slim hand cradling his cheek.

Lord De Lisle waved a hand. "This is Lunasa," he said almost conversationally. "He is my son."

Lord Thorne gasped. The Earl shook his head. "That is not possible, your son is already here."

Lord De Lisle smiled. "I forgive your misconception. Of course, I refer to my *real* son, born of the purest blood: mine and the living reincarnation of the Star Maiden. I had suspected that Miss Templeton was somehow connected to the Star Maiden. It always seemed prudent to link myself to her. Our son was born and raised outside of time, so that he knows nothing of us, or the Quest. He is a pure soul and his love for me is pure too."

He went out to the light beam and held up his arms. "Look, Lady. I bring to you a worthy sacrifice. Here is love that has been shared and proven between father and son. I will give him to you."

The Earl fell to his knees beside the body of the boy. "You cannot do this, Bricin," he said in a voice that trembled. "This is the murder of an innocent."

"I would have thought you would be pleased," said Lord De Lisle, his eyes fixed upon the light. "Isn't this going to give you what you've always wanted? Soon, the

Maiden will stand here in the flesh and who do you think she will reward? The one who has finally set her free of course!"

"This is madness," said Mr Allan. "We must stop him." He turned to Lord Thorne. "Help me!"

Lord Thorne gazed at the beam of light, it was moving carefully and inexorably towards the body of the child. "I cannot," he said heavily. "I am sorry, Ciaran."

The light moved gently forward. It covered the sleeping child and wrapped itself around it. Minutes passed and the silence was only broken by the far away sound of the waterfall. At last, the light burned another message.

THE GIFT IS ACCEPTED.

Then several things happened all at once. Firstly, Mr Allan sprang upon Lord De Lisle and flung him to the ground. The Earl leapt to separate them, but Lord Thorne stood watching the light through narrowed eyes. It became brighter and brighter, until even he had to avert his eyes. Then suddenly all the light disappeared and the upper chamber was plunged into total blackness. It caused Lord De Lisle and Mr Allan to disengage. The Earl groped through the gloom and, by touch alone, found Lord Thorne. They sat together in the darkness. Around them was complete emptiness, a bitter cold and silence that made even the two Perdurare shiver.

"If this is the end," said Lord Thorne, "there is something I must say." He paused and swallowed. "I know you love Theora, but I do too. Will you forgive me?"

"There is nothing to forgive," said the Earl. "If she loves you, I would be glad."

"Touching indeed!" said Lord De Lisle contemptuously through the darkness.

"If you don't shut up!" threatened Mr Allan.

"Oh for pity's sake," said Lord De Lisle irritably. He was about to say more but suddenly a soft glow surrounded them and the upper chamber became light again.

The glow became defined and formed a shape and Lunasa stepped from within it, but his eyes were no longer visible. Now they were flaming with a white light.

"Welcome to you, my children. It has been long since I walked among you, but now I am returned."

"Are we in the presence of the Star Maiden?" asked the Earl in a low voice.

"Yes. Now, I can speak to you more freely. Come forward so that I can look upon you properly, for, so far, you have been in shadow and I wish to greet each of you."

The Lords rose and walked forward, shading their eyes.

The Maiden/Boy looked upon them. "So, four of you yet remain, bearing the blood of the sacred ones. I am glad to see you again. Soon all will be as it was."

The Maiden/Boy walked forward until she reached Lord Thorne.

"I do not yet know you," it said to Lord Thorne. "Will you give me your hand?"

Lord Thorne extended it slowly and the Maiden/Boy grasped it between two palms and the burning eyes shut for a moment. When they opened again the Maiden/Boy was smiling. "My Lord Aidan has courage and nobility and the Lord Ciaran, kindness and truth. You have all these gifts and many more. You are fair hearted, wise and strong. I give you my promise that soon you will have the peace and purpose that you have always craved. Your name will be remembered throughout eternity."

Then the Maiden/Boy released Lord Thorne and turned to Lord De Lisle. "Here is the force behind my resurrection. What reward do you seek, Bricin De Lisle, Moon Lord and father of Moon Lords? What can I give you in return for the sacrifice you have made?"

Lord De Lisle kept his head lowered. "I sought no reward, Lady. It is enough to see you restored to your rightful place," he said and although his voice was low, it was silky smooth.

"You lie," said the Maiden/Boy and the childish voice was harsh and cold. "Your true purpose has always been to prevent the completion of the Quest and leave me sleeping for all eternity. When you perceived that Lord Aidan's forces might be the stronger, you thought that by giving me your son, you would be able to become my master, for you know full well that this body will not last long. You planned to use your connection to Lunasa to control me. Your plan has failed, for the child, who is with me now, would rather die a thousand times, than become your instrument of destruction. He loves you truly, but he knows you too well."

Lord De Lisle leapt to his feet. "You are wrong!" he cried suddenly and his face was drawn and haggard with strain. "It is true that I wished the Quest to fail, but now that the moment has come, I cannot let Lunasa go. I beg you, give him back."

The Maiden/Boy regarded him. "I will require another host," she said flatly. "Will you be the willing sacrifice?"

"Yes," said Lord De Lisle wildly, "anything, but release him please."

"Very well," said the Maiden/Boy. "But, you must also stop the slaughter of the mortals. For I require peace between you all before I take another form. Once all conflict has ceased, I will return."

Then the Maiden/Boy gave a sigh and the body of Lunasa crumpled and fell to the stone floor. Lord De Lisle went to it at once and Lord Thorne followed.

"Is he still alive?" he said.

Lord De Lisle took his hand from the child's throat. "Yes." He picked the boy up and carried him to a sofa where he set him down gently. He stroked the dark hair for a moment then straightened up.

"I must go now and stop the battle. Aidan, you will come with me?"

"Of course," said the Earl. "Argus, Ciaran, will you stay with Lunasa until we return?"

"Gladly," said Lord Thorne. He went to Lord De Lisle and said rather awkwardly, "What you are doing is truly remarkable."

"Yes, sometimes I amaze myself," said Lord De Lisle drily. Then he followed the Earl.

The two Lords walked briskly matching strides, their tall figures merging into one bold shadow on the passage wall. They continued in silence until they reached the curtain chamber. Lord Nechtan was there. He started when he saw the Earl and Lord De Lisle together.

"It's fine," said the Earl quickly. "Lord De Lisle is here to help."

"Then you have succeeded?" said Lord Nechtan with relief.

"We are close," said the Earl. "There is just one more task. Will you release the curtain and let Lord De Lisle and I outside please. I think we need to do this together, or we are likely to be disbelieved!"

"I agree," said Lord De Lisle, "but once we have spoken, if you will permit me, I would like to return briefly to the 1930s and pick up a few things."

The Earl stared at him. "What things?"

Lord De Lisle looked self-conscious. "I'd really like to change my suit," he said reluctantly.

The Earl laughed. "Yes Bricin, we owe you the chance to look your very best, at the very least. But now, let us deal with the moment in hand."

At his sign, Lord Nechtan spoke to the waterfall and the curtain slowed and parted in its centre, so that it formed a gothic arch through which the two Lords walked. Then it closed behind them. Outside it was dark and there was no sign of the two armies. "They have returned to Botreaux," said the Earl turning his gaze out across the fields. "Was it your intention to double back and board Victory?"

"Something like that," said Lord De Lisle, also looking into the distance. "We need to get there quickly." He whistled and far across the valley they heard two neighs.

"Othello is with Apollo then?" said the Earl startled.

"You shouldn't be surprised," said Lord De Lisle. "Even though we became enemies, I am afraid I never successfully persuaded my horse to take sides."

They mounted and within a short time they reached the headland. The two armies were closely engaged. King Henry's banner could be seen at the forefront.

"Let me go first," said Lord De Lisle urgently. "If I call off my troops at the shore, you can get a signal to Victory."

He didn't wait for an answer but turned Othello and rode forward. It soon became clear that, although Lord De Lisle's troops understood their commander's instruction, they were reluctant to comply. The battle continued with only small groups falling back. Part of this was due to the fierce engagement by King Henry, King Louis and the other knights, who, seeing their advantage, pressed forward.

The Earl dismounted from Apollo and walked to the edge of the cliff. He made a throwing motion towards the great ship whose bright lights shone out over the harbour. Then he remounted and rode down to the two kings.

On board Victory, the ship had been made ready for battle but not a shot had been fired. The protection that surrounded the ship was holding and the enemy ships could not penetrate it.

Lord Nelson was in his cabin when the signalman came to him.

"What is it, Pascal?"

The sailor held up what looked like a glass casket, lit from within.

"This fell onto the deck just now. Captain Hardy bade me bring it to you, as he thinks it may be a message."

"A message from Lord Sulien?"

"We believe so, my Lord, but I think only for your eyes. There are words within the light, but we cannot read them."

Nelson took the casket and held it up. As he did so, the glass fell into nothingness and he was left with a slip of parchment. On it was written clearly, *Withdraw*. Nelson ran his finger along the words. When he looked up he was smiling.

"It is from the Earl, it is a mind message and the written word contains his thoughts. He tells me that the Maiden has asked for the battle to cease." He crumpled the paper. "Come, we must issue an instruction to the fleet."

In Captain Hardy's quarters, Theora and Irving were sitting together waiting anxiously. The remains of an untouched meal lay before them.

"I cannot bear this waiting," said Theora miserably. "How long do you think it will be?"

"You have asked me that five times already," sighed Irving. "How about a game of cards? It will take your mind off things. There's no point using up your energy by worrying."

"You are right, of course," said Theora reluctantly.

She returned to the table and sat down. "You were going to teach me something new," she said with an effort. "What is the name of this game please?"

Irving dealt with a practised hand. "Poker."

"Poker," echoed Theora. "Why call a card game after a fireside tool, pray?"

"I could tell you," said Irving, "but if this really is the end of everything, I'm not sure it's worth bothering. Let's just play shall we."

He started to explain the rules and Theora tried hard to focus upon what he was saying but her mind was elsewhere. She was desperately worried about the Earl, but her thoughts turned repeatedly to Lord Thorne. Somehow, instinctively, she felt that he was at the greatest risk, but she could not understand how. Then the door opened and Captain Hardy came in.

He bowed briefly. Theora threw her cards down. "You have news?" she said eagerly.

"Yes, Ma'am, great news. We have been asked to withdraw. Instructions from the Maiden herself! The battle is to cease and all troops withdraw."

"Oh then they have succeeded," said Theora breathlessly. She jumped up, "Where are the Earl and Lord Thorne? Can we not join them?"

Captain Hardy shook his head. "Not yet, I'm afraid it would be dangerous. Lord De Lisle's troops are still all over the glen, although they are falling back and dispersing. The Earl has instructed that you both be safely installed in the village and await him there. Victory will return to Portsmouth with the fleet, for our task is done."

"Well that's a relief," said Irving. "Will you be landing soon?"

"Very soon," said Captain Hardy. "I'll be back for you as soon as we make shore."

In less than an hour, Theora and Irving were ready to

leave. Lord Nelson met them on deck. He shook hands with Irving and then bowed to Theora.

"I wish good fortune to you both," he said. "It has been a privilege to know you."

"I think it's the other way around entirely," said Irving.

Nelson gave his thin-lipped smile. "I thank you." He turned to the hovering Midshipman. "Full salute if you please, Mr Bridger."

At that, all the officers removed their hats and, to the sound of whistles, Irving and Theora were lowered into the waiting rowing boat. As the ship pulled away, they could see Nelson standing on the quarter deck, his slight figure in its red coat, bright, yet somehow fragile, against the might of his ship. They strained their eyes to watch him, until at last he disappeared into the darkness.

Irving let out a breath. "You know, I've met some pretty famous men in my line of business and some pretty good ones too, but that guy is the tops." He yawned and stretched. "It's been a long night. Still, we'll soon be back on land and then we can get some sleep, or some breakfast."

"Breakfast?"

"Look there's the sun rising."

Theora followed Irving's pointing finger. A thin ribbon of light could just be seen upon the horizon.

As the sailors pulled steadily away, the light increased and soon the lapping waves and, at last, the green cliffs could be clearly seen. A soft wind was blowing to break up the mist and, as they stepped onto the quayside, the sun rose properly and gave each of the simple white cottages an outline of rosy gold.

"It's great to be back on solid ground again," said Irving. "Where are we going?"

The young officer who had commanded the boat

touched his forehead respectfully. "To one of the cottages in the centre of the village, just beyond the Spread Eagle."

"Ok let's get to it," said Irving briskly.

They set off, Theora holding Irving's arm. The path wound down the side of a great cliff which was draped with cascading mounds of pink thrift and golden trefoil. When they had descended into the valley, a cobbled road led them across a stone bridge and they soon saw the lights of the Tavern, warm and inviting opening up before them. The officer stopped and pointed. "That's where you need to go. Robin Cottage it's called. The one with the blue stable door. Just down that road."

"You're not coming with us?" asked Theora.

"Oh no, Miss," said the officer. He glanced at his burly companions. "I have a message for the Landlord."

Irving smiled. "Looks like a chance to get the best drink you guys have had for a long time. Am I right?"

The two other sailors grinned. Irving looked wistfully at the Tavern's entrance. "Almost tempted myself," he said.

Theora smothered a smile. "Well why don't you go then?" she said.

Irving shook his head. "I'm not going to leave you alone, just so I can get a drink."

Theora laughed. "Well I'm not going in with you," she said. "It's only a short way. Let me go on and we can meet up later for breakfast."

Irving glanced down the street. "Ok," he said. "But you go straight there and stay there!"

Theora curtsied. "Yes, Sir."

Robin Cottage was part of a small line of terraced cottages that backed onto a sheer cliff in the village centre. Theora was met at the door by a small, rosy-cheeked lady. She immediately made Theora comfortable by providing her with dry slippers. She then suggested tea in the parlour, whilst she waited for Mr Irving.

"I thought I might perhaps rest in my room," said Theora.

"Well of course if you wish" said the Housekeeper doubtfully. "Only the gentleman did say that when you arrived, he would like to see you as soon as possible."

Theora stared at her. "You mean either the Earl or Lord Thorne is already here?" she said with excitement.

The Housekeeper beamed. "That's right, Miss. Such a fine-looking gentleman and so polite he is!"

Theora laughed. "In which case it must be Lord Thorne. I will be very glad to see him."

The Housekeeper opened the door. "Miss Templeton, Sir," she said. Then she stood aside as Theora entered the room and, once she was through the door, shut it quietly behind her.

Chapter Twenty-Four

Theora stopped and leaned breathlessly against the door. It was Lord De Lisle.

He was sitting at a small gateleg table, spread with a red and white checked cloth. Behind him the window was open and warm sunlight and the sounds of the village springing to life poured through. He picked up the tea pot and poured a cup.

"Please do take this," he said, holding it up. "You really do look as if you need it and I'm afraid there's nothing else."

Theora sat down, helped herself to milk and drank. The warm liquid was reassuring but she felt both confused and disorientated. Despite Captain Hardy's assurance that the war was over and the obvious fact that Lord De Lisle had agreed to a truce, she could not prevent her instinctive fear at seeing him again. The fact that all she could remember regarding their last meeting was his arrival on Victory, made her doubly uneasy. The only other time in her life that she had failed to remember anything, was when the Earl had rescued her from the highwaymen. The reason for that memory loss was something she had resolutely put to the back of her mind. She forced herself to meet De Lisle's gaze and surprised an expression which she could not interpret. She guessed that he wanted something from her, but she could not imagine what that could be. Otherwise he was exactly the same sleek, well-groomed model of calm sophistication. She wondered if he knew that Mr Irving would be joining them, but suspected that, even if he did know, he didn't care. Irving was patently not the reason for him being here. She decided to conceal her fears and confront the situation head on. Setting down the cup, she placed her hands in her lap.

"Whilst I am of course aware of the honour your Lordship does me by making this call, I am sure I must be distracting you from other far more important things. Please do not let me hold you up. Mr Irving will shortly be here to keep me company."

"I would have thought you would have wanted a change of company after all those months with Irving abroad," said Lord De Lisle cheerfully. "A wonderfully talented man, of course, but he's never struck me as the greatest of conversationalists. Whereas, you and I... well we've never had any trouble in that department have we, Theora?"

"What is it that you want?" demanded Theora. "The Quest is completed and the war concluded. Shouldn't you be at the Maiden's side awaiting her instructions, instead of drinking tea?"

Lord De Lisle looked idly out of the window. A large bumblebee banged briefly against the glass and fell winded onto the sill. De Lisle picked it up and blew upon it gently. The bee's fluffy body shone. It sat on De Lisle's finger for a moment, stretched its wings and then flew off with renewed vigour.

Theora clenched her hands. "Will you please answer me?" she said fiercely.

He looked back at her and his smile deepened. "Actually, I am doing exactly what the Maiden requires. I need you to come back with me now. If you don't, the Quest will fail and there will be more casualties."

Theora got up and walked around the small room. It was simply furnished. Apart from the table and chairs there was a well-dressed fireplace and a few pictures, including a neatly stitched sampler in red crewel. She was overwhelmed by a sudden sense of foreboding. Somehow it was as if all her life had been leading up to this one moment, when everything would change and there would be no returning to the familiar and comfortable. She felt like the bee, trapped and winded.

"What do I have to do?" she whispered.

De Lisle stood up. "You already know that, Theora," he said. "You didn't need to put on the Moonstone to understand your connection with the Maiden. If you had not been constrained within Aidan's Domain, with all its codes and rules and conventions, you would have realised your true lineage long before now. I sensed it when we first met and, once I had learned the secret of the Quest, I knew exactly why Aidan had taken such pains to bring you under his protection. You are the living image of the Maiden you see, but oh, so much more than that. I really hoped that my original plan would prevent your sacrifice, but alas, at the very last, I hadn't the strength to exchange our son's life for yours."

Theora backed away from him and stood by the door. "What do you mean, our son?" she said in a voice that shook.

He walked to her and took her cold face between his cupped hands. "Of course you can't remember," he said sympathetically. "Let me refresh it all."

He looked deep into her eyes, then he stood back. Theora's face became drained. Her grey eyes glazed and then brightened. "You used me," she said at last, shivering with the shock of the truth.

"Yes, I did," he said evenly, "but I am not going to apologise. It was to a purpose and that purpose was to save lives. You see, I do care for you, Theora, but not in the selfish, silly way that Aidan and Argus do. They are both such hypocrites. They pretend to respect mortals, but they actually treat you as a shepherd might many sheep. They are glad to tend the flocks and always pleased to see them strong and healthy, but no more. So, when a mortal loves them and they feel love in return, they are ashamed.

Whereas I have never made a secret that I see mortals as beneath me."

Theora walked away from him and sat down again. The full knowledge of what he had done played over in her mind.

"You also wanted the Quest completed," she said thoughtfully, "but on your own terms. I believe you sought to overpower the Star Maiden, which is why you offered your own child instead of me. That is why Lord Sulien and Lord Thorne are the more honourable, because they sent me away."

"No, they sent you away because they knew the Maiden would not accept you," said Lord De Lisle patiently. "You see, Aidan knew for certain that the Quest required a pure love sacrifice, which meant that someone who had loved and been loved in return would need to voluntarily give up their life. He established that you were the image of the Star Maiden and had you brought to Temple Court specifically to prepare for the sacrifice. He then ensured that you were put in my path. He expected that you would fall in love with me and that your charms would be sufficient for me to reciprocate. But this plan was doomed from the start, for you fell completely in love with him at first sight. Aidan realised after the highwaymen incident that he loved you truly, but, alas, when he declared it, you didn't believe him! So, from that time you became useless as a sacrifice. He was forced to hope that my grown up son, whom he had ensured had loved and been loved by his own daughter, would be a suitable alternative. It was an extremely risky strategy. He has gambled and lost."

Theora was trembling. "You knew that Mr Allan was your son?"

"Not at first," he said. "I knew Jenny was pregnant. I also was aware that when I turned my back on her she was likely to scuttle off to either Argus or Aidan and ask for protection. I didn't concern myself, for she had no power to hurt me and, at that time, I knew nothing about the actual Quest. It was only after I knew the full truth that I suspected that Ciaran was Jenny's child. Then I made it my business to find out the particulars."

"So, you took me and created another boy and raised him for a sacrifice," said Theora chokingly. "You are a monster."

"You may choose to think so," he said indifferently. "I preferred to see the child as an unavoidable casualty of a long standing war. As it is…" He hesitated. "Well, the truth is that when the moment came I could not give the child up. I love him too well you see." He looked at Theora and she was astonished to see the sadness in his eyes. "So I offered myself instead. Alas, the Maiden has rejected me. She wants to walk again in the body of a mortal woman as she did before. She has looked into our minds and chosen you. That is why she sent Aidan and I back to call off the battle. That was just an excuse, so that I could persuade you to return."

Theora stared at him. "If I refuse, you will bring me back by force I suppose?"

"If I have to, but I don't think that you will refuse. You know what is at stake, for if the Maiden is not resurrected, mortals are instantly condemned to oblivion. Joining the Maiden will give you the opportunity to save Old Earth."

"Is that what it would be," asked Theora, "a joining?"

"In some sense yes," he said, "but I will be truthful with you, what that will mean exactly, I do not know. What I do know is that not only will you save existence, but also our son will be safe. For if the Maiden leaves now, her people will not allow my kind to continue as guardians of time."

Theora stood up. "Look at me," she commanded. He did so, meeting her gaze. After a moment she looked away. "I believe you are speaking the truth," she said. "I will go with you, but before I give myself up, I want to see my son. Show him to me now."

"I cannot do that," said Lord De Lisle. "He is still in the cavern."

Theora laughed bitterly. "Even now you try to trick me. I know perfectly well that you can take us both out of time and forward into the future you created for him. Do it now. I think your Maiden will understand and wait a few more moments for us. She has waited an eternity already."

She saw that he was still hesitating and her face hardened. "You will do this for me, my Lord, or I will never join with the Maiden."

After a moment he nodded. He placed his hand on her forehead and at that moment the little room disappeared completely from view.

*

Theora found herself standing in front of a huge glass window, staring out onto the vista of a city. Her first action was instinctive, for as soon as she moved she realised that she was no longer wearing a grey travelling dress. She looked down her length and attempted to assimilate her extraordinary, masculine attire. Then she heard a familiar laugh and saw Lord De Lisle walking towards her. He too was wearing different clothes, but she was forced to acknowledge that they suited him extremely well. He came directly to her and his knowing smile told her that he realised her discomfiture and was excessively amused by it.

"Why am I dressed like a man?" asked Theora horrified.

"You look quite charming," he said, "and most

fashionable. I thought you would enjoy a change. Besides, Lunasa is a child of this time and he would stare if you appeared before him as a 19th-Century gentlewoman."

"Where are we?" said Theora looking around.

"We are nearly at the top of the Montparnasse Tower," said Lord De Lisle. "I promised Lunasa that I would bring him here on Christmas day to see the lights of Paris."

"Paris, France," said Theora.

"Yes. Lunasa has been brought up here since he was a baby. The year is 2017 and it is December 25th. Earlier today we enjoyed an excellent dinner and Lunasa opened his presents. He is now enjoying the view from the very top of the tower."

"How old is he," whispered Theora.

"Just turned seven," said Lord De Lisle.

"What have you told him about me?"

"That you are a lady friend of mine who is meeting us here for a drink."

Theora gave a slight sniff. "How convenient. I assume you have introduced him to lots of other lady friends?"

"Lots and lots," said Lord De Lisle carelessly. He glanced across the room. "I suggest you take that despising look off your face as he is coming now."

"How long do we have?"

He hesitated. "One hour, I can give you no more I'm afraid."

He walked away from her and pushed through the crowd. Theora hastily manufactured a smile and tried to look relaxed as she watched him steer the boy back across the room.

"Lu, I'd like you to meet Theora, the friend you've heard me speak of," said Lord De Lisle.

The slim boy held out his hand. "Hello, Theora," he

said.

Theora took the hand and gazed into the clear blue eyes that looked up at her. "Hello," she managed.

"Ok," said De Lisle. "Now, I'm going to get us some drinks. How about you show Theora some of the sights?"

"Fair enough," said the boy. He had a very soft voice, lighter than Lord De Lisle's but with the same musical lilt.

De Lisle then strolled away to the bar, leaving Theora and her son together.

"What's the best view, I mean what do you recommend I see first?" stammered Theora awkwardly.

"Most people look at the Eiffel Tower first," said Lunasa and his expression of ill-concealed scorn at her ignorance made him a small, mirror image of his father. Despite her nervousness, Theora could not repress a smile at the likeness.

"Well we should start there then," she said pleasantly. She walked with him to the window and they stood and gazed at the tower, which shone with its myriad of lights, topped with one that revolved and flashed. It was so beautiful that Theora gasped. "It reminds me of a lighthouse I once saw, but this structure is so fragile and fine in comparison. I wonder it does not blow over! How can it stand up alone? Is it magical?"

Lunasa looked at her curiously. "It's engineering that makes it stand up, not magic." He rummaged in the bag on his back and held out a slim box to her. "Here, this tells you all about it."

Theora stared down at the illuminated pictures in front of her. "That's amazing. I've never seen such an extraordinary device."

"It's only an old phone," said Lunasa. "Dad won't get me a better one because he says I'll lose it."

"Would you please read what it says to me," said

Theora hastily. "I am afraid I have left my spectacles at home."

"Sure," said Lunasa. He started to read out the history of the tower, jumping between paragraphs, and finally recounting his own first memory. "Dad took me up to the very top and I nearly threw up when I saw how far down it was," he confided.

"Threw up?" said Theora questioningly.

"Yeah, you know, felt sick enough to spill my guts," said Lunasa. "But since then I've been up loads. You'll have to go up sometime. It's really, Gucci, you know, cool."

"I should imagine it is very cold at the top," agreed Theora.

He glanced up from the phone and looked at her thoughtfully. "Are you for real?"

Theora looked perplexed. "What do you mean?"

He thrust the phone back in his bag. "Well, you are very pretty but you seem pretty stupid too, unless you're just joking me?" His face cleared. "That's it, isn't it, you're making fun?"

Theora forced a smile. "Of course."

"Well that's ok then. A lot of the girls Dad brings home *are* stupid, but the way he spoke about you and the fact that he's brought you here on Christmas day, did make me think you might be a bit different and not just good for sex."

Theora flushed furiously. "I am not your father's…" She broke off in confusion, but fortunately a diversion was created by Lord De Lisle's reappearance.

They all sat down. Theora looked suspiciously at the glass in front of her. "What is this?"

"An Old Fashioned," said Lord De Lisle. "I thought it appropriate."

Theora sipped cautiously. She glanced at Lunasa.

"What are you drinking?" she asked, peering at his glass which had *Coca Cola* stamped in red on the side.

Lunasa grinned. "More jokes, or just a way to get a taste?" He pushed forward the glass. "Here, I didn't want it all anyway." He stood up. "Can I go upstairs again, Dad?"

"Yes, but we will all need to go soon, so five minutes, that's all."

"Ok, I'll leave my bag here then," said Lunasa.

He glanced at Theora. "Do you want to come with me? It's a much better view than in here."

Theora looked at Lord De Lisle who nodded.

On the roof the view was spectacular, but Theora was more interested in watching the vivid, handsome face of the young boy beside her. Like Lord De Lisle he had the same directness of manner as well as the same keen blue eyes. But, his pale colouring and coal black curls were identical to her own. He was clearly highly intelligent and with his inquiring mind and quick comprehension, she saw much in common with herself at the same age. The minutes passed too quickly. When Lord De Lisle joined them, she cast him a look of such speaking hope that he almost appeared sorry for her, as he shook his head.

"I am afraid we must go now," he said. "Say goodbye to Theora will you, Lu."

The boy turned back and instantly came up to Theora. "Goodbye, Miss Theora," he said cheerfully.

"Goodbye," said Theora. She watched as he walked with De Lisle to the door. But then he stopped, whispered something to his father and ran back to Theora.

"Did you forget something?" Theora asked.

"Not exactly," he said slightly breathlessly. "I just wanted to say…"

She couldn't resist reaching out to push a stray curl from his face. "What?" she said gently.

He coloured up. "Well, just that you are very, very pretty so even if you and Dad aren't having sex now, I'm sure you will be soon," he finished encouragingly.

Then the room spun around again and the new world fell away and Theora was outside the great waterfall, with Lord De Lisle laughing beside her.

"I see nothing to be amused about," said Theora furiously. "My own son thinks that I want to… that we are… Oh heavens I can't say it!"

De Lisle continued to laugh. "I don't know why you should take such offence, he meant it purely as a compliment." He wiped his eyes and regarded her. "Anyway, you have met your son. Do you now understand why I couldn't give him up?"

"Yes I do," said Theora. "Whilst I cannot excuse or condone what you have done, I do now see clearly what I must do. Take me to the Maiden."

He put his hand to his pocket. "I need you to say nothing when we are back in her presence. It is important that Aidan and Argus do not suspect anything."

"I understand," said Theora and as she grasped his hand, they both were again standing in the cavern where the Earl, Lord Thorne and Mr Allan were waiting. Lunasa remained asleep on a couch.

De Lisle glanced briefly at him and then went to the Earl. "So, Aidan, the battle is finished and we are reunited once more."

"So it would appear," said the Earl. "I also see you have returned with Miss Templeton. Why is that?"

Lord De Lisle sighed. "She insisted upon coming with me."

"Where is Mr Irving?" said Lord Thorne sharply.

"I have no idea," said De Lisle. "In the village asleep after a few drinks I expect. He became distracted and I saw no need to disturb him. He has undoubtedly played his part. Now if you will permit me, I suggest we summon the Star Maiden." He looked at Lord Thorne. "I assume that after I depart, I can safely leave you to look after both of my sons?"

"You need not ask that," said Lord Thorne heavily.

"Thank you," said Lord De Lisle. "Then let us begin." He looked up and spoke clearly. "Hail, my Lady. I have returned and everything is now as you requested."

As he said this a finger of light came down from the sky. It touched the heads of each of the Lords in turn, finally coming to rest upon Lord De Lisle. He turned and looked at Theora directly. "Goodbye," he said and then he knelt down.

As he did so, the light flashed over his back and landed upon Theora, enveloping her completely. Lord Thorne gave a shout and the Earl flung himself forward but they were too late. The light was locked around Theora and they could not breach it. The Earl immediately swung round and swiftly stopped Lord De Lisle with a blow that caused him to fall back again.

Mr Allan flung himself on top of the prone body, pinning him squarely to the floor. "I have the traitor," he cried.

The Earl took a deep breath. "I would have spared your life if your offences had just been against me, but I cannot forgive this," he said. He drew his sword and the blade had a deep, fiery glow that was only outshone by the brilliant white light that bathed the rest of the upper chamber. De Lisle struggled within Mr Allan's grip.

"I am merely obeying the orders of your precious deity," he said.

"How dare you suggest that," said Lord Thorne furiously, but Mr Allan's sudden exclamation stopped him saying more. They all watched as the light around Theora swirled and rippled and then disappeared.

"He speaks the truth," said a voice which was still that of Theora Templeton, but intensely precise. "Let him go."

The Earl glanced at Lord Thorne who reluctantly nodded. They stood back and the Earl sheathed his sword. Mr Allan rose too. Lord De Lisle remained upon the floor looking up at the Maiden.

"You have done well, Moon Lord," she said in that flat even voice.

The Earl swiftly knelt down. "My Lady, this woman has done you no harm, please let her go."

"No," said the Star Maiden. "I have chosen this vessel and I will use it as I wish. You knew in your heart that this would happen, for this woman walks in my likeness. You hoped that I would choose you instead, but you are the last Sun Lord and I need you to live on in my service. Now hear this. To attain my full strength, all mortal memory of Jane Templeton must be erased from history so that I can take her place."

She beckoned to Lord De Lisle to rise. "You two, Lords of the Sun and Moon, can do this for me. Go now and do what you must. I command you."

Lord De Lisle looked at the sleeping form of Lunasa. "What about our son? If the mortal memories of Theora are lost, will my son not also pass?"

"I do not forget that it was through this child that the Curse of my father was broken and so I will spare him. Destroy his memory of Theora and no harm will befall him," said the Maiden.

Lord De Lisle straightened up. "Well then," he said. He turned to the Earl. "I am ready, if you are."

The Earl made a gesture of assent. He seemed unable to speak.

"I will stay here with Ciaran until you return," said Lord Thorne.

The Earl nodded. "I am sorry, Argus," he said sadly. "I didn't know this would happen."

"Of course you didn't," said Lord Thorne. "You have nothing to reproach yourself for." He embraced him. "Now, let us finish the Quest. This is the oath we swore so long ago and we must fulfil it, whatever the cost."

He stepped back and the Earl and Lord De Lisle walked together to the edge of the chamber. The Earl spoke and they both disappeared into the blackness of the rock. The Star Maiden did not move, but Lord Thorne went and sat down next to the sleeping Lunasa.

Mr Allan came forward. "I am sorry too," he said, staring back at the strangely immobile figure of the woman they had known, still shining with light. "I had a great respect for Miss Templeton."

Lord Thorne took off his cloak and placed it over the boy. "But, does it necessarily follow that because there appears only one path to follow through the darkness, another may not be found?" he said almost conversationally.

"I don't understand," said Mr Allan.

"No, I know you don't," said Lord Thorne. "I wasn't addressing you." He got up and faced the Star Maiden.

"Claudite ostium, et claude ostium non crinem est irritum key aperire vita mea pignus," [22] he said clearly.

There was a terrible rending sound, as if the very walls were being pulled from their foundations. Mr Allan fell to his knees and covered his ears, but Lord Thorne remained standing, looking directly at the Star Maiden.

"So, Moon Lord," she said. "You have locked us

---

[22] Shut the door, bar the gate, break the lock no key can open, my life, my pledge

outside time, beyond the reach of your companions. Yet you know that I can easily break free if I choose to."

"I simply wished no outside interference until you have heard my offer," said Lord Thorne. "Please listen to me. You have not yet fully searched my heart. I bear a pure love. Take my life force and let the soul of this woman be spared. I give myself to you freely." He knelt before her and extended his hand.

The Maiden beckoned to him to rise.

"Worthy words, but you have yet to prove this love and have it reciprocated, Moon Lord," she said.

Lord Thorne sighed. He looked down at the Maiden and drew his hand lightly across her hair and across her brow, tracing the line of her cheek with his finger. Then he kissed her. As he did so, all the torches in the room blazed and the cavern seemed to throb with a suppressed energy which caused the walls and floor to shake. Some of the stalactites came loose and fell to the floor, smashing and causing clouds of dust to rise which enveloped the space, so that the Maiden's light was dimmed. Mr Allan, peering through the gloom, his eyes streaming, saw the two figures still in an embrace, but to his amazement he heard the Maiden was now laughing.

"Enough," she said and the dust cloud evaporated and the shaking within the chamber ceased. "There is no need to bring this place down about us. Yours is indeed a strong, steadfast love and Theora Templeton returned it. I feel her spirit reach out to yours. I also do not forget that I have promised a reward for your strength and goodness. So your gift, Moon Lord, will be this. Although all mortal memory of her will be lost, the spirit of Theora will be saved. I will transfer it to the Moonstone that you bear. You must then hide it within time, so that it can never be found. Bind yourself to it and you will be joined to Theora's soul throughout eternity."

Lord Thorne bowed. "You have offered me more than I could ever have hoped for."

Mr Allan stumbled to his feet. "But this is crazy," he burst out. "You can't mean this Argus. There is no need for you to die too."

Lord Thorne shook his head. "Please do not grieve for me. I am truly glad to do this."

He looked at the Maiden. "I am ready."

The Maiden leaned forward and touched his forehead with her lips. "Go then, with my blessing."

"No," shouted Mr Allan and he lunged at Lord Thorne in a desperate attempt to drag him away. As he reached out frantically, the Maiden spoke a word and both Mr Allan and Lunasa disappeared.

"Where have you sent them?" asked Lord Thorne.

"To the Sun Lord's house in his own domain," said the Maiden, "They will be safe, do not fear."

"Thank you," said Lord Thorne.

"And now let me give you what you wish," said the Maiden. She reached out and took the Moonstone pendant from Lord Thorne's breast and held it up above her head. As she did so, it began to glow and pulsate and was filled with colour and brilliance.

The Maiden held it out to him. "Here then is what you desire. Remember that when you finally sleep, so will she. May you both have everlasting peace."

Lord Thorne stretched out his hand and the Maiden placed the stone within it. Then he turned and walked into the wall of the cavern and passed forever out of mortal sight.

Chapter Twenty-Five

In the library in the Cavern of the Perdurare, the Earl and Lord De Lisle sat together. Each had in front of him a pile of books. Pages from many more were burning on the fire as the Lords identified a reference to Theora Templeton in each separate life history and then erased it. Although a cantus had been used to speed up time so that they could complete the task in hours instead of days, they had worked incessantly. At last Lord De Lisle looked up.

"I think we are nearly finished," he said, tossing more pages away and watching as they flamed and then fell to ash.

"Yes," said Lord Sulien. Although his voice was calm, it did not deceive De Lisle.

"I am sorry, Aidan," he said.

The Earl drew the final book towards him, looked at it for a moment, then he put it on the fire. When it had burned completely he spoke one word and the grate was empty, clean and cold once more.

"It is done," he said. "Now we must return to the Maiden."

He went over to the globe, but as he touched it, he let out an oath for the surface was burning hot.

De Lisle went to him quickly.

"What's wrong?"

"I don't know," said the Earl, nursing his hand. "This has never happened before. But one of us must make contact or we are never going to get back. You try."

De Lisle shook his head. "No thank you."

The Earl looked at him with exasperation. "If you don't, we're liable to be stuck here together for the rest of eternity."

De Lisle sighed. "I suppose that faced with the

prospect of incessantly staring at your sad face, a burned hand would be a small price to pay."

He stretched out his hand, but, even as he did so, the globe suddenly began to spin and the speed of its movement made a vortex which threw both Lords back against the wall. Then the room too spun round, the globe was flung off its pedestal and shattered on the floor. The Earl shouted out, and the room stopped spinning and the Lords fell to their knees. As they stood up they saw they were no longer alone. Mr Allan had joined them.

"Ciaran," said the Earl joyfully. "How did you manage to get here?"

"By the Maiden," said Mr Allan.

"She sent you?" said the Earl eagerly.

"Yes. Something is wrong," said Mr Allan, stumbling over the words. "The Maiden cannot heal reality until we are all in our correct places in time. She has sent me back to help you return to the 19th and 20th Centuries. That is why I had to break the globe. If you tried to use it now, you would be destroyed."

Lord De Lisle was brushing off his coat in apparent disinterest, but he now looked keenly at the younger man. "Why send you and not the Schoolmaster, I wonder?"

Ciaran couldn't meet that piercing glance, but the Earl answered for him.

"I suppose it makes sense that she would want Argus with her to protect her until her strength is fully returned."

"That's right," said Mr Allan swiftly. "Now, let us go. I have brought Lord Thorne's watch and yours. With both, we should have enough energy to make the jump."

He held them out. The Earl took one and, after a moment, Lord De Lisle took the other.

"Then this is goodbye," said Lord De Lisle.

"For the present," said the Earl. "However, unless the

Maiden wills it, we remain Domain Lords and connected through time. So, let us just say, au revoir."

De Lisle looked at him and his lips twisted as if he wanted to smile but could not. Then the three men stood in a circle. Light fused around their fingers as they gripped the watches and then disappeared into the void.

Lord De Lisle was through first. He landed roughly, rolling onto his side. As he recovered his breath, he realised that it was night time and he was again back in Versailles. He stood up unsteadily, blinking as his eyes adjusted to the dim light. He was in the Hall of Mirrors and a clock was chiming. Then he spun around; behind him there was the sound of a match striking as someone lit a cigarette. A slim, dapper figure, was sitting in one of the gilded chairs.

"Guy, well I certainly didn't expect to see you!"

"I would imagine not," said Mr Irving. "How are you feeling? Looks like that last journey had a bit of a kick to it!"

"You could say that," said De Lisle, rubbing his neck which had twisted as he fell.

"What are you doing here?" he said at last, with weary curiosity. "Did Ciaran send you?"

"In a way," said Irving. He stood up. "He thought you might need a lift home."

"And made the arrangements to get you here just at the right time," finished De Lisle. "How very obliging of him. I didn't think he was that concerned with my comfort!"

"I think he also wanted me to keep an eye on Lunasa, until you got back," said Irving.

"Thank you for that," said De Lisle. "How is he?"

"Fine," said Irving. "Doesn't remember a thing."

"No, of course not," said De Lisle. "Well, I suppose I'd better be getting back to him and wait for instructions.

I am expecting the Maiden will want me back at some point to just tidy up the loose ends, but there is no need for you to hang around. He lifted up his watch. "I have my own transportation you see."

"Yes, I do see," said Irving. He walked up to the wall mirrors.

"Incredible how these reality splinters can magnify your powers like this. I assume that when reality is healed again, all the portals will be closed forever."

"Highly probable," said De Lisle. "Thank you again, but now I really must go." He opened up the case and let out an exclamation. The interior was black and lifeless.

"That's strange."

"Something wrong?" said Irving, looking over his shoulder.

"Yes," said De Lisle. "It must have been damaged. Still, not to worry, I can use the mirrors. They may not get me straight back to my apartment, but I can always get a taxi from the Luxembourg Gardens."

He snapped the case shut. "Goodbye, my friend. Perhaps we can meet soon at Delmonico?"

Irving bowed. "I would be delighted." He smiled. "That's assuming that everything will be back to normal and we do meet again."

"I have no doubt of it," said De Lisle. He saw Irving was hesitating. "Is there something else?"

"I was just wondering if you would let me have the watch as a keepsake. You know, a memento of all these adventures."

De Lisle held it out to him. "Why not?" he said easily.

Irving took it off him. "Surprisingly heavy," he said and then with sudden speed and flawless accuracy he turned and threw it at the mirror.

It hit the centre and disappeared. As it did so, the glass shattered and fell in a rain onto the polished floor. The sound was an avalanche of noise, but as the pieces hit the surface they dissolved into nothingness. In seconds, the glass was utterly gone and only the painted wooden frame remained.

De Lisle stared at the empty space. His lip was bleeding where he had bitten it and he took out his handkerchief and wiped it.

"So the realities are actually healing and I have been duped to return here by my son," he said. "How very clever of him. Was Lunasa being here also a lie?"

"No," said Irving. "He's with Miss James at her suite." He held out an envelope. "Here are the directions and here are the keys to your car."

"You're not coming with me?" said De Lisle pocketing both.

"No," said Irving. He picked up his hat which he had left on one of the gilded chairs. "I have to get back to New York and my wife."

Oh I see," said De Lisle. He gave his glinting smile. "I am looking forward to seeing the lovely Gala again. Shall I give her your compliments?"

Irving stiffened. "If you wish."

He walked to the door and paused. "By the way, you might want to get that car of yours into the garage when you get back. In my hurry to get here, I'm afraid I had a slight altercation with a hay wagon. Left a few scratches and bumps. Sorry about that, but I've never handled anything more tricky than a Duesy." He put his hat on his head, swung his jacket over his shoulder and walked breezily out, leaving De Lisle tense and furious behind him.

*

In 19th-Century England, the Earl and Mr Allan were sitting in the saloon at Templeton Court. Juliet, after her initial greeting and obvious relief, was uncharacteristically silent. The fate of Lord Thorne and Theora (as hastily described by Mr Allan) had cast an undoubted pall over their homecoming.

"I wish I could have done something to stop it," said Mr Allan desperately, "but the Maiden sent me here with Lunasa and, although I tried to get back, she stopped me. All I could think of was to find the transportation devices and get them to you as soon as possible."

"Where is Lunasa now?" said the Earl.

"I sent him forward to the 1930s," said Ciaran, "so he could be with his father."

"He is your father too," the Earl reminded him gently.

"He is also a traitor, a rapist and a liar," said Ciaran and his pleasant voice was cold and harsh.

Juliet shivered. She looked at her father fearfully.

The Earl rose and spoke to the fire. Flames sprang to life and he stretched out his hands to warm them.

"Argus and I are partly responsible for what Aidan has become," he said sadly. "Secure in our friendship and focused upon completion of the Quest we neglected him. We failed to understand that, although he quickly grew to manhood in physical strength and intellect, emotionally he was still a child, who wanted both admiration and love. Denied this, he lost his way and became dangerous. We could have guided his path, but we either ignored or scolded him. Still, at least now he has some chance of redemption. With Argus gone, he will be able to join with us and serve the Star Maiden in the time that remains."

Mr Allan who had been holding Juliet's hand in his, released her abruptly and walked to the window.

"We don't need him," he said over his shoulder.

The Earl glanced at him and his green eyes were suddenly very hard and bright. "What have you done?" he said abruptly.

Mr Allan didn't answer. The Earl crossed the room in

three strides and caught his arm.

"Answer me!"

Juliet ran forward. "Papa don't hurt him."

The Earl looked deep into Mr Allan's eyes and then dropped his hand. "You've left him stranded in the future," he said grimly. "A future that will be much changed from what he knew, now that the Maiden is restoring reality."

"What are you going to do?" said Mr Allan with quiet defiance.

The Earl went to the bell and rang it. When Meadows came in he said, "Bring the racing curricle around, with the greys put to."

Meadows bowed. "Yes, my Lord."

"Quick as you can," said the Earl and something in his voice caused his manservant to run from the room.

When Meadows had gone he turned to Juliet. "Please wait here for us, Kit. I have to go with Ciaran on an urgent errand. Ciaran, come with me."

Without bothering to wait for a reply he strode out into the hall. Juliet and Mr Allan followed. Meadows appeared with the Earl's topcoat and gloves. The Earl took his gloves, but waved away the coat. Outside an East wind was blowing.

"Go in, Juliet," he said briefly. "It is too cold out here for you to wait."

"Yes, please do, my love," urged Mr Allan. Juliet went to him and rested her hands upon his chest. "You will be back soon?"

"Of course," said Mr Allan. He bent and kissed her.

Moments later the carriage appeared. The Earl jumped in and took over the reins, nodding to the Groom to get down so that Mr Allan could take his place. He spoke a word and the pair leapt forward.

"Where are you taking me?" asked Mr Allan.

"To find your father," said the Earl, "hopefully, before it is too late." Then he bent over the reins and the greys, now given their heads, galloped down the carriageway.

The Earl pulled up some twenty minutes later, outside Rodsall Church. The village was deserted, but an old man was scything the grass around the graves. The Earl went directly to the chapel and the tomb of the Ancient Knight.

"What are you looking for?" said Ciaran breathlessly. He stopped as he saw that the tomb was now glowing brilliantly white. "I didn't know this was one of our sacred places."

"It wasn't," said the Earl, "but it has become one now."

As he spoke the light dimmed and they saw that the tomb was no longer aged and dusty, but clean as if newly placed. The figure of the Knight was sharply defined and in the pommel of the long sword a pale stone blazed.

Ciaran dropped to his knees. "Lord Thorne rests here," he said.

"Yes," said the Earl. He reached out a hand and touched the visored head. "He is indeed at rest, with the spirit of Theora Templeton beside him for all eternity. Now we have just one chance. His last gift is a way to reconnect with your father."

Ciaran turned his head away. "I won't help you with that," he whispered.

The Earl caught his arm and hauled him to his feet. "Now listen to me," he said fiercely. "Even with reality healing, the Maiden cannot do her work alone. With Argus gone, there are no longer three connected Lords with the knowledge to preserve the domains. Without that balance, we stand to lose everything. We must connect with Bricin and have access to his knowledge, until the Maiden has fully regained her strength. If we do not, everything we have achieved so far will have been in vain and the very essence of our existence will disappear."

Ciaran stared at him. "I didn't know that was the case," he faltered.

"I believe you," said the Earl, "but if you want to see your wife again, you must trust me now. Together we must use the passing strength of my dear friend to light our way to Bricin's future."

He walked to the glass windows behind the tomb. He shut his eyes and then opened them and gazed directly at the shaded panes. At once the glass changed and started to form a shape.

"Quick now," said the Earl. He drew his sword and reached back to touch the Moonstone with its tip. Then he extended the sword towards the glass. "Take my hand," he said urgently and, as Ciaran grasped it, flames ran up the blade of the sword and into the centre of the window. The shape in its centre writhed and twisted, broke apart and then joined again. All the glass shattered and fell out onto the ground, but the shape remained and out of it stepped Lord De Lisle.

He looked slightly shaken but not at all surprised. "Well how very clever you are," he said. "I would never have thought you could reach me that way. I see you have brought my prodigal son." He looked Ciaran up and down. "How extremely unpleasant to see you again!"

Ciaran clenched his fists. "I too hoped to be spared such a fast reunion."

"I am sure that you did," said Lord De Lisle. "Be grateful that I have an essentially merciful nature. Otherwise, who knows how this meeting might end."

Ciaran drew his sword. "I am at your disposal, my Lord," he said hoarsely.

Lord De Lisle stepped quickly forward but the Earl raised his hand. "Enough," he said. "We have only a short time before Bricin is naturally pulled back into his own time stream. We must work together."

He looked at Lord De Lisle. "Will you help me, Bricin, and so save the life of my daughter and both of your sons?"

De Lisle sighed. "Put like that I have no choice," he said. "What do you want me to do?"

"Transfer your knowledge of the future to me, using the energy stream that we have enabled," said the Earl.

"If I do that, there is no guarantee that the future will not change or that my established place in it will continue to be secure," said De Lisle swiftly.

"I know," said the Earl. "But this is the only chance now the true connection is broken."

"As far as I am aware, no Lord has ever been connected to future and present simultaneously. The shock could destroy you," said Lord De Lisle.

The Earl gave a short laugh. "A prick of conscience at this late hour?"

De Lisle grinned. "Just being practical!"

"Of course, we wouldn't expect you to show any true concern," said Ciaran angrily.

Lord De Lisle sighed. "Trust that I have no wish to be obliterated. If Aidan cannot take the strain, none of us will live to see another morning. Still, I suppose we must just hope our luck holds."

The Earl took a breath. "I am ready," he said.

"So I see," said Lord De Lisle. "But there remains the question of how we actually do the transference. If you were a woman, it would be so much easier."

The Earl raised his eyebrows, "Even to save Old Earth, I won't make let you make love to me!"

"That wasn't what I meant," said Lord De Lisle impatiently. "Do you not remember the first lesson? That powerful thoughts can be passed more quickly to an unconscious mind? I am just wondering how best to get you unconscious."

The Earl faced him. "Do what you must," he said brusquely. "But be quick about it."

"Very well," said De Lisle. "Just let me put my coat down first." He bent to place it carefully and, as he did so, he swung around and caught the Earl full on the chin with his right hand. The Earl was flung backwards and fell, hitting his head against the tomb.

Ciaran ran to him. "Did you have to hit him so hard?" he said angrily.

"I did indeed," said Lord De Lisle. He shook his hand to restore feeling and felt the Earl's pulse. "Excellent, he's out completely. That was lucky. I didn't fancy trying that again. Anyway, let's get him sat up."

Ciaran helped the Earl into a sitting position. "Will this do?"

"Perfect," said De Lisle. He went behind the Earl and placed his hands over his eyes, forcing the lids open. "Now we can begin."

He began to chant. Ciaran, watching both the Lords closely, saw that De Lisle's eyes became at first blank and then sharply intense. His facial expression changed rapidly and sometimes he blinked. When he did so, the Earl mirrored him exactly. Once the Earl groaned and swayed, but De Lisle held him still. At last he removed his hands and the Earl fell forward.

Ciaran caught him. The Earl was sweating heavily.

"Will he recover?"

De Lisle stood up. "In a little while. He seems to have stood the strain quite well."

"What should I do?"

De Lisle put on his coat. "You just need to get him back home," he said. "Doubtless the Maiden will contact him in due course. In the meantime, he will need time to adjust."

Adjust to what?"

De Lisle considered. "The enormity of it all," he said at last. "You, who know only this domain and what scraps of the past and future Argus permitted you to see, have no idea what the infinite, forming world is really like. Neither did Aidan. It was his choice, I would have gladly shown him before, but he refused. Now, he knows everything and it will be painful for him to accept."

He went to the glass window. The shape was beginning to form within it again and the shards of glass were flying up to crystallise around it. "It is time for me to go."

"Wait," said Ciaran. He leaned the still unconscious Earl against the tomb edge and went over to De Lisle. "What will happen to you?" he said awkwardly.

De Lisle looked amused. "Do not tell me you actually care about that?"

Ciaran hesitated. "Not exactly," he said. "I just wondered, if..."

"If you would ever see me again?" De Lisle finished. He looked steadily at the younger man. "I think it highly likely," he said at last. There will need to be a reckoning."

He put his hands upon the window ledge and climbed upwards. "Goodbye, my son. Enjoy your life, however long it lasts." Then he stepped into the shape and in an instant he was gone. The old-fashioned glass shone briefly and then became once more clear. But this time, instead of being blank, it contained the picture of a man with dark red hair and gleaming eyes, with a drawn sword.

Ciaran gazed at it for a moment. "Until our next meeting," he said then he went back to the Earl. He was still unconscious. Ciaran went outside. In the churchyard the old man had finished his grass cutting and was now weeding flower beds. Ciaran ran to him.

"I need your help," he said urgently. "I have a sick man in here."

The old man stood up. "'Tis the Earl you mean?"

"Yes," said Ciaran. He watched as the old man carefully set down his spade. "Will you hurry please?"

The old man looked mildly surprised. "I am hurrying, Sir," he said. He followed Ciaran inside and together they managed to get the Earl up and into the curricle. Ciaran took the reins. The old man eyed him dubiously.

"Think ye can drive them, young Sir?" he said.

Ciaran grinned. "Truth be told, I've been longing to! Now get away from their heads if you please!"

The old man stepped back and the greys flashed past, raising a cloud of dust. When they pulled up, sweating, but still keen, in the Temple Court stable yard, the Head Groom came running out. Mr Allan stepped down. "We need to get the Earl inside." He helped the Groom lift the unconscious Earl down and they carried him to the house. Juliet who had been watching from the window came running out.

"Papa is hurt," she said in consternation. She threw herself into Mr Allan's arms. "And you too," she said, noting how he was flexing his hands.

Ciaran laughed. "Not at all," he said. "Although I must confess that I found those greys more of a challenge to drive than I expected. As for your father, we must get him to bed as soon as we can."

Juliet instantly went to call the servants. The Earl was soon in his room and, the following morning, they received the good news from Meadows that he was awake and asking for them.

Ciaran went to him at once. The Earl looked pale, but, otherwise, well enough. Ciaran was startled to find him shaving.

"You feel able to get up?" he asked.

The Earl set down his razor and picked up a towel. "I am not an invalid, Ciaran," he said. He mopped his face. "A little tired perhaps."

He turned to the mirror to tie his cravat. "I am glad you are here," he said unexpectedly. "Will you stay?"

"Of course," said Ciaran warmly. "As long as you want me too."

"I do not know when the Maiden will return," said the Earl. "So, I must wait here until she does. She needs the knowledge that I now hold to close and heal all the realities."

"The Maiden will return soon, surely," said Ciaran.

"She does not measure time as we do," said the Earl. "But, I hope that it will be soon."

"What will you do in the meantime?" asked Ciaran.

"What I have always done," said the Earl, "wait, hope, and manage my affairs. Talking of which," he said, a slight glint in his eye, "who gave you permission to drive my greys?"

Ciaran dropped his eyes. "I could hardly ask you and the situation was desperate," he said tautly.

The Earl smiled. "Yes I know. Well, from what I hear, they have come to no harm. Although, I am relieved that they are safely back in the stable and out of your hands."

"Thank you," said Ciaran briefly.

The Earl shrugged himself into his coat which the valet was holding out. "Let us go down now, Juliet will be waiting."

They descended the stairs. Juliet was waiting for them in the hall. She was holding a bundle of brown, black and white fluff that wriggled in her arms.

"Look what Papa has given me," she said holding out the struggling puppy. "Isn't he sweet?"

The dog, obviously fed up of being so held, gave a

convulsive leap and landed with surprisingly good balance on the marble steps.

He danced up to Ciaran and wagged his tail energetically. He was a tiny little fellow, with a long silky coat, large brown eyes and outsized ears.

Ciaran looked questioningly at the Earl. "A present from King Louis," he said. "Apparently, he gave the dog to the Queen and the bitch to his mistress and they made an illicit assignation. The court was soon full of puppies, so he was glad to pass this one on."

Ciaran picked the puppy up and it licked his face. "He's delightful," he said examining the squirming creature closely. "What's wrong with him?"

"Nothing at all," said the Earl, "except that he has only one brown patch over his eye where he should have two." He patted the dog and it licked him frantically.

"I believe that Juliet is going to call him Buccaneer. Now come with me and I'll show you the rest of your wedding present."

He walked out of the door not waiting for Ciaran to answer. Ciaran looked questioningly at Juliet but she merely smiled and picked up the puppy. He looked down at her in appreciation. She was wearing a dress of pink sprigged muslin. As always, the sight of her fresh, unspoiled beauty warmed his heart. He bent and kissed her, but they were interrupted by the puppy who scrabbled impatiently for freedom.

"Damn the little beast," said Ciaran, reluctantly pulling away as sharp claws dug into his wrist.

"Oh don't scold," said Juliet. She took the dog into her arms again. "Go now and see what Papa has for you!"

"Are you not coming?" said Ciaran.

She smoothed the pup's silken ears. "I need to go and redress my hair and this young gentleman needs his breakfast," she said demurely. "But I will see you later, I promise." She gave him a push. "Go now, Papa's waiting."

Outside, the Earl was standing beside a gleaming new racing curricle. Emblazoned on the side door was the emblem of a sickle moon.

"I thought," said the Earl, "that since you showed such a talent for racing, you should be given the chance to demonstrate your skills more regularly. Juliet has her new puppy and a selection from the Sulien jewels as her wedding present. This is for you."

Ciaran gasped. "It is too much," he said finally. "Thank you, my Lord."

"Don't thank me until you have tried it," said the Earl. He whistled and the Head Groom appeared, grinning broadly and leading the two greys. He proceeded to couple them to the carriage.

"I don't understand?" said Ciaran.

"Do you not?" said the Earl.

He picked up the reins and led the horses forward. "Take them, my boy," he said, "with all my blessings."

Chapter Twenty-Six

The spring of 1804, following the noumenon,[23] broke gently. All around Temple Court, clustering blossoms nodded in time to the vital, satisfied humming of bees. The lane that led to the moor was gathered with a belt of primroses. Wood violets fringed glistening banks of dog mercury and the air was spiced with the scent of wild garlic.

It was on one such perfect day that the Earl decided to ride out. It had been some months since he had done this, for he had not previously had the heart to do so. It had never occurred to him that to complete the Quest would mean severance from the man whose strength and companionship he had valued above all others. Although he had heartily welcomed Mr Allan to Temple Court and was glad to have him and Juliet remain there, he missed Lord Thorne greatly. Coupled with this was another, deeper, grief which made it hard to think or sleep or do anything but create a basic pretence of normality.

He went to the stables and ordered Utopia saddled. When the Head Groom made the point that Apollo also needed the exercise, the Earl shook his head. "No, today I will ride Utopia. But, I would like you to take Apollo out later."

The grooms were startled as their experience was that nobody but the Earl was allowed to ride Apollo, but they did as instructed and soon the Earl had left the yard and was heading towards the park.

*

---

[23] Kantian philosophy – an event that exists independently of human sense and/or perception.

The Earl at first rode slowly through the woods, but when they reached the grassland he allowed his mount to canter and then gallop. When at last he drew rein, both of them were blowing, but the little black stallion seemed the better for the run. He tossed his head and appeared more cheerful than when he had been led out. The Earl patted the shining neck. "I cannot replace your master, but I promise to get to know you as well as he did. Now I must leave you for a while. I pray you, wait here for me." The horse raised his head and looked steadily back at the Earl for a moment. He waited as the Earl dismounted and looped the reins over a post. Then he stood and watched him walk through the gates and out towards the moor and the summoning stone. The Earl climbed to the top and stood looking out over the heath. Far above his head he heard a gurgling call and his spirits lifted as he saw his first swallow. He had found that, since the reincarnation of the Star Maiden, his powers had not disappeared completely, but it was definitely more difficult to channel them. Since his return to the 19th Century, he had not attempted to communicate across time. Now he concentrated deeply and sent his thought out across the void. Unlike before, there was no answering touch. Lord Thorne could no longer connect with him. For only the second time in his long life, Lord Sulien, Earl and Sun Lord, gave way to tears. He leaned his head upon his arms and wept.

When at last he raised his head, the sun had gone behind a cloud. The morning was passing. The Earl sighed and began to descend the steps. As he did so, Utopia let out a neigh, a sound of such gladness and hope that the Earl was startled. The stallion flung his head to free himself and, snapping his bridle, headed off at full gallop across the moor. The Earl breathed an oath and prepared to follow him, but stopped in his tracks at the sight of a light forming beyond the distant ridge of hills. It was a series of arcs that merged as they came closer and formed a glistening mirage of flowing colours, blending the light of both sun and moon. So gold and blue, green and pink, violet and silver shone distinctly yet, also, flowed seamlessly together. Then the light faded into a soft, silvery, shining mist and the shape became clearly that of a white mare. Walking beside her was the Star Maiden.

The Maiden stopped and the white mare looked over her shoulder at Utopia who had galloped up to them. The Maiden nodded and, as if it was a signal, the two horses walked away together, down towards the orchard. The Maiden continued walking until she was standing before the Earl. The Earl sank to his knees. The Maiden smiled down upon him.

"So, here I am at last, Sun Lord. It has been a long, weary wait for you. Did you perhaps fear that I might turn my back on this world and pass away forever to the realm of my father?" The Earl nodded and the Maiden signalled to him to rise. She looked out across the moors towards the northern sky, where the last of the mist still lingered. "That path still remains open to me, although I have not yet chosen to take it. The wounds of this world are not yet fully healed. Would you be willing to help me complete my work?"

The Earl bowed low. "You know that I will gladly do anything that is required. What is it that you wish of me? My sword and my life have always been yours to command."

The Maiden nodded. "Yes, as was your father's and your father's father and back through the long years when Owain walked with me at Rheged. How well I remember him and you are very like to him, although, I think, even stronger and wiser in mind and heart."

The Earl flushed. "I am honoured that you think so."

The Lady smiled again. She sat down upon the grass and removed the white veil and wrap that she wore. She was wearing a dress of silver, girdled with moonstones, and her black hair shone loose upon her shoulders. She stretched her hands out into the warm wind.

"How sweet and fresh it is," she said with a shiver of delight. "How pleasing it is to feel such things after my long sleep. You, who were born in mortal form, do not realise how truly blessed you are and yet, how little you know of all the wonders of this Earth."

"Will you not teach me?" said the Earl seriously.

The Lady looked up at him. "You have the intuition of your forebears and have guessed what I have not yet asked. But know this: helping your people to learn how to live well and wisely will not be a quick or easy task. I have taken the form of a mortal again, but the life force that lies within me will outlive this vessel and I must then depart forever. When I leave, who then will guide the mortal folk and protect them? For, I tell you this, there is still danger to be faced and it will grow again. It requires more than your wisdom and the blades of your knights to ensure future safety for Old Earth."

The Earl looked back down towards the orchard. Through the gates he could see Utopia and the white mare grazing together. The sight was beautiful yet it brought tears to his eyes again. He went to dash them away, but the Lady stayed his hand.

"Do not be afraid to show me your grief, Sun Lord. I know how much the one you called Argus meant to you. I sorrow for his untimely death. I wish I had foreseen what he would do, but his mind was closed to me at the last. Even if I had reached it, I do not know if I could have changed it. He loved the woman Theora Templeton. To continue to live without her was more than he could bear.

Take thanks that he is now at peace and his spirit and Theora's can never be parted. But there is another deeper burden that you have personally carried. Even now your heart burns with it. You cannot become my champion and defend this world until that wound is healed and the memory forgotten."

After a long moment, the Earl spoke again. "Alas, Lady, I fear that you must then find another champion. For my part, I do not wish to ever forget, although the pain is hard to bear."

The Lady reached out and took his hand. "Yet," she said, "there may be a chance for you to keep your memories and be truly healed, if you will let me show you the way."

The Earl looked at her with hope and his eyes held an unspoken question, but the Lady shook her head. "No, I cannot bring back Theora Templeton. I have taken her physical form and her spirit is gone. I am now a mortal, though I have the power and knowledge of all eternity to guide me. I can last for only one Old Earth year, before this body fails and I will follow my father's path into the Star Realm. So, I have come to you with a request. Stay with me for one year, as my husband. During this time, I will teach you what you need to know to protect the Earth and, through our child, we will furnish this world with a future champion. I promise that I will give you as much love as Theora Templeton would have done. For she did love you, my Lord, although she renounced that love and cleaved to another who needed her more." The Lady halted and stood up. When she spoke again her voice was low. "I pledge that I will make you happy." She extended her hand.

The Earl stood up. There was a glitter in the green eyes that had been missing for many days. He took the white hand in his and kissed it.

"You do me a great honour," he said unsteadily. "I accept, my Lady, and I will do my best to make you a good husband."

"All ask is that you love me," said the Maiden.

Her voice, so gentle and yet so like Theora's in its expression, made the Earl smile. "I will certainly try to," he said unsteadily. They stood regarding each other for a long moment and then the Earl extended his arm. "Perhaps we should go in now, my Lady, for, alas, I can no longer easily control the weather as I once did. I suspect there may be rain on the way."

"You think so?" she said. "Yet, now, for the first time in so many long years, I believe we both truly feel the warmth of the sun."

And with that she stepped forward and kissed him.

Epilogue

Within the auditorium of the Chinese Theatre in New York, the audience sat in breathless silence. It had been a spectacular evening. The opening of any film from the celebrated Director and Producer Mr V, were always exciting, but this one had been the best yet. There had been a massive publicity campaign beforehand and no detail had been left to chance. Sid Grauman, Managing Director and joint owner of the Theatre (sat in his usual box), had no doubt this picture was going to be a success. The build-up had been perfect. The series of parties hosted by Mr V had been elegant, yet lavish. His arrival at the Theatre with Gala James on his arm had been followed by an 'impromptu' dance by Miss James and Guy Irving in the lobby. This had created a frenzy of anticipation. Everyone had sat down expecting to be entertained and they had not been disappointed. The film, dubbed, 'the Musical to keep you mesmerised' had certainly done that. Now the final shots were rolling. The scent from the Theatre's incense burners, sickly, yet not overpowering, filled the air. On the screen, the figure of the tall, fair-haired man, holding the hand of the slim dark woman walked away across the green meadow. As they faded into the mist, they were replaced by Gala and Guy, dancing, on clouds. Then they too faded and the plush red velvet curtain with its golden palm trees enfolded the screen. There was silence and then an eruption of applause that rocked the room. Guy and Gala stood up and acknowledged the crowd. After a moment, Mr V did the same. They were all soon engulfed by the press. After a while, Mr V fought his way out of the crush and excused himself to go to the Executive Men's Room. Once there, he made a discreet exit through the back door. Soon, he would need to return and host the celebration party, but he wanted a moment alone. He leaned back against the smooth wall and looked up at the stars.

"Great film," said a voice. Mr V turned. He saw with distaste that it was a grubby little man in a green coat. One of the 'local hacks' who would report in the morning papers, but not one of the major press lords. The man was plump, with bright eyes, sharp and darting as a weasel's.

"Can't you see I'm busy?" said Mr V coldly.

"Yeah," said the little man. He took off his hat. "So, I guess that counts as one good day at the office for you. This one's gonna make lots of bucks. Not that you need it. Whereas me…" He wiped his bald head. "Well, I need a hot story."

"Is that why you've forced your way into a private party?" asked Mr V.

The man grinned. "I know you're a real busy man, so I don't want the whole scoop, just a spoonful."

Mr V looked amused. "What would you call 'a spoonful'?"

The agent produced a notebook. "How about you give me the inside on your two 'unknown and uncredited' stars."

"So, you expect me to exclusively reveal the big secret of the entire movie? Why would I do that?"

The agent grinned again, but more widely. His teeth were uneven and there was a conspicuous gap off centre. "I'd suggest because if I don't get this story, I might publish another. How about one around the unexplained death of your ex-girlfriend, Miss Layton? My friend at the morgue told me that it was as if all the life had been burned out of her. Yes, 'burned out', those were his very words."

Mr V sighed. "You really are a weasel aren't you? Very well, I'll tell you. My two stars were filmed without their knowledge. The footage is their true story. Does that help you?"

The agent's eyes glistened. "You bet it does. Anything else?"

"Just that I expect to meet with them very soon," said Mr V. "Now, I must return to my guests."

The agent hastily pushed his notebook into his coat. "Sure, of course. Thanks, Mr V. I really appreciate this." He turned to go and then hesitated. "This will be an exclusive won't it? I mean you won't be telling anyone else?"

"I assure you that only you and I will ever know about this," said Mr V. He held out his hand. "Well goodbye, Mr?"

"Brooks," said the agent. "Sure was great to meet you."

"A pleasure," said Mr V smoothly, shaking his hand. "How about I reveal one more secret?" his hand tightened abruptly. Brooks looked down in horror as, from hand to wrist to arm to shoulder, the life was drained from him. As the process reached his brain, his legs buckled and he fell to the ground. His last memory was of the red-haired man bending over him and speaking into his ear. "Not a burning for you, Mr Brooks, just simple energy withdrawal. Good evening."

Mr V, known in other places and times as Bricin, Lord De Lisle, straightened up. He adjusted his tie, smoothed his jacket and, leaving the twitching corpse behind him, walked back into the glittering splendour of the Chinese Theatre and the adulation of his fans.

In the American papers the next day there were two major stories: the spectacular opening of the incredible film called *My Dance Please* and the transient lunar phenomenon (which showed glowing red spots on the surface of the unusually large full moon) on the same night. Buried in the back pages was also a brief mention of the unexplained death of a minor press agent. The unexplained death story quickly faded into obscurity, but *My Dance Please* broke all box office records and was a major news sensation for the rest of 1938. The public clamoured for more and were ecstatic when Mr V promised them a thrilling sequel.

About The Author

Andria Marston started writing imaginative fiction to escape the trials of commuting whilst working as a public sector consultant. 80% of her novel, Perdurare was written on the daily train journey from York to Sheffield. Andria is inspired by the English countryside, the United Kingdom's history, myths, traditions, and the possibilities presented by alternate realities.

Andria also writes short stories and comic poetry. In 2012 her work was included in a poetry anthology published by Forward Poetry for the Queen's Diamond Jubilee.

Andria Marston hails from Surrey. She now lives in Yorkshire with her husband where they enjoy supporting wildlife, antique collecting, allotment gardening, and amateur bee-keeping.

www.blossomspringppublishing.com